The
WANTING

The WANTING

Campbell Black

McGRAW-HILL BOOK COMPANY
New York   St. Louis   San Francisco   Bogotá   Guatemala
Hamburg   Lisbon   Madrid   Mexico   Montreal   Panama
Paris   San Juan   São Paulo   Tokyo   Toronto

The Author and Publishers gratefully acknowledge the following for permission to quote from copyrighted material:

"Bad Moon Rising." Copyright © 1969 by Jondora Music. Used by permission. "Mellow Yellow" by Donovan Leitch. © Copyright 1966 by Donovan [Music] Ltd., London. All rights administered by Peer International Corporation. International copyright secured. All rights reserved. Used by permission. "Substitute." Words and Music by Peter Townshend. © Copyright 1966 Fabulous Music Ltd., London, England. TRO–Devon Music, Inc., New York, controls all publication rights for the U.S.A. and Canada. Used by permission.

1 2 3 4 5 6 7 8 9 D O C D O C 8 7 6

ISBN 0-07-005564-5

LIBRARY OF CONGRESS CATALOGING-IN-PUBLICATION DATA

Black, Campbell.
The wanting.
I. Title.
PR6052.L25W36   1986   823'.914   86-2750
ISBN 0-07-005564-5

Book design by Kathryn Parise

For Sally and Colin, good friends,
this small feast of bones

The
WANTING

1973

P ROLOGUE: Officer Metger thought there was something purify-
ing, something uplifting, when it rained here in the California pine
forest. A cleansing action that left the air sharp after the dry days
of summer.

But this rain was different, hard and sinister and cold. Already it had
soaked through his uniform and he could feel it press against his flesh. He
raised a hand, wiped large drops from his eyebrows, and then gazed back
toward the forest, which was more secretive than usual; the rain wove a thin
curtain between the trees. A spidery, gray camouflage.

Metger cupped his hands and tried to get a cigarette going but he gave
up in despair, his fingertips covered with flakes of damp tobacco. He raised
his face to the sky. Low, heavy clouds shadowed the landscape and the forest
caught the rain, echoing its sounds like a million unsynchronized pulsebeats.

He shivered. Water had seeped inside his boots and his socks squished
against his ankles. But the discomfort he felt could not be attributed simply
to his wet condition.

It was the slicing rain, the way it created a conspiracy in the landscape.
He could sense the forest stretch on for mile after wet mile, the washes
running like liquid ribbons, bedraggled birds perched in the inadequate
shelter of trees, animals lurking in the cavities of trunks.

He blew into his hands for warmth. Something streaked through the air
in front of him. A sleek buzzard, wings spread vainly against the angle of
the rain, hovered over the trees a moment, then was gone. The forest, Metger
thought, is never still; it's always shifting, stirring, whispering. You can
never step into the same forest twice.

And now apparently it had swallowed a child.

As he stared at the trees he had the feeling that it wasn't going to give the child back easily either. It wasn't going to make him a gift because it wasn't a generous entity. Unyielding, unresponsive, it staked its claims and held them hard and tight; it was furtive and indifferent and its moods completely whimsical. Now the trees seemed to come closer together in the rain, closing ranks against the policeman as if they had sniffed the presence of the enemy.

You could lose more than a child up here, Metger thought. You could lose all the little threads that held your sanity together.

He wondered if that was what had happened to the parents of the child. If they had somehow lost it. He turned and looked up at the sun deck of the house behind him and observed the faces of the man and the woman, understanding that they were waiting for him, a cop, a representative of law and order and regulation, to do something to find their missing kid.

Metger was suddenly angry. Why the hell did people bury themselves out here anyhow? Why did they come up from their big cities to spend weeks and months in this hostile, unfamiliar environment twenty-one miles from the town of Carnarvon?

Back to nature, he thought. That's what they called it. Back to the primal landscape. Back to the soil, if only for a while. Liberated from freeways and traffic fumes and the general ungodliness of the cities.

In the rain the faces of the parents were pale and moist, white and expressionless as blank paper. They were silent with the intense silence of parental anxiety. Already they were imagining their stray child dead and waterlogged in one of the fast-running washes. Or carried away by some massive animal that was the beast of a nightmare.

It was more likely that the kid was out there lost. Probably sheltered beneath a tree and sobbing her little heart out.

Metger moved, mud sucking at his feet, toward the trees. Although he knew this forest vaguely, although he had lived all his life around here, its desolation always got under his skin just the same. His area of patrol included the forest and he was sometimes obliged to drive the dirt road that skirted the edge of the trees, but that was all as far as he was concerned. Just another area that fell within the dominion of the most junior officer in the Carnarvon Police Department.

Conscious of the man and woman watching him, he moved farther between the trees. And all at once it came to him that there was something odd about this whole situation. He pushed aside an overhanging branch and he stopped, studying the trees ahead. As rain drummed against his cap he wondered now why the parents chose to stay behind at the house instead of accompanying him on his search—wasn't that strange? You'd expect the parents to be out here digging trees up by the roots and hacking the whole goddamn forest apart to find their missing kid.

But Mr. and Mrs. Ackerley had remained behind on the deck, faces bleached by rain, white hands clasped tightly on the rail. Although he wasn't a parent himself, Metger imagined that if it were his kid no force on this earth could keep him out of the forest.

He stopped and looked back the way he had come. The house was no longer visible, hidden behind the screen of trees. He tried once more to get a cigarette lit—a minor success this time, a few quick puffs before rain slid down his fingers and extinguished the thing.

He felt suddenly very lonely out here. Even if the house was only a hundred yards or so away, it might not have existed at all, so dense was the cover of pines. He walked a little farther. Rain dripped from needles and cones and slithered from the visor of his cap down his cheeks, his neck and throat, dampening the collar of his shirt.

Were the Ackerleys scared of the forest? Was that it? Scared to leave the security of their rented house? Mr. Ackerley, a law professor from Seattle, had said that he and his wife would remain in the house on the chance that their daughter would come back. They wanted to be there, he said. Metger had looked into the pinched face of the professor, seeing in those guarded eyes a flicker of pain—but maybe he'd misinterpreted that expression. It could have been fear of what might lie out here in the forest.

Mrs. Ackerley, a dyed redhead who clung to her husband's arm, hadn't looked Metger straight in the face during all the time they had talked together. She just kept watching the trees and twisting her wedding band around and around on her finger. What Metger sensed was that the couple had had a disagreement of some kind, although he couldn't say what.

Maybe the husband hadn't wanted the police called in just yet and the wife had insisted. Or it might have been the other way around. Whatever, the atmosphere around them had a tense, cutting edge—a sharp thing that wasn't entirely connected to the missing kid. Metger had the feeling you got when you walked into a room at the end of a violent argument, when the air was heavy with the clamminess of domestic discord.

"She was wearing blue jeans. Red sneakers. A jacket. Brown, I think," Mrs. Ackerley had said, offering Metger a description he thought was superfluous because it wasn't as if he was going to run into *scores* of kids out there in the vast forest. It wasn't exactly the most populous place on the planet.

Apart from the redwood house the Ackerleys were renting, there was only one other home within miles. That was where Dick Summer and his wife lived, a reclusive old couple Metger had seen only a couple of times. They gave new meaning to the word "privacy," Metger thought. Once, he'd actually seen them in Carnarvon, shuffling along the sidewalk together, arms linked as if each were afraid of losing contact with the other. They came to town rarely, though, presumably only for essential provisions. Metger had wondered what they did up here in the pine forest all the time and had decided that they had perfected the goal of all recluses, that of keeping yourself to yourself with a vengeance.

"Her name's Anthea," Mr. Ackerley had said. And there was an undercurrent in his voice, as if he were repressing something. When he spoke his daughter's name his expression changed—he blinked his eyes and swallowed hard and then gazed down at the floor like someone rendered suddenly shy. Then a current of some sort had passed between husband and wife, like an electric jolt coursing the length of a metal tube. Metger picked up on it.

"She's twelve," Mrs. Ackerley added. "Only twelve . . ." The voice had been filled with an odd uncertainty. The red-haired woman glanced at her husband and then added, "She looks . . ."

Infuriatingly, this sentence died on her lips as well.

"She doesn't look her age," Mr. Ackerley put in.

"She's tall? Big? Is that what you mean?" Metger asked.

Now, as he plodded across the mud, he realized he hadn't received an answer to his question. It was a simple enough question, but the parents had evaded it, somehow managed to slide their way around it.

She doesn't look her age, Metger thought. Whatever. Out here, it didn't matter if he was searching for a giantess, a twelve-year-old Amazon or a stunted dwarf—because if he ran into a child at all it was sure to be Anthea Ackerley.

He collided with the arch of a drooping branch, which swiped him damply across his forehead. He cursed, walked a little way, then stopped. It was funny, though not altogether in a comical sense, how the forest seemed to lean on you, pressuring you, as if it were a conscious act of resistance on the part of the trees. Rain, blown at tattered angles by a sudden wind, filled his eyes and blinded him.

It was hard to avoid the conclusion that the Ackerleys were concealing something, he thought. In a halfhearted way he toyed with the fantasy that perhaps they had murdered their own child and were busily creating a false impression of deep anxiety. But he rejected that notion at once as a trick of his mind, something inspired by rain and fueled by the dreary menace of the pines.

He had asked the Ackerleys if the child was given to wandering through the trees. The couple had been quiet for too long a time, and then Mr.

Ackerley had said the girl often went to visit the Summers. He said she often spent afternoons over there.

Something in the way he uttered this simple sentence reinforced the idea in Metger that Mr. and Mrs. Ackerley were not being entirely forthcoming with him, that they were obfuscating. Your kid is missing, so why fudge around the truth like this? he thought.

"She wouldn't have gone over there today," Mrs. Ackerley said.

"Why not today?" Metger asked.

"I understand the Summers have gone, Officer."

"Gone?"

"A trip. They said something about a trip, I believe."

"Maybe your daughter's over at their house—"

"But the place is empty—"

Metger interrupted the law professor's wife. "Which might make it attractive to a kid. Right?"

The couple said nothing. "When did you last see Anthea?" Metger asked.

"Early this morning," the mother answered.

"How early?" Precision, Metger thought, I need precision.

"Seven." Mrs. Ackerley looked at her husband for confirmation.

"Seven is about right," the professor said.

Metger examined his watch. "Ten hours."

Ackerley sighed with some impatience. "Officer, I feel sure she'll turn up, she'll come home. Maybe this is just a waste of your time."

So it was the professor who hadn't been eager to call the cops. It was Mrs. Ackerley who had insisted, Mrs. Ackerley whose eyes were suddenly filled with tears and who pressed her face into her husband's chest. There's grief here, Metger thought. And he was dogged by the feeling that it was more than something caused by a child who might have wandered too far into the pines.

"Now that I'm here, I might as well look around," Metger had said.

And here he was now, looking around but not seeing very much.

Rain rattled branches and wind shook limbs and the pattering sound of water on the feeble plants of the undergrowth suggested the scampering motions of small animals. Then there was another noise, one that grew as he moved—the splutter of foaming water hurrying through a wash.

When he reached the wash he observed the swirling muddy foam and the broken branches that were sucked down this narrow funnel in the land. Opaque and swift, the water yielded nothing, no drowned child, nothing but the surface debris of nature which the maddened water had grabbed on its twisting way through the fold in the landscape.

Somewhere beyond the wash was the house where the Summers lived. To get there Metger would have to ford this crazy swollen river, this defiant bastard of the rain—not a prospect he found any pleasure in.

He scrambled along the bank looking for a likely place. The roar of water filled his ears and he realized his discomfort had become intolerable.

A good fire, dry clothes, a tumblerful of scotch—his desires were simple ones right now. Anthea Ackerley, why did you wander off on such a day? If indeed you have wandered. If indeed that was your choice.

He studied the shifting wash like an explorer assessing his chances of survival. He peered at the opposite bank at the cluster of rainswept trees. He slithered down the bank, then paused.

Over the roar of water and the incessant bickering of the rain, another sound came to him, one that he could neither locate nor identify at first. But it had a weird effect on him—the prickling of the hairs at the back of his neck and a coldness, nothing to do with the weather, that seemed to form in the marrow of his skeleton.

His immediate instinct was to place his hand on the butt of his pistol, something that struck him later as uncharacteristic, because in all his six years in the Carnarvon Police Department he'd never drawn the weapon—indeed he'd come to forget that the damned thing hung at his hip.

He turned his face and looked back the way he had come.

The sound came again. Human, certainly, but unlike anything he could remember ever having heard before. It was both a scream of grief and a cry of madness and it assailed his senses as if it were the incomprehensible utterance of something alien.

He scrambled up the bank and then the trees were surrounding him again and he was trying to run, to trot back to the redwood house as fast as he could, despite the impediments of the landscape and the rain—serrated, sharpened by wind—which blew into his eyes.

When he heard the gunshot he stopped moving, a response that wasn't a professional one, but the sound, muffled by wet branches, seemed to hold him paralyzed a moment. There was a feeling inside him that was close to pure dread.

He started to run again. When the house came in sight he glanced up at the sun deck, empty now, strangely desolate as the rain swept across it, discoloring the redwood slats. The entire house, stained and dreary in the gray-green drizzle of the landscape, might itself have been completely empty.

Metger moved around to the front porch. He took his pistol from its holster and he thought of how complete the silence had suddenly become, filling all the spaces around him, a big wet world of total quiet.

And he was afraid, scared to go inside the house, scared of pushing the door open and stepping in—the way a man given to nightmares might be afraid of falling asleep.

He steadied himself, leveled the gun in his hand even as he felt ridiculous about having removed it from the holster, and he nudged the door with his knee.

The living room was empty. He could see clear across it into the kitchen. The silence that had begun outdoors tracked him inside the house like some damp dog moving on his heels. When he reached the kitchen he gazed up at the recessed fluorescent light and the tiled ceiling, catching a smudged image of himself in reflection. He could hear rain clicking against the windows of the house.

"Mr. Ackerley?"

There was no answer.

"Mrs. Ackerley?"

A hallway opened out in front of him. There was a curious smell in the air, bitter and clinging and utterly unfamiliar to him. It gathered in his nostrils, then it seemed to prickle the back of his throat like something he'd tried to swallow—a fishbone, something that had become lodged at the back of his tongue. He felt nausea, cleared his throat; the smell remained.

"Mr. Ackerley?"

Now he found himself staring at the Ackerleys, who were standing apart from one another at the end of the hallway. Their bodies were motionless —they might have been the two subjects of a badly composed photograph, limp and listless, uncertain of their focus.

Ackerley turned his face and his glasses glistened in the dull light of the hall. The law professor's face became a patchwork quilt of incoherent emotion. A nerve worked under his eye, and his hands, which he raised loosely in the air in a gesture of futility, trembled visibly.

Metger looked at Mrs. Ackerley. She wasn't here, she wasn't in this house, she wasn't of this world—she had gone, been transported to another zone. Her eyes were blind and blank.

Ackerley said, "She came back," and he jerked his head stiffly, indicating that the young cop should go inside the bedroom at the end of the hall. There was a half-open door, a slat of liquid light.

"Your daughter came back?" Metger asked, surprised by the rawness in his voice.

Ackerley said nothing. He was staring at his wife, and there was a look of profound sorrow in his eyes.

Metger felt something slip in his own heart.

Whatever the grief was in this sad house, it was something Ackerley and his wife were going to carry around with them for the rest of their days. Metger became aware of a quiet, creaking sound, repetitive and understated. It was coming from the bedroom that faced him.

He wiped a cold hand across his damp face and then he reached out and pushed the door and it swung back into the room. The creaking sound was slowing, fading. But the smell remained, strong and pervasive and dreadful.

He stepped inside the room. At first he was conscious only of the motion of a small rocking chair, the kind of chair built for a child.

Back and forth, forth and back, ticking like a clock.

Then he had the impression of redness that slid down the walls of the room beyond the moving chair.

Metger placed one hand nervously over his mouth. He stilled the empty rocking chair. There was blood on his fingertips.

He stepped forward. It lay at his feet. He almost stumbled over it.

When he looked down he saw the bloodied shape of what might have been a child only he couldn't tell for sure because the head had been blown away and the remains of the face were so scorched and indistinguishable that only one cold eye was left intact; it stared back at him with the bleak intelligence of death.

He moved back. Even the Remington 870 shotgun that lay on the bloodied rug alongside the dead child wasn't a real artifact in a real world.

He closed his eyes a second and wished the nightmare away.

Later, he would remember the blood and the violated tissue and the way the solitary eye had regarded him so closely and the long strands of fine white hair that lay like unexpected threads among the human wreckage. And he would remember the hands—the dead child's hands, which were wrong, all wrong.

1986

1 Louise could think of only one thing—the need to get out of this city, far away. The prospect created a pressure she could feel at the back of her head like a buzz saw cutting bone. There was still so much to do, so many last-minute items to attend to, and she was sure she'd forget something extremely important.

She looked at Mr. Banyon. He was a small fussy man in a dark blue suit. A white carnation was perched in his buttonhole. His hair, greased back and center-parted in the style of another age, reflected the light from the window.

"These," Mr. Banyon said, "are the keys."

He placed a ring of keys down on the surface of his desk and Max picked them up.

Louise watched her husband stick the key ring inside the pocket of his old tweed jacket. The damned pressure in her head was rising.

She studied Banyon's small hands a moment. Manicured nails, a big fat ring on the middle finger of the left hand, glassy skin. Ever since the Strangler's exploits had begun to appear in newspaper headlines, Louise had found herself examining the hands of strangers she saw in restaurants, checkers in supermarkets, bag boys, noticing the shapes of fingers, bulbous joints, gnarls.

The Strangler had killed his first victim in a parking lot near Fisherman's Wharf. A twelve-year-old girl. His second victim had been a boy of nine whose body was found in Golden Gate Park. The killer, whose speciality was that of assassinating his victims with short lengths of five-and-dime-store twine, had been active for about three months. Four kids were already dead. And the shadowy character known as the Strangler had been reduced in her mind to a pair of large disembodied hands she couldn't visualize with any precision—and yet she could always sense them nearby, as if by divination.

"You take Interstate Five to Redding," Banyon was saying. "Then High-way 299 as far as Carnarvon. Beyond Carnarvon, say nine miles or so, you'll come to a roadhouse called the Ace of Spades."

Banyon paused and smiled. He had a realtor's smile, thin and yet convincing. "Take a left at the roadhouse. The pavement runs out. Go twelve miles down the dirt road. The house is easy to find. Redwood. Sun deck. There's an old-fashioned sundial out front, I recall. Anyway, you can't miss it. It's the only property out that way."

Louise looked at Max, who was gazing out of Banyon's window, seemingly lost in contemplation of the San Francisco skyline. The late afternoon sun was red.

She thought how typical it had become of Max lately to tune himself out. He drifted away from the core of things. His eyes would glaze over, and although he might nod his head and make noises, you could tell he wasn't really paying attention. *Burnout:* he had worked too hard and too long without any kind of a break and he'd forgotten how to relax. There were times when he looked quite unhealthy, almost haggard.

Banyon said, "It's a pleasant house. Pleasant countryside. You'll enjoy it." A wistful pause: "I haven't been up that way in, oh, let me think, years . . ." He waved a hand and the rest of his sentence faded out. He stood up and looked at Max and his tiny red face creased into a beam.

"I expect you're looking forward to this vacation, Dr. Untermeyer," he said.

Max changed the position of his long thin legs. "My wife keeps telling me I need some peace and quiet."

"And you'll find it, Doctor. You'll certainly find it up there." Banyon caressed his carnation briefly.

Louise asked, "What kind of town is Carnarvon?"

Did it make sense to rent a house for a whole summer without ever having seen the place? She wondered briefly, then turned the question aside. Banyon had shown them a bunch of color photographs of the property, and the place looked absolutely perfect for what they wanted. Maybe the indefinable unease she experienced had another source. Maybe the real question was whether it made sense to bury oneself in the countryside for three months, connected to all the things you knew only by a frail telephone line.

But we need this break, she thought. We all need it. Max and me and Dennis. We need to get out of this city. . . .

She rubbed her eyelids. The buzz saw was droning against the fragile surface of skull bone. There were still so many things left to be done before they could leave in the morning—and suddenly her life seemed an assortment of lists written on scraps of paper she'd somehow contrived to misplace or lose completely.

Banyon said, "Carnarvon is a picturesque place. It has a significant tourist trade during the summer months. Local crafts. Arts. That kind of thing. I'm sure it will provide anything you might need, Mrs. Untermeyer." He rubbed his hands together and smiled at Louise. "When do you intend to leave?"

"Tomorrow," Louise answered. She saw Banyon's hand move across the desk. His fingers came to rest on the check she'd made out for the rent.

"Allow about six hours for the trip," Banyon said. "Splendid drive. Wonderful countryside."

There was a brief silence in the room. Louise glanced at her husband. Max was rattling the keys in the pocket of his jacket; it was a nervous little sound and it contributed to the slight edge of anxiety she felt. It wasn't just the trip. There was also the fact she wasn't altogether happy about having rented their own house to a rather weird professor of anthropology from Georgia in the Soviet Union.

There was, she had told Max, something a little sinister about Professor Zmia. It was in his secretive dark eyes and the odd way he smiled, as if he knew something about you that you didn't know yourself. And his extraordinary politeness, which bordered at times on the unctuous, wasn't quite as charming as she should have found it. But Banyon, who'd suggested the professor as a tenant when they had first come to see him, said that the man's references were impeccable, they couldn't *possibly* find a *better* tenant, and moreover didn't it make good economic sense to rent their home while they were gone? There was also a security factor, Banyon pointed out: an occupied house is less attractive to a potential burglar than one obviously empty. Banyon had a smooth way of making the obvious seem utterly irresistible.

Max was standing up, looking at her, and she realized the transaction with Banyon was over. The realtor followed them across the rug to the door of his office.

"Call me if there's anything," he said. "Plumbing. Leaks in the roof. That sort of thing. Call me."

"We'll call," Max said.

There were handshakes, quick flutters of Banyon's tiny fingers.

"Enjoy, enjoy. Have a good summer. I know Professor Zmia will take exquisite care of your property. Worry not. . . ."

Then they were outside in a long fluorescent corridor and walking toward the elevators.

They rode down to the street level in silence. When they were on the sidewalk Max looked this way and that, trying to remember where he might have parked the station wagon. A gust of wind tugged at the hem of Louise's light cotton dress. When they found the car Max unlocked the door. Louise slid onto the passenger seat.

Max slipped the key in the ignition. He stuck the Volvo into first gear and joined the late afternoon traffic. When he braked for a stoplight a tall girl in a red dress walked in front of the car. She had long brown hair that floated behind her, tendrils caught in an updraft. He rubbed the back of his wife's hand, feeling the warm metal of her wedding ring.

Louise said, "I keep wondering about Professor Zmia."

Max smiled at her. "I bet he's going to hold orgies as soon as we're gone. Girls in every room. Strange Eastern sexual rites. Incense sticks. The whole thing."

"Then maybe we ought to stay," Louise said. "We might be missing out on something."

Max watched the girl vanish on the other side of the street. There was a dryness in his mouth and at the back of his throat. His hands felt unsteady against the wheel.

He was not even thinking about Professor Zmia. He was not pondering Louise's odd little misgivings about the man. He was thinking how he had his own very private reasons for getting far away from San Francisco.

Louise surveyed Professor Zmia's belongings, which cluttered up one corner of the entranceway to the house. The professor had been moving his stuff in on a daily basis from his temporary living quarters in Oakland. For a while Louise had wondered if the neighbors perhaps suspected illicit undertakings when they saw a small man come and go at odd hours with canvas bags, suitcases and bizarre carvings—fertility statues the professor claimed he had brought from an expedition to Borneo.

Louise leaned against the wall and sighed. How could one man possess so much? The statues were brutal and primitive, squat faces suggestive of ancient magical powers. They had been crudely hewn out of wood. The unsettling thing about them was in their eyes, which were blind and blank and yet still seemed capable, in some unnatural way, of sight. She stepped over suitcases and made it to the living room.

She flopped on the sofa, her legs spread, her arms dangling by her side. She looked around the room with a slight feeling of dispossession. Already Professor Zmia had taken over the house; his physical tenancy was the only thing left to make the takeover complete.

Louise heard a tiny strident voice inside her skull. *Cancel*, it screamed. Stay here in San Francisco.

She rubbed her eyelids and watched Max flick through the pages of one of the many arcane medical journals to which he subscribed. "Do you think we're just a little crazy?"

Max looked over the edge of his magazine. "Crazy?"

Louise said, "Let's face it, we don't really know anything about where we're going. We don't know what life up there is going to be like. We're not woodsy people, are we?"

"Woodsy," Max said, amused by the word. Sometimes he'd suck on a word like a lozenge, turning it over in his mouth as he tasted it.

"Well, we're not. Especially you," she said.

"Especially me—why?"

"Your idea of the great outdoors is a backyard barbecue, Max." The pain in her head was located behind her eyes. "At least I was a Girl Scout once."

Max smiled at her. "We're renting a house, Louise. A solid structure. Wood. Masonry. We're not going to be sleeping under canvas. A house, dear. A telephone. TV. Washer and dryer. Electric stove."

She said, "I know what's *in* the house, Max. I read Banyon's little brochure. Just the same . . ." She let her sentence slide away, unfinished business. She looked at her watch. It was almost five, which meant Dennis would be home soon from the roller-skating rink.

Max put his magazine down. "It's the right thing, Louise. It's a good decision. I won't be sorry to get out of this town for a while." He stared across the room at his wife. "I'm sick of broken bones and varicose veins and drug salesmen. And Ed Stallings is a damn fine doctor, so I'm leaving the practice in pretty good hands. I was lucky to find him."

Louise, restless, stood up. She walked to the window, folded her arms under her breasts and looked across the street. The narrow frame houses were stacked one against the other like so many dominoes. It's the right thing, Louise.

She thought of Dennis out there someplace and felt a small panic at the idea that she wasn't one hundred percent certain of his exact location at this precise moment. The Strangler was always out there these days. Sometimes he would even take on a specific characteristic in her mind—cold green eyes, a harelip, a certain kind of walk—but mainly he remained a terrifyingly oblique menace with nothing else on his mind but the murder of her own son, whom he had obsessively singled out from hundreds of thousands of kids in the San Francisco area.

"It's not as if you won't be able to do your own work, Louise."

"You're right," she said, turning to her husband. She smiled. "You're absolutely right." She walked across the room and, bending from the hips, kissed Max on the lips. Then she went to the kitchen and poured a cup of coffee. She sat at the kitchen table, lit a cigarette, sipped the stewed brew, swallowed two Tylenol. She gazed at a scrap of yellow paper attached to the refrigerator door by a magnet in the shape of a tiny bird. It was a list of things still to be done.

> empty refrig
> trash
> cancel paper
> spare key for Zmia

So many trifling last-minute chores and tasks. So many little demands. *Spare key for Zmia* . . . She shut her eyes. The professor had told her he lived a spartan vegetarian life; he gave the distinct impression of surviving on nothing but lentils and oxygen and she wasn't even sure about the oxygen. Zmia gave new resonance to the word "ascetic."

Max appeared in the kitchen doorway, leaning against the frame. "It's the perfect situation," he said. "It's absolutely the perfect situation. Do you know how sick I am of sick people?" He approached the table, sat down, took her hand between his own. The quiet pressure of his fingers had a soothing effect. For a long time she didn't move; in her mind she had left San Francisco and was living in a house surrounded by the mysterious silences of a forest. She could feel the darkness of trees press against her and smell air that had been purified by the pines. She could hear the furtive crying of birds.

The vision was rudely broken by a loud clattering sound from the hallway. The explosion of a twelve-year-old boy.

She opened her eyes and smiled at Max. "Here comes the Menace," she said, and rose from the table.

"Bobby Pinkerton says Professor Zmia is going to keep a harem here," Dennis said.

Louise stepped back against the wall as the kid roller-skated past her. She was about to say that skates should not be worn indoors, and most certainly should not be used as a means of transport on an expensive old oak floor, but she let it all slide away.

Not today, she thought. Today she didn't have the energy for haranguing the boy or arguing about Bobby Pinkerton's claims, which were frequently of a preposterous nature. She wondered if Dennis ever believed anything his best friend ever told him. A harem, she thought. She saw rooms filled with veiled women who drifted back and forth awaiting a summons to sexual activities. Professor Zmia naked. Her mind swiveled.

"Bobby Pinkerton's full of it," Dennis added as he rolled into the kitchen.

From the kitchen she could hear Max welcome the kid, followed by an assortment of noises—china rattling, water splashing inside the sink, a refrigerator door slamming shut, and the constant accompaniment of small wheels.

Louise moved to the kitchen doorway. Dennis, leaning against the sink, chewed into an apple. She studied his small, serious face a moment. Sometimes she could see Max in there, a little reflection. At other times she caught a slight glimpse of herself, as if in a mirror at the end of a long hallway. You fall in love with your kid on a daily basis.

"How was the skating?" she asked.

Dennis shrugged. His world was filled with tiny indeterminate gestures. A shrug, a flip of a hand, a twist of his mouth. She wondered if there was a special meaning attached to any one of them.

"Does that mean it was good? Bad? Indifferent?" she asked.

"It was the usual," Dennis said.

"I'm glad you clarified that," Louise said.

She moved to the table and sat down, reaching out with one hand to caress Max's wrist. Her husband, her kid, this family; she lowered her face and caught the faint familiar aroma of Max's cologne.

This family. Suddenly it seemed to her an indestructible entity. Inviolate, protected by love.

And she realized that she was afraid of the city. It wasn't simply the fantastic notion of a killer moving through dark streets—no, it was the city itself, the way it grinds you down like rough metal rubbing on rough metal, the way it makes you spin so that you are always hurrying, always rushing to defeat some clock, always moving as if the concept of just sitting still were too terrifying to contemplate. The separation of lives, the individual schedules that erode the structure of family.

Everyone had his or her separate commitments. Max had his patients, the sometimes impossible demands of the practice. Dennis took guitar lessons twice a week and baseball practice on three nights. And she was always working upstairs in her office, always seemingly threatened by the guillotine of some deadline or other or forever running back and forth with her portfolio in her car and going to endless meetings with editors and publishers. These were more than separate commitments. They were separate lives.

She moved across the room to her son and slung one arm around his shoulder, drawing his face close to her own. He permitted this affection for as long as he thought it was *cool*, then shifted slightly away, embarrassed.

It's going to be good, she thought.

During the whole summer that lay ahead of them they would begin to make connections again. They would be whole again, safe in a place where the strident demands of the city couldn't touch them, where there would be no threats against their unity.

She looked around the kitchen. It's going to be damn good. And the prospect expanded inside her. The forest. The isolation. *The family.*

The summer that lay in front of them assumed the tantalizing aura of an oasis, a cool green lovely place where one might be still for a time.

2 Max crossed the floor of the untidy bedroom, edging his way around the suitcases that lay in a pile and two huge boxes of books and magazines he intended to take with him. Books he hadn't had time to read—he never had time for anything any more. He stared absently at titles. *The Arthurian Legends. Heading Toward Omega. World Religions.* These books arrived in neat little packages each month from the book club he'd joined; sometimes it was weeks before he even bothered to unwrap them.

He sat on the edge of the bed gazing at the pale summery light that lay upon the window, the color of a bleached rose. From downstairs he could hear the sounds of Denny and Louise. Could you lose yourself in books? he wondered. Could you just shut yourself away in a forest and be free? His hand trembling, he rubbed his eyelids for a time.

He rose from the bed and went to the window. He ran one hand loosely across his jaw as he stared out into the street, which ran steeply downward and along whose curbs cars were parked at angles that defied gravity.

The tension that ran through him was almost painful. He took a small silver pillbox from his pocket, removed a pale blue tranquilizer tablet and swallowed it dryly. He noticed there were only twelve pills left in the box, which meant he would have to fill certain prescriptions before he left town. He'd drive to different pharmacies the way he usually did, filling a prescription here and another there, feeling the way he always felt—like a criminal, a junkie, somebody who couldn't climb down from the cross of his own addiction. Then he rejected the idea of addiction; what he was going through was something else, a temporary condition, some unwholesome infection at the center of himself.

He went back to the bed and sat down. He was tense because he knew he shouldn't be using the telephone in the bedroom to call Connie. What if Louise picked up the downstairs receiver? What if she listened in to his conversation?

Voices still drifted up from below. Your wife and son, Max.

Max gazed at the bedside telephone and his hand went slowly toward it. Forget it, Doctor, he thought. Let it go. It isn't going to make a damn bit of difference now. He turned to look at the open bedroom door and dialed the number.

There was a sigh in Connie's voice when she answered.

Max said, "I'm going. First thing in the morning."

"I figured you would."

He was silent. He wanted to hang up. An image of Connie Harrison went through his mind and he could see her standing with the receiver pressed to her lovely face, strands of hair falling against her cheeks, her fingers twisting the cord around and around. There was an ache of longing inside him.

"I have to," he said.

"If you think it's what you want, Max."

"Look . . ." And he started to fish through his mind for a definitive statement, a suitable epitaph to put on the grave of the romance. Nothing came.

"Well," the girl said. "It's been nice. Maybe it could get even nicer someday. I'll console myself with that thought. How are you going to console *yourself*, Doctor?"

There were footsteps on the stairs. Imagining Louise coming up, Max said good-bye hurriedly and replaced the receiver. He stared at the dead black telephone for a time, then the sounds from the stairs stopped and a silence, as unexpected as it was ominous, pulsed through the entire house. Connie, he thought. He stood up.

Connie Harrison was a graduate assistant in the English department of City College, a girl with a strangely fragile quality. She was emerging from a divorce and she'd first come to Max about four months ago because of her insomnia. He'd prescribed Halcyon. Some weeks later she came back to ask for something stronger because she was still suffering bouts of sleeplessness. This time he'd given her Dalmane in thirty-milligram capsules. She returned a third time. She talked about her personal concerns, her anxiety about her thesis, her loneliness, the death of her marriage. The girl's unhappiness echoed inside Max.

He was attracted to her. When she sat close to him in the office he had the urge to touch her, to make love to her on the floor beside his desk. It was the first time in his entire married life he had ever been tempted, the first time the prospect of infidelity had ever occurred to him.

And it scared him. The girl was willing, he knew that from the beginning. And so was he.

He stared into the palms of his hands and saw a thin film of moisture. He remembered the first time he had touched her—a quick embrace, a soft kiss in the parking lot of a downtown bar. And she had done nothing more than hold him tightly against her, her anchor in the stormy fuss of everyday life.

He held his hands out in front of himself to see if they were steady yet. *How are you going to console yourself, Doctor?*

He lay back across the bed. He shut his eyes. The diazepam in his bloodstream had begun to calm him but it was a temporary relief at best. He saw, with a vicious clarity, the hotel room with the window that over-looked the Bay. He saw Connie Harrison standing alongside the bed and the way the lamplight had shadowed her features and how she'd taken off her blouse and skirt and sat down on the edge of the mattress beside him. He saw himself bend his face toward her breasts, felt the palms of his hands against the curve of her hips. She made love gently, slowly. What he remembered was how she didn't close her eyes, how she kept staring at him with an intensity that excited him. She wanted to see everything; she wanted to do everything. And Max wanted her in return, again and again and again.

The lies came very easily to him. He'd been surprised by his own facility for them. A medical conference, Louise. A last-minute emergency, Louise. The guy's appendix ruptured right there in the goddamn office, Louise. Dear Christ, he'd built a fragile construction of mistruths that some god-awful hurricane was going to blow away, revealing the truth, raising all the skeletons he feared.

The lies came as easily as the prescriptions he'd started writing for himself, using fictitious names as recipients. The Valium. The Darvon. The Nembutal. Anything to kill the ache. Anything to defuse the anguish.

And now he was running away.

He was running toward what he knew best. His marriage. His family. This safe little life he'd made. A life he had always imagined stretching ahead of him like a highway with no detour signs. He did not want to inflict hurt and pain on his wife and son.

He was aware of Louise standing alongside the bed. He raised his face, looked up at her. The pale light stroked her skin, made puzzling little shadows in her cheekbones and the corners of her mouth. Had she heard him on the telephone?

She asked, "Well, Doctor? You ready for the great outdoors? You all psyched up about splitting this scene?"

I love you, Louise, he thought. "I'm ready," he said.

As she sat down beside him he caught her hand and pressed it against his lips, a gesture that surprised her.

"You sweep me off my feet," she said.

"And you thought romance was dead, didn't you?" He lay back across the bed, head propped on one hand, and looked at her. Why did he keep hearing some of the things Connie Harrison had said to him only the night before? *You'll never be happy without me, Max. We have an affinity for each other.*

An affinity, he thought. A bond. I know you, Max. He felt an edge of despair.

"I had my suspicions," she said. She was silent, looking around the chaos of the bedroom. "I can't wait, Max. I can't *wait* to get out of this town. Now I know we're really going and it's not just some wild dream, I'm impatient as hell. And I don't care if Professor Zmia has a harem or cooks up weird concoctions in the kitchen or holds strange rituals . . . I just don't care."

3 Dennis Untermeyer sat in the backseat of the Volvo and watched an unfamiliar landscape unfold. The city had vanished hours before and now little towns flickered past in the late afternoon light. *Willows. Artois. Corning.* Every so often he'd listen to a snatch of conversation between his parents up front, but mainly he tuned them out because they talked about people he didn't even know—one of his dad's patients, an author whose books his mother illustrated. The conversation became a drone, like two flies buzzing in an enclosed space. *Charlie Wisdom wants pastels, nothing but quiet pastels zzzzz like he's never heard zzzzz of bold colors. I told her zzzz you need a zzzz psychiatrist zzzz not a GP. . . .*

Dennis shut his eyes and chewed on a stick of spearmint gum. He wondered about the wisdom of spending three months buried in a forest but that had not been his decision to make; like most families, his was not exactly a democratic institution. It had all started simply enough last April when out of the blue his father had mumbled something about how he'd like to get away for a while. His mother had picked up on this in a casual kind of way.

What do you have in mind? she'd asked. Max had mumbled again; he really didn't have anything special in mind—it was just a notion he was entertaining and how did she feel about it and wouldn't it do them a whole world of good to get away from San Francisco for a time?

From this innocent beginning a whole series of decisions had been spawned in an accelerated way. A house in the country had been located. A replacement physician found for Max. Three months set aside for the purpose of "retreating," as his mother had once phrased it.

What Dennis noticed in the course of these decisions was how little they seemed to involve him. He hadn't exactly expected to be consulted, but it was as if in their weird haste to flee San Francisco—and it did seem a little weird to him because they'd always struck him as stable people and now here they were rushing out of the city to a house they'd never seen—his parents had somehow overlooked his existence. Not once had he been asked whether he had his own plans for the summer. Not once had his parents asked him how he felt about this vacation. Of course glowing little attractions had been held out in front of him. *There's bound to be good fishing, Denny. Maybe we can camp out some nights.* Stuff like that. And maybe it *was* going to be an okay summer finally.

He gazed out the window again. A sign said PARADISE. Dennis thought of angels on Main Street. People sitting on little clouds. The lady in the Baskin-Robbins store would have a cash register that sounded like a harp and maybe God himself was the manager of the Alpha Beta.

He shifted in his seat restlessly. He picked up his portable radio and placed the lightweight speakers against his ears. There was a blast of rock music from some distant station—Motley Crüe—and then static. He fiddled with the tuner for a time but didn't manage to find any music again. He hoped the reception might be better wherever it was they were going—*the end of the world*, he thought. Twenty-one miles from Carnarvon, which itself was a million miles from nowhere.

A few nights ago he'd checked the place out on a road atlas. There were some peculiar names in the region. Yolla Bolly Middle Eel Wilderness, for one. Shasta and Yreka and Whiskeytown and Hooker. Carnarvon itself was situated on the edge of the Rogue River National Forest, which stretched on up into Oregon, where it faded out around a place called Ruch.

Ruch, the boy thought. It sounded like an old man coughing up phlegm. He took the earphones from his head and leaned forward against the driver's seat, tapping his mother lightly on the shoulder.

"How much longer?" he asked, aware of his mother's eyes in the rearview mirror.

"Two hours. Maybe three," Louise said.

Dennis slumped back in his seat, playing with the Sony, turning it over and over in his hand. The conversation of his parents had subsided somewhat. Now they weren't talking about people they knew. Now it was *I thought the traffic might be heavier* and *We should be at Redding pretty soon.* Polite chitchat, the kind of talk that did nothing more than fill a vacuum of silence. Dennis sighed. He gazed at his father in the passenger seat; you could see Max's scalp under the thin strands of brown hair. Sometimes, when he looked at his father, Dennis had the feeling he was peering into his own future. He was going to be like Max—long and thin and balding, with serious eyes that burned behind spectacles and hands that shook almost imperceptibly. God, he thought. Please let me be more like my mother, the good-looking one. Don't let me lose my hair and have to wear glasses.

He glanced at Louise in the rearview mirror. She had vaguely sad eyes and high cheekbones and a firm little nose above a mouth that was full and generous. Small lines ran from the edge of her nostrils to the corners of her lips, and her hair, which was mostly glossy black, sparkled here and there with small flecks of gray. Once, Bobby Pinkerton had told Dennis that Louise was a real nice-looking *broad* and Dennis hadn't known whether to be pissed or pleased. Bobby was generally well-disposed toward Louise. Dennis remembered the time he'd shown his friend a book with Louise's illustrations in it and her name on the title page. Bobby had been impressed to the point of speechlessness and from that day on had acted like a kid with an impossible crush whenever he was around Louise.

Dennis turned his eyes away from his mother's reflection. Sometimes he caught in his mother's face a certain nervousness; as if she lived in fear of something terrible happening. She had a hyperactive imagination. She could take a distant event and somehow make it close and personal. The Strangler, for instance. There were times when Louise talked about the Strangler as if she saw him every day at the supermarket. She had taken the horror of newspaper headlines and made them real in her own mind; now the Strangler was like an old family acquaintance.

It was the same with the book illustrations she did: she devoured the text and pulled vivid pictures from it, trapping them brightly in watercolors. They were kiddie books and kiddie illustrations, but somehow Louise managed to give another dimension to the simple words. Whenever Dennis glanced over her shoulder while she was working he'd invariably see a cheerful yellow sun in a turquoise sky or a small train chugging bravely across a landscape or a couple of rascally gnomes peering from behind a toadstool. Even though these were painted with small kids in mind, the look on Louise's

face was always one of immense concentration and belief, as if she were a
passenger on that little train or she knew the gnomes personally. She was
always *inside* her paintings.

Dennis looked out of the window. He was thinking how there were some
jokers at school who'd hide in clumps of shrubbery and suddenly leap out
at you with their hands upraised and their fingers stretched, pretending to
be the Strangler. He wasn't one of them because he'd decided that that kind
of behavior was more than a little undignified. If you were going to pretend
to be somebody, why waste your energy on a scumbag like the Strangler?
Why not pretend to be somebody *good*?

A place called Red Bluff was coming up. Dennis saw a sign that said
HIGHWAY 99, which apparently led—beyond Red Bluff—to a town named
Los Molinos.

"Is anybody hungry?" Louise asked, smiling at Dennis in the rearview
mirror.

"I could manage a few bites, I guess," the boy said. It was a standard
routine with them. Louise would always ask Is anybody hungry? knowing
what the answer would be. And Dennis would always respond in the same
way. These little rituals of family, insignificant as they seemed, made him
feel good. They filled him with a soft warmth. They reminded him of the
beat-up old security blanket he'd always fallen asleep with until about two
years ago, when he'd reluctantly decided to give it up as a sign of immaturity.
At the age of twelve, he needed reminders like this. It was a shifting world,
things kept changing, and sometimes you couldn't keep up with them.

Louise turned to Max. "What about you?"

Max nodded. He passed the palm of one hand across his forehead. "You
want to stop here?" he said.

"It looks as good a place as any."

Louise drove around until she found a steak house called The Pits. It had
the skull of a long-dead steer hanging above the entranceway. Hollow sockets,
a spidery crack along the jawbone, teeth that appeared to be smiling about
some black secret. As he stepped out of the Volvo Dennis gazed up at the
skull. Lit by the pale yellow light of a late afternoon sun, the great skeletal
head was filled with pools of shadow.

"Poor thing," Louise said. "Remind me to become a vegetarian, Denny."
She gave a little shiver.

Dennis smiled. He passed under the skull, following his parents into the
restaurant, which was made up of large, gloomy interconnecting rooms. A
hostess showed them to a table by a window. Dennis noticed there was a
good view of the parking lot. Before they sat down Max excused himself
and went off in search of the men's room.

Louise examined the menu briefly, then she set it down and reached out across the table to grab Dennis's hand. "He's been working too hard. He hasn't really had a break in seven years," she said. "He needs this time, Denny."

The tone in her voice puzzled him. She was talking about Max as if he were an invalid. It was the kind of tone you used when you were referring to somebody bedridden in the next room, confidential in a wary, hushed kind of way.

Louise said, "I think he needs this break more than he even knows."

Dennis moved his head. Was his father sick or something? He glanced at the menu. His stomach rumbled briefly. Because he felt his mother was waiting for his agreement, he said, "I guess he does."

"We all need it, Denny."

"Yeah."

Louise, who had been frowning seriously, threw back her head and laughed. Dennis wondered if he had missed a small joke somewhere. She was vigorously rubbing the back of his hand now.

"We're going to have a good summer, Denny."

"Let's hope so."

"No, I take that back," Louise said. "We're going to have a *terrific* summer."

Dennis said, "The best."

Louise picked up her menu again. "The very best," she said.

4   The man, who wore his hair back in a ponytail with a rubber band, and whose navy-blue T-shirt had the faded emblem EVERYTHING IS ROTTEN across its chest, beat on the back of a skillet with a wooden spoon in time to the music that issued from the Sanyo tape deck of his old VW van.

I see a bad moon rising . . .
I see trouble on the way . . .

The man used the spoon now to stir the mixture that was brewing on his Coleman stove. Beef, red peppers, mint leaves, teriyaki sauce and onions. The fragrance of the food activated his tastebuds so much that he had to move away from the hissing stove.

He went toward his van, which contained everything he owned in the world. Apart from the stereo, there was a pile of T-shirts, several pairs of blue jeans, some cutoffs, sneakers, sandals, books, and an old clay bong that he kept as a kind of souvenir of his past—his *hippy* past—even though he didn't indulge in weed these days.

Some things, after all, you had to set aside.

Don't go round tonight
It's bound to take your life . . .

He lay down on the foam pad at the back of the van. The VW was equipped with a small skylight, and the man stared at the darkening sky through the opening. Already pale stars were visible. He sipped a little lukewarm California red and pondered the great expanse of forest that lay all around him. It was twenty-one miles to the nearest town and, unless you counted the old couple who lived two miles away, there were no neighbors. He didn't include the weekend hunters, those parties of good old boys who came up into the forest to shoot such menacing creatures as quail and deer with all the ferocity of people intent on endangering as many species as they could.

He had seen the old folks from time to time on their slow strolls through the trees. Clutching each other, they hobbled patiently along, imparting the impression that they were not two separate individuals but rather one, almost as if they were joined at the hip.

Sometimes he had noticed them standing in the distance, half hidden by pines, and they seemed to be observing him with a kind of curiosity. At first this awareness of being assessed by silent strangers had spooked him, but then he'd accepted the fact that he played some kind of role in their sheltered lives. He had spoken with them on only one occasion, to ask whether they needed any odd jobs done. They had been extremely polite in their refusal, as if they were sorry they had no work for him. Looking around their yard, which had the appearance of a dump, he could see a hundred things that needed to be done.

What the hell. You couldn't deny other people their eccentricities. Maybe they liked the way their property looked. Maybe they enjoyed being surrounded by an assortment of discarded objects, the way some people felt uneasy unless they had a white picket fence around their home.

He crawled out of the van and went to the Coleman stove, where he stirred his food. He sat cross-legged beside the flame, his skinny body bent forward from his hips like a half-broken stick. All around him the spaces between the pine trees were filling up with darkness.

There's a bad moon on the rise . . .

The cassette stopped and the silence around him was profound.

This last year, winter and summer alike, he had spent here in these woods. He went into town only when he had to, mostly to buy groceries or use the public swimming pool.

He spooned some food from the skillet onto a metal plate and ate quickly. Then he gathered the utensils together and went down a grassy bank toward a narrow, sluggish stream. He cleaned the plate, skillet and spoon, squirting a glob of Dove over each item before plunging it into the dark water.

He climbed back toward his van, where he removed the rubber band from his ponytail and shook his hair out. The hair was thick and full, perhaps a consequence of the Zen macrobiotic diet he had followed so religiously in the late sixties, those heady years of pretension and optimism, faddism and naïveté—how weird that trip seemed to him now.

He went inside the VW and opened his glove compartment. He groped around with his fingers, found what he was looking for, and started to count his money under the absurdly thin light that fell from the dashboard stereo.

He was down to nine bucks and twenty-nine cents, and his provisions were dwindling. Which meant Odd Job Time. He sat behind the wheel, his face tilted back, and finished the bottle of wine.

He remembered three days ago he had seen a van parked outside the empty redwood house located three miles down the dirt road that led to the Ace of Spades. The van had a logo painted on its side: CARNARVON CLEANING SERVICES. This presumably meant that the house was about to be rented, which in turn suggested that he might offer his services to the tenants when they arrived. Weeding, clipping, trimming, chopping, cleaning—he did it all.

Turning, he crawled into the back of the VW.

He thought about the forest that stretched away on all sides and in his mind's eye he traveled the terrain, floating from the crusty little log house where the old couple lived to the sleek empty redwood and then all the way up the dirt road to the Ace of Spades, where there was a jukebox filled with country music and sullen types played eight ball.

He did not go to the Ace of Spades often, except on those rare occasions when he felt like picking up a girl. His success ratio wasn't very high, partly because few of the female patrons of the Ace of Spades wanted to ride into the forest in a beat-up old VW. But mainly it was on account of himself and how he looked, like he was a relic of a time most of those young girls had never experienced. And the name he was known by—Frog—was an echo of a suspect hippy past when even a plain John Smith could turn into something like Shenandoah Goldenghost.

He lay with his eyes open and listened to the impressive silences of the forest, a great wall of quiet that was broken only intermittently by the cry of a bird or the paw fall of a foraging animal or the sly whisper of the breeze as it stroked black branches.

It was the kind of vast starry night on which, several centuries ago, he would have dropped a tab of acid and sat up waiting for the sunrise while his brain self-destructed in the laboratory of the skull. He smiled at the thought.

5

It was almost dark when they reached Carnarvon and rolled along the narrow main street.

Louise looked at the lit storefronts. The stores were small and trendy, the sidewalks done in cobblestone, the lamps on every corner facsimiles of Victorian gaslights. She glanced at the names of the shops. The Coffee Beanery. A restaurant called La Chaumière. A place called Crafty Things, its window stuffed with scrubbed wood artifacts. An art gallery named Framed.

And then suddenly the town was gone and the road ahead was dark and all Louise could see in the rearview mirror was the afterglow of the lamps, which spread across the reflective surface like a faded decal.

"Boy, that was quick," she said.

Max said, "It's amazing—you think you're out in the middle of nowhere and suddenly there's a small trendy town, all bare pine and macramé and Italian cheeses and Scandinavian furniture."

Louise leaned forward, peering at the way her headlights sliced the darkness and touched the trees that pressed in from either side of the road. She had the sensation she'd just left civilization behind, that there was no going back.

"I assume this is *woodsy* enough for you," Max said.

Just ahead there was an incongruous slash of neon in the darkness. A big electric card, an Ace of Spades, blinked on and off like a lascivious eye. Then a roadhouse loomed up and through an open doorway Louise could see a large room filled with tobacco smoke and the shadows of people clustered around a bar. A sound of country music filtered out.

Max touched the back of her hand. He slouched in his seat and closed his eyes, enjoying the darkness; a sense of relief coursed through him suddenly. Here in these dark woods he could hide himself away, insulated from the world outside. He felt a calmness, a quieting of nerves, pulses still. It was more than just the medication he'd taken back at the restaurant in Red Bluff, more than twenty milligrams of Valium, could make him feel. Maybe up here in the green security of the forest he could make himself whole again.

Turning, he looked at the darkened face of Denny, who was asleep. Neon slinked over the boy's closed eyes as the roadhouse slipped past. It was another world here, Max thought. What he had left behind were messy fragments of himself, like the fingerprints of an amateur burglar at the scene of a botched crime. He wanted to hold his wife and tell her how sorry he was. He wanted to make—if he could—a fresh beginning. And then he was thinking about the various pills and capsules he'd stashed inside his suitcase under his shirts—he'd dump them. He'd throw them away. It wouldn't be difficult.

He put his head out the window and inhaled the dark air. Fresh and sweet, it filled his lungs with the sharpness of pure water. It was the clearest air he could remember ever having breathed. You could only be whole in a place like this—how could you be anything else? He felt the breeze push through his hair as the Volvo turned down a twisting dirt road. There was the sound of loose pebbles drumming on the undercarriage with the ferocity of hailstones.

"Here we go," Louise said. "Good-bye, San Francisco."

She turned the full beams on. All around the car the trees grew thicker, their trunks closer together now. She had the impression of great expanses of pine reaching away forever on either side into an impenetrable secrecy.

"Look for a house with a sundial," she said to Max.

He laughed quietly. In the dark you could see hardly anything. Night and forest combined to impose blindness on you. He moved one hand, resting it against Louise's knee.

Louise leaned forward over the wheel. The Volvo rattled and shook in the ruts. She thought she saw a dark shape ahead, a shadowy structure barely visible between the trees. She braked gently as the structure assumed form, taking substance from the forest around it.

"Could it be?" she said.

Max said, "It's the only house we've seen since the tavern."

She swung the Volvo carefully into a narrow driveway and the headlights picked out details of the redwood house. A porch. Downstairs windows. A glass-fronted door. An impression of first-floor windows melting into the dark beyond the reach of the car's beams. Louise jumped out of the Volvo and stared at the house.

She had seen the photographs, of course. And she had liked what she saw.

But it was a different experience to stand outside the house, confronted by the reality of it. She folded her arms in front of her chest and she thought, I like it. I really like it. It welcomes us. Somehow it welcomes us.

Max was coming around the front of the car. He stood beside her, clearing his throat. She pushed her arm through his and they moved up the steps on to the porch. Max had taken the key out and was trying to fit it into the lock. But there was no need for the key.

"It isn't locked," he said.

"Why would anyone need a lock out here?" Louise asked, laughing with nervous excitement, pushing the door, stepping inside.

"I wonder why it wasn't locked," Max said, more to himself than to Louise. Why was he letting such a small thing trouble him? A key in one's hand was a form of expectation—you anticipated turning it in a lock, after all. And when you found you didn't need the key in the first place, there was a sense of slight disorientation. Fatigue, he thought. That was all. Suddenly he was tired.

Across dark spaces a feeble bulb burned. A stove light in the kitchen.

"Why was that left on?" Max asked. He had found a switch and suddenly the room in which they stood was white with electricity. Louise moved toward the kitchen and Max followed her.

She said, "To welcome us. So that we wouldn't stumble into a house that was totally dark." She touched the edges of the stove, which was more modern than the one she had in San Francisco. Self-cleaning. Touch-control buttons. A digital timer.

Max shrugged. An unlocked door. A light burning. These were incidental things. They weren't important. This wasn't San Francisco, where such occurrences would have had you calling the cops in a flash. He had to relax—the pressures were all behind him.

"I guess the realtor had somebody come out and clean the place up, Max. And they left this light on for us." She turned to face him, aware of the white kitchen gleaming all around her like an island of light afloat in the dark center of a pine forest. Stainless-steel sink. Dishwasher. Lots of counter space. Ceramic tiles across the floor. "I love it, Max. I really love it."

Max was opening the big refrigerator. He peered inside, then said, "Look at this."

She moved toward the appliance.

There were two apple pies sitting on the center shelf. Freshly baked. Crusts golden. Two apple pies in old-fashioned glazed stoneware dishes, antique pieces inscribed with a pale blue floral pattern of a kind Louise hadn't seen in years.

"Isn't that nice, Max?" she said. "Doesn't that make you feel at home already?"

Max shut the refrigerator and smiled. "I better wake Denny."

She watched him go across the kitchen floor, heard him cross the porch, and then there was the reassuring sound of car doors opening and closing. She opened the refrigerator again and she thought, Whoever has left these antique dishes here will surely come back for them pretty soon.

She would thank them for their thoughtfulness.

6 Professor Pyotr Zmia, who had degrees from several institutions of higher learning around the world, flexed and unflexed his hands slowly. He stood in the center of the living room with his eyes shut, concentrating hard on a patch of color that existed only in his mind. After a time, when the rate of his pulse had been slowed and his body felt completely loose, he opened his eyes.

He looked around the living room. He had a sense of ownership. He could *feel* the house all around him—its rooms, its spaces, its dark corners. Before too long he would come to know this house intimately. He moved slowly, crossing the living room and stepping inside a smaller room, which contained a large piano. The instrument, which sat in the center of the floor like some huge bat with an upraised wing, was black and glossy. The professor went toward it. He laid his hands over the keys but didn't strike them. He tilted his head back a little in the fashion of a man listening to a purer kind of music than any piano might ever produce—an inner symphony of some kind.

He moved away from the piano. He gazed from the window out across the street. Houses similar to the one he stood in faced him, glowing in the last light of day. The professor smiled. Although the houses were exact copies of one another, there were striking differences in their colors, their wood trims, their front doorways. Americans, he thought. They were a race of people running after an elusive individuality. They wanted to leave little marks to tell you that they had existed—*I* painted this house yellow, *I* had a racing stripe put on *my* Dodge Colt, those are *my* initials carved in this tree. They wanted a kind of immortality, so they wrote their names or left signs of themselves wherever they could.

He shrugged very slightly as he turned from the window. It was twelve years since he had last been in the United States and he found it little changed. There were the usual excesses of energy to be seen everywhere—new freeways, new shopping malls, high-rise buildings going up at an impossible rate while older structures, with many years of use still ahead of them, were being torn down. Americans were a restless crew. In their urgent quest for their destiny, they had never learned how to sit still. They had never mastered the art of silence.

The professor stepped toward the kitchen, a big gleaming room hung with copper pans. A window looked over a narrow backyard. He imagined the woman, Louise Untermeyer, standing at the sink, perhaps peeling an onion.

He sat at the kitchen table, his small hands stretched on the surface. He tried to see the man, Max, standing in the kitchen doorway. But Max was blurry to him because Max carried a disturbance around with him. He always had a slightly tortured look, the professor thought.

He moved on to the boy.

Dennis was easy to envisage. He was open and good-hearted, despite his adolescence—a time in his young life which would push him toward secrecy, which would bring him furtive qualities and awkwardness of emotion.

The professor stood up. He would go upstairs now. Bedrooms were very informative places in which to prowl. In the narrow hallway, where his delicate bare feet slapped against the shiny wood floors, he paused beneath a little gallery of family photographs. There was one that depicted all three Untermeyers sitting under a red parasol on a beach, grinning. The boy had a Popsicle in one hand and his lips were purple from the stain of artificial grape. Louise wore a silly straw hat.

The next photograph showed Dennis alone. It was obviously a studio portrait because it captured none of the boy's inner self. It was staged, deliberate, and bland. The professor stared at it for a moment. Then his thoughts were interrupted by the sound of the doorbell ringing. Westminster chimes: *bing-bong, bong-bing.*

Everett Banyon was standing outside. Although the night was dry and the skies clear, the realtor carried a rolled-up umbrella. Professor Zmia held the front door open and Banyon stepped inside.

"I was in the neighborhood," the realtor said. "It occurred to me I might drop in. See how you're settling. Nice house, don't you think?"

"Very nice," said the professor. His "V" sounds always came out as "Ws." *Wery nice.*

Both men went into the living room. Professor Zmia sat down and was silent. He watched the realtor move to the window, where he glanced out a moment before he lowered himself onto the sofa.

Banyon moved the tip of his umbrella on the floorboards, inscribing a loose circle. "Do you have everything you need, Professor?"

"Indeed."

Banyon sighed quietly. Professor Zmia could read the uneasiness on the realtor's face. A single sliver of perspiration slinked down across Banyon's brow from his greased hair.

"What makes you so nervous?" the professor asked.

"Am I nervous?" Banyon smiled.

"It shows."

"Then I should try to relax."

"If you want a long and healthy life, yes," said the professor.

Banyon breathed deeply for a time. Then he leaned forward, adjusting the cuffs of his jacket, pulling them back so that one-quarter inch of shirt showed at his wrists. "Has it changed in twelve years, Professor?"

Professor Zmia was silent. He tended to regard all questions carefully, no matter how trivial they seemed. And the English language made him more wary than usual—it was so full of land mines and pockmarks and words with many meanings that you had to take your time. He said, "All change is relative, Mr. Banyon. Some things change only to remain as they were. Other things change because they have to make way for what is new. Two objects cannot occupy the same space simultaneously."

Banyon sometimes felt he was talking to a fortune cookie. He poked the floor with his umbrella. He had the feeling that the professor had misunderstood his question. He would ask it again, this time with a different emphasis. "Has *it* changed in twelve years? That's what I wanted to know."

Professor Zmia smiled. It was a bright expression, a benign white sun crossing the brown face. He sparkled whenever he smiled. Over the years many people had been hypnotized and charmed by that same expression.

"Has *it* changed?" the professor mused. He shook his head very slowly. "I hardly think so. It remains the same as it always was, Mr. Banyon. Always the same. Why should it ever change?"

Mr. Banyon wiped the sliver of perspiration from his forehead and for a long time studied the greasy spot it left on the tip of a finger.

7   "Banyon's photographs didn't do this place any justice," Louise said. She was sitting on the redwood deck with Max, drinking coffee, chewing on a slice of apple pie. The early morning light that sneaked

through the pines was the color of soft pearl. "They didn't quite capture the space here. They didn't get the *feel* of things, did they?"

Max shook his head. He was only half listening to his wife. A hawk had drawn his attention and he was watching the great bird create graceful patterns in the sky. He drained his coffee cup and looked over the rim at Louise, whose expression was one of satisfaction.

From the lower part of the house there was the sound of music from Dennis's portable radio. Reception was poor and the music came in short bursts before it was obscured by throaty static.

"You sleep okay?" Louise asked.

"Fine. Did you?"

"It took me a few minutes," she answered. More than a few, she thought. She'd lain awake for perhaps a half hour, hearing noises to which she was quite unaccustomed—the rustling of trees, the querulous sound of an unfamiliar bird, the stealthy whisper of something moving around the house.

An animal, she had thought—a badger, a skunk, some dark furry thing wandering in circles. Sometimes its body brushed against the outside wall, and once she thought she heard it grunt directly beneath the deck.

She looked at her husband a moment before she spread her hands in her lap and studied her wedding band. "The air up here seems to have a positively horny effect on you," she said, and there was a mysterious knowing look in her eyes.

"Does it?" He knew what she was talking about. He glanced at the hawk again, which had flown close to the house.

"Forgotten already, Max?" She feigned disappointment.

"I haven't forgotten a thing," he said. Which was true enough. He remembered how, after they had explored the house last night, after Denny had crawled into bed in the downstairs bedroom, he had drawn her out here on this deck and pulled her down to the boards and made love to her with an urgency he hadn't felt in years, as if something inside himself had become rejuvenated. Afterward, he had been unable to sleep. Somewhere in the middle of the night, after he was sure Louise had finally dropped off, he'd located his pills in his suitcase and swallowed three capsules of Dalmane—gazing with mild disgust at his own reflection in the bathroom mirror, telling himself, I don't need these things.

"You astonished me," Louise said. "Took me quite by surprise."

I surprised myself, he thought. He rose and moved to the handrail that ran around the deck. He studied the patient movements of the hawk until it was gone. And then Louise was standing behind him, pressing her body against his spine.

"You think the air up here is an aphrodisiac, mmm?" she asked.

Max smiled. He turned and faced her, placing his hands on her hips and drawing her toward him. "I think I should bottle the stuff if it is," he said.

She pressed her face against his shoulder, thinking how he had acted like a young kid who couldn't wait to get laid. The way his hands fumbled at her and how unashamedly noisy he'd been—positively *adolescent*. It had reminded her of the first time they'd ever gone to bed together, when she'd been an art student at UCLA and Max was in his third year at medical school. What had drawn her to Max back then was an endearingly clumsy quality he had. If he gave you a rose, its stem was bound to be broken. If he gave you chocolates, they were certain to have been crushed in transit somehow. A quality of awkward bewilderment—his fingers seemed too large for his hands, he was awful at undoing buttons, and he handled the hooks of a bra like a man reading braille. For some reason too obscure to explore, she had loved him for these inadequacies. Back then, too, he had carried a certain excitement about him—he was forever describing his studies, amazed by each new wonder he'd discovered, astonished by what he had still to learn.

One time, she remembered now, they had made love in her small apartment in Westwood and afterward Max started to talk about the pancreas and what this gland did inside the human body, and although she hadn't really listened to what he was saying—what did she know of enzymes and hormones?—she hadn't been able to take her eyes away from his face, which was flushed and excited, as if he were telling her something that nobody else in all the world knew. The pancreas wasn't the most romantic subject on earth, God knows, but when Max talked about it he was like a small boy on Christmas morning. How could she resist that infectious quality?

The years since had buffed the edges of his wonder. The grind of a general practice had worn him down. But last night, right here on this deck, she had listened to old echoes of the Max she'd first loved and she'd been enchanted by his lovemaking, by the silences of forest and the starry arch of sky.

She caught his face in the palms of her hands. And then she turned toward the trees, the thickets of greenery that covered the landscape like fur.

"I love it here," she said. "I love it. The view. The house. The whole thing. Who remembers San Francisco anyhow?"

She sighed quietly, happily. Last night's exploration of the house had provided one pleasant surprise after another. The living room had seduced her, with its brick fireplace that covered an entire wall, the comfortable furniture, the woven oval rug that lay across floorboards whose glossy surfaces

suggested deep brown mirrors. The downstairs bedroom was perfect for
Denny. It had its own bathroom, which impressed him, pale blue ceramic
tile with matching fixtures.

The upper part of the house consisted of a large master bedroom and a
small adjoining room she could use as a study. There was enough space for
her easel and brushes and paints. Work seemed so incredibly distant from
her all at once.

From the bedroom, sliding glass doors led to the deck. Space and light,
glass and redwood and pine. She had caught herself thinking in the breathlessly abbreviated jargon of a realtor: *2 bds, 2bths, dk, frplc.*

Now, as the forest absorbed her, she held her breath—she hadn't expected
an encounter with perfection, hadn't anticipated anything like this. And
what she felt, with the pines reaching toward the sky and Max standing
beside her, was a curious sense of freedom, a quiet soaring inside, as if what
filled her lungs was not oxygen but helium, something that rushed to her
brain and made her light-headed and dizzy in the most pleasant way she
could imagine.

And then her attention was taken by a faint shadow out there among the
trees. For a second she wasn't sure what it could possibly be that drifted up
so lazily into the gray sky. Of course—it was smoke, a thin spiral of smoke
that rose almost imperceptibly before it disintegrated.

"Look," she said to Max and pointed. It was hard to estimate distances
out here, but she judged the source of the smoke to be a quarter of a mile
away.

"Maybe it's a campfire," Max said.

"Or a chimney." She narrowed her eyes. She hadn't considered the possibility of neighbors. Now a slight breeze tugged at the smoke, twisting it,
blowing it haphazardly.

"A chimney." Max appeared to turn the word around in his mouth.
"Who'd want to build a fire on a humid day like this?"

Humid? All she had felt was the weight of a comfortable warmth in the
air, but no moisture, no clamminess. She glanced at Max. He was lifting a
piece of apple pie to his lips. He chewed a moment, then made a face. He
parted his lips and spat crumbs out into the palm of his hand.

"Jesus," he said.

"What's wrong?"

"It's bitter—"

Louise watched as he placed the remains of the slice back on the table.
"I thought it was sweet."

Max sat down, put his feet up on the table. "Whoever was kind enough
to bake those pies for us must have used crab apples. Or left the sugar out."

• • •

Dennis thought it was strange about the radio. At times he could tune in a station clear as he wanted, and then, quite suddenly, it would become silent. He positioned the antenna this way and that, with no measurable success, then he took the portable GE outside and tried it there. He was determined, with an inquiring mind, and he was not about to be cheated out of his music because of some atmospheric freak.

Behind the house, not far from the shadows thrown by the sun deck, he twisted the antenna with grave concentration. He was rewarded by a sudden burst of rock music, followed by silence. He stared down through the trees a moment, then decided he needed a higher position, above the tree line if possible. Pines, he knew, were not the best climbing trees in the world because of the scratchy branches.

He made his way some distance from the house, looking for a likely candidate to scale. When he found one he tucked the portable radio against his side and shinnied up the trunk to the lower branches.

Clinging to a branch, he caught his breath. He turned the radio on and jiggled the antenna and, distantly, he heard the voice of a deejay saying, "*Hey hey hey out there fellow travelers in realms of rock, it's approaching the hour of eight ai emmmmm right here at good ole KBBC in the capital city of sweet Sacra-Mmmmmento!*"

The voice sounded as if it came from a distance too far to measure. But then it died, and Dennis, tucking the radio beneath his arm again, clambered higher into the tree. When he stopped he realized he had a good view of the sun deck—overlooking it, in fact, seeing empty coffee cups and a slab of pie on the round table. That mysterious pie which had turned up out of nowhere. Deee-licious.

Branches slapped at his cheeks and needles pricked his hands. When he stopped again he realized that his position was precarious. He pressed himself as close to the trunk as he could, wrapped his legs around it, and watched a colony of ants excavate a long thin crack in the wood in front of him.

It would be a drag, he thought, if he found out he could really get good reception only at a height of thirty feet. What was he supposed to do then? Scale a tree every time he wanted to listen to a few tunes?

He turned the ON switch.

He fiddled with the tuner. Damn, there was nothing.

He shut the radio off, conscious of a thin smell, an aroma blown by a faint breeze through the trees, something he knew was familiar but couldn't quite put a name to it. It was sweet and alluring and he turned his face this way and that to see if he could detect its source. Maybe it was coming from the kitchen, maybe his mother was making something—no, she was busy unloading suitcases and boxes.

He looked upward through the branches. He was close to the top of the pine. And he wasn't confident of scaling it any farther because the trunk had begun to quiver each time he moved. The scent hit him again. It was like toffee, sweet and almost unbearable. His mouth watered and he could almost feel the stuff sticking to his teeth.

Perching awkwardly, he shut his eyes.

He suddenly thought about the time when he'd gone to the Santa Monica boardwalk with his parents and the air had been rich with the scents of cotton candy. Mouth-watering, almost painful in intensity. It was like that now, only more so. His stomach made a noise. He opened his eyes and flattened his body against the trunk of the tree. The front of his SAVE THE WHALE T-shirt was pierced by tiny pine needles. It was time to get out of this flakey tree.

He made his way down, catching his clothes against the rough bark. When he was on the ground again the scent had disappeared entirely. He turned and looked through the trees, his body motionless, as if he were waiting for the aroma to come back so that this time he might track it down and find its origin. But it had dissipated.

He went inside the house. His mother was standing at the kitchen sink, rinsing out a coffeepot. She turned her face toward him and smiled. "Been exploring?"

Exploring, the kid thought. Sometimes there was a tone in his mother's voice he didn't appreciate. Like the way she'd used the word "exploring"— she still spoke to him as if he were five years old. Maybe mothers couldn't help that creeping condescension. Maybe they didn't like their babies to grow up. It reminded them of their own mortality, he figured.

"I climbed a tree," he said.

"You see anything?"

More trees, he wanted to say. "Somebody's baking something out there," he remarked. "There was this wonderful smell."

His mother was quiet a moment. "I saw some smoke before."

"You think somebody lives nearby?"

Louise shrugged. "I guess."

Dennis sat down at the table. He put his portable radio down and gazed at it. "I wonder who."

Louise was drying her hands in the folds of a paper towel. "I imagine we'll find out soon enough."

8 Frog opened one eye, aware of a metallic dryness in his mouth. He raised his head and the muscles in his neck creaked and he peered at the youthful puffy face of the girl who lay alongside him in the back of the VW.

You got lucky, you sly old fart, Frog.

The girl was still asleep.

The beauty he thought she possessed just before the Ace of Spades shut was an illusion that faded in the pale light of morning. Puffy from alcohol, her nose a little too large for her face, she was plain—but she was young, maybe eighteen or nineteen, and her body was firm and her ass (ah, sweet Christ, her ass) hadn't yet fallen down her legs.

Just the same, as he rose from the sleeping girl, he wasn't very happy with himself. He didn't know the first thing about her, couldn't remember anything she'd said except for her name, Roxanne, and—the real kicker— he couldn't remember much that had happened after he'd brought her back here to his spot in the woods.

He shoved the cover aside and tried to get up before the girl stirred because he wanted to go down to the stream and wash himself. He moved very slightly. *You, old Frog, have turned into a chauvinist pig.* Using a young girl like this. Is there no shame in you? Moreover, he had squandered his last few bucks, which meant that he'd have to go down to the redwood house and look for work as soon as he could get himself together.

The girl's eyes sprang open and it took her a moment to focus on her surroundings. She pushed black hair from her eyes and looked at him and said, "Oh, shit. Shit shit *shit.*"

Frog said nothing. He caught his hair in a tail and slid a rubber band around it. Now comes the moment of painful recognition. How drunk had they both been last night?

"I'm up shit creek," the girl said.

"That bad?" Frog asked.

"You don't understand." She examined her arm, as if she expected to find a wristwatch there. "What time is it?"

"I don't have clocks out here," he said.

"Is it nine? Do you think it's after nine?" Her voice was filled with panic.

Frog glanced through the window of the VW and pretended to take the measure of the sun. "Relax, it's only eight. What's the big deal about nine anyhow?"

The girl smiled for the first time. "Nine is when Robbie comes home."

"And who's Robbie?"

"My husband."

"Ah. Now that casts another complexion on matters," Frog said. Robbie and Roxanne, he thought. They might have his and hers bath towels. He had not set out last night to make a cuckold of anyone.

"He works night shift," the girl said. "Can you drive me back to Carnarvon?"

Frog felt bad, demoralized. He had his own code of ethics and it did not vindicate cuckoldry, although there were serious lapses usually born out of ignorance. Naked, he slipped out of the van and stretched his arms, listening to the sluggish whimper of the stream nearby. The girl stuck her head out, her black hair falling forward on her bare shoulders.

"Where you going?" Roxanne asked.

"To freshen up. To perform ablutions." He grabbed a towel and a skinny bar of soap and started to move toward the stream.

"Hey, wait for me," and the girl came out of the van and followed him down the incline in the land to the water. She stared at it with an expression of horror. "It's stagnant," she said. "You can't bathe in stagnant water."

"Your eye deceives you. There are undercurrents." Frog stepped into the greenish water and felt its coldness against his hips. After a moment—as if after having cuckolded her husband she saw stagnant water as only one other step in her moral deterioration—the girl joined him. Frog watched her splash herself tentatively.

She sank downward until her face was submerged and her long hair floated out like black seaweed. He waded toward her. Now this is quite perverse, he thought. This sudden arousal he felt through the folds of his hangover. The last thing I need.

The girl surfaced. "Gimme the soap," she said.

"At your service," and he passed the slippery bar toward her.

He watched as she slid it between her breasts and then her hand went down into the water and she was soaping herself between her legs. Frog sighed like a man made weary by his own rebellious libido. To what do I owe this reaction? he wondered. He looked past the girl a moment in the direction of the trees, as if he might put this new temptation out of his mind. He didn't need the moral complications of all this.

The girl was looking at him with an unmistakable light in her eyes. "Come on," she said. "What are you waiting for?"

A stand-up performance, he thought. Hampered from the hips down by water. She pressed herself against him and he could feel her legs swing around him, an interlocking of limbs.

When she kissed him her mouth was wet and open and her tongue moved inside his lips. It was a forceful, hungry kiss.

He pulled his face away from her shoulder, feeling her hand go under the water toward him. This aquatic fucking was a young man's sport, he thought. Now she was clinging to him and the quick way her breathing came suggested a kind of desperation.

Hold on, he wanted to say. Let me get my bearings, baby. Pressed against her shoulder again, he found himself gazing absently up the bank toward the trees. A visual exercise in detachment, in control.

And he saw—thought he saw—something or somebody moving just beyond the screen of the trees. His impression was of little more than shadows, gray as the light of the sky.

He shut his eyes because this kind of submarine pounding took all the concentration he could muster—and when he felt the girl shudder against him and the long painful raking of her fingernails on his spine he realized it was all over and he could go limp in the chill water. Limp, relieved. And not very happy with himself.

When he opened his eyes again his visual field was still, devoid of movement. But he *knew*. Who else could it have been but the old couple? Who else? Out on one of their strolls, casually taking the morning air, they had stumbled over his watery indiscretion and perhaps had inadvertently watched for a moment, with something akin to astonishment on their faces. An unexpected sideshow here in the forest! Naked people sporting in a stream! Come See Frog Fuck! He felt a burning sensation on his cheeks. What was it? A sense of shame? Some old bourgeois coyness resurrected?

What the hell—he didn't like people to see him in the throes of coitus, that was it. Not even the old folks, whose own recollections of similar couplings in their own lives must be little more than dim memories by now.

He staggered up onto the bank and the girl came after him, laughing as she moved. From behind, she reached up under his buttocks and caught him gently by the testicles. These young girls, he thought, these *kids*— they just don't know when enough is enough. He was too old for this shit. Depleted, he sank into the grass and lay there wondering what the old folks were thinking about now. He imagined them perched out on that little porch of theirs, looking like two ancient squirrels who disapprove of the world around them. Can you believe what we saw in the stream? Maybe it was an hallucination, dear.

Frog smiled. On the other hand, he thought, the spectacle in the stream might have inspired them to antique fumblings of their own. It was quite a thought.

•   •   •

Metger parked his patrol car in the lot of the Ace of Spades and went inside the tavern, where he hauled himself up on a stool at the bar. He ordered a beer and sipped the froth from the head of the ice-cold Coors.

He lit a cigarette and watched as Martine, the barmaid, folded her arms on the counter and leaned toward him. Years ago, when he had been a young officer, not sheriff of Carnarvon, when he hadn't been a married man weighed down by a life of domestic responsibilities—a swimming pool and a home and a 1984 Chevy, all owned by one bank or another—he had had a sweet thing going with Martine.

She had aged pretty well, he thought. Maybe a thickness at the hips and pronounced circles under the eyes, but these were surface things, and as you got older you learned to look a little deeper than that.

"Well, stranger," Martine said. She had wonderful, thick black hair, almost the intense black-blue of a raven. "We don't get to see you in here very much these days. Crime wave in Carnarvon keeping you busy?"

Metger set his glass down. "Somebody ripped off a stereo from Radio Shack. And a stray dog was run over by vacationing Texans in a Winnebago."

"No shit," Martine said. "A real crime wave."

Metger nodded. "I tell you, no place is immune these days." He drained his glass and watched the woman draw him another beer. "How's business?"

She patted the back of his hand. "Fair to middling. How are you? How's married bliss?"

Metger said, "I can't complain, Martine." He had been married for two years. "Nora's pregnant. Seven months."

"That's nice," Martine said. "You must be looking forward to the big event, Jerry."

"I am. I guess I really am."

He was conscious of a memory in Martine's eyes, the way it had been back then when both of them were younger and more carefree and caution was something other people brought to their behavior. Not them, though, not when they had been as free as goddamn birds and there had been long wild nights of wine and lovemaking. The memory stirred inside him like a soft wind. He had married Nora and he was glad things had worked out, but there wasn't any harm in a little nostalgic indulgence now and again. If it didn't get out of hand. Martine, he knew, had never married.

"How's your dad, Jerry? I heard he wasn't too well."

The thought of his father depressed him. The old man was stuck in the nursing home at the edge of town; he spent long hours secretively counting candy he hoarded. When you spoke to the old guy you were never sure what kind of answer you were going to get. At times Metger Senior was lucid, but more often he was tuned to different frequencies from those of anyone else.

Metger said, "He's not good. It's weird. I still can't figure it out. One day he was fine. The next day his mind was gone. Just like that. As easy as blowing out a match. I always thought he was indestructible."

Martine looked at him sadly. "That's too bad. You get a chance, Jerry, you give him my best."

"If I catch him on a good day," Metger said.

They were both silent for a time.

"You didn't say what brought you out here, Jerry."

Metger was quiet for a time. "Well, I heard in town they'd rented out that redwood house for the summer."

Martine leaned nearer to him. "Is that right?"

"That's what I heard."

Metger shifted his weight against the bar, then pushed his empty glass away and frowned at Martine's suggestion that he have another.

"A family," he said. "Married couple with a young kid."

Martine didn't speak.

"They haven't rented that place to anybody with a kid for some time," Metger said.

"I didn't know Joe Lyons had gone," Martine said.

"Last spring. I heard he moved down to San Diego."

"He'd been there a long time."

"Eleven years," Metger said. With certainty. Joe Lyons had been the tenant for eleven years and now he was gone and a new couple had moved in with their kid and this distressed Metger—even if he knew his unease wasn't exactly rational. He looked past Martine's face at the rows of liquors along the shelves, then he said, "I was thinking of going down there. A courtesy call."

"So that's why you're out this way," Martine said. "And I was flattering myself that you wanted to see me."

Metger smiled. "Introduce myself. No big deal. Just a quiet visit. Make them feel at home."

"Like the Welcome Wagon," Martine said.

She took his empty glass and filled it with Coors and this time she added a shot of rye to the beer. "It's good for you. Drink it."

Metger tasted the mixture, then set the glass down.

9 For the next two days Louise was involved in household tasks—rearranging furniture to please herself, driving with Denny and Max into Carnarvon for supplies, checking out the stores, getting the phone company to install service—something Max was curiously reluctant to do. Did he want to cut himself off entirely from his patients? What if there was some kind of crisis Ed Stallings couldn't handle?

She had no time to sit down to her own work, even though she had an upcoming deadline for a series of illustrations that were going to be used in a book for first-grade kids. She set up her drawing board, arranged her paints and brushes, but even in idle moments when she thought about the illustrations or when she leafed absently through the spare text of the book, she invariably found herself drifting through the glass doors to the sun deck and just staring at the forest.

The trees pulled her away from her thoughts, as if she were the willing victim of a magical spell. She would simply lean against the deck rail and let the quiet undertones of the pines fill her mind. A seductive lethargy had overcome her.

Peace, she thought. The tiny miracle of peace here in the middle of the pines. She enjoyed the silent telephone and the absence of traffic and the sense she had of somehow stepping outside the boundaries of time.

At night she would sit out here with Max and drink a couple of glasses of wine. Sometimes Denny joined them and she'd experience the true sense of family for the first time in years.

If there was anything that troubled her, even in a minor way, it was the fact she hadn't become attuned to the night sounds of the forest. It wasn't so much the occasional unexpected cry of a bird or the way the night breezes would rattle the trees, it was the noise of the animal that came every night to prowl around the house.

She assumed it was the same beast both nights. Now and again she'd been tempted to take a flashlight and go out and identify the thing once and for all, but somehow the unbroken blackness of this place prevented her. There were secret pools of dark that moonlight didn't penetrate, hollows beyond the reach of stars.

She lay awake and listened to it roam, shuffling, circling. Was it stalking something? Or was it simply a scavenger drawn to the house by the prospect of food or the attractions of trash cans? In the mornings the cans were never disturbed. And she could never find any tracks, paw marks, any sign of the creature's passage.

She had vague dreams, indistinct images that sneaked into her brain like light passing through the lens of a camera. Once or twice on waking she remembered the snout of an unidentifiable animal, wet and black and quivering, and she recalled small amber eyes that held her in some hypnotic manner.

On the morning of the third day when she was in the kitchen and wondering about the two antique pie dishes that nobody had bothered to come and collect, she heard the unexpected sound of a vehicle pulling up outside the house. She walked out onto the front porch and saw an old VW van turn into the driveway, its side panels streaked with mud and its windows dirty. At one time it had obviously been painted in Day-Glo colors, a kind of psychedelic camouflage, but they had faded over the years into pale yellows and bleached reds.

Louise went down the steps and saw a man emerge from the van. He had his hair in a ponytail and he wore a T-shirt with the legend LET FREEDOM RING. He wore cutoff blue jeans and had sandals on his bare feet and he looked like somebody suffering from malnutrition. A freak, she thought. A superannuated hippy coming out of the forest.

The man came up the driveway, his arm extended and his hand open in a gesture of greeting. She took his hand and felt the vigor of his grip.

"James Arnott Bartleby," he said, grinning. His teeth were good and his hair clean and strong, but it was the glow from his eyes that captivated her.

"Is that really your name?" she asked.

"Call me Frog."

"Frog?"

He looked beyond her at the house for a moment. "We're all a little ashamed of something," he said. The eyes were pale blue and they burned in his head. But the quality wasn't anything manic or drugged-out; rather, there was a kindness, a warmth, an openness she found herself liking at once. "Why Frog?"

"You don't want to know."

"I do. Really."

"Ancient history." He shuffled his feet around. "You remember communes? Those dens of hippy evil?"

"Communes, sure."

"I was once in a commune in Colorado," he said. "In those days a lot of people were not exactly in their right minds. Those were the days of chemicals. Well, yours truly apparently lost whatever trifling control he might have had and spent one entire night thinking of himself as a frog. Making frog noises all night long. Rebbit. Rebbit. Amazing what you can do with your time when you're really applying yourself, isn't it? The name stuck."

"Frog," she said. "It might have been worse. You might have imagined yourself a hyena. A worm." She smiled and shrugged. She could catch the whiff of instant nostalgia here. During the mid-sixties, when she'd been a student at UCLA, she had lived for one entire semester in the purple haze of marijuana. Those lazy days when you let everything hang out. Brain cells were popping all around her as her friends swallowed acid or sat up night after night in amphetamine bewilderment or took reds to come down. Even Max back then had been known to eat speed, which, as a med student, he had easy access to, but he'd given up foreign substances when his weight started to plummet. When he'd dwindled from a healthy one forty-three to a spindly one twenty and couldn't stop his hands from trembling, he'd decided it was time to call it quits.

"Settled in?" Frog asked.

"Pretty much." She paused. "What can I do for you?"

"Don't ask what you can do for me. Instead, ask what I can do for *you*." He stuck his hands in his pockets. "I weed. I trim. I tidy around. At a pinch I can cook gourmet meals. Your fancy. It's been a long trip and I've picked up a few skills along the way."

She smiled at him. "My name's Louise. Louise Untermeyer. We're from San Francisco. We're going to be here for the summer."

"Is that the royal 'we'?" Frog asked slyly.

"My family. My son somewhere. And a husband upstairs reading."

Frog surveyed the grassy area alongside the driveway. He pointed. "Look, Louise. Weeds. Stinging nettles. Curled dock. Ragwort. I'd say you need my services around here."

Louise stared at the weeds. "Where do you live, Frog?"

He pointed to the VW.

"Where do you park it?" she asked.

"My address is General Delivery, care of the forest. No zip. If you really want to know, you follow the wash back there until you come to a stream of sorts. Hang a left and keep going. That's where you'll find me. We're neighbors."

Louise thought about the smoke she'd seen rising out of the trees a couple of days ago and she asked, "Is there anybody else in the vicinity? Other neighbors?"

Frog, bending to scrutinize the weeds, glanced up at her. "Beat the woods with a big stick and you'd probably scare out fifty people. Dope dealers. Lovers. Bums. Fugitives from the FBI. Illegal aliens. Moonshiners—"

"Seriously," she said.

"Seriously, there's only an elderly couple over that way," and he pointed a finger absently. "I say elderly. Old would be better. Very old. I'm talking Wrinkle City, if you pardon the phrase." He paused, licked his lips, tugged at the end of his tiny beard. "What the hell. We're all headed for Wrinkle City." He smiled at Louise. "You want these weeds pulled?"

"I'm not sure—"

"A weed is an affront. Nature's pests. A bane to mankind."

Louise laughed. "If they're that bad," she said, "why don't you do what you have to do, Frog?" Then she turned and went up the steps of the porch and Frog watched her go. In the doorway she looked around and raised one hand in a small, delicate gesture, then the door swung shut and she was gone.

He studied the weeds, then he went to his van to get his gardening tools. Shears. A weeder. A black plastic trash bag. On his way back to the weeds he looked at the sleek house and thought, Good-looking woman. A class act.

He bent down to start his assault on the ragwort.

As he did so, a kid appeared around the side of the house, smiling at him shyly. Dennis, who had been behind the house trying to fix a snag in his fishing line, was surprised to see the skinny bearded man hacking away at the weeds. For a moment he wasn't sure what to say, how to introduce himself; sometimes he had trouble with adults when it came to basic social skills. They seemed to observe you as if they expected you to perform. Tell us about your girlfriends. How are your grades? But the bearded man wasn't like that at all. Dennis understood that right from the start. The guy skipped through the weeds and flipped the palm of his hand over so that Dennis could give him five.

"Frog," he said. "You must be the boy about the house."

"That's me," Dennis said. Frog? he wondered.

"Got a name or do you go by a number?"

Dennis smiled. "You can call me Denny."

"Well, Denny," the man said. "What do you think of it so far?"

"Think about what?"

"All this," and the guy made a huge circle with his arm. "Nature's greenery. The woods. The silences. Too quiet for you?"

"It's okay. I guess."

"Do I detect a tone of uncertainty?" Frog had a huge smile on his face.

Dennis shrugged. He wasn't sure about the tone in his own voice, nor was he certain what he thought about living out here. He'd gone on several walks into the forest and had even penetrated a place where, some three or four miles from the house, the pines grew so close together you almost had to turn your body sideways to slip through the spaces. "I'm not used to it,

I guess," he said. He wanted to add, Sometimes the forest gives me the creeps. Sometimes I think I'm going to get lost out there. Sometimes I miss the city so badly I want to yell.

"Give it time," Frog remarked. He switched his scythe from one hand to the other. "It takes some getting used to. When I first came up here about a year ago, I thought I was going crazy. How was a city boy like myself supposed to cope with all this goddamn quiet? Where were the video games? Where were the poolhalls? What was I going to do all the time up here! You get used to it. It sorta gets under your skin after a while. Either that or you go insane totally, in which event the environment doesn't matter a damn anyhow. Who knows? Maybe you've got to be a little loony to live up in these woods."

"What do you do?" Dennis asked.

"Try to stay alive and healthy."

"Is that a full-time occupation?"

Frog looked at the kid and laughed. "Yeah. Yeah it is when you think about it. Anything else is bullshit, Denny."

The boy was silent. He liked it when an adult used a word like "bullshit" casually around him because it meant he wasn't being treated like a kid. It conferred upon him the status of acceptance. Usually, adults didn't swear in front of him—at least his parents' friends didn't. They cussed in private, but not when a kid was around. Dennis knew it was a hypocrisy.

"You live in your van?"

"It's comfortable."

"You're free."

"I'm working on it," Frog said.

"I like the idea of living in a van," Dennis said. He stared at the vehicle in the driveway. "No landlord and no mortgage to pay. I like that. You could take off any time you liked."

"Yeah," Frog said. "So what do you do all day?"

Dennis kicked at a clump of weeds and watched a red butterfly rise upward and float away. "I go for walks. I watch a little TV."

"You get any kind of reception up here?"

"Fuzzy," Dennis said. "Sometimes it's just snow."

"Where do these walks take you?"

Dennis thought about this question a moment. "Here and there," was what he finally said. "I've been on the lookout for someplace to fish. You know any good spots?"

"Sure," Frog said. "Ten miles on up the dirt road brings you to Canyon Lake. Sometimes you'll find bass up there."

Dennis thought that ten miles sounded like a long way. He'd have to talk Max into driving him—if he could somehow get his father activated. Max had retreated into the big bunch of books he'd hauled up here with him and whenever he had his face stuck between the pages—which was most of the time—he was lost in his own space. Book in one hand, a glass of scotch in the other. Louise called this process of reading and drinking "unwinding." Last night, when they had all been out on the sun deck, Max had lost his balance momentarily and slipped against the handrail. Louise, entranced by the trees, hadn't noticed it. But Dennis had and the little incident bothered him. He'd never known his father to drink to excess before.

"Well," Frog said. "I better get on with it. Your mother's paying me to cut her weeds." He turned away, then hesitated. When he looked back he added, "See you around, Denny. Nice meeting you."

"You too," Dennis answered.

"If you see my van out there in the forest, come visit me. Okay?"

"I'll do that."

"You like rock and roll?"

"Yeah."

"I've got some good tapes. Feel free."

Dennis watched the guy walk back toward the weeds. Frog raised the scythe and began hacking furiously, the muscles in his thin arms tensing as he worked. When he paused once he lifted his face and smiled in the boy's direction.

"You met your neighbors yet?" he called out.

"I didn't know we had any."

"Old couple by the name of Summer. They live back that way"—Frog pointed loosely—"about three quarters of a mile."

"What do they do back there?" Dennis asked. He couldn't imagine anyone living out there in the direction Frog had indicated, but then he remembered the sweet scents that had drifted down through the trees just the other day. Maybe that's where they had come from, the Summers' house.

Frog said, "I never asked them. Maybe they spend all spring growing cucumbers and all winter pickling them. Who knows?" He winked and went back to work.

After a time Dennis drifted back around the house again and lay down in the shadow of the sun deck.

Nice kid, Frog thought, and stuck his old meerschaum between his lips and worked as hard and as fast as he knew how. He trimmed and snipped and cut and hauled weeds, his whole body a frantic instrument of activity. He was sweating and his muscles ached and his hands bled from various snags he'd caught, but he understood it was only good business practice to work like a fucking *whirlwind* the first time, because then you left a terrific impression and they always asked you back.

The woman came out once and offered him a glass of lemonade but he refused it, wiping streaks of sweat from his forehead. The Puritan impression. Nothing interferes with work. She went up on the porch and watched him for a while before she stepped back inside the house. Without his audience, Frog slowed his work rate, though not by much.

When he'd finished with the weeds he carried the heavy plastic trash bag to his VW and dumped it inside. He wiped his wet hands against his shorts.

The woman came back on the porch. "You through?"

Frog nodded. "You had a heavy weed problem," he said.

"But not now?"

"Weeds always come back, Louise."

She watched him, her arms folded beneath her breasts. A curious little smile lingered on her lips. "We're just about to have coffee. Want some?"

Frog stepped into the house, wiping his feet on the doormat first. He followed the woman through the living room to the kitchen. Her husband, a long thin guy with glasses and brown, thoughtful eyes, was already seated at the table with a coffee mug in one hand. He introduced himself as Max.

Frog sat at the table, where Louise poured him coffee. He took one sip of the strong black liquid and shut his eyes like a wine expert taking a sample. "Kona," he said.

"Right," Louise said. "Was knowledge of coffee something else you picked up on your trip?"

"I drink Maxwell House when I'm at home. Instant."

"Where's home?" Max asked.

"The van out there," Frog said.

Max nodded. "A free spirit," he said.

Frog stared into his coffee cup a moment. "I try. It ain't easy."

"You worked hard out there," Louise said. She sat down and faced him.

"A tornado," Max put in.

Frog smiled. "It's all sleight of hand. I wasn't alone out there. I had a gang of helpers. Didn't you notice? A bunch of dwarfs. Modest little guys. They don't ask for much."

He emptied his cup and Louise filled it up for him again. She regarded him with curiosity. "What else do you do, Frog?"

"This and that. So long as it's legal."

"Frog cooks, Max. Did I mention that? Gourmet stuff."

"Is that right?" Max said.

Frog nodded. He understood what was going down here—it was a kind of polite interrogation. He couldn't blame the couple. They had every right to know who they invited inside their house. Was he really just an itinerant weeder? Or a mad ax killer? He looked at them, his eyes switching from wife to husband. Of the two, he received the warmer vibrations from the woman. The husband was stiffer, although you had the impression he was trying.

Frog asked him what he did for a living.

"I'm a GP," Max answered.

"No kidding? I was in premed once. Jesus, it seems like a long time ago."

"Where did you go to school?" Max asked.

"Boston."

"You dropped out?"

"First time I saw a fetus in a pickle jar I decided it wasn't for me." Frog paused. He could still remember that baby, umbilical cord and all, floating in a glass jar of formaldehyde. Its eyes were shut and its expression was one of eternal annoyance. Both mother and child had expired during delivery. It seemed unfair to Frog that your destiny, after a nine-month gestation, was to be displayed in preserving fluid for the edification of generations of gaping medical students.

"Some people don't take to medicine," Max said. "What did you do after that?"

"I spent a semester at Columbia," Frog answered. He glanced at Louise, who was smiling at him. "That was around '68, I guess. Time gets away from me. I never finished, though. I had a political disagreement with the authorities." Political disagreement, he thought. He had been unceremoniously kicked out on his ass after an occupation of the administration building and a bonfire of personnel records. He recalled, with uncomfortable clarity, being dragged down Amsterdam Avenue by a big red-faced cop who was making free with his nightstick.

"I wasn't much of a student," Frog said. "There were too many things that sidetracked me back then. There was a war nobody liked very much. There was a butcher in the White House. I got bogged down in the politics of protest, which seems damn childish to remember now. Funny. I don't have the energy for politics now. If I had to vote, I'd vote the apathy ticket. If there was such a thing."

There was a silence in the large kitchen. He concentrated on his coffee, slouching over the mug. The quietness compelled him to add something. "But I had one or two beliefs back then. You know how it was."

Max said, "I remember."

Another pause.

"Tell us something about our neighbors," Louise said.

"Neighbors?" For a second Frog lost his place. He couldn't imagine what the woman was talking about. Sometimes he had moments like that, when there was a kind of slippage in his concentration. He wondered if it had to do with his past drug excesses—some form of brain damage—or if it was just the harbinger of eventual senility—an old broken-down man with pee stains on his pants. Who'd look after him? How could he survive cold winters in a VW van, for Christ's sake? Panic Time. The way to defeat that kind of desperation was simple—you just refused to think of a future.

"You mentioned an old couple—"

"Oh, the Summers." He nudged his empty cup away from him. He could already feel caffeine jangle inside him. "I don't know anything about them, really. I talked with them only one time. I was looking for a job." He spread his thin hands and examined the lines in his flesh. "I saw their place and I figured they'd be happy to hire me . . ."

He looked at Louise. She was listening with obvious interest, her dark eyes alert. Maybe, he thought, she's hungry for social news already. Hungry for snippets of information about neighbors she never suspected she had. Conditioned by her urban environment, coffee with the girls, the chitchat of the city.

"What's wrong with their place?" Max asked.

"Charitably, it's a dump." Frog paused. "Anyhow, they didn't need help. They were emphatic about that in a polite kind of way. I got the impression I was the first being they'd seen in half a century and they weren't sure where I'd parked my spacecraft. I'd venture to say they're mildly eccentric."

"Eccentric neighbors," Louise remarked. "They sound intriguing."

"Yeah," Frog said. "They're intriguing all right. You ought to visit them sometime. Pay a courtesy call."

He stood up, hitching the belt of his cutoff shorts. Max and Louise seemed a little disappointed at the prospect of his departure. He felt vaguely flattered. "Off and running," he said. "This business. It's cutthroat, I swear. I never know when a competitor is going to underbid me."

Louise laughed. "How much do we owe you?"

"Twenty," he said in a tentative fashion.

She found her purse and passed a brand-new bill to him. Max, who was standing up, said, "Come around some night for dinner, Frog. We'd be glad to see you."

"You might even cook for us," Louise added.

"My Chinese is best. Hunan. Szechwan. Cantonese."

"It's a deal," Louise said. "We get the ingredients, you do the rest."

"All I ask is a wok," Frog said. He moved toward the door and noticed how they tracked after him politely, seeing him off the premises.

"Denny loves Chinese," Max said.

"I just met him," Frog remarked. "Friendly little guy."

Louise shook her head. "He must have wandered off somewhere, I guess. New territories to explore." She was quiet a moment, then she added, "At least I don't have to worry about him so much around here. It's not like San Francisco."

Frog opened the front door and paused a moment. "I like kids," he said. "Kids and puppy dogs."

He waved, hearing the door close behind him.

When he reached his VW he imagined he heard the sound of a child from nearby, but he looked around and saw nobody. A cat maybe, he thought. There were lots of wild cats up here in the woods, turned out of their domestic bliss by weary owners. Evicted from suburban comfort and left to forage for themselves. It was a hard world.

He climbed inside the van, looked at his suntanned face in the rearview mirror. It was the face of a man, he decided, who *did* like kids and small dogs.

10 Simple curiosity took Dennis out into the trees. The idea of neighbors living out there in the forest somehow struck his fancy. How did they survive the winters here? *What did they do with their lives?* Then he had a picture of this landscape filled with clean white snow and two old people trudging through it, their arms linked together. It was like having a Christmas card inside his head.

He moved quickly until he came to a kind of funnel in the land, like a dried-up streambed. The place was strewn with rocks and pebbles and all kinds of rotted stumps and branches; blue flies zinged back and forth over everything.

When he reached the other bank of the streambed he paused, tilting his head to one side as if he were listening for something. But there was nothing except for the hollow screech of a jay and the flustered sound of some quail nearby. He moved down the bank, realizing when he looked back the way he'd come he couldn't see the redwood house any longer. The forest might have swallowed it whole.

He went deeper into the pines. Thin midday sunlight filtered down through the branches. The air was slightly humid around him and he had the feeling he was walking through tepid water. He paused again. It would be dreary here when the winter settled in on the landscape. Everything would be gray and bleak. Everything would be depressing. The trees. The silences. The isolation.

Something in the notion of isolation appealed to an aspect of Dennis's personality. Since the age of six or seven, when he'd stopped to consider possible futures for himself, possible jobs, he had been drawn to occupations that involved long spells of solitude. A long-distance trucker. A forest ranger in a lookout tower. These essentially lonely occupations struck chords inside him—he wasn't sure why. Once his mother had said it was because he had a streak of the romantic in him, a description that brought to mind pirates and buccaneers and characters swinging on vines through impossible jungles. He wasn't altogether sure, even now, what it meant to have a romantic streak inside—he wasn't altogether sure he liked the idea either. It implied being a dreamer. And Dennis liked to think he was much more practical than that narrow description allowed.

He moved on. The pines grew closer together. When he looked up he saw a gray-blue sky scarred by pine needles. Then it hit him quite suddenly.

The air was perfumed. It floated around him, danced and weaved in the air he sucked into his lungs—a wondrous scent of chocolate baking, burned sugar, pastry rising. It was what he had smelled the other day when he'd been up in the tree pursuing the lost cause of bringing music into his life. It was the same smell but it was intensified, pervading everything, seeming to cling to his skin and invade the fibers of the clothes he wore.

It was coming from a place nearby. A distinct hunger bit him sharply. It seemed to him that he'd actually *stepped inside* the aroma, that he was powerless to do anything except follow it.

The land rose upward almost imperceptibly. Dennis climbed the gentle slope, and when he reached the top he saw what he'd come to see. A clearing. A small house.

Dennis shook his head. What he saw in front of him was a wonderland, a run-down wonderland filled with the carcasses of all manner of things— the skeleton of a pickup truck, rolls of rusted chicken wire, piles of lumber in various stages of decay, an amazing array of old tools whose names and functions he couldn't begin to know, a mountain of tires, the broken sticks of discarded furniture, oil drums, sewage pipes. A museum of the broken and the useless and obsolete. And still the smell rushed around him. Now he saw pale smoke rising from the chimney of the house.

He gazed at the chimney, the way the roof sagged. He absorbed the sight of the porch and how it sloped toward one end. But it was the sight of the junk that attracted him most. You could play for days—weeks even—in all that stuff! It was like one huge rummage sale to which nobody had ever come. You could find a thousand things to do there. He moved into the clearing and, glancing once at the house, which, except for the smoke, seemed lifeless, walked around the ruin of the old pickup. He opened the door and climbed into the driver's seat, laying his hands on the steering wheel and gazing out through the spider's web cracks in the windshield.

It was an old Dodge with a long gearshift, which the boy manipulated back and forth. In his mind he was suddenly steering this jalopy down the hilly streets of San Francisco. He was gathering speed, swerving around traffic, running stoplights.

Brrrmmm, brrrrmmm, he said, twisting the wheel. It was childish—he knew that on some level. But he'd forgotten the fact he was twelve, he was supposed to be gaining maturity, he was supposed to be *cool*. Sitting up in the high cab with one hand gripping the wheel and his feet on the pedals and the knob of the big gearshift in his fingers, it was easy to forget you were all of twelve and heading for junior high.

Ahead of him, birds flew out of log piles, no doubt panicked by the presence of the Mad Driver. He tipped his head back, glanced at his face in the rearview mirror—in his opinion he had too many freckles—then let his hands fall into his lap. His attention was drawn out through the window and across the junk-filled yard to the house, where he noticed the front door lay open in deep shadow. What if he'd been seen? he wondered. What if the old people were unfriendly and didn't want kids hanging around? What if they were like his Untermeyer grandparents, who hated him for the way he left fingerprints on paintwork and crumpled their antimacassars and spilled little trickles of sugar? Old people got cranky; at times they were like babies.

He climbed out of the cab. There were streaks of rust across his black T-shirt. He moved toward a mountain of old tires, feeling the urge to take a headlong dive into them. Smoke, drifting toward him from the chimney, teased him with its perfume. He was astonishingly hungry now. His stomach creaked like old wood planks. He glanced back at the house. There

were no curtains at the dark windows. Two ancient deck chairs were placed
side by side on the porch. Their canvas straps sagged. Was somebody
watching him? Would the old couple step out at any moment and chase
him off their land? He had the impression that the house was empty. Maybe
the occupants had gone for a walk, leaving something delicious to bake
in the oven.

He skirted a rusted-out pile of old gardening tools—rakes and scythes
and shears that were grown over with cobwebs and tangled in barbed wire
—and he paused at the foot of the steps leading up to the porch. Beside
one deck chair lay a clay pipe in an ashtray that was nothing more than an
empty Bumble Bee tuna can. Alongside the other was a crochet needle.
Dennis wondered if he should go knock on the door; maybe, if they were
at home, they'd ask him to come inside for milk and homemade cookies.
Just maybe. And if they weren't at home . . .

The steps made groaning noises as he climbed. The scent reached out to
embrace him from the darkened kitchen beyond the open door. *He couldn't
stand it. He had to eat something!*

He raised his hand, rapped his knuckles on the door. No answer. He
knocked again. Then, encouraged by silence and yet wary of the fact that
he was actually trespassing, he stepped into the room. There was an old
stove and shelves that contained dishes and little porcelain figures—animals
and fish and children, all of them covered in dust. Here and there the
desiccated corpses of dead flies and the skeletons of dried moths hung to
fragile cobwebs. There was a desk, a table, a couple of chairs, a tall dresser
made of cherry wood. His attention wandered to the dark shadows on the
far side of the room where he could see a fragment of staircase that led up,
through increasing folds of shadow, to the top part of the house.

"Anybody home?" he called out. He stared at the shut door of the stove,
longing to throw it open and discover the goodies baking inside. "Anybody
home?"

He wandered to the bottom of the stairs and peered up through the
dimness. A floorboard creaked somewhere at the top. The shadows up there
changed abruptly. There was the sound of a hand on the banister rail.

Dennis looked up, trying to make out shapes. He rehearsed what he was
going to say and how he'd say it. He'd smile and be nice and ask if they
could spare a glass of milk. He'd be very polite about it all and maybe they'd
throw in some of whatever was reaching perfection in that stove.

He heard the hand squeak on wood, the flat palm causing friction on
the handrail. And then a voice came down through the shadows, a voice
that was both cracked and cheerful. A man, a woman—Dennis couldn't
tell.

The voice came again, closer. "Well, this is a pleasant surprise," it said. "This is truly a pleasant surprise. Welcome to our home, young man."

Out of the gloom a hand appeared on the wooden rail. It was the oldest hand Dennis thought he'd ever seen.

11 What Max dreaded most was the telephone. During the two days before it had been connected he had experienced a strange sense of serenity, as if he were somehow floating through time, adrift from the things that harried him. He wanted to say it was freedom, but he wasn't sure how to define that. He knew only that he was liberated in some narrow sense of the word and the feeling was one of muted exhilaration. But now that Louise had the phone hooked up, his tranquility was menaced—he was accessible to Connie Harrison. She could call Directory Assistance, get the number from them, and pick up her own telephone in the city. She could punch in the digits. Connections would click. Wires would fill with sound waves.

And then the telephone would ring in this house with a shattering sound.

He sat on the living-room sofa. The potential of the black instrument to disturb him seemed unlimited. What the hell would he do if Connie called and Louise was in the room, as she was right at this instant? How could he carry that off? He rose and walked nervously to the window. There was the edge of a slight hangover rubbing at the center of his skull; last night he'd gone overboard on the scotch, which hadn't mixed well with that wretched medication. He resolved to abstain and yet the sense of threat he felt made him so nervous that he thought automatically of the pills. He drew one hand over his face.

Louise, who was flicking through the manuscript of the book she was to illustrate, looked up at him. "He seems pleasant enough," she said.

"Who?"

"Frog. Pleasant. A little quaint. He reminds me of old friends I haven't seen in twenty years."

Max nodded his head. The trees on the far side of the narrow dirt road appeared oppressive to him suddenly. A squirrel dangled from a branch, then swung nimbly out of sight. He strolled around the room, glanced once at the telephone, listened to Louise leaf through the script. Once she laughed at something; he didn't ask what. His mind was filled with a picture of Connie Harrison picking up her receiver. She wouldn't do it, though. Why would she put him in that kind of awkward situation?

Max stood behind his wife looking at the neatly typed words on the paper she held.

He read:

> . . . if only the bird would sing again
> Richard would be very happy . . .

Enthralling, he thought. Poor unhappy Richard.

He returned to the window, his hands behind his back. The book he'd been reading—a boring tome on allergies—lay open on the coffee table. He was tempted to pick it up, but instead he continued to look out through the window at the trees. Lighten up, he instructed himself. Breathe deeply. Relax. She isn't going to call.

When the telephone suddenly screamed he felt himself jump—the sound seemed to be located inside his own skull. He turned to the instrument quickly, but Louise had already picked it up and was talking into it. Max held his breath even as he thought he was being ridiculous. What would prompt Connie to call? She wasn't the kind of person who wanted to make trouble, was she?

Louise said, "Professor Zmia?"

Max breathed out. Not Connie after all. He sat down in an armchair and gazed at his wife, who was smiling at him even as she talked to the professor.

"Trouble with the dishwasher," she was saying. "Yes, I guess it does take time to get the hang of the buttons. . . . Yes, yes. . . . If you'll look . . . if you'll look in the kitchen cabinet over the stove you'll find the instruction booklet. . . . I know, I know. . . . What? . . . Oh, we're fine . . . very pleasant . . . Max is fine. And Dennis is always out exploring some-place. . . . The woods are very pretty—"

Louise laughed at something the professor said.

"Well, everything's so computerized these days. . . . I guess not. . . . I hope you can figure it out from the booklet. Good-bye, Professor."

Louise set the receiver down. She looked across the room at Max. "Poor man couldn't make the dishwasher work," she said. "He couldn't figure out the cycles."

Max reached for his wife's hand.

"He asked after you," she said.

"I gathered that."

"And Denny too. He wanted to know if we were enjoying ourselves."

Max nodded. "How's he doing down there?"

"Aside from the dishwasher, he seems to be doing all right." Louise closed the folder of the manuscript. There was a sticker on the cover with the title *The Day the Canary Wouldn't Sing*.

She turned to Max and smiled. "He's so much nicer on the phone than he is in person somehow," she said. "Maybe it's because I don't have to look into those funny eyes of his."

"What funny eyes?" Max asked.

"Didn't you notice how they just seemed to bore right through you?"

Max shrugged. "I can't say I did." He paused. He was feeling better all at once, back in control of himself. "Did you hear any orgiastic sounds in the background? Girls squealing? Anything like that?"

Louise shook her head. "The only background noise was music."

"Balalaika? Something exotic?"

"It sounded more like Mantovani. Actually, I think it might have been 'Moon River'."

"What a disappointment," Max said. "I thought the professor's tastes would be more eccentric. 'Moon River'!"

"Maybe he was only playing that music to lull us into a false sense of security." Louise stood up, the manuscript clutched in her hands. "He probably changed the record as soon as he hung up."

"You think he's that devious?"

"I wouldn't be the least surprised." Louise stepped into the kitchen. After a time, Max went and joined her.

12 The man in the misshapen three-piece tweed suit paused at the corner of First Avenue and Delaney Street. Sweating in the midday humidity, he gazed across the street at the windows of various stores and recalled a time when Carnarvon had not been quite the tourist haunt it had grown into—when there had been *real* shops and not these overpriced boutiques designed to trap the tourist dollar. A time when greedy realtors had not taken everything over and weren't pulling in the bucks as fast as they could be printed. But that was Carnarvon nowadays— a paradise for quick-buck property developers who dreamed at night of erecting condominiums and filling them with seasonal occupants, flocks of migratory suckers who thought time-sharing was the greatest notion since sliced bread.

The names of the shops irritated him. Hanging By a Thread was a clothing store whose window was filled with designer jeans and shirts with patterns that resembled spilled paints. Bits 'n' Bytes sold computer software. If you wanted a haircut you went to Hair Hair or if you needed to buy used books you went to The Page Boy. Sometimes he half expected to find McMahon's Funeral Home renamed The Dead End. It was all too trendy.

He crossed the street, noticing the out-of-state plates on the vehicles around him. Big Winnebagos from Texas, campers from New Mexico and Colorado. Carnarvon had once been a sleepy little place—back in the golden days before tourists discovered it and a hyperactive chamber of commerce had seen fiscal possibilities in turn-of-the-century architecture, leafy back roads, and miles of unspoiled pine woods.

Then the smart money had flowed in from L.A. and San Francisco and Dallas and all the old stores had been converted into what they were now and all the fine old taverns had been turned into restaurants serving up whole-grain bread and bean sprouts and that unsatisfying food known as *nouvelle cuisine*.

The man poked one thick finger under the damp collar of his shirt. He moved along the sidewalk and stopped when he came to the intersection of Delaney and Fourth. It was quieter here. There were less shops and the traffic was thin. He thought a moment about the phone call from Sheriff Metger. I'd like to meet with you, Miles.

The man felt uneasy, without really knowing why. Metger wanted to talk with him—okay. But he hadn't seen Jerry Metger in months. He rarely saw anyone these days. What could the sheriff of Carnarvon want with a retired physician anyhow?

You could melt on a damned day like this, he thought. He had some trouble catching his breath and his lungs felt like old sponges. He raised a hand to his mouth and coughed into it. The hacking sound distressed him as it always did. Sixty-seven-year-old lungs—you couldn't expect them to work like new, especially after a lifetime of cigar smoking. His eyes watered.

When he reached the end of Delaney Street he stepped inside Bascolini's Tavern, the last bar left untouched by the holocaust of change that had swept through Carnarvon. Bascolini's hadn't surrendered to the urge to install stained-glass windows and plants in brass pots—it was a dull, dark, cool place smelling of spilled beer and old tobacco smoke. It was comfortable. It was a place whose only function was that of drinking, without needless ambience, distracting signs, hanging ferns that threatened to smother you, funny windows that made your skin look as if you had scarlet fever or the yellow plague.

The man saw Jerry Metger at a corner table. He hesitated a moment before he went across the floor toward the cop. Metger raised his face and smiled, half rising from his seat to assume an awkward little crouch over the table.

"Been a while, Miles," Metger said.

Miles Henderson squeezed himself in between table and chair. The palms of his hands left damp slicks on the wood. He gazed at the cop. It was hard to believe that this young man was the sheriff—the face was smooth and unlined and the hair soft and boyish. He reminded Henderson of a young evangelist; he had that kind of energetic light in his clear eyes. An intensity that Henderson instinctively didn't like. Intense people were scary—they could become fanatics right in front of your eyes.

"You still drink gin?" Metger asked.

Miles Henderson nodded. Metger waved to the barman and a drink was fetched and Henderson raised the glass and sipped.

"Don't see you around," Metger said.

"I don't *get* around," Henderson replied. He tapped his leg and added, "Circulation's bad. Sometimes they just stiff up on me. Too much mileage. My tread's worn. If I was a goddamn radial tire I'd be through to the steel by now."

Metger ran a fingertip around the rim of his beer glass. "Can't you do something about it?"

Henderson shrugged. "I get medication. Helps now and then. That why you asked to see me, Jerry? To get the lowdown on my blood problems?"

Metger smiled. It was like a small light bulb going on in the center of his face. "I wanted to talk to you, Miles."

Henderson took another sip of his gin. He felt it slide warmly into his bloodstream. He was tempted to drain the glass entirely but he understood he needed to pace himself because if he went at it wholeheartedly now he'd be drunk on his ass before five o'clock and Henrietta would be a harridan. He said, "If it's a medical matter, I don't need to remind you I retired years ago and all that's left of my practice is a couple of mildewed prescription pads and a mind full of useless bullshit, Jerry. . . ."

Jerry Metger leaned across the table. "It's not medicine, Miles. It's something else."

Miles Henderson leaned back and closed his eyes. He tired easily these days. Especially when it was humid like this, he could feel his strength evaporate through his pores. Aging was a bitch, a perfect bitch. *Something else*, he thought. Jerry Metger's phrase went through his mind like bats flapping down dark tunnels.

Miles Henderson opened his eyes. He had a sudden insight into what was on Jerry Metger's mind and he didn't want to talk about that, didn't want

the subject raised, didn't need any of it. Good Christ, he was retired, he
had his gin and his computer chess game and his classical music collection
and his old books, and he was set on a placid journey through retirement
to death and he didn't need anything dredged up from those years when
he'd been the coroner of Carnarvon County because all that was long gone
and he wanted to forget.

"It's that goddamn house, isn't it, Jerry? It's that goddamn house again.
Tell me otherwise."

"It's been rented," Metger said. "A family. One kid."

Henderson burped gently into his hand. He wanted another gin. When
the barman brought it Henderson drank it back quickly and smacked his
thick lips and saw tiny spots dance before his eyes. He rose a little unsteadily
and looked down at Metger, shaking his head from side to side.

"So it's been rented. Big deal."

"Family from San Francisco."

Henderson tapped the side of his skull and smiled. "You've got a bee
loose in your hive, sonny. I hear it buzzing from where I stand."

Jerry Metger stood up. "You don't want to think about it, do you?"

"You're damn right, Jerry. I don't want to think about it and I don't
want to talk about it."

"It was your case, Miles—"

"Yeah, and it's twelve years old and I've forgotten the half of it and I
don't see any goddamn connection between then and now, Jerry." Henderson
made a gesture of finality with his hand, chopping the air swiftly. "Leave
it alone. Just leave it alone. The older some questions get, Jerry, the less
chance you have of getting any answers. You understand me?"

Metger sat down again, played with his empty beer glass in a resigned
way. He reminded Henderson of a forlorn kid tinkering with a toy.

"It's time for my nap," Miles Henderson said. "That's what I do these
days, Sheriff. That's what old men do best. They nap and they like it."

He turned and made his way across the floor.

He heard Jerry Metger call out, "Wait! I'm not through yet. . . ."

The murky sunlight on the street made him blink and he was a little
disoriented from the gin he'd drunk too quickly. He peered along the
sidewalk. The inside of his mind felt like a map that had been left in the
rain. He put a hand to the side of his face and shut his eyes, imagining the
colors of the map running every which way across the sodden paper.

It was twelve years ago and it was cold to him now. Cold and dead. He
was damned if he was going to let Metger get to him on this subject.
Damned if he was going to reopen an old puzzle like some scar tissue that
hadn't quite healed.

He'd go home to Henrietta and drink some more gin and maybe he'd sleep and the sleep would be untroubled and drunken and dreamless.

Louise painted a small yellow bird. She moved the brush slowly, taking care over each detail—the brightness of a blue eye, the layering of feathers, the pink claws. She understood that if her work had any real merit, it was this attention to small detail. Once or twice she'd tried to create more impressionistic watercolors but she'd always felt uneasy about them—the kids who read these books and examined the pictures were sticklers for every little detail, every shadow, every color. They wanted authenticity. Now, leaning over her easel, she examined the canary that gazed out at her from the paper. She'd painted it in mid-flight, wings extended and claws spread. Somehow it seemed unintentionally menacing, coming out of the paper like a weird bird of prey.

She added more blue to the eye, as if this might take the edge off the menace, defuse the threat in the bird's expression, but it didn't do it. She sighed and put her brush down and gazed at the creature. What was she supposed to do? Paint a smile on the bird's face? Give it a jaunty upward turn of the beak? She removed the paper from the easel and set it down on the floor beside her. She'd try again. This time she'd paint the bird in a stationary position, perhaps situated on its perch. It would alleviate the menace. Maybe she'd put it in a cage, which was the way most young kids first saw domestic birds anyhow. There would be a comforting familiarity in that.

Years ago, around the time when she first met Max, she had been doing abstract oils, great swatches of color—mainly shades of green in geometrical shapes—on large canvases. She painted twenty hours a day, driven, it seemed to her, by an enthusiasm that was almost evangelical. The green canvases mounted up until they filled her small apartment. She hadn't sold any of them. Once a small Los Angeles gallery, a fringe establishment, had hung a few—an act of uncritical kindness, she thought now. Nobody had bought any and the only review, in an underground paper now defunct, had savaged them, calling them "derivative," "unfeeling," and "without any spark of creativity." From that point on she'd never done any more of the large green canvases and whenever she thought about them now she felt a strange little embarrassment—they had been youthful creations and unspeakably trite. Even Max, who had been charitable about her work back then, the way any lover might be about his loved one's creations, said that sitting in her apartment was a bit like being trapped inside a green nightmare.

After graduating she spent a couple of years in an advertising agency where she discovered a knack for certain kinds of illustrations—small red-cheeked children and dogs and butterflies and cute little automobiles. Her illustrations were charming and she was highly paid for them by West Coast publishing houses. Now and again she'd done some greeting cards, usually of a sentimental nature. Get-well cards for five-year-olds, heartbreakers, and tearjerkers. Christmas cards depicting a plumply healthy boy sitting on the lap of robust, florid Santa. The children in her illustrations always had plump little hands and puffed-out cheeks and curly hair, usually blond. The thing she always thought saved her illustrations from being sickening was a humor that crept into them, a mischief. Her kids sometimes had bruises on their knees or scruff marks on their shoes or an unruly curl sticking up out of their heads or a toothless smile—tiny things that suggested blemishes in an otherwise perfectly cozy little universe.

She cleaned her brushes and massaged the sides of her neck. She glanced once at the canary that was frozen in mid-flight, then stood up and walked out on to the sun deck. She surveyed the trees. Immediately below she saw Max, sitting with his back to a tree trunk, a book open in his lap. His head hung to one side and his eyes were closed—the embodiment of idleness. Why shouldn't he be lazy? she wondered. He had worked too long and too hard to build up his practice, rarely taking any time off except for occasional long weekends. Watching him, she was conscious of circles under his eyes; the bald spot at the center of his skull was visible. Dear Max, she thought.

He stirred, opened his eyes, smiled up at her. "I must have fallen asleep," he said.

"You were snoring," she called down.

"I never snore. Physicians know how not to snore. It's a special skill they learn as interns. It's rude to snore during an operation even if you've slept only three hours out of the last forty-eight. We learn that in the first year."

Louise leaned against the handrail. A wood dove went flapping past in a flurry of falling pinecones.

"If you meet me in the kitchen, I'll make some coffee," she said.

"Agreed." Max got to his feet. Louise went downstairs. In the kitchen she filled the coffeepot with water and placed grounds in the basket.

Max wandered in, the book tucked under his arm. He yawned, shook his head. "What time is it?" he asked.

"Three-thirty."

Max sat at the table. The angularity of his body always amused Louise; at times he gave the impression of having more limbs than he knew what to do with. He spread his long fingers on the surface of the table and his wedding ring glinted.

"Where's Denny?" he asked.

Louise shook her head. "I was beginning to wonder about that. He didn't come back for lunch."

Max leafed through some pages of his book in an idle way. "Was it the sound a blue spruce makes/ in the wind at night, owls huge among its needles/ or was it the echo of a footfall/ springing among wet leaves and cedar boughs/ on the riverbank?"

"What's that from?" Louise brought coffee to the table.

"This book of poems. Somebody called Lewis Turco."

"When did you start reading poetry?" she asked.

"I'm full of surprises," Max answered.

"Aren't you just?" She looked at her husband a moment. The whites of his eyes were faintly pink. Suddenly she caught the scent of his breath—there was a trace of stale scotch. Last night he'd consumed about five or six good-sized shots. Maybe what she smelled on his breath was the aftermath of that. Unless—unless he'd been drinking again today while she was upstairs working. She had never known him to drink more than one glass of liquor at any particular time and certainly never during the day. What the hell, it was part of the process she'd described to Denny as *unwinding*. Max was like a little kid playing hookey. Nobody was going to call him about an urgent appendectomy in the middle of the night, were they? Nobody was going to have to be rushed to the hospital at 3 A.M. for a cesarean. It wasn't as if he had to be stone-cold sober for his patients.

"Somebody left this book in the reception room," he said. "I just happened to pick it up."

Louise sipped her coffee. She looked at the title, *American Still Lifes*. She put her cup down and thought about her son. "I guess he's okay," she said.

"Who? This Turco person?"

"You know I'm talking about Denny. He's bound to be hungry."

Max sighed. "He can't be too far away. Maybe he ran into Frog. Maybe Frog's regaling him with tales of forest lore or reminiscing about the glorious sixties."

"Maybe," Louise said. She gazed through the kitchen window at the rectangle of sky visible over the tall pines. She had the sudden impression that the forest went on without any end, mile after mile of dark trees stretching to infinity.

"I'll go out and look for him if you like," Max offered.

"It's strange he didn't come back for lunch."

"Kids don't know about time," Max said. "Time doesn't exist for them. He never wears the watch I gave him last Christmas because he says the band makes his wrist sweat. That's how much he thinks about time."

Louise drained her coffee. "He doesn't usually miss meals, though."

She was silent for a while. She felt an echo of a dread she had intended to leave behind in the city. Out here it was different, she told herself—there's only the safety of the trees, nothing else. But how was one small boy managing to amuse himself out there for such a long time? There were only so many trees you could climb, after all.

Max touched her hand. "Look, Louise. Green trees. No city street corners. No dark alleys. Just trees and sky. What could *possibly* happen to a kid out there?" He paused. "There are no child molesters in the forest, my dear. No stranglers. Nothing."

"Actually, I wasn't thinking about the Strangler. I was thinking about accidents. Like falling out of trees. Tripping on something and maybe breaking an ankle. You never know."

For a moment she imagined these woods alive with weird characters—moonshiners, hillbillies with hunting rifles, madmen on the run from the law, sinsemilla growers, crazed trappers, all kinds of loonies who scratched out some kind of living among the pine trees. She imagined Dennis encountering any one of these creatures.

You imagine too much, Louise. What are these bizarre figments except rustic extensions of the Strangler?

She walked into the living room, carrying her coffee. Max followed her slowly. They sat down together on the sofa. She thought, I have to learn how to silence the tiny screams of anxiety. These woods mean no harm to anyone.

Max said, "He'll come bounding through the door at any moment telling us how he got lost. Louise, it isn't like *Deliverance* out there, you know. You've got to turn down the pilot light of your imagination, sweetheart."

"I'm okay, Max. Really." But she wasn't altogether okay—she imagined Denny lying in a ditch with a broken leg and it struck her that she wouldn't know where to begin looking for him. There were no street signs in the forest. There were no haunts where a child might hang out.

She got up from the sofa and wandered to the window.

As she did so she saw a car turn into the driveway and she felt an odd icy clawing around her heart. The vehicle was a cop car. A beige sedan with unlit roof lights.

For a second Louise couldn't move, couldn't think. Cop cars belonged someplace else, not up here in the forest. Not here. They belonged in humid San Francisco nights, their lights flashing and sirens screaming. They belonged where there was blood, a homicide victim tossed into a dumpster or a young kid strangled on a vacant lot.

Denny. *Something to do with the boy.*

She looked a moment at Max; her expression was one of confusion. And then she was hurrying out of the room, Max striding after her. When they went outside on the porch a cop was emerging from the sedan and gazing toward them with a smile.

They don't smile, Louise thought, if it's bad news. *They look grim then, don't they?* They look like morticians when it's something bad.

The cop took a pack of cigarettes from his jacket and lit one casually. He wore a crumpled chocolate-brown uniform but no cap, no hat.

Louise said, "Is something wrong?" She was conscious of the forest stirring—a quick breeze fluttered through it and for a second the sound of branches whispering suggested secretive voices carrying a message she was too dumb to understand. She felt Max's hand against her arm, the pressure of his fingers. Denny, she thought. Why else would this cop be here?

Her world tilted. She was conscious of gray sky, the path of a bird, the sun concealed by a cloud.

"Is something wrong?" she asked again. She couldn't keep the shrill edge from her voice. And then she was trapped on a downward spiral of panic and recrimination, a flood of guilt: I could have been watching out for my son. I could have kept better track of him.

The cop shook his head. "Hell, no. What could be wrong?"

"I imagined . . ." Louise said, with an intense rush of relief.

"I know," the cop said. "People see me and they always imagine the worst. They seem to think I don't do anything but deliver bad news. Sometimes I feel like a messenger of doom. It's an unfair image."

He stuck out his hand and Louise shook it. She heard herself utter a small shrill laugh, a nervous sound. Max took the cop's hand next.

"Name's Metger," the cop said. "And no, I don't have bad news. I found out in town you were renting this place and I thought I'd say hello. Nothing more sinister than that."

Louise laughed, a little too sharply. She introduced herself, then Max, and she realized that relief had brought a breathless quality to her voice. She glanced at the police sedan. The side panel had the word SHERIFF in dark blue letters.

"Nice to know you," Metger said. His hair was the color of sand and his muscular body filled out his uniform. "How long are you figuring on staying?"

"The summer," Max said.

"A wise choice. You don't want to spend a winter up here." The cop glanced at the house a moment. He had an open, honest face. The eyes suggested some kind of inner strength; it was the face of a man who knew his own limitations. It was also deceptively young. If it hadn't been for the tiny lines around the edges of the eyes, you might have supposed him to be in his mid-twenties.

"You've got a son, I understand," Metger said.

"When you drove up that was my first reaction—that something had happened to him," Louise said.

Metger smiled. "Is he around?"

Louise made a vague gesture toward the pines. "He should be," she said. "He went for a walk. He's a little late. You know how kids can be—"

Max said, "Why don't you come inside? We've got some coffee. . . ."

The cop shook his head. "I'll take a rain check on that if you don't mind. I don't have the time right now." He was looking at the front of the house again. "Good-looking place. I expect you folks are comfortable here."

Louise said they were.

Metger looked upward at the roof of the property. He had the cop's practiced manner of casually taking things in, his eyes deceptively lazy now, almost glazed. He tugged at his belt buckle. Louise noticed the weight of his gun shifting.

Then he turned his face toward the trees for a moment. It was almost as if he were searching the landscape for something. The breeze came again and the pine branches whimpered and then there was silence.

Louise had a strange impression just then—that this cop hadn't come here to introduce himself, he hadn't come out here just for the purpose of getting acquainted—it was something else altogether, only she couldn't think what. The way he looks at the house, the way he *studies* it. He is like a man trying to compare reality with a memory.

He put his hands on his hips and his body swayed a little. "It's good to have a family out here for a change. The last guy who lived here had this place all to himself. Joe Lyons. I always wondered what he did with himself in a place as big as this. If it was me living all alone out here, I think I'd go crazy. Especially in the winter." He smiled, then started to walk back toward his car, where he stopped. "Your boy like it out here?"

"I think he's getting used to it," Louise said.

"Maybe next time I'm out this way I'll get to meet him," Metger said. "This could be a good place for a kid. So long as he's careful."

Careful? Louise wondered. She was about to ask him what he meant by that, but he was already climbing into his car. She saw the cop wave, then watched as the car backed out of the driveway. For a long time the sound of the engine reverberated through the air before the silence came back again. She leaned against the porch rail. She was drained. You overreact, Louise. Sometimes it's too much. There's nothing wrong with Denny. Christ. You take a tiny flame and fan it and before you know it you've got a whole goddamn bonfire burning in your mind. She placed a hand over her heart, which was still kicking against her ribs.

"Our friendly sheriff," Max said. He had his hands stuffed into the pockets of his brown cord pants. "Did you really think he was coming to tell you something bad about Denny?"

Louise smiled thinly. "It crossed my mind."

"Save your imagination for those books you illustrate. At least you get paid for that." Max placed his hands on her shoulders and drew her toward him.

She said, "We still don't know where Denny is, do we—"

Even as she asked the question there was the sound of laughter from the side of the house and the boy appeared around the corner.

He wasn't alone.

Dennis introduced them as Dick and Charlotte Summer. There was a curious similarity between the two old people, such as you see on the faces of couples who have been married for a lifetime. Dick had thin white hair and an easy smile that turned his face into something resembling a crumpled map; he wore dark brown suspenders outside his plaid shirt and his gray flannel pants were baggy and one of the fly buttons was loose, hanging a little awkwardly. Charlotte's hair matched Dick's in color, but hers was still thick, held in place by orange barrettes at the sides of her skull, which gave her an odd girl-like quality, Louise thought. Her shapeless dress was of pale green wool and she had sandals on her white, veined feet. A trace of lipstick was visible on her tiny mouth. Both Dick and Charlotte had bright blue, almost youthful eyes, watchful as those of a bird.

Dennis was babbling as he introduced the couple. You should see their house. You should see the old things they've got. There's this ancient pickup truck and Dick says I can help repair it and Charlotte bakes all this wonderful stuff and they've got old tools like I've never seen before and old books and old photographs . . .

The Summers smiled and nodded until the boy ran out of steam.

Dick said, "Fine boy you have there."

"Real fine," Charlotte put in.

"He likes dabbling with things," Dick said.

"Couldn't get him away from that old pickup," Charlotte added.

"Fascinated him," Dick said.

"He's never seen one that old, Dick, that's why."

Louise smiled. "Won't you come inside?"

The old people looked at each other. Charlotte said, "Can't stay. Not really. I've got something in the oven. Got to keep an eye on it. Hate it when something burns."

"We thought we'd introduce ourselves." Dick shrugged loosely. He winked at Dennis. "Brought you a small offering."

"You shouldn't," Louise said.

"Nonsense. It's nothing." Charlotte produced an old china dish, over which had been stretched a slice of aluminum foil. Her wrinkled fingers, which were bulbous with arthritis, swollen at the joints, pulled the foil away. "Fudge. Did it myself. Always do my own cooking. Can't trust stores these days. Store-bought foods are filled with additives. Mono-this and sodium-that. Who wants to eat that trash? Not me."

"Nor me," said Dick.

Max reached out and raised the dish to his face and made a show of sniffing. "Smells terrific," he said.

"Wait till you taste it," Dennis said.

"It's really very kind of you," and Louise smiled, because the two old faces—these two occupants of what Frog had called Wrinkle City—were clearly waiting for her approval. "I'm sure it's delicious."

Charlotte scratched the side of her nose. "Been meaning to ask for my pie dishes back."

"*You* baked the pies?" Louise asked.

"Surely did."

"They were delightful. I wasn't sure where they had come from, which was why I didn't return the dishes. I thought maybe the cleaners had left them." Louise looked at the couple. It was utterly impossible to estimate their ages—they could have been anywhere between seventy and ninety. Only their eyes, trapped in those two worn faces, seemed to suggest life. And then she wondered if they had a key to this house or if the place was left unlocked even when nobody occupied it. What did it matter? This was the country and people here were real neighbors who didn't bolt their doors and turn on their burglar alarms the way they did in paranoid San Francisco.

"I really must thank you for your kindness."

Dennis went indoors to fetch the pie dishes.

Louise said, "I hope he wasn't any trouble to you."

Dick laughed. The sound reminded Louise of air escaping from a steam pipe. "He can come over whenever he likes. We don't get visitors up here. It's nice to have somebody young around the place. It gets way too quiet sometimes. He's a good kid."

"Fine boy," Charlotte said. "Anytime you folks want a night out on the town, you talk to us. We'll baby-sit him. Even if he isn't what you'd exactly call a *baby*."

Both Dick and Charlotte laughed this time. Hers was a girlish sound, clear and strong and melodic. It emerged incongruously from her face. The small mouth opened, revealing small yellowish teeth and pale gums. The old couple laughed in unison, as if they had infected each other with mirth. Louise had the impression of two people who had become uncannily attuned to one another's lives—mind readers picking up on every little nuance.

"That's really good of you," Louise said. "Maybe we'll take you up on that some night."

"Very kind," Max added. "A very kind offer."

Dennis came out with the dishes. As he handed them to Charlotte, Dick Summer patted him on the head a couple of times. Dennis, who normally would have been embarrassed by this kind of gesture, didn't seem to mind. He accepted the pats the way a dog might.

"Nothing to it," Charlotte said. "Only thing, we don't have a telephone. You'd have to walk over. About a half mile."

"More like three quarters," Dick said.

"I'm sure we'll come and visit you sometime." Louise leaned against the rail of the porch. She glanced at Charlotte's hands—they might have been two artifacts badly carved out of pinewood. They suggested pain, restricted movement. The fingers were thick, the knuckles twisted. As if she were conscious of Louise's gaze, the old woman concealed her hands under the pie dishes. Louise looked away.

"Have you been living up here long?" Max asked.

"Stopped counting the years ages ago," Charlotte answered.

"Too depressing," Dick said. "The way they keep rushing past. Hell, who wants to count time?"

"That's a healthy attitude," Max remarked.

There was a moment of silence now. The Summers were smiling at Dennis. The boy stood between the couple, framed by their old bodies.

"Well," Louise said. "Are you sure you don't want coffee or maybe a beer—"

"Another time," Charlotte said. "Got to get back and check that oven. Burned things don't taste so good." Charlotte laid a hand on Dennis's shoulder, rubbing it slowly. "We'll look forward to seeing you real soon. All of you."

The Summers turned away together. Louise watched them go. As they reached the corner of the house they did something she found oddly touching and yet somehow a little strange—they grasped each other's hands and walked away, swinging their arms like two teenagers experiencing love's first shy connection.

When they were gone she turned to Max and said, "Romantic."

"It's the only word for it," Max said.

"Nice." Louise slung an arm around Dennis's shoulder and drew the boy against her side. "I like your new friends, Denny."

"Me too," he said, disentangling himself from his mother's arm and vanishing inside the house.

13 From beyond the bathroom door Metger could hear the sound of his wife, Nora, talking to him. Because the door was closed, she had her voice raised a little higher than usual. He was barely listening. He looked at his face in the mirror; his lack of color appalled him. He filled the washbasin with cold water and plunged his face into it, opening his eyes under the surface.

"Charlie Badecker called when you were out, Jer . . . something about a life insurance payment . . . told him you'd call back . . . your father called—"

"My father?" Metger asked through the closed door. The old man rarely called from the nursing home and when he did he always sounded confused, as if uncertain of whom he was talking to, and suspicious of the instrument at the same time. "What did he say?"

"He didn't make a whole lot of sense, Jerry."

Metger turned the thought of his father around in his mind a moment. Because the sight of the man—who was once so vital, so alert—depressed Jerry Metger, he didn't visit his father as often as he should have and he felt guilty about it. He tried, and always failed, to justify this neglect. *I'm too busy. I have a pregnant wife to take care of. There's the spare bedroom I'm trying to knock into a nursery.* None of these excuses worked for long. The guilt always came back like a nagging tide.

His father had been one of those figures people say are larger than life. Everything Stanley had ever done he did to excess and with the gusto of a man to whom life is a splendid array of appetites to satisfy. And stories, Metger thought, always stories. Metger's childhood had been filled with tales and legends of old Carnarvon that the elder Metger relayed in his characteristic animated fashion. Some of the stories were whoppers. Others were simple exaggerations concerning the way the early Welsh settlers had lived here, amazing narratives of deprivation and hardship. Most of these stories kept changing in the retelling. It didn't matter. Metger Senior always told them with a tremendous relish that suggested authenticity, and Jerry—wide-eyed, listening intently—swallowed it all without question.

Now, as Metger pulled his dripping face out of the water, he remembered from somewhere in his colorful, crowded childhood his father's tale of a boy who had died in a highly unusual way—but the recollection was vague and confusing to him, as most of his father's stories had become over the years. In this case it was nothing more than a whisper that faded into silence whenever he tried to pin it down.

A boy, he thought. The name eluded him. But he linked it somehow in his mind with the death, twelve years ago, of Anthea Ackerley.

And then there was something else. There had been a kid in his first-grade class who had attended school for maybe a week before they'd taken him away. Robert Hann, that had been the kid's name. Bobby. Nobody knew where he'd gone. A sick boy. A terrible sickness.

Odd links. Connections. Threads so pale they could hardly be seen.

He shook his head. Sometimes he wanted to laugh at himself, at the suspicious turns of his own mind. Somehow he couldn't do it, couldn't release it that simply. A phase, Metger thought. This stuff concerning the redwood house and his father's half-remembered stories and the kid known as Bobby Hann—all this was a phase.

You'll get over it. When? Tell me when. It's been twelve years already.

He thought of Miles Henderson now. That old fart knew something, more than he was prepared to say, but there was no way of getting inside his pickled head to find out for sure. Henderson didn't want to look back into the past these days. He had closed the doors on all those rooms. He had locked them. But he knew *something*—Metger was convinced of that much.

Metger buried his face in the folds of a towel, then he checked to make sure the door was locked. Satisfied, he climbed up on the toilet and raised his hands to the air-conditioning grille near the ceiling.

He paused. This is something you don't need, Metger. Balanced on the toilet, he pressed his face against the wall. A phase, he thought again. That was charitable. There was another word: "obsession."

He took out a pocket knife and used it to remove the screws of the air-conditioning grille. Then he reached inside the vent; his fingers encountered an eight-by-ten manila envelope. He undid the metal clasp and looked inside.

There they were—photographs that had been taken by a disinterested police photographer twelve years ago. Photographs of Jerry Metger's obsession.

Suddenly he could feel the same old rain soak through his clothes and between his hands was the sodden butt of an extinguished cigarette and then he was walking through the wet pines and staring upward at an empty balcony and hearing the sound of a gunshot all over again.

Then they weren't just pictures anymore, they weren't mere recordings of past events, *he was standing inside that room of death and he was looking at that girl and he was trying, Christ he was trying, to make some sense out of it all like a man who stares at a puzzle and knows it can never come out quite right no matter how hard and long he works at it.*

Nora was tapping on the bathroom door. "Jerry, you okay in there?"

"Fine," he answered. He stuck the pictures back inside the envelope. He replaced the envelope in the air vent. He felt like some sad old man who hid a collection of pornography from his wife.

"You sure?"

"Really," he answered.

But not really, he thought. Not fine at all.

He opened the bathroom door and looked across the room at Nora, who was folding clean clothes, placing them in tidy little piles. Metger's here. Her own there. She was huge in her pregnancy and she looked strangely satisfied by her condition, as if she shared some enormous secret with the child inside her.

"You're pale," she said. She was a tall woman, almost as tall as Metger himself.

Metger moved toward the bed and sat down.

Louise and Max Untermeyer. And their kid.

He shouldn't have gone out there today. He shouldn't have bothered it all over again. It was old, a bleached bone, it should have been buried back there in the past the way he had buried so many of his dad's old narratives. But he had a grim sense that he was doomed to keep on making the same resurrection time and time again—a man digging a hole that never gets any deeper no matter how furiously he shovels.

Nora came across the room and sat down beside him.

He held her hand in his own and smiled at her. He didn't like himself for hiding the photographs from her, for keeping those old pictures in a secret place where she couldn't find them and be disturbed by them. What you need to remember, he told himself, is that this is your reality right here. This woman. The unborn child inside her. *This is all that matters.*

But even as he thought this he was filled with a curious, damp dread.

14 It was early morning and there was both sun and moon in the sky simultaneously. Frog had slipped out of his VW and, dressed only in cutoff blue jeans and a sweatshirt, he jogged. It was the most tedious exercise ever designed. The reason Frog bothered with it was some hangover from the days when he'd been a health-food freak. Now, since he didn't indulge in a diet anymore, since he had given up eating like a squirrel, jogging was the only thing he did that seemed remotely calculated to promote well-being.

Even then he wasn't sure if it really helped. He sweated some and his body ached and he felt as if he were melting like a wax candle inside his sweatshirt and the soles of his feet burned—what was so goddamn wonderful about all that? It was the aftermath, he supposed, when you collapsed in a heap and lay there—your heart banging away like a drum and your eyes popping out of your head—and you just felt *good*. You could brag to yourself about how you'd just run twenty miles, even though you knew it was only ten at the most. Joggers, like fishermen, boast cheerfully and lie without scruples.

Jogging was the pits. He puffed down through the trees and hit the dirt road. His ankles were weakening and perspiration was already soaking through his shirt and creating a tiny puddle around his crotch. Blood beat inside his head and small spots danced in front of his eyes. Way to go, Frog, he thought. This is the life, huh?

When you jogged your mind acted peculiarly. Odd little thoughts popped in out of nowhere. Mildewed memories reared themselves up and you thought of people and places you hadn't pondered in years. Now, his feet pounding the surface of the dirt road, he remembered the night on the commune when—so many fucking years ago!—he had swallowed LSD and assumed the stance of a frog and gone hopping down through the bulrushes to the edge of a stream where he'd *rebbitted* all through the hours of darkness, attracting a variety of toads and frogs to his throaty call. Back then it had been easy to believe that you'd become a form of reptilian life, at one with the currents of the stream and the whisper of the rushes and the night sounds of every living thing.

Which was all just so much Zen shit to him these days.

Frog. As Louise Untermeyer said, it could have been worse. Imagine a maggot.

He reached the redwood house. He was losing his breath rapidly. He noticed Denny moving down the path toward him. An early riser, Frog thought. Sweat ran into his eyes.

"Frog!" the kid called out.

"Can't stop." Frog was unable to speak coherently; imminent collapse was on him. "Miles to go. Do I look stupid or what?"

Denny fell in beside him for a hundred yards. It galled Frog that the kid ran so gracefully.

"Can't talk," Frog said. "Out of wind."

Dennis moved without effort. "You want company?"

"Sorry. Always. Run. Alone." Frog groaned. He felt his skeleton rattle around inside his body. Actually, he might have been glad of company, but he couldn't put up with the shame of having this kid watch him fall into an untidy pile at the end of the run.

"No problem," the kid said in a knowing kind of way. "See you later."

"Right." And Frog was gone, trying to sprint for the boy's benefit, up through the trees and out in the direction of the Summers' house. When he glanced back once, Denny was shaking his head, as if the sight of a forty-three-year-old ex-hippy jogging through a forest was lamentable.

Up and up into the trees. He wondered if Denny thought he was rude, refusing his company that way. What the hell. He'd make it up somehow later. Meantime, he was approaching the clearing where the Summers' property line began.

He staggered against a tree and fell down flat on his back and lay gazing at the sky, thinking he would die out here. Coronary infarction. His chest heaved and his lungs felt like two old furry mittens filled with mildewed air. With an enormous effort, he hauled himself up into a sitting position. He peered through the foliage of some shrubbery. Across the clearing, beyond the piles of junk the Summers seemed indecently attached to, he could see the small log house. Thin smoke rose out of the chimney. The windows were in shadow, dark glass reflecting nothing. Lying flat on his stomach now, Frog observed the porch, a ramshackle affair that tilted at one end.

The Summers, barely visible in the shadows, sat on deck chairs. The man smoked a pipe, which he sometimes tapped against the handrail of the porch. The woman was apparently crocheting something. They were unaware of his presence.

I spy, Frog thought. Why did the Summers interest him anyhow? Was it because they were all fellow travelers in solitude, in rustic loneliness? There was a certain serenity to the view Frog watched, the way there is something comforting in a Norman Rockwell illustration. Two old folks, eccentric in the way all old people have the right to be, enjoying the sunset years of their life together. Frog experienced a twinge, thinking of himself alone in the VW. Old Graybeard, the Madman of the Forest. Tourists would drive out to take his picture and there would be a presidential telegram on his hundredth birthday. *Ah, blissful solitude.*

The man set his pipe down. At precisely the same moment the woman laid her crocheting aside. It was almost as if a prearranged signal existed between them, something imperceptible. For some reason Frog felt a curious tension—he was holding his breath without knowing why. The Summers sat motionless, staring out across their property. Then the old man moved his hand slightly at his side and his wife, without looking, reached out to take it.

Frog thought of young lovers. He watched, as the Summers must have watched him in the stream only the other day. Fair's fair, he thought—you watch and I watch.

On the porch, the old couple stood up. Still holding hands, they inclined toward each other, face to face, lip to lip, in a slow kiss. They stood, body pressed against body, for what seemed to Frog like a very long time. He suddenly felt awkward, intruding on an intimacy like this. He shut his eyes a moment. When he looked again he saw the Summers were going inside the house, still holding hands as if they were desperately afraid to let go of each other.

They moved with the kind of urgency that could only have been a prelude to sex and yet they didn't seem to be moving at any great speed, as far as Frog could tell. It was simply an impression he got—*the old folks were going indoors to make love.* He saw the Summers go into the house, watched the door close, noticed how the porch vibrated slightly from all the movement. And then there was silence through the clearing.

A little unsteadily, he rose to his feet. They make love, he thought. At their age. But why did that surprise him? What else was there to do out here anyway? Good luck to them. Bon appetit.

He turned away from the clearing and was about to move slowly down through the trees when a sound from the porch made him look back. He saw the woman hurry out of the house, the man appearing seconds later. They stood together on the porch and it was clear to Frog—from the man's imploring gestures and the way the woman's face was averted—that their little skirmish with passion had turned out badly. Although he could hear nothing that was said, Frog thought he saw the picture. *The old guy couldn't cut it anymore.* It was as simple as that. He watched them embrace, but it was different from before—it had been defused, their passion derailed, it was nothing more than an embrace of comfort, a moment of consolation. Two old folks who couldn't get it on anymore.

Frog could almost feel the old guy's disappointment and humiliation. As he moved away, his legs hurting and a headache beginning to pound at the back of his skull, he realized that their faces were turned toward him now. They could see him, he was sure of that. What did they think of him— some forest voyeur, a creep of the dark green places?

Maybe they figured he was spying on them. Which, he thought, was true enough. A touch embarrassed, he dragged himself back through the trees and along the edge of the dry wash, unable to shake a vague depression that had fallen over him.

In the early morning light the woman climbed the steep path that led through St. Mary's Cemetery. A sullen sunlight slanted through trees, illuminating the headstones with a kind of gloomy certainty. The woman walked slowly, with her head down and her body bent forward a little from the hips, as if she were struggling against a wind.

Florence Hann was fifty-eight years old and her thin face had an element of unshakable sorrow. It was not the kind of face you could imagine breaking into uncontrollable laughter. The eyes were like rusted mirrors that kept light locked in; the lips were tight and dry and mirthless. She wore a heavy gray coat, which, despite the clinging warmth of the early sun, was buttoned to her throat.

When she reached the summit of the path she paused and looked back down at the town of Carnarvon spread beneath her. A faint smoke-blue haze hung around the rooftops. Beyond, the woods created a thick green band around the town.

Florence Hann could see traces of moisture clinging to the faces of head-stones. All the rows of the silent dead, she thought. So many of them. *So many.*

She walked a little way, glancing at the graves. Sometimes, when she came up here on the anniversary of Bobby's death, she imagined she could hear dead voices whispering. They were unintelligible, barely audible, but they seemed to rise out of the earth as if from some dark chorus far below.

And sometimes she thought she heard Bobby's voice among them. No words. No sentences. Just a certain *tone*, a suggestion of the boy's voice that created little tremors in her heart.

She sniffed the flowers she carried. Six dark red roses, one for each year of the child's life. One for each suffering, wasting year.

She paused at a place where the pathway forked. Each year it seemed to her more and more difficult to recall the child's face, more and more difficult to bring to mind the color of his eyes or the way his hair looked or how he felt when she touched him. It was bitterly unfair. She had been robbed of the boy once when he had died; now she was being robbed again, this time by the deterioration of her own memory.

She continued to walk, slowing as she always did in the vicinity of his grave. It was a modest headstone but it was all she had been able to afford because her husband, Frank, had deserted them shortly after the boy started to get sick. She couldn't bring herself to blame Frank any longer. She was too tired of apportioning blame. These things just happened. That was all.

No. They didn't *just* happen. Nothing ever just happened. Something made them happen.

Her shadow fell across the stone. The words were simple.

ROBERT "BOBBY" HANN
1949–1955
Before His Time

Dear God, the woman thought. So well before his time.

Her eyes watered. She raised her face upward to the sunlight. Six brief years. Six blood-red flowers.

She went down on her knees in the grass and laid the flowers against the stone. She closed her eyes and she thought of how she knew of at least one other grave in St. Mary's Cemetery exactly like Bobby's. At least one other.

A shadow fell across her, obscuring the words on the headstone. She turned her face. The man who stood behind her with the sun throwing his face into shadow was tall and wide-shouldered and he stood with his head tilted questioningly to one side. For a moment she didn't recognize him, but then he moved his face and the sunlight filled in his features.

"What brings you up here?" she asked.

Miles Henderson shrugged. He had a big white face and a small mouth and his smile was like a tiny hole punched in the center of an unbaked cookie. "I was walking, that's all."

"You walk up here often?" Florence asked. She raised a hand to the collar of her coat. She had a suspicion that Henderson had been drinking, but she didn't say anything. Although she hadn't seen the retired physician for several years, she'd heard the rumors about his colossal drinking activities—binges that were said to last two, maybe three, days. It was a wonder he wasn't a dead man.

"Now and then, Florence." Miles Henderson set his feet apart and balanced his overweight body as best he could. "Anniversary," and he nodded his head at the grave.

"You might say." The woman stood up, her arms hanging at her sides.

"It's been a long time," Henderson remarked. "Thirty-one years, Florence."

"Like you say, a long time." She looked at Henderson's face. The eyes were bloodshot and the tip of the squat nose was lined with broken red veins.

"And you're no farther along, are you, Doctor?"

She hadn't meant to say that, but it had come out of her mouth before she could stop it and now she felt a vague resentment directed not only at the death of the boy and the physician but also at herself, as if she had failed dismally in ways she couldn't quite comprehend.

"There's still no cure," Henderson said quietly. "Researchers are working on it all over the world. But . . ." He shrugged and swayed a little on his spread legs. He took his hands out of his big overcoat and rubbed them together. Big red hands that hadn't been able to save this small boy's life.

"A cure wouldn't be much good to Bobby now," Florence Hann said. She gazed away from Henderson down the side of Cemetery Hill toward the town. Smoke drifted out of the forest, miles away.

Henderson said, "I retired, Florence."

"I heard that."

"Out to pasture. Just like some old horse." He sighed; his shoulders slumped.

The woman gazed at the grave again.

"I don't miss it," Henderson said. "Let some young guy cure the sick. Somebody with a commitment to it. Let somebody else perform autopsies. You get to a point where you start to see life only in terms of death and you don't know what the hell the point of anything might be." He was silent for a moment. "Whatever happened to pure old joy?"

"You're asking me?" She glanced at him.

Henderson ran one of his large hands across his mouth. "I couldn't do a damn thing about your boy. You know that, don't you?"

"I know it."

He flapped his arms and his overcoat made a rustling sound. "I couldn't give him life, Florence. Nobody could have done that."

The woman looked down at the headstone again. And then, raising her face, returned her eyes to the distant pall of smoke that came rising out of the forest. "You knew I'd be here today, didn't you? Maybe you've got something you want to say to me, Doctor. Is that it?"

Henderson shook his head with uncertainty. "I wasn't sure . . ." A look of pained confusion crossed his face. "I'm not sure of much these days. Something went out of me the day I retired. I forget things. I get confused. I don't remember details. Why am I up here? I don't know. I don't know."

"You've been drinking, Doctor."

"A little."

"It'll kill you."

"Something's got to."

Florence Hann sighed. "How many are buried up here?" she asked. "Like Bobby. How many like Bobby, Doctor?"

Henderson moved almost imperceptibly away from her. "I don't follow you, Florence. I'm sorry."

"Don't you?" She stared at him. Then she was looking back down at the town below her. She saw sluggish tourist traffic move along the main street, the big buses that would disgorge retired couples and Japanese tourists drawn to Carnarvon by its quaintness, its turn-of-the-century atmosphere, its *authenticity*. All they ever encountered was the surface of this town, its appearance; they didn't penetrate the substance of the place. How could they?

Miles Henderson stepped toward her and placed one hand on her shoulder. She shrugged it aside.

"Bobby died. And you're upset. And I'm sorry I couldn't do anything. But I just don't follow what you mean, Florence."

The woman felt cold suddenly. "Maybe some places are *cursed*, Doctor. Maybe it's that."

"You're talking nonsense, Florence. Places aren't cursed. Sometimes people have more than their share of misfortune, but it doesn't mean that a geographical location is bad in itself." The physician laughed quietly, but it was a mirthless sound.

The woman turned away from her child's grave. "I know what I've seen," she said icily.

She walked several yards quickly, then paused, turning back to look at the physician. Then she walked away.

15 When he was sure Louise and Dennis had gone, when he was certain they were out of sight between the trees and well on their way to visit the Summers, Max took a couple of Darvon and washed them down with a glass of scotch. There had been bad dreams and he'd awakened with a feeling of impending disaster. And when Dennis had come up with the suggestion of going to see Dick and Charlotte— quaint neighbors, Max thought—he'd declined, saying he thought he was coming down with a cold.

He listened to the voices of his wife and son until they faded among the pines, and then he went inside the living room, where he sat down on the sofa, balancing his scotch between the palms of his hands. The dreams, he thought—were they the artifacts of his guilt?

He couldn't remember them now with any certainty, but something had been circling the house, this redwood house, time and again in the dark of night. Something that appeared to shuffle, a creature he couldn't identify.

Around dawn he'd gone out onto the sun deck and scanned the trees, scrutinized those blind places where light hadn't fallen. He had remained on the deck for thirty minutes, gazing out at the landscape like a man who expects to see something move. Once he noticed an empty reverberating branch that might have been set in motion by a departed bird. He had had the feeling of standing in a place where dream and reality collided in such a way the edges were blurred, the distinctions gone. Had he dreamed the creature circling the house? Or was the act of standing on the sun deck the dream and the creature the reality?

Max rubbed his eyes and looked at the telephone. The Darvon created a kind of glaze between himself and the things he perceived. He felt as if he were sitting inside a clear plastic box. It wasn't unpleasant. He rose and wandered to the window. Then he turned back to the telephone again. What was he supposed to do? Call Connie just to tell her not to call him here?

He picked up the receiver and punched out the number. It rang for such a long time that he began to wonder if she were home. The notion that she might be out somewhere, perhaps even with another man, touched him with a jealousy, which took him by surprise. Jealousy, Max? What does that imply?

He replaced the receiver, ran the cuff of his shirt over his warm forehead, then picked up the phone again. He dialed the number a second time. Connie answered almost at once.

"Was that you before?" she asked.

"Yeah," Max said.

"I was in the shower." Silence. "I had a feeling it was you. I'm glad you called."

The shower, he thought. Had she been alone there? He was filled with a great longing for the woman, a desire to see her, hold her, take her to bed.

"How is the bucolic life?" she asked.

"Quiet," Max replied. Why had he called, for God's sake? He hadn't come all the way up to this forlorn place just to drag the past with him like this. He had come for a different reason. He was here to reestablish his love for his wife and son, which is what he should have been working on. Instead he was digging up something he wanted to bury.

"Can you stand it?"

"I think so."

She was quiet for a while. "I drove past the hotel the other day. You know, the one overlooking the Bay. It's silly, but I wanted to go in and take a room. I wanted to sit at the window and look at the view."

Max shut his eyes. He had to put a stop to this nonsense, he had to tell Connie once and for all that they were finished, through, it was over.

"I think about you, Max. Do you think about me?"

His voice dry, he confessed that he did.

"Can't you come to the city? Can't you find some excuse to come see me?"

"I don't know how I could do that, Connie."

"You're good at making up stories, Max. Why don't you think of something? I miss you."

Max gazed at the window, where a bleak sunlight fell. He said, "I don't feel very inspired, Connie."

"What's the matter with your voice? It sounds thick. Are you ill?"

"I'm fine."

"Will you come see me?"

"I don't see how I can—"

"Find a way, Max."

Max tried to think of something to say. The silence on the line was a great void into which he felt his life was spilling. But nothing came to him.

"I want you, Max," the girl said. "And I know what *you want. I know what Max likes, don't I? I know how to satisfy* you, Max."

She had lowered her voice until it was a sultry whisper. Max felt the beginning of an erection. It was preposterous—he was going through some retarded adolescence, something he'd missed on the first go-around because he'd been too busy working toward his goal—the Physician, the Healer. He'd never wanted to be anything else since the age of seven, when a kindly old GP called McNamara had given him a shot of penicillin to fight an infection Max had developed in his ear. McNamara had leaned toward the frightened seven-year-old boy and whispered, "I've got a magic needle, Maxie. And this magic needle is going to cure you."

A *magic needle*. It had all started there. Max wanted to be like McNamara. He wanted his own magic needle. And here he was, thirty-two years later, making a goddamn mess of everything. It was a slide he had to stop, a breach he had to shore up somehow.

"If you won't come down here, Max . . ." The voice turned.

"What, Connie? You'll do what?"

A pause. Max fidgeted with the phone cord. "Connie . . ."

But she had hung up abruptly. Max put the receiver down.

Had she threatened him just then? He wasn't sure. He went into the kitchen and took a cold beer from the refrigerator, popping the tab quickly and swallowing the chilly liquid down into his dry throat.

I love my wife, he said to himself. I love my wife, my son. My family.

He crumpled the aluminum can in his hand.

Miles Henderson understood that it had been a mistake of judgment to go up on Cemetery Hill, today of all days. Now, as he walked down Delaney Street, limping past the tourist buses and the out-of-state campers, he needed a drink.

He crossed Delaney. A warm gust of wind caught the hem of his overcoat and flapped it against his thigh. His legs ached, which meant his circulation was all screwed up again. By the time he reached Bascolini's his legs were barely functional. He limped inside and ordered a double gin and tonic and carried it to a table at the back of the room, where the shadows were deep and cool.

I delivered Bobby Hann, he thought. I brought that baby into this world. And he'd been a good healthy baby. Strong and loud and hungry. It was only later that the sickness came.

He sipped his drink. *I also did the autopsy on the body*, which he didn't need to remember now because he had set aside the knives and instruments of his dead craft. He took a cigar from its aluminum tube and lit it with a flourish of his hand. Sweet Christ, why was he trembling? The exertion from walking? Or something else?

The encounter with Florence Hann.

But that was your own fault, Doc, for going up there in the first place. You knew you'd see the woman—did you want to be reminded of something? Was that it?

"Crap," he said to himself. He looked into the bottom of his empty glass. He rose clumsily and went back to the bar for a refill. When he had it, and the slight alcoholic panic activated by the empty glass had passed away, he returned to his table. He was cold suddenly, shivering inside the folds of his coat. The inner thermostat was breaking down with age; all the clocks that regulated you were in need of winding except you couldn't find the right keys for them. Time was always a precise killer, always punctual.

"Doc."

Henderson looked up to see Jerry Metger standing over him, his body pressed against the side of the booth.

"Mind if I join you?" the cop asked.

"Goddamnit, I *mind*. What the hell is this, Jerry? You following me or something?"

Metger slid into the booth, the seat facing Henderson. He had a beer in one hand and an infuriating smile on his face.

"I saw you coming in here. I figured you might want some company, Miles."

"Company is what I *don't* want." Henderson drank from his glass. He could feel the gin high coming on, like a reliable locomotive that followed its timetable religiously. He could feel it rush along the slick railroad inside his head, transporting him to a pleasing destination.

Metger said, "I went out to that house yesterday."

"What house would that be, Jerry?"

Metger ignored this question. "The tenants seem like nice people—"

"You want a suggestion? Dig a big hole, Jerry. Drop this thing inside it. Then when you've done that, jump in yourself. I went through all this with you yesterday. It's a dead issue. Finished. I can't make it any clearer than that."

Metger sipped his beer. "I've been thinking."

Henderson shut his eyes and sighed. The train was making an unscheduled stop, and he didn't like that.

"The Ackerleys. I keep thinking about the Ackerleys," Metger said.

"Ancient history."

"I was twenty-one years old at the time," Metger said. "Twenty-one and highly impressionable. It was the first time in my whole life I ever saw a dead body. That particular dead body was a startling introduction to violent death. It stuck in my mind. Over the years, it comes back to me." Metger paused. "And every now and then I think about it. You know how it is."

"Leave me alone," Henderson said.

"There was something very wrong about that corpse. Something *very* wrong, Miles. And you know what that was, don't you? You know and I know. The Ackerleys, wherever they are, also know." Metger's expression was now one of introspection and doubt. "I keep coming back to that coroner's inquest, Miles. That's what bothers me all over again. Your report on the child's suicide. Nowhere in that report did you mention the child's . . . condition. I wonder about that."

Miles Henderson, in the manner of a man stalked by troublesome ghosts, reached for his drink. "You're sick. You need a long vacation, boy. If I was still in the business, I'd make you out a prescription for sedatives."

Metger took out a cigarette but didn't light it. He surveyed it in the manner of someone trying to kick the habit, rolling it back and forth in the palm of his hand. "I'm not sick, Doc. Just a man who's puzzled and who finds the puzzle coming back at him more often than he wants it or needs it—"

"Lemme ask you this, Jerry. Why did you go on down to that house yesterday? What exactly are you afraid of?"

"I'm not sure."

"Damn right you're not sure! You know what your problem is, boy? You're one of those guys in love with mysteries. You lie awake nights dreaming about conspiracies. You're like a kid who can't help but pick at a scab, Jerry. You worry it until it opens and starts bleeding all over again. You know what the same thing is to do? Cover the goddamn thing with a Band-Aid and forget it."

"Forget Anthea Ackerley?"

"Forget what you have to." Henderson could feel his heart pumping in the center of his chest. "Quit scrounging around looking for old gossip or superstitious nonsense—"

"What's superstition got to do with it?" Metger asked, leaning across the table.

"Forget, boy. Just forget." Henderson got up. His head was swirling; his reliable old locomotive had been sidetracked, shunted into some bleak railroad yard where it lay motionless.

"I asked you a question, Miles," Metger said. There was an edge to his voice all at once. "Why the hell are you avoiding an answer? *What's superstition got to do with it?*"

"I answered, goddamnit. You chose not to hear."

Miles Henderson went toward the door.

Sunlight came through high glass windows and struck his face; for a brief moment he felt he was being exposed beneath a hot spotlight. He went out into the street and the door swung shut behind him.

He didn't want to go home and sit under the scrutiny of Henrietta's sharp little eyes. There was another bar nearby where perhaps he could find a little peace. He passed the crowds of tourists who sat on the terraces of restaurants or meandered in and out of the gift boutiques as they searched for some overpriced souvenirs of Carnarvon. When he reached the Hawk—which looked more like an art gallery than a tavern—he went inside.

Metger and his idiotic persistence. Why couldn't he leave everything alone? Florence Hann and her wild talk. She was insane, of course. Deranged by an old grief.

He pushed toward the bar and laid some crumpled notes on the counter. When his drink came he carried it through the throng of customers to a quiet corner of the room where he stood with his back to the wall.

Bobby Hann.
Anthea Ackerley.
How many others down the years?

16 Denny hadn't stopped talking since they'd left the house. Louise, who had discovered a fundamental truth of motherhood—survival meant having to tune out your child every now and then—listened to him on a selective basis. She gleaned enough to know that Dennis was anxious for her to like the Summers as much as he did. He couldn't stop talking about how he and Dick were going to work on the old pickup and get it running, or how Dick knew the ancient secret recipe for a special fishing bait guaranteed to land a whopper every time you cast your line, or how marvelous a cook Charlotte was. What was it? she wondered. What was it that had made Dennis like the old folks so much? Maybe it was something simple, such as that they were surrogate grandparents—God knows, Denny's real grandparents weren't very good at the job. They watched the boy as if they just knew he was going to leave indelible fingerprints on their most treasured possessions. They criticized him every opportunity they could get, with the result that Denny was always sullen and defensive around them. Maybe the Summers were diametrically different; maybe they didn't care about the smudges of childhood. On some other level perhaps they liked Denny because he was company, somebody different for them to fuss over.

"I wish Dad had come," Denny said suddenly.

Louise paused to remove a burr from inside her sneaker. "He said he wasn't feeling too good. He didn't look all that good either, did he?"

Dennis was silent for a moment. "Since we came up here, he's hardly said a word to me."

"Aren't you being a little hard on him, Denny?"

"It's true, though."

"Give him a little time," Louise said. She was surprised at the tone in the boy's voice. There was a hurt behind the words. "Look, you know he's pretty tired, he just needs time to get used to having no pressures on him—"

"He's drinking too much," Dennis said.

"He isn't—"

"Why are you defending him, Mom?"

"I am *not* defending him, Dennis—"

"You are too."

Louise hesitated. "Be patient with him——"

"You always talk about him like he's sick. Is he? Is he sick, Mom?"

Louise smiled. "He's not sick at all, Denny. The thing is, physicians are often under a whole lot of stress. People don't really realize. Your father . . . well, he's like any other physician. The pressures . . . the important decisions he's got to make every day that affect people's lives." She faltered a moment. She realized the boy was right—she *was* defending Max. "When you remove a man like your father from all that pressure, Denny, there's a period of adjustment. He's got to learn how to relax, and that's hard for somebody like him. He'll be all right."

Dennis, who thought this was so much bull, didn't say anything. He had never actually known his father to be quite so withdrawn before. Sometimes he looked so far away, so distant, he was positively ghostly. Just the same, he wished Max had come with them. He kicked at some dry pine needles underfoot. Without his father, the family felt unfinished, incomplete. He took a piece of fudge from his jeans, picked off some lint, popped the candy into his mouth, and chewed.

"He'll come next time. We'll make him come," Louise said. She looked at her son and saw hidden depths and fragile surfaces; you had to be careful how you walked. Was Max conscious of how little time he'd spent with his son since they'd come up here? She supposed not. She'd wait a couple of days and if the situation hadn't changed, she'd drop some unmistakable hints.

The trees ahead yielded to a sudden clearing. Louise stopped.

The small log house that appeared in front of her was literally besieged by trash; it had the look of a dwelling plopped down in the center of a dump. For a moment she didn't move. There was so much junk strewn around the clearing that she couldn't take it in all at once. A whirlwind might have come this way, gathering ruined items from all over the country and simply dropping them in this spot.

"This is it," Dennis said. "Terrific, huh?"

Louise nodded her head slowly.

"They don't keep the place too tidy," the boy remarked.

Too tidy. Louise had seen neater places condemned by health inspectors. "What do they want with all this *junk*?" she asked.

Dennis said, "It's only junk to you. It might mean something more to somebody else."

She gazed beyond the great collection of trash toward the house itself. Flowerpots on a broken porch, dead plants, wilted leaves. The impression she got was of lifelessness, strangulation, things being choked to death amid all the junk. Flowers dying in dry soil and plants choked amid coils of chicken wire and discarded piles of cedar roofing and rolls of fluffy insulation material. Dennis would see all this as a kind of wonderland, she thought. A big playground.

"There's the pickup," he said. "See it?"

Louise gazed at a very old Dodge truck, which lay beyond a pile of tires. The windshield was broken and the hood upraised; all four tires were flat. She thought, If that truck were a person, it would be terminally ill. "And you're going to get it *running?*"

"Yeah. Dick and me."

"You've got your work cut out, kid."

"Dick's a wizard," Dennis remarked. "He knows about tools and engines. He told me he could've repaired it years ago, but he was waiting for a helper to come along."

Louise shielded her eyes against a sudden stab of pale sunlight and she looked in the direction of the house.

Charlotte and Dick appeared on the porch. At the same time the air was filled with the sweet scent of whatever was baking in Charlotte's oven. It floated out through the open door, almost tangible in its intensity.

"Welcome," Dick said, with genuine warmth.

"Glad you dropped over," Charlotte added, running her thick fingers through the folds of her apron.

Louise went up the steps to the porch.

Charlotte said, "Oh, I couldn't say how long we've had that old thing. Years, I guess. Maybe Dick would know."

Dick Summer shrugged. "I can't rightly recall."

Louise turned the copper chafing dish over in her hands. She knew from a course she'd taken once in antiques that it was a dish by Gustav Stickley dating from the turn of the century, a reasonably valuable item. "It's very beautiful," she said. She smiled at the Summers and wiped dust from her fingertips as she set the dish down on a shelf.

"And so is this." She reached out to touch a pewter candelabra that was probably close to a hundred and fifty years old. A few strands of dried-out spiderweb came away in her fingers.

"Just old things," Charlotte said, laughing quietly. "Almost as old as us, I daresay."

"You have so many lovely things," Louise said. What she wanted to say was, It's a goddamn shame you're letting them rot like this, but the whole place was filled with old treasures and each one was covered with dust or rusted or blackened by the passage of time. It was sad to see so many desirable pieces in such a condition.

A yellowing mother-of-pearl pitcher that had to be a hundred years old. A lovely cameo glass vase by Émile Gallé, its surface encrusted with old dust. A tarnished silver Athenic vase, which had been designed—if Louise remembered correctly—by William Codman. There was a Tiffany silver serving dish, more than a hundred years old, that had been allowed to grow dull and lackluster over the years.

But these items reflected the condition of the rest of the house. Gorgeous furniture—a large oak armoire, a beautiful mahogany rolltop desk, a splendid walnut dining table—sat dull and cracked and lifeless. The explanation for the neglect was obvious—the Summers didn't have the energy to keep the place up.

"There are some wonderful things here," Louise said.

Charlotte, who wore bright green barrettes in her hair today, smiled. "We're so familiar with all these doodads, I suppose we don't really notice them. Do we, Dick?"

Dick Summer shook his head. "Guess we don't."

Louise paused at the foot of a stairway. Presumably there was a bedroom up there. She glanced upward at the murky shadows, and then she looked at the Summers again. They were watching her as she examined things, their bright little eyes following her around. Dennis, too, was observing her from the doorway.

"Would you like something? Tea, perhaps?" Charlotte asked.

Louise shook her head, smiled politely, stared through the window across the junk in the clearing. She saw a squirrel vanish over a pile of logs.

"Lemonade," Charlotte said. "I think we have . . ." The old woman looked around the kitchen, her expression one of confusion. She started to move toward the refrigerator, then she stopped by the stove, an enormous Acme Royal with ornate carvings.

"It's okay," Louise said. "Really. I don't want anything. I only wanted to see your home, say hello. What are you baking in there, Charlotte?"

"Something for Dennis," the old woman said.

"Lucky kid. It smells magnificent."

"Special cookies," Charlotte said. "Special boy. Special cookies."

Louise glanced at her son. He was sitting at the table now with a big grin on his face. Dick Summer was standing behind him, one old shiny hand on the boy's shoulder.

"He's special all right," Louise said.

Charlotte nodded her head in agreement, then moved to stand at her husband's side. All three of them—Dennis and the old couple—might have been taking up positions for a group photograph, a composition of line and shadow, youth and old age, extremes. For an instant Louise felt a strange awkwardness, as if she were being excluded from something. The way the three people faced her—it was like a club to which she didn't have membership.

Dick said, "Well, young man. What you want to do? Start right in on fixing the truck? Or you want to brew up a batch of that wonder bait I promised you?"

"Let's make the bait," Dennis said eagerly.

Louise understood—she was supposed to leave the boy here. He was going to spend the rest of the day with the Summers. Somehow this decision, which had been made without consulting her, took her by surprise. She'd imagined a quick visit, a gesture of politeness, and then she'd go back home with Dennis. But he obviously wanted to stay. New friends, she thought. Unlikely new friends. And he enjoys them.

"Are you sure he's no problem?" she asked. "I wouldn't want him to stay if he's going to get in your way or anything."

"No problem," Dick said.

"He's welcome here," Charlotte added. "Besides, maybe you want to spend some time alone with your husband."

Louise looked at the old woman; there was a vaguely conspiratorial smile on the creased face. One woman to another. Go home, honey, spend a little time with your man. We'll take the kid off your hands.

"Well, if you're sure," Louise said.

"Sure," Dick said.

Louise moved toward the door, stepped out onto the porch. She turned and stared back inside the shadows of the house. Dennis was smiling at her. She said, "Be back before dark."

"We'll see to that," Charlotte answered.

Louise waved. She went down the porch steps slowly, then paused at the bottom and looked out across the yard.

A black crow watched her from a heap of old tires.

From inside the house she could hear the faint sound of Dick Summer's voice, interrupted now and again by Dennis asking a question. The old man seemed to be reciting a list of ingredients.

A clove of crushed garlic.

A half cup of moist dough.

Two tablespoons chopped parsley.
A teaspoon of rancid cat food.
Rancid cat food. God.

She moved toward the trees, then stopped and turned to gaze back at the house.

She couldn't hear Dick Summer's voice anymore. All around her the landscape was filled with silence.

17

There was no hospital in the town of Carnarvon. Instead, there was a small facility, the Carnarvon Medical Center, which was located on the edge of town, tucked away from view behind a stand of tall pines, as if to keep the place concealed from tourists. The center, staffed by two physicians, one part-time, and three nurses, had four beds but no operating facilities.

Jerry Metger parked his car in the parking lot of the center, opening the passenger door for Nora. She had an appointment for her regular checkup with the part-time man, an Englishman by the name of Dr. Scoursby.

Metger escorted her up a short flight of steps and into the waiting room, noticing how short her breath had become and how ungainly her movements. The receptionist, a gray-haired widow called Marla Tubbs, smiled from behind her desk. "Doctor won't be a moment, Mrs. Metger."

Nora placed her hands flat on her huge stomach and sighed. "You don't need to stay, Jerry. I'll be okay. I can call a cab when I'm through here if you've got something to attend to."

"I want to stay."

"You're overprotective. You know that? You spoil me. You'll make a lousy father if you treat the kid the way you treat me."

Metger took his wife's hand. Her fingers were swollen. The wedding band seemed to cut right into her flesh. Sometimes he couldn't remember what she'd been like before the pregnancy except for certain flashes he'd get of a slim, vivacious woman. This baby was draining her. It was the first, and everybody told him the first was the worst.

"I like to spoil you," he said. "I want my wife to be healthy. And I want our kid to be healthy as well."

"We're fine," Nora said. "This kid has the kick of a mule."

Metger leaned back in his chair.

Beyond the receptionist's desk he saw Dr. Pelusi passing out of one door and vanishing behind another. Pelusi was a squat, dark man with solemn ink-colored eyes who had taken over the clinic after Miles Henderson's retirement. Between Scoursby and Pelusi, Metger thought, there was some competence, but he still didn't have the confidence he needed in them. He wasn't altogether sure why. Maybe he didn't want his kid born in Carnarvon, that was all.

What kind of thinking was that anyhow? He got up from his chair and looked out the window.

He'd been born in Carnarvon himself and it hadn't hurt him any, had it? And they didn't even have the medical center back then—a midwife had delivered him in his parents' bedroom. Safe and sound and complete, all eight pounds of him. Still, as he stared at the stand of pines, he felt uncomfortable.

Nora said, "Something wrong?"

"Just thinking."

"You want to tell me?"

Metger went back to his chair, crossing his legs as he sat down. He didn't say anything.

"You worry too much, Jerry," his wife said. "The baby is going to be fine. You'll see. And I'm a big girl. I'll survive."

Metger scratched the tip of his nose.

"You always do that when you're troubled," she said.

"Do what?"

"This." She ran one fingernail around the tip of her own nose. "I know you, Jerry. I know when something's bugging you. You've been like this for days."

Metger uncrossed his legs and shuffled his feet in the pile of the rug. Was he so damn obvious? He took out a cigarette, remembered where he was, then stuck the pack back in his jacket.

The receptionist said, "Dr. Scoursby will see you now, Mrs. Metger."

Nora got up awkwardly and moved toward the door. She turned around and smiled at her husband.

Metger said, "I'll wait."

"Okay."

Metger watched her go out of the room. In another office Scoursby would check her blood pressure, her pulse, her heart; he would poke at her in his curiously offhand manner, then announce she was coming along just splendidly and remind her to take her vitamins and get a good night's sleep and watch what she ate. It was routine, it was the same damn thing every visit, and the pregnancy was coming along as expected—so what the hell was this vague, gnawing unease that was getting to him?

He stepped outside and lit a cigarette. In the distance he could hear the drone of traffic coming along the two-lane highway that ran through the heart of Carnarvon. Tourists, bringing life, blood, and money to a town that would normally have died in the natural course of things when the old silver-mining operations folded fifty years ago. Without these visitors, Carnarvon would have no reason to exist.

He took smoke deeply into his lungs. It was a morning of rare beauty; the sun made the trees appear silken and luscious and there was a warm breeze blowing up. His thoughts turned to the Untermeyers in the forest —maybe he'd find the time to take a run over there later just to see that they were fine.

Jesus, Jerry. Old Miles Henderson was right. You don't know when to leave things alone. Of course the Untermeyers are okay. Of course their kid is fine.

A little irritated with himself, Metger dropped his cigarette and stamped it with his foot, then went back inside the building. Because a tragedy happens to a family called Ackerley twelve years ago, do you *really* imagine gruesome history could repeat itself? And because, years before that, a child called Robert Hann became sick, you want to see connections all over the place, don't you?

What is it, Metger? You tired of being a cop in a tourist town? Tired of having no bank robbers to catch and no rapists to apprehend?

He stood in the corridor of the center absently gazing at health bulletins tacked to a bulletin board. There were reminders about getting tetanus shots. Dietary information. An antitobacco poster.

"Sheriff, how are you? And Nora—how's the better half?"

Dr. Pelusi had appeared at the end of the hallway. His manner was always that of a man flustered, somebody forever on his way to a place where he simply had to be.

Metger smiled. "She's being checked over," he said, making his wife sound like an automobile.

"She's in good hands. The best." Pelusi took a fountain pen from the breast pocket of his white coat and rolled it in his hand. "Andy Scoursby's a good man. For a Brit." Pelusi smiled, his plump little lips welded together.

Metger leaned against the wall. "See much of Miles these days?"

"Last time I gave him some AA literature. He more or less threw it back in my face. I don't know any other way to put this, but there's one guy that wants to kill himself." Pelusi had an expression of resignation on his face.

"Why?"

"I'm no psychiatrist, Jerry. I don't know Miles Henderson well enough to speculate."

Metger watched a nurse disappear through a door at the end of the hall. She was shaking a thermometer in one hand and her white shoes squeaked.

"So what's new around town, Doc?" he asked. "Any devastating medical emergencies I should know about?" He kept the questions light around the edges, almost flippant. He wondered what it was that he really wanted to hear.

"I had a tourist with a fractured arm. Fell out of a bus, I guess. Then a woman suffering Valium withdrawal. Not a whole lot, Jerry."

"Nothing unusual?"

Pelusi laughed. "You fishing, Jerry?"

"Just keeping my ears open, that's all."

"There's been nothing but run-of-the-mill stuff recently, I suppose." Pelusi was silent a moment, trying to remember. "There was one man, guy of about forty, with a broken pacemaker. But nothing I could write up for a medical journal, if that's what you mean."

Metger looked up a second at the fluorescent strip of light overhead. Pelusi was right, he supposed. He *was* fishing. But it was like casting your line into murky, stagnant water when you couldn't see a damn thing under the surface and you didn't know what you expected to catch in any case. Quit, he thought. For Christ's sake.

"How long have you lived in Carnarvon, Doc?"

"Oh . . . four years going on five."

Four years going on five, Metger thought. It wasn't very long. Maybe it wasn't long enough to understand the place, to hear any of the rumors and gossip that ran in the bloodstream of a small town.

Pelusi frowned now. "You got something on your mind, Jerry?"

Metger gazed into the palms of his hands. "Nothing, Doc. Just killing time, I guess. Idle curiosity."

A nurse appeared at the end of the corridor and called to the physician. Pelusi turned away.

"See you around, Jerry."

Alone, Jerry Metger moved back inside the reception room.

Nora was already waiting for him.

She reached out for his hand. "Take me to breakfast, Pops. I got a clean bill of health."

He draped an arm around Nora's shoulders and went with her out into the morning sunshine.

Maybe that was what lay at the bottom of all his recurring concerns, his half-assed anxieties, his troubles—a clean bill of health for both his wife and baby.

His unborn baby.

18

Louise put her brush down and drew a hand across her face. Her mind wasn't on her work. She stood up, gazing down at the child she'd painted. He was what she thought of as her Standard Boy—his eyes were large blue saucers, his mouth a plump pink heart. Today, she thought, this kid makes me sick.

She wandered around the bedroom. The house seemed hollow and empty. Dennis had risen early and departed, to visit the Summers again. She strolled to the window and looked out at the trees. Max was out there, sitting beneath a pine, his back to the trunk. She observed him a moment. He flipped the pages of a book, then closed it and tilted his head back against the tree with his eyes shut. His face seemed strangely gaunt.

She turned away from the window and went downstairs. In the kitchen, she brewed coffee. She was remembering yesterday, when she'd come back from the Summers, how she'd found Max asleep on the living-room sofa. She'd lain down beside him, pressing her body against his, whispering in his ear, We've got the whole place to ourselves, Max. Anything you feel like doing?

Max had opened his eyes, stared at her. There was something cold at the center of his expression, as if he were emerging from a bad dream and didn't recognize her. It was a look she'd never seen before and it froze her. When he had focused, when he'd snapped himself back into the present, he muttered something about a nightmare in a voice so thick it was almost unrecognizable. *Hold me, Louise. Hold me.* There was an urgency in the way he spoke. As she cradled his head against her shoulder, stroking his hair, whispering to him, it crossed her mind that Max was somehow drifting away from her, that she was losing him in a way she couldn't quite grasp. But that was nonsense, a random notion, one of those uninvited thoughts that gate-crash your brain now and again. Where's the real Max? she wondered. Where is the man I love? He trembled as she held him, shaking like someone with a high fever.

And then they'd made love on the floor, Max driving away at her with what she thought was panic, his body stiff and unyielding. He wasn't participating in anything—he was using her to drive away whatever demons might have been inside him right then. A strange Max, a different man,

coarse in his actions, rough. And the perception filled her with anxiety—
you live with somebody a long time and then suddenly another facet of that
person is abruptly revealed and you're lost all at once. He had never made
love to her so selfishly before; she might not have been there.

She sipped her coffee now as she walked into the living room. What was
wrong with him? And why hadn't she noticed anything before? Even Denny
had seen something different in his father. It's because you don't want to
see, Louise. You don't even want to look.

She rose and walked through the living room, absorbed the silent telephone
and the dead TV (whose reception was appalling in any case), and went to
the cabinet that contained the liquor they'd bought in Carnarvon the other
day. They had brought home three bottles of scotch, three bottles of red
wine, a fifth of rum, and some cocktail mixers. The rum and wine were
untouched, but there was only one full bottle of scotch remaining. How
much was Max drinking, for God's sake? She hadn't been conscious of his
consuming *excessive* amounts—a little more than normal, perhaps, but not
excessive. Did he drink outdoors? Did he drink in secret?

She shut her eyes. All these thoughts battered at her. Yesterday, hadn't
she said something to Denny about a period of adjustment? It sounded feeble
to her now. How long did it take for somebody to *adjust* anyhow?

Her attention was drawn to the sound of somebody moving on the porch.
Denny, she thought.

She went to the door, opened it. It wasn't the boy.

Frog, clutching a brown paper bag, smiled at her. He was wearing a
T-shirt with the motto STYLE IS EVERYTHING. Louise held the door open
for him and he came inside, his ponytail swinging against his neck.

He raised the paper bag in the air and said, "I bring goodies from Carnarvon. Freshly baked croissants from the bakery known as the French Quiche,
which I understand is some kind of play on words."

"Great. I just brewed some fresh coffee."

They went into the kitchen. There was a strong, fresh, soapy smell coming
from Frog. His hair was soft and shiny and he moved with a quick little
spring in his step. He opened the bag and removed two croissants, one of
which he handed to Louise. She thought, I need Frog right now. I need
somebody upbeat.

She said, "I was trying to get into a working frame of mind."

"Did it catch on?" Frog brushed crumbs out of his thin beard.

"Let me put it this way, Frog. I welcome the interruption." She poured
a cup of coffee for him and set it down on the table. "Kona. Like before."

"What kind of work do you do?"

She told him.

"Ah, you poison the minds of the very young with a distortedly cheerful view of reality," he said.

"Actually, I only illustrate texts that are distorted to begin with."

Frog sipped his coffee. "Good stuff. Where's Max?"

"Buried in a book," and she waved a hand loosely. She didn't want to talk about Max right now. "Do you go to Carnarvon often?"

"Once a week. I use the public baths there. Makes a change from the stream I usually bathe in. I can't make up my mind whether a chlorinated pool has it over a sluggish green stream." He finished his croissant and rubbed his fingers together. "Where's the kid?"

"Gone to visit our neighbors," she said.

"The old people, you mean?"

Louise said nothing. She gazed past Frog toward the window, the trees beyond. She wondered when she might get sick of this forest, when she might fall victim to a green claustrophobia.

"He likes it over there," she said eventually. "The old people like him. I guess he brings a little liveliness into their world." She poured more coffee. "You were right about their property, Frog. It's a dump. But inside the house they have some stuff you wouldn't believe—antiques, treasures. And it's all just rotting away."

Frog plucked another croissant from the bag. "So they've taken a shine to Denny, huh?"

"Looks that way. What's more interesting is how he's taken a shine to *them*. We're talking about an incongruous relationship here."

Frog nibbled the edges of his croissant. "I keep meaning to run over there and see them," he said. "I figure if they employ me to knock their place into shape, it would be a reliable source of income for a while."

Frog got up and brushed crumbs from his T-shirt. He collected them conscientiously in the palm of one hand and dusted them off inside the trash can. "Neat freak at work," he said. "For this kind of behavior, you could be expelled from a commune and have your name blackened forever among old-time hippies everywhere."

Louise watched him. He moved very lightly on his heels. Although he was skinny, he gave a comforting impression of strength. "I wonder how long the Summers have lived up here, Frog."

"Since dinosaurs roamed," he answered.

Louise smiled. Frog skipped in and out of flippancy, like a man afraid of being taken too seriously, especially by himself. She had a warm feeling right then toward him—it was as if they had been friends for a long time.

The brotherhood of the sixties, she thought. That was it. They shared something of the same water that had swept, with a depressing swiftness, under the same bridges.

He came back to the table and sat down. "Old eccentrics aside, how are you adapting to the woods?" He pushed a croissant toward her, holding it as though it were a microphone.

"Fine," she answered, nudging the croissant away from under her nose. "Except for the night noises."

"The forest never sleeps, they tell me."

"I guess. But whatever it is that doesn't sleep out there, it has the annoying habit of waking me up at night. It doesn't happen every night, but sometimes I hear this animal wandering around outside the house. It seems to *brush* against the walls. You're the resident expert. You tell me what it could be."

"Probably an aardvark," Frog said.

"Seriously."

"Okay. Could be a raccoon. A skunk. A fox. Might be a beaver or a deer looking for something to eat. You've got quite a choice around here."

Louise had an image of a whole congregation of furry things gathering in the darkness and pressing against the house. She hadn't been disturbed in her sleep for the past three nights or so, but just the same she wanted to put some kind of label to the animal that foraged just under her bedroom window in the darkness. It would be consoling simply to know.

Frog got up from the table now. He yawned and stretched his arms. "Well, I better be running along. Shame I didn't get to see Denny. Next time. I'll check your weed situation on the way out."

"You only just did them," Louise said.

"They grow, Louise. In the dark, when you're not listening, those little monsters are forcing their way up out of the good earth. When it comes to weeds, you can't be too careful. Don't forget that."

Then he was gone with a quick smile and a flurry of ponytail, and the house silently settled down once again around Louise. She wandered restlessly down the hallway, stopped outside the door of Denny's room, which was halfway open.

She went inside. As soon as she entered the room a terrible smell hit her with the force of a small hammer. She crossed the floor quickly, pushed the window open, gasped—the stench was indescribable, choking.

It might have been the aroma of a long-dead, rotted animal. It had the bittersweet pungency of corruption.

She roamed around the bedroom, trying not to breathe too deeply.

Saliva formed at the back of her throat and she thought she was going to be sick.

And then she found the source of the horror. It came from a small unstoppered glass jar on the bedside table. The jar contained something shapeless, dark brown.

She knew what it was. Dick Summer's Wonder Bait.

19 Outside the Alpha Beta, Florence Hann paused. The big windows had posters advertising various special bargains. Now and then, when the glass doors slid open, she could hear the voices of checkers over the intercom system. *Price check on Number Six. Harry, please come up front. Harry.* These voices seemed to emerge from an unknown dimension. They were disembodied and strange, somehow shrill to Florence Hann's ears.

She stared at the advertised specials. But she wasn't really seeing them. Instead, her attention had been drawn to the sight of Jerry Metger, who was moving down the covered walkway toward her. She pretended she didn't notice him. She gazed at an illustration of a cow, its body diagramed into various sections. Rump. Prime rib. Sirloin. She didn't want to talk to Jerry Metger.

But he was on her before she had a chance to hurry inside the market. The automatic doors slid open and she heard an amplified voice ask, *Bobby, where are you?* But she knew that *had* to be a mistake, something she hadn't heard properly.

"Nice afternoon, Florence," Metger said.

It didn't seem right to her that somebody as young as this should be sheriff of Carnarvon. She had liked the old sheriff, Big Tom Altman, because he hadn't seemed like a law officer at all, more like your next-door neighbor. And he'd been kind at the time of Bobby's death. She'd always remember that.

"How are you these days?" Metger asked. He put his hands on his hips. The butt of his pistol caught her eye and she felt a tiny, inward flinch. She looked into his eyes now.

Why was she suddenly reminded of a recurring nightmare she had? It was a bad dream of a yellow school bus and Bobby's face was staring out at her from every window. Behind each pane of glass, the same weary face. There was no expression on the faces other than resignation to a fate over which there was no control. They were all going to their end without question. All these blank, leathery faces. The big yellow vehicle was a bus of death.

She could hear the door hiss shut. The roar of tires.

She must have swayed, or lost control somehow, because Metger was holding her by the arm and asking if she was all right. She said she was fine. But the bus was still lodged in her mind and all the faces behind glass wouldn't go away. She concentrated on Metger's eyes now.

"You sure you're okay, Florence?"

"Perfectly fine, Jerry."

"You had me worried there. I thought you were going to fall over."

"That would look good, wouldn't it? Falling over outside Alpha Beta. People would think I was drunk." She forced a little laugh into her voice, but she knew it didn't sound convincing.

Jerry Metger was staring at her strangely. She turned her face to the side. "I'd get a reputation like Miles Henderson, wouldn't I?"

Metger smiled. "You'd need to work pretty hard to get *that*," he said.

"So what are you doing, Sheriff? Grocery shopping or something?" Her voice seemed reedy to her, like wind in a wooden cylinder. "Or are you out catching *real* criminals?"

"Who are the real criminals, Florence?" Metger was still smiling but it had changed somehow—it had become a stiff expression in the middle of his face.

"Don't you know the answer yourself, Sheriff?"

Metger said, "No. You tell me."

She looked through the window of the supermarket and saw a fat woman dragging a sobbing child by his hand. A perfectly normal sobbing boy. There was a tight fluttering around her heart.

Metger said, "I'll tell you what I think, Florence. I think there *aren't* any real criminals in Carnarvon."

"No?" She waited a second, almost purposefully, before she looked at him with a bitter smile. "Who killed the children, Sheriff? You got an answer for that one?"

Florence Hann moved toward the door of the supermarket. She tripped the automatic device and the door slid open noiselessly. A stream of cold air rushed out at her. She was conscious of Sheriff Metger looking at her and she imagined he was going to pursue her right inside the store, but all he did was stand on the sidewalk and shake his head from side to side. As if he pitied her. As if he thought her mad.

She remembered something—if Bobby Hann had lived, he would be exactly the same age now as Jerry Metger. And another thing: for a short time, a week or two, until it had become too unbearable for the boy to go to public school, until the pain and the humiliation had become more than he could justifiably take, he had been in the same first-grade class as the sheriff.

If Bobby Hann had lived . . .

The glass door slipped shut behind her and she turned once, but Metger had already gone somewhere across the sunny parking lot.

Dennis nibbled his way around the edges of a chocolate-chip cookie. It was really the only way to eat them—begin on the outside and munch your way into the dead center. Charlotte had put a whole plate of the cookies in front of him. He ate three, then pushed the rest aside, feeling just a little bloated. Dick and Charlotte liked to feed him, to spoil him. They watched him as he ate, apparently enjoying the sight of his pleasure.

"Had enough?" Charlotte asked.

"Yeah. I think so."

"Always eat enough to keep your strength up. It's very important. 'Specially at your age."

Dick, who sometimes echoed his wife, nodded. "Very important."

Charlotte asked, "You eat that fudge I brought over?"

Dennis said he had. He belched quietly into the palm of his hand. Then he looked at Dick, who was cleaning some silverware. The old man dipped each knife into a dark liquid solution, turned the blade around a couple of times, then dried the knife off. Today was the day Dick had promised they'd begin work on the pickup, but so far he hadn't raised the subject. At times the Summers seemed to forget things, but that was part of growing old anyhow, Dennis thought. Your memory wandered. He suppressed another belch. The cookies were delicious, like everything else Charlotte baked. But why did they fill him up so much?

He drummed his fingers on the table. "How long have you been married?" he asked.

The Summers chuckled together, as if this question amused them mildly. "More years than I care to remember," Charlotte said.

"Did you have a honeymoon? Where did you go?"

"This boy asks a whole bunch of questions, doesn't he, Dick?"

"He surely does," Dick said.

"Dad says it's the only way you ever get any answers."

"Your dad's right," Charlotte said. She looked thoughtful a moment. "We've had a few honeymoons, Denny. We've had a few. Most folks have only one in a whole lifetime. But that wasn't the way for Dick and me." A kind of glaze went across the old woman's face as she remembered something. "We went different places. Niagara Falls. One time we went to Vancouver up in Canada. Another time Dick took me down to Mexico. We went a whole lot of places."

"Why did you have so *many* honeymoons?"

"Love, child. Love," Charlotte replied. "We've always believed you fall in love with each other more than just once in a lifetime. It's a process that goes on and on. Doesn't stop just because you're old."

Charlotte closed her eyes for a time. Dick gazed down at the floor, lost in his thoughts. A shaft of sun pierced through the open door of the house and illuminated their old faces and Dennis thought of a bright flashlight falling on crumpled white paper. It was hard for him to imagine two people as old as the Summers being in love; he always associated love with youth. Now he glanced at Charlotte's hands. He was fascinated by how they appeared, gnarled and misshapen and raw. He wondered if the Summers ever made love together; he couldn't see Charlotte's ungainly hands caressing Dick. It was a picture he couldn't quite make.

Charlotte stepped away. "I'll show you something. Promise you won't laugh?"

"I promise," the boy said.

He watched her go to the stairs, where she climbed up into the gloom. Her bones creaked as she went. Dick was still dipping silverware inside the cleaning solution. Knives shone. In the glittering blades Dennis could see his own reflection thrown back twenty times.

"Sometimes," Dick said. "Sometimes the past's the only thing you got to look forward to."

Dennis smiled as if he understood this, but he didn't.

"You'll see for yourself one day," Dick added.

Dennis was quiet a moment. If Dick wasn't going to bring up the subject of the truck, he'd have to do it himself. He cleared his throat. "Yesterday you said we could get under the hood of the Dodge. You remember that?"

"Sure I do. Soon as I finish this silverware, we'll go out there." Dick smiled. "You remember to do what I told you about that bait?"

"I kept the lid off the jar, just like you said."

"Good. Thing is, if you expose the bait to the air, it matures that much quicker."

"It stinks, though."

"Doesn't stink to a fish," Dick said and winked. "Which is what really matters."

There was silence now. Dennis closed his eyes. He found this house serene in some way. He could relax here because the Summers didn't bother him about anything. There was no pick up after yourself, Denny, or put the cap back on the toothpaste or you've spilled paint all over the floor! There was none of that parental stuff. Nor was there a moody father to contend with.

He opened his eyes. Dick was watching him.

Dennis turned to look at a shelf of old clocks, their glass cases so covered in dust that the hands and faces couldn't be seen. He tried to imagine what the room would sound like if all these clocks began ticking at once. The Summers had so much old stuff here it was like a museum nobody attended to. There was a liberating quality for Dennis in all the dust and the cobwebs and the junk outside—a wonderful sense of disorder, of chaos. Back home, Louise rarely allowed chaos into their lives, which Dennis thought a pity.

Charlotte was coming slowly back down the stairs, smiling to herself. In one hand she clutched a photograph. There was an expression on her face that Denny thought was secretive, as if she were enjoying herself immensely.

"See," she said, placing the picture down on the table.

"That old thing," Dick said. "Haven't looked at that in years."

Dennis gazed at the photograph. It depicted a man and woman, both around the age of twenty, standing on a quay with a steamship in the background. After careful scrutiny, Dennis could vaguely recognize Charlotte and Dick—but it wasn't easy. How could these two young handsome people have grown so *old*?

"Honeymoon," Dick said.

"Yep," Charlotte remarked. "San Francisco."

"When was this taken?" Dennis asked. The photograph was sepia, the surface faintly cracked.

"Before you were born," Dick said.

"Long before," and Charlotte laughed.

"Can't remember the year," Dick added.

Dennis, who stared at the picture for what he thought was a politely long time, smiled at the Summers. "You look so different in this," he said finally.

"The boy says we look different, Dick."

"Boy's right," Dick said.

The Summers laughed together for a moment.

Then Dick remarked, "Charlotte, the boy doesn't want to see old pictures of us! He wants to get working on that truck! That's what this boy wants. Am I right?"

Dennis nodded. "I'd like that."

Charlotte approached the table. She placed the palm of her hand on Dennis's shoulder; there was a smell of lavender water. "A young man in a hurry," she said. "You won't always be in such a hurry, mister."

"I guess," Dennis said, a little puzzled. As far as he knew, he wasn't in much of a hurry about anything.

"You keep that picture, Dennis," Charlotte said. "Keep it as a memento."

"Thanks," Dennis said uncertainly.

"When you're back in San Francisco maybe you'll think of us sometimes."

Dick slapped the palm of one hand upon the table. "Roll up your sleeves, sonny! Let's get that Dodge rolling!"

Dennis followed the old man outside into the sunlight. Charlotte came out on the porch and watched them. She sat on a deck chair crocheting with stiff fingers, looking up every now and then to observe her husband and the boy putter around under the upraised hood of the old truck.

20 Max had his feet propped up on the sun-deck table. He stared upward at the inscrutable blue of the sky. In the distance was a thin spiral of pale smoke rising from the location of the Summers' house.

"Charlotte must be baking again," Louise said.

Max nodded in a drowsy kind of way. "I tried her fudge," he said. "I don't know what she sticks in her cooking, but it tastes bitter to me. I couldn't eat any of it."

"Denny seems to lap it up."

"Obviously." Max turned his face in the direction of the smoke.

"He's over there again," Louise said.

"Well, if he's enjoying himself, I don't see any harm."

Louise was silent a moment. Then she said, "Why don't you take him fishing, Max? Maybe you could take the tent and camp out with him. I know he'd like that."

Max smiled. "Make a night of it?"

"Sure. It would be fun. You haven't camped out with him since he was seven, Max."

Max reached down and picked up a book that lay on the floor of the deck. He placed it in his lap and stared at the cover. "I've been remiss, haven't I?"

"A little," Louise said. "Call it oversight."

"Oversight," Max said, as if he weren't convinced. He smiled—a little sadly, Louise thought.

Max got up and walked to the edge of the deck. He gripped the rail between his hands, turning his face toward the forest. Louise watched him. At least he understands his shortcomings as far as Denny's concerned, she thought. But what about his behavior yesterday? What about the inconsiderate way he made love to me? What about the drinking? Is he conscious of these things too?

She went to him, pressing her face against his spine, clasping her arms around his chest. "It's nice he likes to visit the Summers, but nothing's a substitute for one's own father, Max."

"You're right. I'll plan something. I'll surprise him."

"That would be wonderful." She paused a second. "I know something else that would be *equally* wonderful."

"What's that?"

"You and me. A romantic dinner in Carnarvon. A night out. Just the two of us."

"And we could get the Wrinkled Ones to baby-sit."

The Wrinkled Ones, Louise thought. "They *did* offer."

"Then how can we refuse? Why don't you ask them next time you see them?"

"I noticed a couple of interesting restaurants in town," she said. "Let's go to the most expensive one we can possibly find. We'll get dressed up—"

"To the nines," Max said.

"And we'll buy champagne—"

"Two bottles—"

"And then we'll come back here and fool around—"

"That's the part I like best," he said.

"Max," she said.

"Max what?"

She shrugged. *Be whole, Max. Don't be a stranger to us.* "Yesterday," she heard herself say in a quiet voice. "You worried me, you know that? You had me really worried."

Max shut his eyes briefly. He said, "I was having this bad dream. I can't remember what it was about. When you woke me I guess I was disoriented. You know how dreams can leave you feeling. I'm sorry about yesterday." He looked at her and he was smiling and it was the first time she'd seen that particular expression in days. You can still do it to me, Max. After all these years, you still have the knack of overcoming my doubts, my fears. And you still turn me on. He was making it easy, far easier than she'd anticipated. The stranger she'd encountered yesterday was gone, replaced by the real Max, the Max she knew.

She held his hand against her breasts. She began to move into the bedroom, pulling him gently.

"You want to try again?" she asked. "Huh? You want to start all over again?"

She drew him back on the bed, her body falling under his. She reached for his belt, working the buckle with her fingers. The kiss was warm, perfect, an enclosed little universe. There was no darkness here. There was no anxiety. There was only a comfortingly familiar passion. She felt his palms slide beneath her shirt and his warm breath against the side of her neck. Beyond his head she could see the smoke rising outside in a clear unwavering line, perfectly bisecting the disk of the sun. And from a great distance away she was conscious of the telephone ringing downstairs.

"Let it ring," Max whispered. "Let it ring."

"I have absolutely no intention of answering it," she said. The last few words of her sentence were lost under the warm pressure of Max's mouth.

Professor Pyotr Zmia allowed the telephone to ring a dozen times before he hung up. A little disappointed, he sat very still for a time on the edge of the double bed in the Untermeyers' bedroom. During the last few days he had learned a great deal about the Untermeyers. He'd discovered a batch of old love letters written by a young medical student to the girl he adored—flowery things that even Professor Zmia, who knew how the amorous heart could babble, found slightly embarrassing. He had not imagined the physician as a romantic. The letters had been concealed inside a trunk in the attic, together with assorted discarded objects—a tennis racket, something called a pogo stick (Americans were given to investing huge sums of money in absurd pastimes—a fact the professor had learned on previous trips), broken medical equipment, and very old shoes. Under the big double bed he'd found and opened a couple of suitcases, which contained Louise's underwear (scanty things, the professor thought) and a variety of birth-control devices as well as copies of old income-tax returns, certificates of deposit, bank statements, and blank prescription pads.

He was peering into their life, digging, driven by his own curiosity. Sometimes he'd go inside the boy's room and sit on the narrow bed and look around at posters of football players, rock stars with extraordinarily weird posters, pennants from Disneyland—that triumph of technology in pursuit of the trivial. He examined the boy's toys, his computer games, his books. Young Dennis, it seemed, was very fond of adventure stories, the kind in which the narrative offered the reader participatory choices at the end of every chapter. If you choose to go to the moon, turn to page forty-three. If you decide you'll stay on Space Base II, go to the next chapter. These books, which Zmia found amusing, suggested that Dennis was imaginative, an active child, but the professor already knew that much about him. A child of high energy, too, if you were to judge from the roller skates, the skateboard, the baseball bat, the framed photographs of athletic activities. All this, as far as the professor was concerned, was very good.

Now he stood up, rubbing his hands together. He'd call the Untermeyers later. He didn't have anything very much to say. He merely wanted to ask how they were getting along.

He moved downstairs, still thinking about the boy's qualities. What it was to have so much energy! So much life! The professor smiled to himself. He sat for a time on the sofa, his short legs crossed, his hands clasped, his eyes shut.

When the doorbell rang he rose immediately, stepping down the hallway. The girl came inside as soon as he opened the front door. The professor said, "My dear," and touched the back of her hand, but the girl, ignoring him, went on to the living room. So touchy, Zmia thought. So very edgy.

She sat down, lit a cigarette. Professor Zmia opened a window. "How are we today?" he asked.

The girl smoked furiously. Her face was clenched, like a closed fist. She stared at Zmia, saying nothing. The professor shrugged, took his checkbook from his inside pocket, wrote a check, and handed it to the girl, who looked at it as if she were dissatisfied.

"I should have asked for more," the girl said.

"Ah." Zmia sighed. "You're unhappy with our arrangement?"

"Very," the girl said.

Zmia sat beside her and held her hand between his own. "Are you very fond of him?"

"I don't care about him remotely, but that isn't the point."

"Explain to me, my dear. What is the point?"

"I don't feel good about it, that's all."

Professor Zmia studied her pretty face. "You are not really required to feel anything."

The girl stood up. She tossed her cigarette into the empty fireplace, watched it smolder. "I'm unhappy."

Professor Zmia was silent for a while. The trouble with Americans, he had always thought, was their propensity to have *feelings*. Emotional currency was the one they most easily squandered, which was why they were forever joining therapy groups or talking with psychiatrists or babbling to anyone who'd listen about their innermost selves. They had not come to realize yet that the self was a transitory phenomenon at best, a shackle to which they imagined themselves bound. Zmia knew how to deal with it in a way the girl would understand.

He took out his checkbook. "Would a small bonus appease you?"

"It might," the girl said.

"Very well," and the professor wrote a second check. He gave it to the girl, who took it and smiled.

"Okay," she said. "What's the next step?"

The professor stood up, hands in the pockets of his tailored pants. He looked across the room at the girl. Her prettiness was really rather bland, he decided, although she had quite a firm body, well proportioned—but he could see it age, he could see how the buttocks would collapse and the breasts sag and the lines develop around the eyes and mouth. But right now she had a marketable commodity—her somewhat serious good looks and her attractive shape. Zmia ran the tip of his dry tongue over his lips.

"Let us discuss that, Connie. Let us talk it over."

The girl shrugged and moved to the sofa. She hitched up her short skirt as she sat, revealing a smooth stretch of tanned thigh, silken flesh that reminded Professor Zmia of how a beach looked when the tide had receded and the moon was burning on the damp sands.

21 Lou Pelusi parked his 1970 Eldorado convertible in the street outside Miles Henderson's home. It was a flashy car in excellent condition and its bright yellow body shone in the late afternoon sunlight in such a way that Pelusi could see his reflection in the metal panels. He patted the car the way a man might his dog, then turned and walked up the pathway to the house.

Comfortable place, he thought. Victorian. Good state of repair. He had an eye for the value of things because he was the kind of man who haggled over every purchase he made. It didn't matter that he had more than one hundred thousand dollars in tax-free bonds and a similar sum invested in, of all things, a prototype cow feed—haggling was one of the few human activities that truly excited him. He zeroed in on possible bargains with the sharp, lustful eye of the experienced predator in a singles bar.

As he rang the doorbell and waited he glanced back at his Cadillac. It looked big and brassy there on the street and he took pleasure in its appearance. He was a man who defined himself in terms of his possessions. Take away the car, the handmade suits, his own remodeled turn-of-the-century home on the other side of town, take away his tax-free bonds and his credit cards and his membership in the Carnarvon Country Club, and what were you left with? A pauper with a medical degree.

Like most people inordinately attached to their physical belongings, Lou Pelusi lived in the fear that one day—overnight, without warning, like a sudden hurricane—somebody would come and take everything away from him. Consequently, he looked for threats in most situations. He had a highly developed sense of menace. As he stood on the doorstep of the Henderson house he could feel his antennae quivering more than he liked.

Henrietta Henderson opened the door. A haggard woman with the features of a hatchet, she looked Pelusi over. She looks like a drunk's wife, Pelusi thought—years of humiliation and anxiety had hardened in her face into self-righteousness.

"Miles is expecting me," he said. He stepped inside. The hallway smelled of mothballs.

"I'm not sure he's awake," the woman said. "Sometimes he has a nap in the afternoons."

"Nap" was the kind of word that would have a useful place in the vocabulary of a drunk's wife, Pelusi thought. How could she come right out and say her husband was probably sleeping off a hangover?

"Why don't you go in the living room and I'll see if he's up?" She pointed to a door. Pelusi stepped into the room beyond.

Big, comfortable, if you liked the overstuffed look. There were framed diplomas on the walls. Old family photographs. He strolled to the window and looked at his Elgin pocket watch, a 1920 gold timepiece he'd picked up in Los Angeles some years back for $25—a real steal.

The time was 4:20. His appointment with Miles had been for half past the hour. He hoped his early arrival wouldn't betray the quiet anxiety he felt. As he was tucking his watch away Miles came into the room wearing a gray cardigan that was baggy at the elbows and long khaki shorts that revealed thin legs covered with silvery hairs. His eyes were red, his hair uncombed. Christ, Pelusi thought. He looks worse than ever—if Miles Henderson were a house, he would be condemned.

They shook hands. Miles Henderson sat down. He let his eye roam all over the room, as if he were searching for hiding places where he might have stashed booze in a drunken stupor. "You sounded vague on the telephone, Lou. What's going on?"

Pelusi said, "I'll come right to the point—"

"When a man says that to me I know he's going to beat the bush half to death," Henderson said.

Pelusi smiled thinly. There were times when Henderson's irascibility irritated him. He could be a truculent old fart. "I don't intend to do anything of the sort, Miles. The fact is, I saw our local sheriff today—"

"Metger? Metger's a royal pain in the butt." Henderson found a cigar and, without lighting it, sucked at it. "What did he want?"

"He asked me a damn funny question."

"It's a habit of his. He's a specialist in funny questions. What was on his mind?"

"He wanted to know if I'd run into any devastating medical emergencies lately. That's the word he used—'devastating.' "

"So?"

"What do you mean *so*? Doesn't it strike you as weird that he'd ask a question like that? Right out of the blue? He was fishing, Miles. It was written all across his face. He was on a fishing expedition. What the hell did he mean by devastating medical emergencies?"

"Goddamn boy asks too many questions," Henderson said. He rose from his armchair and walked around the room, chewing on the dead cigar. "He's been nagging me lately too."

"How?"

Henderson stopped at the window and looked out into the front yard. He didn't answer Pelusi's question directly. "I know what's eating him. This baby he's got on the way. That's what's bothering him. The usual prenatal anxieties of the father. Is the kid going to be healthy? Will it have seven toes? Webbed feet? Will it be a hermaphrodite? He's young and anxious, that's all. And in that condition he's vulnerable to extremes of his own imagination."

Henderson made a wheezing sound as he turned around. Pelusi imagined the older man's lungs. They had to be frightful.

"You don't need to worry about him, Lou. Your problem is you're paranoid. Soon as somebody asks you a question, you read about sixteen different meanings into it."

Pelusi shrugged this aside. "It was the way he just came right out with the question, that's all. I wondered if he *knew* anything."

Henderson returned to his chair and sat in silence for a while, studying the design of the rug. "None of us knows anything, Lou. And we're *trained* to know such things. So what could this small-town cop understand? Jesus Christ. What could he possibly know when people like you and me haven't got a goddamn clue?" The old man waved a hand in the air; his voice had a strangely bitter ring. "No explanations, Lou. Just tragedies."

Pelusi detected something else in the voice now. A sadness. A weary futility.

Henderson finally found a match and held it to his cigar. A big cloud of blue smoke enveloped his skull. "We help at birth. We repair broken bones. We write prescriptions. Sometimes, when the circumstances demand it, we cut folks open when they die. But what are we? What the hell are we, Lou? We're goddamn technicians who don't understand what the hell we're doing most of the time and who don't know the real secret of it all. We scratch surfaces, for God's sake. And you're looking at one man who got pretty damn tired of scratching."

Henderson leaned back in his chair. His large face, puffy from drink, was an unhealthy gray color. "We don't know why one person gets flu while the guy in the next house escapes the virus. Something *that* simple, and we don't know the answer. We don't know why one person succumbs to a wretched disease and thousands of others don't."

Pelusi looked at his watch. He was suddenly restless. It bothered him when anyone, especially a fellow physician, pointed out the inadequacies of his profession. It took something away from him, made him uneasy and less valuable in his own sight.

"If I was you, Lou—and that isn't altogether a pleasant speculation—I'd put Metger right out of my mind," Henderson said. "What could he *possibly* know? Let him ask his questions, let him do all the asking he wants—"

"Miles," Pelusi said. "You're not being realistic. What if he wants to . . ." Pelusi paused, searching for a suitable phrase. "Rock the boat?"

Henderson laughed. "You're a scared little man, Lou. Aren't you a scared little man? Rock the boat! So what?"

Pelusi felt a flush of blood rise to his scalp. "I'm trying to find the worst possible scenario—"

"Scenario!" Henderson laughed again. "What a ridiculous word. *Scenario.* You got any more stupidly fashionable words tucked away, Lou?"

"Miles, I'm only trying to cover this situation—"

"And I'm trying to tell you to go home, forget, go play golf, whatever it is a prosperous physician does these days. Don't worry about Metger. Take a ride in that big pimp mobile of yours. Screw it."

Pelusi went to the door, struggling with his anger. He knew that suitable responses would come flooding into his mind later, when they would be useless to him. But right then he couldn't think of a snappy comeback, a quick insult, a barb. He opened the door and stepped into the hallway, where a grandfather clock ticked solemnly.

"You know what I wish, Miles?"

"Tell me, Lou. Treat me to your inner desires."

"I wish I had never heard a goddamn word about this whole thing."

"Too late, friend," Henderson said. "Much too late for that now."

Hands covered in grease, oil stains inscribed all over his shirt, his forehead smudged darkly from poking around in the engine of the Dodge pickup, Dennis made his way along the bank of the dry wash. A few late afternoon buzzards made patterns in the sky above the trees, flying in the concentrated circles that suggested carrion nearby. Dennis wiped his hands on his jeans. The Summers had insisted he wash up before going home but somehow he'd managed to get out of that one. Now, satisfied by his oily condition and the fact that he and Dick had actually made the Dodge engine turn over, he slithered down into the wash, kicking up dust and small stones.

He paused in the arroyo, looking this way and that. As the light faded —slowly, imperceptibly—the woods around him appeared to dwindle, the trees growing closer together. He took a cookie from his pocket and chewed on it; Charlotte had insisted he take a couple home with him. But he didn't quite feel like going back to the redwood house just yet. What he wanted to do was find Frog, who had held out the shimmering promise of rock and roll. Dennis had been amused by the sight of the man jogging with such a terrified look on his face. He ran like a man afraid of heart seizure.

The boy moved up the wash, away from the direction of the redwood house. He had already come to recognize various landmarks, seeing differences in a landscape that might have looked monotonously regular to most people. For example, there was a strange twisted pine on the edge of the wash, which was where he would take his bearings when he was heading back from a visit to Dick and Charlotte. When he reached it he paused once more. An odd tree—it looked like it might have been touched by lightning long ago.

He moved on, scrambling up the bank of the wash. He knew, from what his mother had said, that Frog lived near a stream, which you reached by following the edge of the arroyo. So he kept close to the wash as he walked. He finished the cookie and fished out another from his jeans. His hand encountered the photograph the Summers had given him, which was creased from having been stashed in his pocket. He took it out and gazed at it, wondering how long ago it might have been taken. To his young eyes it looked ancient. Charlotte and Dick appeared happy in the picture, young married people about to embark on a honeymoon. Had they boarded the steamship in the background? He turned the picture over. On the back was the photographer's name in faded blue ink: J. DURSTEWITZ, PHOTOGRAPHS & PORTRAITS, GEARY STREET, SAN FRANCISCO, CALIFORNIA. He wasn't absolutely sure what he was supposed to do with the picture, but he thought it was kind of touching that the Summers had given it to him.

There was, Dennis thought, something a little mysterious about Dick and Charlotte. It was connected partly with their great age. Dennis thought old age a mystery—you lived that length of time and you must have seen almost everything there was to see, which meant accumulated wisdom and deep secrets and a rich memory. But there was another thing he couldn't unravel, and that was why they chose to live out here in the isolation of the forest. He'd never asked them and they hadn't volunteered the information. Why would old people want to live in such an inaccessible place?

He ran one greasy hand over his black forehead. The slipping sun poked through the trees. Dennis imagined it was around five, five-thirty, he wasn't sure. He kept close to the wash, expecting at any moment to come across Frog's van. The land rose upward a little and he climbed quickly, avoiding the pine branches that loomed around him.

And then he heard it—the soft slap of water running, little more than a steady background whisper. Through the trees he saw the outline of the VW and he headed down the slope toward it. Frog was hunched over a Coleman stove, concentrating on the food in a skillet. He looked up when he heard Dennis come out of the trees. Whatever Frog was cooking smelled delicious.

"My man," Frog said, smiling.

Dennis liked this welcome—it was cool, laid-back. He approached the stove and gazed down into the skillet, where tiny pieces of meat lay amid sliced vegetables.

"Out walking?" Frog asked.

"Yeah." Dennis sat down. "You said I could visit."

"You smelled the food," Frog said. "Admit it."

Dennis's stomach squeaked. His hunger took him quite by surprise. Only a half hour before he'd eaten two tuna sandwiches Charlotte made, and then there had been all those cookies.

"I guess the air makes you hungry up here," he said.

Frog stood up, shaking one leg, which had fallen asleep. "I'll put some music on." He went inside the VW and after a moment the air was filled with the sound of a guy singing:

> *Electric banana, is gonna be*
> *The very next craze . . .*

It had a strange, antique sound to Dennis's ears. It reminded him of the music his mother sometimes listened to when she was working. He gazed down into the food again, which Frog was stirring with a wooden spoon.

"Donovan," Frog said. "I guess that's before your time, huh?"

Dennis nodded. It was the kind of music he could easily tune out. It was a little bland for him.

"I don't have heavy metal or anything," Frog said. "I'm not sure I should apologize for that omission, though."

"That's okay." The boy shrugged.

"What happened to you? You fall into a cesspool or something?" Frog asked, stroking his beard.

"I was working on Dick Summer's pickup."

"Yeah?"

"We got the engine to start."

"Good going," Frog said.

"It's a 1941 truck."

"A classic."

"I guess."

Frog stirred the food. It glistened inside the skillet. "You get along real well with the Summers, don't you?"

Dennis heard the song change. Now the guy was singing something about an elevator breaking down in the Brain Hotel. Weird stuff. "They're lonely, I guess," he said. "I figure they like having somebody young around. Maybe they wanted kids at some time only they couldn't have them. I don't know."

Frog turned off the Coleman stove. "Want to share this with me?"

Dennis nodded eagerly.

Frog dished out two portions and Dennis ate quickly.

"You don't know about chewing, Denny? You never learned that knack?"

The boy smiled. "I don't know why I'm so hungry all the time."

Frog chewed every mouthful carefully. "You're a growing boy. That's my guess."

"I didn't have much of an appetite back in the city."

Frog finished and lay flat on his back, gazing up at the sky. Dennis spooned the last few morsels out of the skillet and onto his plate. "This is so good," he said. He was still hungry when he'd finished the last of the food. "What do you call this stuff?"

Frog said it was Mongolian beef. He yawned. "What do they talk about?"

"Who?" Dennis asked.

"The old folks. What do they talk about?"

Dennis shrugged. "Stuff."

"That's informative."

"Well, it's hard to say, Frog. I mean, I don't know what they talk about when I'm not around."

Frog lowered his head again. "Good point," he mumbled.

Dennis added, "They speak about the past sometimes."

"I figured they might." Frog propped himself up on one elbow. The early evening sun laid a film of orange over his face and burned in the silvery hairs of his beard. "When you get to their age, what else have you got?"

"I guess," the boy remarked.

Frog stared at Dennis a moment. "Hey, maybe you could put in a good word for me with them. Tell them I'm a terrific weeder, a hard worker. Tell them that when it comes to shaping a place up I'm Mr. Amazing."

Dennis smiled. "Yeah. I'll try."

"Don't enthuse or anything," Frog said, tugging at his little beard.

Dennis was quiet for a time. He listened to the soft undercurrent of the stream, which was lost somewhat in the noise of the music.

> *I'm just mad about Saffron*
> *Saffron's mad about me . . .*

"I get the feeling, Frog, they don't care much for company."

"You're company."

Dennis shook his head. "It's like they think of me as their grandchild or something. That's different. I don't know exactly how to explain it."

Frog found a twig and worked it between his fingers. He gazed up at the sky, then he said, "Don't think I don't like your company, my man, because I do—but does your mother know you're up here with me?"

"I guess not."

Frog slapped his thigh. "I'll walk part of the way back with you then. I need the exercise."

Dennis rose reluctantly. "Isn't jogging enough for you?"

Frog put his arm around the kid's shoulder. "When you're an excessive personality like me, you can't get enough of anything. Including pain and humiliation."

They walked a little way in silence. Between the trees there was already the suggestion of night falling, murky pools of shadow developing. Dennis was glad of Frog's company—when the sun disappeared the forest changed. A weird silence fell over it, a dormancy broken only now and then by the sound of an animal or the dark cry of a bird. Sometimes, especially at night, Dennis would lie awake watching the pattern of branches imposed by moonlight upon the window of his room or listen to the footfall of some animal drawn by curiosity to sniff around the house—the forest had a night life all its own, and it was just a little *spook-eee.*

"What brought you out here, Frog?" Dennis asked.

Frog thought a moment. "Where else do you go when you've grown out of communes and you're too old to get your hair cut and find a job as a postal clerk or something?" He laughed to himself quietly. "Can you see a guy called Frog holding down a position in a bank?"

Dennis shook his head.

"I didn't really grow up," Frog said. "I kinda grew sideways, if you see what I mean."

Dennis wasn't sure what he meant but he nodded anyhow. Between the trees he could see the outline of the redwood house. The sun deck jutted out into branches of a pine.

"You going to come in with me?" he asked.

"I'll pass this time," Frog answered. "Next time you're hungry, stop over."

"I'll do that."

"Or next time you feel like some company that isn't entirely ancient, see me. At least I'm only middle-aged."

Entirely ancient, Dennis thought. Was Frog criticizing the Summers in some way? Or was he implying, obliquely, that Dennis shouldn't hang around old people all the time? The boy wasn't sure. Maybe Frog hadn't meant anything.

Dennis moved quickly in the direction of the house, pausing once to look back. But Frog was already gone, swallowed by the darkening forest.

22   "Surprise surprise," Martine said. She was standing, arms folded, behind the bar at the Ace of Spades. She looked tired, Metger thought, as he climbed onto a stool. Circles under the eyes, little lines at the corners of her lips—it was just after ten and she'd probably been tending bar for eight hours or so.

"Couldn't sleep," Metger said.

Martine leaned against the bar, inclining her head toward him. "Does your wife know you're out, Jerry?"

Metger smiled. "I was careful not to wake her." He had risen in the darkened bedroom and dressed silently in old jeans and sneakers and a windbreaker. He had left the house quietly, with no particular destination in mind. All he knew was that if he lay in bed any longer, tossing and turning and seeking the dark reaches of sleep, he'd go crazy. He couldn't relax, couldn't switch off the old electric light in his brain. And so he'd driven down through the night streets of Carnarvon, unable to shake loose his encounter with Florence Hann.

Martine opened a bottle of beer and slid it toward him. She supplied a glass and watched him pour. "Problems?"

Metger shook his head. Problems, he thought. Some things you couldn't define quite that simply.

Somebody in one of the booths at the back of the room went to the jukebox and punched in coins. Two half-drunk cowboys played a casual game of pool over in the corner. There was the sound of balls clicking.

"Did you ever go to that house?" Martine asked.

"I made a courtesy call. Nice couple. I didn't get to meet the kid, though."

Martine moved a strand of hair away from her forehead. She lit a cigarette, which she placed in an ashtray. The smoke rose toward Metger's eyes. He shifted his head slightly as he sipped the cold beer, which left a metallic taste at the back of his mouth. Now the jukebox kicked into life. It was one of those whining country tunes Metger disliked. "I Fall to Pieces . . ."

He said, "I ran into Florence Hann today."

"Who?"

"Florence Hann. You remember her."

Martine looked puzzled a moment, then she said, "I don't see her face. I remember her kid, though. What was his name?"

"Bobby," Metger said.

"He had that sickness."

"Right. He came to school for maybe a week . . . A month . . . I don't rightly remember. Then he vanished."

"Shame about that kid," Martine said. "He died, didn't he?"

"Yes." Metger tapped his fingertips on the bar. He went down inside the shadowy places of his own memory for a moment, reaching for a recollection of Bobby Hann's face. When he had it the image was surrounded by clutter—spilled watercolor paints, chalk dust, Miss Gabriel's shrill voice, the sight of Florence Hann waiting in the school yard every day for Bobby to get out. And then they'd both disappear inside a car and go home and

the car was spitting out great black clouds of smoke. Metger recalled
wondering why they rushed away like that each day, why Florence Hann
didn't allow Bobby to linger in the yard like everyone else. Now he understood, as he hadn't at the time, that it was because Florence Hann couldn't
stand the idea of her son undergoing the torture of other kids laughing
at him.

Normal kids.

Then one day Bobby Hann didn't come to school and nobody ever saw
him again. It created a mystery in Metger's young mind.

"Do you remember you used to wear a blue ribbon in your hair back
then?" he asked.

"Red," Martine said. "It was a red ribbon."

"You're confused, Martine. Blue. I used to pull it."

"Red, red, Jerry. I ought to know. Even then I was conscious of what
colors suited me. I never wore blue."

Blue, red—what difference did it make now? Metger wondered.

"So why all this nostalgia, Sheriff?"

"I guess it was because I ran into Florence, that's all." But that wasn't
all. There was more. Only he couldn't quite get a handle on what the rest
of it was—he understood simply that it bugged him, that he couldn't leave
it alone. It was the same feeling you got when you had a word on the tip
of your tongue only you couldn't say it because there was some bewildering
short circuit in the coils of memory, something that wouldn't quite connect
for you.

He finished his drink. Martine opened a second bottle for him. He studied
the label for a time. Sometimes these days his mind seemed to him like a
coat that didn't quite fit. It was too tight and it made him uncomfortable
and he wanted to throw it off.

He said, "I felt the baby kick yesterday."

"Yeah?"

"Strange sensation. I put my hand on Nora's stomach and the kid launched
a terrific kick." He realized he had a stupid paternal grin on his face all at
once.

"How did you feel?"

"I can't explain," he answered. "Proud. Scared shitless. Awed. Afraid.
All of the above."

Martine smiled and patted the back of his hand. "Afraid of what?"

"Who knows?" He sipped his beer, glanced at the pool players, tuned
out the jukebox and the sound of Patsy Cline's voice. "It's probably a common
experience for expectant fathers."

"You'll make a wonderful father, Jerry," Martine said. "You'll be kind and attentive and indulgent."

"I don't know about indulgent," he said. Scared, he thought. Scared of the impending birth. There were times when he lay in the darkness of the bedroom with his arm circled around his wife's big belly and he'd try to imagine the kid floating inside the amniotic sac and he felt queasy, uncertain, hoping the child was all right in that blind moist place but not really knowing for certain.

Martine was silent a moment. She reached out and touched the surface of Metger's beer bottle. "You were kind and attentive and indulgent when it came to me, Jerry. Once upon a time."

"Once upon a time," he said. He smiled awkwardly. He finished his beer and spread his hands on the bar. Martine picked her cigarette out of the ashtray and drew on it before setting it down once again.

Metger drifted back to Florence Hann once more. Moths and flames, singed wings. You should leave it all alone.

What came to his mind was the strange question she'd come out with, the way she'd looked when she'd asked it: *Who killed the children?* Wasn't that the question? Who killed the children?

What children?

Who was she talking about? Her own son, obviously—but why did she couch her question in the plural? She couldn't have known about Anthea Ackerley. How could she? Maybe she was referring to the boy Metger's father had once talked about. Bewilderment, spirals of confusion—Metger felt he was on some watery downhill slope with no hope of ever stopping. His mind seemed to him now like a series of highways that weren't connected to one another, freeways along which his thoughts hurtled without purpose, without direction. Anthea Ackerley dies. Bobby Hann dies. A baby is about to be born. New tenants move into a house of tragedy.

There are no links, he thought.

Goddamnit, there are no connections.

You, Metger, are a troublesome fool.

He pushed himself away from the bar now, turning his face toward the door.

"You have to leave?" Martine asked.

He nodded.

"I'm always here," she said.

He turned from the bar, then he paused and looked back at the woman. "Can I ask you something?"

"Go ahead."

"Did you ever hear of anybody else being sick like Bobby Hann?"

She seemed disappointed. He realized she had expected a different kind of question, something more personal. Maybe we can get together sometime, Martine, go out for a drink, old time's sake, what do you say?

"Like Bobby?" she asked.

"Yeah."

"Never. Did you?"

"I don't know, I don't know for sure." He thought. "Something my father told me once. Or might have told me. Or else I dreamed it."

He smiled at her and stepped outside into the dark and he stood for a while in the glow of the neon sign that filled the night. Across the parking lot, in a place where the neon couldn't reach, the forest began. It lay there, crouched and black and silent, like a creature of infinite patience observing the ways of the night. Metger thought of the people from San Francisco who lived down there across the darkness. He thought of their redwood house with perhaps a couple of feeble lights from windows trying to make tiny holes in the night. He thought of the other residents of the forest. That old couple, the Summers. The dropout who lived in a van.

He stared upward. The moon came sailing out of clouds and laid silver snowlike tracks across the landscape. These threads of light did nothing to dispel the feeling he had right then—which was fear, indescribably complex.

23 Louise said, "It stinks your whole room up, Denny. I don't know how you can stand it, frankly. Doesn't it bother you?"

Dennis was propped up in bed, watching his mother. He was leafing through the pages of an adventure story. Louise glimpsed the title: *The Lost Moons of Earth.*

She turned her attention to the bedside table, where the gleaming brown bait lay inside the glass jar and looked for all the world like a huge amorphous slug. Dennis had removed the stopper and now the putrid aroma drifted around her nostrils.

"I find it offensive," she added.

"The air makes the bait mature. Dick said so."

"Did Dick also tell you that it was likely to *sicken* your mother?"

Dennis smiled. He reached out and put the stopper back. "There," he said.

"Thank you," Louise said.

Boys, she thought. Why do boys love disgusting things? Once Dennis had dragged home a maggoty cat, long-dead and stiff, insisting it have a decent burial in the backyard. Why couldn't she have had a daughter, dammit? Someone with just a little more grace, a little more sensitivity. She sat down on the edge of the boy's bed. The scent was still strong, repellent. She tried unsuccessfully to ignore it.

"You really think fish will like that stuff?"

Dennis nodded. "They love it."

"According to Dick."

"Right."

"I thought fish would have better taste," she said.

Dennis flipped the pages of his book. Despite the fact he'd taken a bath—which Louise had forced him into—there was still black grease beneath his fingernails. My boy, the mechanic. She leaned over and kissed him on the forehead. Propped up against the bedside lamp, adjacent to the bait, was the photograph the Summers had given the boy. Louise picked it up and held it flat into the light. Although she'd tried before, she could barely see any resemblance between the old people and this young couple captured in the picture. She wondered idly when it might have been taken. Charlotte wore a white gown into which flowers had been stitched—white floral details on a white background. She flipped it over, looked at the inscription on the back—a photographer's name and address—and then she set it down. Why did she think it a curious thing to give a twelve-year-old boy? It was a keepsake, a memento, nothing more.

"I only came in to say good night."

Dennis put his book down. "Good night, Mom."

"Got any plans for tomorrow?" she asked when she reached the doorway.

"I guess we'll work on the pickup again."

"Ah." She stepped out into the corridor, closing the door of the boy's room quietly. She paused briefly at the foot of the stairs. She could hear Max up in the bedroom, opening and shutting one of the closets. She needed air. The rancid scent of the Wonder Bait still filled her nostrils. She stepped out onto the front porch.

There was a bright moon surrounded by ghosts of clouds. Unlike any city moon, which was usually ensnared in gasoline fumes and industrial smoke, this one seemed pristine, a cold transparent disk in the dark blue sky, clear and pockmarked and aloof. She leaned against the wall of the house, folding her arms. The night air had a sharp edge to it. She sucked it deeply into her lungs. Perfection, she thought. *Almost* . . . Dennis intended to visit the Summers again in the morning. Why did that bother her?

The answer was easy. She and Max and the boy should have been planning something together. Why did he have to find pleasure in the company of two old people who were practically strangers to him? The thought irked her a little. Max had said he'd surprise Dennis—so far he hadn't mentioned how he planned to do it.

She moved to the edge of the porch steps. Maybe tomorrow he'd have a scheme worked out; let him sleep on it. She shut her eyes, breathed deeply, relaxed. The forest stirred faintly as a thin breeze whimpered through the trees, blowing smells of pine resin at her. Somewhere nearby there was a soft dropping sound—a pinecone tumbling through branches to the earth.

Or was it something else? She opened her eyes.

The woman appeared in the driveway. Just like that. Louise felt her heart jump. She peered through the dark, narrowing her eyes.

"Charlotte?" she asked. "Is that you?"

The old woman came toward the porch, where the faint light falling from the hallway illuminated her. She looked up at Louise, smiling. She wore a robe, loosely belted at her waist, and her face—whether from moonlight or some kind of makeup, Louise didn't know—appeared flat and white, a blank oval adrift in the darkness.

"Insomnia," Charlotte said. "Can't sleep some nights."

Louise recovered quickly from her surprise. "Can I get you a glass of warm milk? They say it helps if you can't sleep." The old woman shook her head and Louise thought of her wandering aimlessly through the dark trees. "Won't you at least come in for a moment?"

Charlotte gazed past Louise at the open door, the hallway beyond. "Nice house."

"We like it—"

"We enjoy your son," Charlotte said suddenly. "He brings something into our house. If you know what I mean. Hope you don't think we're stealing his affection or anything."

The thought hadn't crossed Louise's mind and she said so now. In fact, she told Charlotte she was happy that Dennis had made new friends, that he had found something to keep him busy. Even as she spoke she had the odd suspicion that Charlotte's insomnia was a small lie—maybe the old woman had walked over here just to explain about Dennis, just to say that he was welcome in the Summers' house as long as he wanted to visit. *Stealing his affection*, Louise thought. It struck her as a quaint turn of phrase, something an old person might use.

"Well," Charlotte said. "So long as you don't mind about him coming over. Cheers Dick up too." The old woman smiled. "And Dick really needs it. At our age . . ." She didn't finish her sentence. Her voice trailed off. She took her hands, which had been deep inside the big pockets of her robe, and spread them out in front of her. Moonlight hacked odd shadows out of the ridges of her knuckles. Louise looked politely away.

The old woman said, "Hope I didn't disturb you just turning up like that. You must have thought I was a prowler or something."

"You didn't disturb me at all. I just stepped out for some fresh air. That bait your husband gave my son—"

"I know what you mean. It sure catches fish though. I'll say that much. Smells like hell but it works." Charlotte smiled. "Some nights I walk as far as the stream. Other nights I come this way. Depends."

On what? Louise wondered. "It's turning cold," she said.

"Yep," Charlotte said. "I'd best be getting back. Maybe this time I won't toss and turn."

"Are you sure you don't want anything?"

"Sure. But thanks." The old woman moved toward the trees. "Be seeing you."

Louise watched her go out of sight, then turned and went back inside the house. She shut the door and leaned against it a moment. There was a sudden sense of peace throughout the house—she could feel it—a certain security, as if the house were a closed fortress against the vicissitudes of the dark outside.

She moved down the hallway. When she reached the foot of the stairs she glanced in the direction of the kitchen, where there was a soft glow from the stove light. A faint sound drew her to the kitchen doorway.

Dennis sat at the kitchen table. There was a large bowl of grapes in front of him and, like some predatory little creature of the dark intent on devouring as much as it possibly could, he was popping grapes hurriedly into his mouth and swallowing them with haste.

Louise said, "Caught you! At last the Great Grape Thief is unmasked!"

Dennis looked up in surprise. "I was famished," the boy said, looking a little guilty.

Louise walked to the table and sat down facing her son. In the pale light from the stove the boy appeared a little haggard. She put one hand over the back of Denny's hand. His skin was cold to the touch.

"Are you feeling okay, honey?" she asked.

Dennis nodded. "Why do you ask?"

"You're so cold."

"I don't feel cold." Dennis placed a grape on his tongue, then closed his mouth.

"I guess you're all right. At least your appetite isn't suffering." Louise stood up. "I love you, Denny."

"Love you too," said the boy.

"Don't eat too much."

"I'm through," and Dennis pushed the fruit bowl aside.

Louise yawned. "Good night again."

"Good night, Mom."

Max listened.

He heard his wife come up the stairs. He listened to the sound of her robe brushing against the wall as she ascended. The bedroom door opened and she stepped inside. He reached for his glass of scotch on the bedside table and sipped.

"A nightcap?" Louise asked.

"It settles the turmoils of the mind," he answered flippantly. "You want one?"

"I don't think so, Max." Louise sat on the edge of the bed. She ran her fingers through her hair, smiling at him. "Have you given any more thought to the camping expedition?"

Max said he was contemplating it. He forced enthusiasm into his voice. He hated fishing and the prospect of a night under canvas was anathema to him. Insects and kerosene fumes and lukewarm beans. But he knew he had to do something to make everybody happy.

Louise said, "We just had a visitor. I found Charlotte Summer out there."

"What was she doing?"

"Couldn't sleep, she said." Louise shrugged. "Actually, it was kind of touching in a way. She wants us to know that she and Dick aren't stealing our son's affections away from us."

Max smiled. "What did you say?"

"I told her she was worried over nothing."

Max drained his glass and looked up at the ceiling. Louise rose and went into the bathroom. A moment later she appeared again, holding a small prescription bottle. Max started—he'd left his goddamn pills lying beside the sink! He ran one hand across his face—the combination of pills and alcohol can lead, he knew, to a kind of careless amnesia.

"What are these, Max?" Louise asked, with a concerned look.

"What does it say on the bottle?"

"One hundred milligram Darvon. It's made out to somebody called Ronald Smythe. Who's he?"

Max got up and grabbed the small brown bottle. Ronald Smythe was one of the stupid pseudonyms he used on his odyssey from one unfamiliar pharmacy to another. He pretended to read the label. He said, "I guess they must have been in my belongings. Smythe's a patient of mine. Maybe he was supposed to pick this up at my office or something. I can't remember."

Louise came back to the bed.

Max put the bottle on the bedside table. His hands were trembling. He felt wretched. When you start to cheat you trap yourself in layers of deceit. You live in a dread that even chemicals can't take the edge off.

He held his wife's hand. "I'll talk to Denny in the morning," he said. His voice was cheerful. "We'll plan something."

And then he heard it as he'd known he would.

It was shrill and piercing and it seemed to fill the entire house. He got out of bed. Louise said, "Who'd be calling at this time of night?"

"Don't know." Max went out of the bedroom. When he reached the landing he realized the ringing had stopped, but only because Dennis had answered the telephone. Max looked down into the hallway. Dennis was gazing up at him.

"It's for you, Dad."

"I'm coming."

"Some woman. Says it's important."

Had Louise heard that? Max wondered. Denny's high-pitched voice was loud and was bound to carry upstairs into the bedroom. *Some woman. Says it's important*. Dear God, what if she'd heard that?

Max picked up the receiver in the living room.

24 There were three men in the wood-paneled recreation room of Theodore Ronson's house. It was a room hung with mounted stags' antlers and the large bleak head of an elk whose big glassy eyes surveyed the world with sullen indifference. Ronson, who had served three terms as the mayor of Carnarvon, was a plump little man whose clothes seemed not quite to fit him. His pants shriveled around his ankles and the cuffs of his crisp white shirt rose over his wrists. The proportions of his body were too odd for the elegance he craved.

As he looked across the room he found himself envying Pelusi, who managed to look passably trim in his rather loud plaid sports coat and polyester slacks, even if his clothes showed an execrable lack of taste. Bryce

Dunning, the mayor's administrative assistant, a silent man with the pallor of an undertaker, looked lean in his camel-hair jacket and dark brown slacks. Ronson thought it a jest of God that he had been born somewhat misshapen—his arms were too short and his legs dumpy—but he often consoled himself with the notion that it could have been worse.

Pelusi was talking about the sheriff, Jerry Metger, and Ronson had to tune his brain back into the conversation around him. Pelusi was saying something about how Metger had come to his office asking curious questions, and then something else about Miles Henderson's state of mind.

Ronson leaned forward a little in his seat, glancing toward the oblong of light suspended over the pool table. He liked this room, his den of recreation. He liked the big guns in the display rack and the hunting trophies and the soft green baize of the pool table. He was at peace in this place. Even as he listened to Pelusi, who was still going on about Metger, he could maintain his equilibrium because the room made him feel a kind of a glow.

Lou Pelusi said, "I don't like the threat Metger represents. It makes me worry. And I don't like Henderson's cavalier attitude either. He's lost it. His brain's sawdust."

"Exactly what threat does Metger represent?" Ronson asked. As mayor of Carnarvon he was best known as a kind of mediating influence, a moderate man who had only the town's best interests at heart. Hadn't new roads been built during his term of office? A new public swimming pool installed? There had been civic achievements, for sure. Ronson never listened to his few critics—those fuddy-duddies who complained that Los Angeles and San Francisco real estate moguls had Ted Ronson tucked in their hip pockets. He was his own man—as much as any small-town mayor could be.

"That's obvious, Ted. He isn't asking funny questions for the good of his health. He *knows* something." Pelusi looked worried, but that was par for the course when it came to the good doctor.

"Such as?"

"How would I know that? I can't ask him straight out. I can't just go up to him and say, Listen, Jerry, how come you're asking these strange questions, can I? I just put him off as best I could."

Ronson swung his swivel chair to one side. "The Metgers are a meddlesome bunch. Like father like son." He was thinking now of Stanley, Jerry Metger's father, who languished these days in the nursing home, his mind flickering like an old candle. Ronson didn't like to think about Stanley much. It was really too bad when you got right down to it, Stanley Metger had been such a vital man in many ways. It was a downright shame. Necessary, maybe, but a shame nevertheless. What had prompted Stanley, at his time of life, to start setting down on paper his memories of old Carnarvon, for God's sake? What weird impulse was it to record stuff? It was one thing to *tell* stories when you had a few snorts under your belt, which was Metger's way, but it was something else to write the goddamn things down and plan to print them in a private edition—something the tourists might buy. By common consent, Stanley Metger's name was never mentioned in this room.

"What could Jerry Metger possibly know?" Ronson asked.

"I don't know, Ted, but he looks like a hound worrying a goddamn bone," Pelusi said. "I don't like it."

"Okay, *say* he knows something," Ronson said. "Is he going to go around telling people about it? I don't think so. He knows how his bread is buttered, doesn't he?"

"Maybe, maybe not," Bryce Dunning said in that strange high-pitched voice of his—he was like a man who had swallowed a whistle. "I went to school with Jerry. He's a straight arrow."

Ronson adjusted the cuffs of his shirt. "I'll have a quiet word with him. Feel him out. See what's on his mind. Jerry Metger doesn't worry me."

"I don't know about that," Pelusi said. "Metger's one of those Boy Scout characters, at least that's the way I've always seen him. Mr. Honesty . . ."

Ted Ronson swiveled in his chair, watching morning sunlight slant through the louvered blinds that hung against the window. "Lou, would you put Jerry Metger out of your mind, for Chrissakes!" He swung around to face the physician. "He's not going to be a problem."

Pelusi put his hands in his pockets. He was forever being told that he worried too much, that he harried things needlessly. A little paranoid— wasn't that what Miles had called him? He gazed at Ronson and said, "I'm scared. That's the bottom line. I'm scared. Conspiracies scare me."

"Conspiracies?" Ronson asked. "I don't see any conspiracy around here. You see anything like that, Bryce?"

Bryce Dunning smiled thinly, a wrinkle of purple lips. "I don't see anything remotely like that, Ted."

Ted Ronson swiveled in his chair again. His short legs barely touched the thick rug. "What I see is protection, Lou. Protection for us. For the people of this town. For our livelihood. I mean to say, Lou, we've got a nice little town here, haven't we?"

Pelusi nodded. He was still thinking about Jerry Metger. Was he just overreacting to the sheriff? Was he letting a simple question alarm him? Maybe Metger had had nothing on his mind, maybe he'd just been passing the time of day. But Metger was one of those people in whom Pelusi perceived ulterior motives—he didn't buy Metger's simple boyish facade, not for a moment.

Ronson said, "We all know this is a good place, Lou. We're expanding. We've got a tourist industry worth a couple of million bucks a year and that's growing faster than we can keep up with it. When the new hotel goes in on Stapely Hill, hell, you won't be able to catch your breath. Our projected estimates suggest a fifteen percent increase in tourism next year *alone.*" Ronson tapped his fingers on the arm of his chair. "The nice thing is, everybody prospers. All the citizens prosper. Nobody's left out, Lou. Including you."

Pelusi nodded, conscious of Bryce Dunning—who spooked him with his funereal demeanor—staring at him. "I know, I know this, Ted. And I don't want to see anybody upset the applecart—"

There was a silence in the room now. Bars of light dappled Ronson's face and he blinked. "All your talk of conspiracies kind of depresses me, Lou. When I think of a conspiracy I feel bad. Sometimes it's necessary for the general well-being of the population"—and here Ronson took a deep breath and his barrel chest swelled up—"that they don't know everything that's going on. Sometimes you have to exclude the people. *For their own good.* Now, I don't call that a conspiracy, Lou."

Pelusi said nothing. Ronson was explaining his own peculiar brand of utilitarian politics, which involved a selective vocabulary. New meanings were given to old words. The thing was a conspiracy any way you happened to slice it. What did it matter if it was for the general prosperity of the town or not?

Pelusi took out his watch and checked the time. He wasn't going to mention to these two men what he had seen last night in a bad dream— *the town of Carnarvon totally deserted, stores and houses boarded up, dilapidated cars motionless on the streets, the highway choked with weeds.*

He wasn't about to share this bleak vision with them. He would play his part in the conspiracy because he wasn't courageous enough to do otherwise—he had grown accustomed, all too easily, to what he considered his comforts.

Ronson clapped the physician on the shoulder. "Don't look so goddamn gloomy, Lou. I'll speak with Metger. I promise you."

"It might be wise," Pelusi said. He looked at both men. The problem he sometimes had was that he still felt like an outsider in Carnarvon. These men, both of them born in this town, shared a common heritage that Pelusi had no part in. He had been hired from outside—he was the newcomer to the conspiracy. How easy it had been to slip into the whole thing, he thought. When Ronson had first explained it, it had all sounded amazingly plausible to him. Why scare the residents? Why frighten off the tourists? After all, Ronson had confided, winking—*it's not like it happens every other month, is it?* And the inflated salary had helped assuage any doubts he might have entertained—Carnarvon paid a hell of a lot better than the hospital in Los Angeles.

Ronson gripped his hand. "Go cure some people, Lou. Or whatever it is you doctors do."

Pelusi moved to the door. Ronson called out to him, "And smile, for God's sake! Physicians shouldn't look like death warmed over. It's bad business practice."

Frog filled his pipe and stretched his legs beneath the kitchen table. Louise poured him a second cup of coffee. It occurred to him that there was a slight tension about her, hovering around her shoulders in the manner of a disturbed aura. There had been a time, once, when he would have sworn he saw auras hanging around people like flimsy scraps of laundry. Louise, on this pleasant morning, was *gray.*

Frog sipped his coffee. Upstairs there was the sound of a shower running. Max, the doctor, performing his morning ablutions. Louise sat at the kitchen table, a preoccupied little light in her eyes—Frog thought she was some distance away right now.

"Didn't sleep well?" he asked.

"I slept okay. I guess." Louise smiled. A frail expression.

Frog rattled a spoon in his saucer. "You look—how shall I say—a leetle weary."

"I swear I'm fine."

Frog was quiet a moment. "Where's Dennis? Don't tell me. Lemme guess."

"It's becoming a habit." Louise rubbed her eyes.

"Do you disapprove?"

She shook her head. "Not really. It's just . . ."

"Just what?"

"I guess I feel that he should be here with us." Louise listened to the rattle of the upstairs shower a moment. "He should be doing things with his parents. His father especially. When I got up this morning Denny was already gone."

She spread her hands on the table, examined her wedding ring. It isn't just Denny, she thought. Not entirely. She got up, fetched the coffeepot to the table. She refilled Frog's cup. Then she sat down again, closing her eyes and tilting her head back out of the sun that came streaming through the kitchen window. She was thinking about Max, about the phone call he'd received last night at bedtime. A patient, he'd told her. Somebody with a problem the replacement physician, Stallings, couldn't deal with. She'd heard Denny call out *Some woman, Dad.* What kind of patient was it who called so late at night? Why hadn't Stallings been able to deal with it? She had lain awake a long time, turning these questions around in her mind. But it wasn't just the questions that dogged her.

It was something else. The intuition that Max was lying. Why did she feel that? And what could Max possibly have to hide? He had looked awkward when he'd come back upstairs to bed, reluctant to discuss the phone call. And even when he'd done so it had seemed to Louise that he was spinning a complicated tale about some neurotic woman she'd never heard of, somebody he'd never mentioned before. She needs a shrink, Max had said. But why hadn't Louise ever heard of this particular patient before? Max always discussed the most interesting people who came to his office. He always regaled her with stories of hypochondriacs and neurotics and the plain loonies who sought him out to cure their imaginary ailments. But she'd never heard of this Mrs. Harrison before. And, as far as she knew, Max had never lied to her before either. Was he lying now? Or was she simply reading complexity into something innocent?

She tried to push all this aside, but it kept returning to her in the most unwelcome fashion. She opened her eyes and smiled at Frog. He was saying something about Dick and Charlotte and Dennis—and she hadn't been following a word of it. She focused in on him.

"I'm sorry, Frog. What were you saying?"

"Sigmund Frog, erstwhile analyst, was simply saying that young people can contribute immeasurably to the lives of the old, and vice versa. It's a give and take proposition. Your son obviously offsets some of the emptiness in the lives of the Summers. And the Summers offer him something—"

"Something he doesn't get here? Is that what you want to say?"

Frog puffed on his pipe. "Hold, Louise. I wasn't going to say that. Aren't we touchy?"

"Just a little. I'm sorry."

Frog gazed at the woman a moment. He took his pipe from his mouth —the goddamn thing always made him feel pompous. "It can be a learning process for young Dennis. Where else would he get the chance to try out his mechanical yearning on a classic Dodge truck, for instance? He can't run down to the local auto shop in San Francisco and say, Hey, lemme work on that classic car, can he? They'd laugh at him. The Summers don't do that. They accept him. And obviously they don't give a damn about letting a kid loose around their property."

Dear Frog, Louise thought. He was trying very hard to cheer her up, but he was coming in from quite the wrong angle. She patted the back of his hand. *Max couldn't have a woman somewhere, that was just too absurd, too ridiculous; Max wasn't a philanderer.* "Speaking of the Summers . . ." she said. She stood up and paused.

"Speaking of the Summers," Frog prompted her.

"I'll show you something." She went inside Denny's bedroom and came back carrying the bait in the glass jar and the photograph. "The old folks give him peculiar things. Such as this so-called amazing fish bait, which stinks like you wouldn't believe. And yesterday they gave him this picture. I assume it's shortly after they married. Dennis says it was taken at the start of their honeymoon."

Frog studied the bait first. He held the glass jar up to the light and made what he thought of as the noises a mad scientist might make. *Mmmmm I see mmmmm ah-hah.* He reached for the stopper.

"Be warned before you open that," Louise said.

"Is a genie about to escape?"

"Less pleasant than that."

"Who knows? Maybe I ought to make some wishes anyhow. Just in case."

He stared a moment at the dark brown goop in the jar and then took off the stopper. The stench assailed him at once, making him dizzy. Whatever was inside came reaching out to crowd his senses and make his eyes water. He thought of a dead dog putrefying in a hot midday sun. He thought of a very old soup that had lain rotting in a covered saucepan for years.

He rammed the stopper back in place.

"Holy shit," he said. "It's no way to start your day, is it?"

Louise wrinkled her nose. "Denny doesn't seem to mind it. He keeps the stopper off the damned thing. Can you believe that?"

Frog shook his head. "What the hell is in that stuff?"

"Mainly rancid cat food, I believe. According to Dick Summer, fish apparently go bananas over the bait."

Frog put the jar down on the table. He stared at the brown stuff behind glass. It had the shape of a malformed fetus.

"Sinister," he said.

"Very." Louise slid the photograph across the table and Frog reached for it.

"Dick and Charlotte," she said. "Can you believe that?"

"When, I wonder. The middle of the eighteenth century?" Frog smiled, turning the picture around in his hands. He brought it up close to his face and squinted.

"I suppose it was taken in the 1920s sometime," Louise said.

"If they married in 1925, that would make this their sixty-first year of bliss. And if they married real young—say in their late teens—that would mean Dick and Charlotte are hovering around the eighty mark."

"That would be right, I guess," Louise remarked.

"It bogs the old mind," Frog said. "Sixty-one years of married life! They must have run out of conversation forty years ago. No wonder they enjoy having your son around."

Louise smiled. "You take the cynical view of marriage, huh?"

"Cynical? Not entirely. I speak for myself. All my relationships have petered out into silences," Frog said. He tilted the photograph a little. "If you look real closely at this, you can make out the name of the steamship."

"Really?"

"Yeah. Look."

Louise took the picture back and peered at it. For a second she imagined herself inside the thing—standing on that sepia quay, smelling the dark brown ocean. For a second she *became* the photographer, asking the young couple to smile, framing them in the lens of her camera.

"You see it?"

"Just," Louise said. There it was, in small blurry letters: *The Cosima*. She set the picture down. "Dick and Charlotte must have sailed off in that ship. I wonder where they honeymooned."

"They don't look too happy, do they?"

"It's hard to say."

"He seems puzzled by something. And her smile is kinda glassy," Frog said.

Louise finished her coffee. The sound of the shower had stopped upstairs; she could hear Max move around. A closet door opened and closed. Frog stood up.

"Are you leaving?" she asked.

He nodded. "I checked your weeds on the way in. They're not coming back fast enough for me to make a profit." He stretched his arms, yawned, and placed a hand across his mouth. "I think I'll have to go on hands and knees to the Summers and beg them to put me to work. Will you give me a reference? Say how honest and hardworking I am."

Louise smiled. It seemed to her just then that she'd known Frog forever. "Do you really need to make some money?"

"It wouldn't hurt."

"Okay. I'll look around the place and see if I can come up with something to keep you busy."

"I'd appreciate that."

Frog moved out of the kitchen. "I really think I will try Dick and Charlotte again. I get a kick out of refusals."

She watched him go, heard the front door close. Then she carried the empty coffee cups to the sink. She rinsed them just as Max appeared—showered, shaved, shining—in the kitchen doorway.

"Dennis gone?" he asked.

"Long gone."

Max came up and kissed her on the back of her neck. She felt his hands against her hips.

"I love you," he said.

25 Metger's office was a windowless, white-walled tomb at the heart of a series of partitioned rooms in the Carnarvon City Hall, a building that had once been the enormous home of a prosperous mine owner in the early 1900s. Now it housed Ted Ronson's office, the Tourist Board, the Chamber of Commerce, the County Assessor's office, the Registry of Births and Deaths, and the Sheriff's Department. It was the aorta of Carnarvon, the central pump through which the town's blood flowed. Metger spent as little time as he possibly could in the place because he believed bureaucracy was a contagious thing and once a man was stricken by that particular virus he became plump and contented with paper shuffling and rubber stamping and something vital went out of his soul.

What he longed for most in his room was a window, a few panes of glass, a view. Instead he had stark white walls and a solitary cork bulletin board and a large desk strewn with files and folders, many of them related to the trivia of his work. Traffic offenses. Domestic disputes. Every time he opened one of these folders he imagined he detected the sound of snoring rising out of the paper.

But there was one folder on his desk that was different from all the others. A blue label attached to the manila cover had the words ACKERLEY, ANTHEA.

Metger opened it, turning the pages slowly.

History, he thought. Fading notes on the death of a young girl. Miles Henderson had been the coroner then.

Metger scanned the pages, his eyes glazed—he had looked inside this particular folder more times than he cared to remember. Over the years, in idle moments, he had turned these same pages. And they had never yielded anything to him—almost as if the entire file were written in a code for which he didn't have the key.

Now, tilting his chair back at the wall, he turned his eyes to the telephone. In keeping with the contemporary feel of the place, it was one of those skinny white push-button numbers that had a penny-whistle sound whenever it rang. Just as he longed for windows, so he had a lust for a good old-fashioned solid black phone with a rotary dial.

He leaned forward, picked the telephone up, dialed Directory Assistance, and asked for the number of the University of Washington in Seattle. He scribbled it on the cover of the Ackerley file, then put the phone down.

Now that he had the number, he wasn't sure what he was going to do with it. He got up and walked around the room. He beat the palms of his hands against his thighs as he moved, like a man fighting an attack of cold weather.

Earlier it had crossed his mind that he should pay a call on Florence Hann because of the enigmatic remark she'd made yesterday outside the Alpha Beta, which still haunted him. He should go ask her some questions—but he had the feeling that she wasn't going to add anything else to what she'd already said.

There was a definite edge of madness to the woman, a slippery thing Metger knew he couldn't quite grasp. The real trouble with madness, he thought, was how it ran off into hundreds of tangents, areas you couldn't altogether follow because sequential thinking had no place in that kind of mind.

And he needed logic. He needed a sequence. Something he could understand and examine. He didn't need further enigmas.

If he had to, if he needed to, he could go back and tackle Florence Hann later, but right at this moment he had the number in Seattle and that was what occupied his mind. What was he supposed to say? Even if he managed to get through to the man, what was he supposed to talk to him about?

Remember me? Metger? We met some time back?

He stopped circling his office and sat down behind his desk. He picked up the lightweight phone and punched in the number. A woman answered.

"University of Washington," she said, a singsong voice.

"Professor Ackerley," Metger said.

"One moment puh-lease."

It was a start. At least the guy was still there; he hadn't wandered off like some academic nomad. Metger twisted the telephone cord around his fingers. There was a slight burning sensation around his heart. Something I ate, he thought.

A man's voice now. "This is Julian Ackerley."

"Professor Ackerley?"

"Yes . . ."

Metger gazed up at his bone-white ceiling. "I'm not sure if you'll remember me, Professor. My name is Jerry Metger."

"Metger?"

There was a long silence. For a while Metger thought the line had gone dead.

"Metger. Yes." The voice, which had been warm and somewhat pleasant before, contained a chill now. An edge of ice.

Metger rubbed his eyes. It comes back, he thought. It just comes rolling back at me—he could see Ackerley's face on that rainy afternoon, Ackerley and his wife standing up there on the sun deck, he could feel the damp trees press against him as he called out a child's name, the spray that rose from pine needles each time he brushed against a branch.

"I know it's been a long time, Professor—"

"Yes. It has. I don't understand why you're calling me, Metger. I don't have anything to say to you."

"It's a loose end, nothing important—"

"A loose end, Metger? How can there be a loose end after twelve years, for God's sake?"

Metger bit his lower lip. This was leading him nowhere. There were just long corridors with shut doors and the echoes of his own footsteps. *A loose end*, he thought. He was making up fictions to justify his obsession. He felt like a man trying to weld together substances that wouldn't respond—wood to water, fire upon ice. Something impossible.

"Really, Metger. You talk about loose ends. Have you any idea how long it has taken me to put my life together since then? Have you?" There was a heartbreaking catch in the man's voice.

Metger felt a deep sympathy. Metger, as sheriff, tried to ignore the pain. "I was going through my old files, Professor Ackerley—"

"I can't help you with anything, Metger. I don't want to talk to you—"

"It's only going to take a moment." Now Metger felt like a salesman hawking magazine subscriptions, the pushy guy who gets one foot inside the door and won't go away. A figure moved across his line of vision a moment, the plump shape of Deputy Shannon, a man whose insensitivities would have qualified him admirably for the task of telephoning Ackerley. Let me call him, Sheriff. I got a way of opening old wounds. . . .

"I don't have the time," Ackerley said.

"A moment, that's all . . ."

Silence. At least the line wasn't dead. Not yet.

Ackerley could be heard sighing. Far away in damp Seattle a man sighs because a closed box of his life is being forced open. Metger picked up a Bic pen and drummed it nervously on his desk. "I know this is difficult for you," he said.

"How did you know that, I wonder," Ackerley remarked. The throaty catch had gone out of his voice and the coldness was back.

"It's about the coroner's report," Metger said.

Ackerley made no response.

"I was trying to close some old files and I notice in the report written by the physician, Dr. Henderson, that there's no mention of your daughter's symptoms—"

"What symptoms are you referring to? It's a long time ago, Metger. I've become an expert at not remembering things."

"I appreciate that," Metger said. "But my problem is that I don't understand why Dr. Henderson didn't remark on those symptoms in his report."

"What is it you want? What exactly do you want, Metger?"

Metger shut the folder in front of him. "It puzzles me, Mr. Ackerley. That's all. It puzzles me why Henderson didn't mention the girl's condition. Wouldn't a physician say something about that?"

"I don't know what a physician would or would not mention, Metger. I've never been one."

Metger let the pen slide from his fingers and it rolled across his desk. He wasn't going to get anything here, he knew that. It had been an act of foolishness even to make this call. Ackerley wasn't going to be sucked back into the past, into the tragedy.

For one terrible moment Metger imagined that he was all alone in the world, and quite demented. That he perceived things nobody else did, that he imagined events which had never taken place. The rainy afternoon, the dead girl, everything else.

"Mr. Ackerley, did your daughter have any symptoms before you came to Carnarvon that summer?"

"Why do you keep going on like this, Metger? Can't you leave this goddamn thing alone?"

"I'm sorry," Metger said. And he was. "I don't mean to drag up something you understandably find depressing. It's just one of those bureaucratic loose ends, like I said."

There was a long silence. Then Ackerley said, "I have bad dreams, Metger. Every one of them is set in a place by the name of Carnarvon. I wake up sweating. I wake up panicked. It doesn't matter that I take sleeping pills. It doesn't matter. I still wake up and my mouth is dry and I'm shaking and I'm back in Carnarvon again—and you have the gall to ask me to remember something about that place! About my daughter!" Another pause. "I wish with all my heart I hadn't come to your town that summer, Metger. That's what I go over again and again. Would my daughter have been okay if we'd stayed here in Seattle or if we'd gone some other place? I ask myself that. I'll tell you one thing—my daughter changed *in that place.*"

The goddamn phone was dead. A connection in Seattle had been severed. He couldn't blame Ackerley for hanging up. Who wants to work over the sorrowful ground of an old tragedy—who except a ghoul? *My daughter changed in that place.* . . .

Metger stood up, stroked his jaw. He looked at the Ackerley folder, flipping it open.

Miles Henderson had written, . . . a verdict of suicide at a time when the balance of the girl's mind was disturbed. . . .

Now *that* was choice language. That was *precise.* The balance of her mind. As if there had been a set of tiny cerebral scales inside the poor kid's brain. Very nice, Miles.

Metger thought he'd get the hell out of this office. Go down, as he seemed doomed to do, in the general direction of the redwood house and the nice people from San Francisco. Go down there, stalking his private phantoms and fears, in the dark green depths of the trees.

Charlotte Summer held a small glass jar between her hands. She turned it this way and that, so that its contents, which were practically weightless, shifted beneath the kitchen light. She heard Dick coming down the stairs from the bedroom. When he reached the bottom he paused.

She raised her face. He was holding something out to her. After a moment she recognized what it was. An old bottle of nail polish.

"I couldn't," she said.

"Sure you could."

She set the glass jar on the kitchen table. The nail polish was dark red. She picked it up, opened the cap, smelled its woozy scent.

"Been such a long time," she said.

Dick smiled. He watched her dip the tiny brush into the blood-red liquid and apply a slick to the index finger of her left hand, which she held out in front of her.

"Well?" she asked.

"Looks pretty."

Charlotte studied the nail for a while. Then she said, "Why did that young man come around here?"

"Who? The fellow that lives in the van?"

"Don't much like him watching us, Dick."

Dick shrugged. "He doesn't worry me."

Charlotte was silent. Then she said, "He isn't going to make trouble, is he?"

"Hell no."

"I couldn't stand it if he did, Dick."

"Don't you worry," Dick said. "Don't you worry your head about him."

Charlotte stared at her nail. "Pretty color," she remarked.

26

"What did he say?" the professor asked. "What did he say when you told him that?"

The girl, hunched over a cardboard cup of weak coffee, lit a cigarette. The ashtrays in the diner where she sat with Professor Zmia were the inverted lids of Mason jars. She looked at the man for a time before answering. The room was filled with steam and condensation hung against the windows.

"He didn't say much. What could he say? I gave him an ultimatum. It shook him up. What the hell do you expect? Did you think he'd be happy?"

Professor Zmia sipped his tea, which was abominable. He placed his fingers over the girl's hands. "Your part is almost over, Connie."

"Almost? What do you mean almost? You've had enough out of me. You got what you paid for." She took her hands away and the professor grimaced. "I don't know why you're doing this and I don't think I want to know, but I'm out. Oh you tee, Professor. Out."

"Such nonsense. Such a delicate moral sense." The professor smiled. He pushed his tea aside. "We are not quite finished yet, Connie. There remains something more to be done."

"Yeah? Well, I just upped the price, Professor. And I don't think you want to pay it. And anyhow, this town gives me the willies. I'm a city person. I want to go home."

Zmia took out his checkbook. He flashed it in front of the girl's face. She pushed a strand of hair out of her eyes, ignoring him. She raised her coffee and blew on its surface.

"Goddamn," she said.

Professor Zmia smiled and took out his fountain pen.

Theodore Ronson usually felt a sense of accomplishment when he stepped into the Carnarvon Nursing Home. Nurses smiled at him, orderlies regarded him with a kind of cautious awe. He was a member of the nursing-home board and had been more than a little instrumental in raising the funds necessary to build the place. This evening, though, the mayor did not experience any of his usual buoyancy. He barely looked at the nurses, even though he normally found them pleasing to his middle-aged eye. He went up the stairs to the second floor, where he moved quickly along the corridor. When he found the room he wanted he knocked on the door tentatively before entering.

The man who sat on the edge of the bed stared gloomily at the TV. He was a big man whose skin seemed to hang like loose cotton on his bones. Down his arms there were pale old tattoos, that now looked like a variety of discolored contusions. He didn't turn his face when Ronson came in.

"Stanley, Stanley," the mayor said effusively. "How are you this evening?"

The man appeared not to hear. Color from the television played across his face like a kaleidoscope. Ronson, hovering on the margins of the room, feeling awkward, cleared his throat. "Not talking tonight, Stan? Cat got your tongue?"

The man on the bed, Stanley Metger, finally turned his face. He regarded the mayor for a second, his look one of nonrecognition. The blankness in his eyes always shook the mayor. Big Stan Metger, the life and soul of any party—where are you now? What have we done to you?

Ronson approached the bed. He smiled, glanced at the TV. "What's on, Stan?"

Metger said nothing. A tiny grunt issued from his mouth. Goddamn, Ronson thought. What made you take on the funny notion you were going to write a fucking book? What put that nonsense in your head, Stanley? Ted Ronson rubbed his hands together. There was a time when he and Stanley Metger had been the very best of friends. A time not so long ago either. Drinking buddies, roustabouts, carefree terrors of the night places. Big Stan, with his stories, his tall tales, his awful jokes, had been welcome anywhere. Ronson remembered the Taffy Owen stories, legends Stanley Metger had gathered about an eccentric Welsh miner who'd been among the early settlers in Carnarvon. He assumed Metger made many of them up—Taffy's polygamous marriages, the night the Welshman had tried to ride a three-legged mule all the way to San Francisco, the gargantuan drinking binge that had ended when Taffy woke up in Tijuana with a new Mexican bride he was obliged to bring all the way back to Carnarvon without knowing the woman's name—in Metger's world you couldn't tell where the truth finished and the embroidery began. In the manner of any storyteller, Metger kept recreating the universe he inhabited.

Ronson sat on the edge of the bed. "How are you, Stanley?"

"Who wants to know," the man said flatly.

It was some kind of response, Ronson thought. How far gone was Metger tonight? The mayor looked at the TV and sighed quietly. He was extremely uncomfortable. It had become his habit to look in on Metger now and then, but what brought him here? Old time's sake? Or was it a touch of guilt? Ronson did not entertain this thought long. He patted Metger's arm for a time. The big man tolerated this momentarily before moving slightly away.

Theodore Ronson stood up, hands plunged inside the pockets of his lightweight sports coat. He was at a loss for further words; he gazed bleakly at the darkening window of the room. A tree knocked upon the pane, blown by halfhearted breezes.

"I just thought I'd stop in," the mayor said.

The big man turned his face. He had great dark eyes, hollow and empty, lifeless as asteroids. "Where's my wife?" the man asked.

Dead, Ronson thought. A long time ago. Saying nothing, not knowing what words were appropriate in any case, he moved to the door and was reaching for the handle when Lou Pelusi came into the room. Pelusi carried his small black bag, all the portable tools of his trade. Ted Ronson stepped back.

"I was just leaving," the mayor said.

"Why? Something you don't want to see?" Pelusi asked.

Ronson shook his head. "This isn't exactly a pleasure for me, you know that. You think I like to see him like this? You think I enjoy this?"

Pelusi opened his bag. He rummaged around inside. "Are you queasy, Ted? Don't like the sight of blood?"

"I don't need it," Ronson answered.

"Somebody has to do it. Right, Ted? Isn't that how you phrased it?"

"You knew what you were getting into," Ronson said. "Don't bitch about it now."

Pelusi turned to look at the man on the bed. "How is he tonight anyhow?" he asked.

"Whatever it is you're giving him, Lou, it's working." Ronson moved to the door.

"Would you want it any other way?" Pelusi asked.

Ronson went out into the corridor, closing the door behind him. Writing your stories down on paper, Stanley—how could you be so fucking *stupid*? The mayor moved toward the stairs. Before he started down he heard Stanley Metger moaning from behind the closed door of his barren little room.

27

Louise said, "It doesn't look *too* bad," and she reached out, fluffing the edges of Dennis's hair, as if she wanted to alter the style Charlotte had imposed there. It looked too flat to her somehow—Dennis's curls were gone. He had lost something of his cherubic appearance. He appeared more mature, older. She dropped her hand to her side when she saw his look of exasperation.

"I *like* it," he said.

"So do I. Kind of." Louise ran a potato beneath the cold-water faucet, then began to scrape the skin. "Did you ask her to cut it, Denny?"

"Of course I did." The boy picked up a peeled potato and crunched into it as if it were an apple. "I wouldn't let anyone cut my hair without permission, would I?"

That tone, Louise thought. That little edge, almost a whine. She glanced at Dennis, smiling. "Something wrong?"

The kid shook his head. He wandered to the table and sat down, tipping his chair back to the wall. "I'm okay," he answered. He scratched at the back of his wrist for a few seconds.

"Insect bite?" Louise asked.

"Just itchy."

Louise placed the potatoes inside boiling water, then wiped her hands on her apron. She removed the apron and hung it on a hook on the kitchen wall. "Did you work on the truck today?"

Dennis nodded.

Louise was quiet a moment. The boy was mining a taciturn vein right then. Opaque adolescence, she thought—like a window you can't see through. It was an age filled with mood swings and elaborate foxholes where you could hide your personality when you needed to.

"Did you get it to run?"

Crunching into the potato, Dennis shook his head.

"How come I get the feeling I'm holding a one-sided conversation here?" Louise said.

Dennis smiled at his mother. "I'm sorry. I've got this headache. Maybe

I'll go take some aspirin." He rose, left the kitchen, wandered along the hallway toward the downstairs toilet. Louise heard the door click shut, then there was the sound of running water. She thought about the boy's hair again; it seemed strange to her that Dennis, always so possessive of his hair, so particular about how it looked, should allow Charlotte to cut it. Should *ask* her even. And she felt a vague twinge of jealousy all at once. Why would the boy let Charlotte cut his hair when he wouldn't even allow his own *mother* to touch it?

It was a brief resentment and she let it pass. Presumably Charlotte had some secret way about her, something that made Dennis trust the woman the way he wouldn't trust his mother. A *knack*, Louise thought. A gift for getting along with kids—another person's kid anyhow. Why didn't you get one of your own, Charlotte?

Louise took a chilled bottle of white wine from the refrigerator and opened it. She poured herself a large glass and carried it to the living room. Max lay on the sofa, a book open on his chest. He had fallen asleep and his hands hung limply at his sides. She poked him in the side and he stirred, opening his eyes.

"Hey," she said. "It's almost time for dinner."

"Dinner?" His voice was dry, a sleeper's voice. Max sat up awkwardly. "I was dreaming that Denny and I were fishing in this huge dark lake. He caught some monster and I had the job of skinning it. Which wasn't altogether pleasant. Thanks for waking me."

Louise sipped her wine. She looked at her husband. He was rubbing his eyes, his long fingers flying around his face. "A fishing dream," she said. "Wonder what that means. Maybe it's one of those future projections. Maybe you're going to take your son fishing."

Max groaned. "Where is the kid anyhow?"

"Bathroom," Louise said over the rim of her wineglass. "He had his hair cut today. By Charlotte."

"Yeah?"

"It's okay except it makes him look about five years older."

"Do I hear disapproval?"

She shook her head. "Not really. Only . . ."

"Only what?"

"Nothing," she answered. She stared inside her wine. Max got up, paced around the room. He paused by the telephone, let his hand dangle across the instrument momentarily, then he moved to the window.

"Are you expecting Mrs. Harrison to call again?" Louise asked.

Max turned, smiling at his wife. Mrs. Harrison, he thought. Why in the name of God hadn't he invented another name for Connie? It had come out without thinking, without planning—it was this absence of instinctive guile that made him a bad conniver. He laid his hand on the windowpane and said, "I asked her not to. I told her I was taking a leave of absence. I told her to talk with Stallings if she had any more problems."

"Firm, were you?"

"Firm," Max replied. "I can't have neurotic women calling me up."

"Is she pretty?"

"No," Max said. He gazed out at the car in the driveway, then let his eyes roam across the dirt road to the trees. Pretty—Connie was more than that. He felt a certain thickness at the back of his throat and small flylike spots shimmered in his vision. She couldn't have been serious last night, could she? She couldn't have meant what she said. Max pressed his nose to the windowpane and wondered what Louise was thinking, whether he'd convinced her with his explanation of a neurotic patient. She couldn't think anything else—she didn't have reasons. Now, like some terrible echo of a voice trapped in his mind, he heard Connie all over again. I've been thinking, Max. Silence. Ten seconds of silence. I want you to leave your wife. I want you to live with me. . . .

Preposterous, Max thought.

But there had been in Connie's tone a kind of determination he didn't like, an implicit menace to him. Dear Christ, how had he managed to get himself into this dreadful situation anyhow? Maybe she wouldn't call again. Maybe. But he couldn't shake that tone in her voice.

"How old is she?" Louise asked.

"It's hard to say."

"She must have provided that information for your records, Max."

"Some women—don't be shocked—lie about their age."

"Can't you guess how old she is?"

"Forty," Max said quickly. "Forty and sagging fast. I don't know why you're so interested in this woman."

"Idle curiosity, sweetheart." Louise came to the window and rapped the rim of her wineglass on the pane. "Actually, I think some of your female patients probably have the hots for you. That's standard, isn't it? The old cliché of the lonely woman falling for her physician. It's your bedside manner that leads them on."

Max snorted. "Bedside manner! I failed Bedside Manner in medical school."

Louise smiled. She reached out and touched Max lightly on the back of his hand. "I don't believe that. I remember you were a pretty persuasive guy back then."

Persuasive, Max thought. Could I persuade Connie Harrison to leave me alone? Could I talk her into not calling me? He slung one arm around his wife's shoulder and hugged her quickly before releasing her. "The cocktail hour approaches," he said. He poured himself a scotch from the liquor cabinet. *I want you to leave your wife, Max.* Just like that. Out of the blue. Come live with me and be my love. . . . He stared at the telephone. Hadn't it been Nimzowich, the chess master, who'd said that the threat was better than the execution? It was what the telephone represented to him—the sheer bloody threat of Connie calling again. It didn't have to ring in order to menace him.

He sipped his drink. His hand shook and cubes of ice knocked on the inside of his glass. If Louise noticed, she didn't say anything. Max gripped the glass in both hands now.

Dennis came into the room.

"Like your hair," Max said.

"It's okay."

"Old Charlotte must be quite a barber."

Dennis nodded. He placed himself on the arm of the sofa and swung one leg back and forth.

Max cleared his throat. "I've been thinking about canvas," he said. "Nights under the old roof of a tent. Casting the rod into the water. Watching the sinker bob up and down. All the magic of the great outdoors."

Louise said, "It sounds good to me."

"Does it sound good to you, Denny?" Max asked.

"You want to go on a camping trip, Dad? *You?*"

"Well, I've been pondering the notion." Max sipped his scotch. "Does it appeal to you?"

The boy appeared hesitant. "I'd like it." A short pause. The kid slid down from the arm of the sofa and squatted on the floor. "The only thing is, I'd like to wait until that bait really ripens. Dick says it takes maybe five more days before it reaches maximum potency."

"Maximum potency?" Louise asked. "How much more maximum does it have to get, Denny? I mean, every time I walk along the hallway and pass your bedroom I can smell the stuff. Couldn't you allow it to maximize its potency outdoors?"

"Uh-huh. Dick says rain shouldn't get to it because that weakens the composition."

"What rain, Denny?"

"Dick says there's a rainy season coming."

"So he's not only a master Bait-Maker, he's a meteorologist as well?"

Louise said. The tone in her voice—why did it come out sounding resentful like that? Did she really resent the attraction the Summers had for her son? She felt suddenly silly, small-minded.

"He's an old man," Max said, coming to the defense of Dick Summer for some reason. "He's probably been around. Old people develop certain feelings for things like the weather. They have internal barometers. Fact."

"Dick knows some things," Dennis added.

"I bet he does," Max agreed. "Anyway, the outcome is that we wait for your bait to . . . well, ripen . . . and then we can take a trip?"

"Right," Dennis said.

Louise finished her wine. It had rushed to her head, creating a small buzz there. At least Max had gotten his project off the ground, she thought. It was some kind of start. As the warmth flooded through her she smiled at her husband, catching his eye as if to say, Thank you, Max. . . .

Dennis was scratching the back of his wrist vigorously.

"Is that still bothering you?" Louise asked.

"Maybe I came in contact with poison ivy or something."

Max said, "Let Dr. Untermeyer take a look." He raised Dennis's arm, staring at the reddened spot where the boy had been scratching. There was a small collection of pale freckles there, tiny flecks created by exposure to sunlight. "It's not poison ivy, I can tell you that."

"What is it?" Dennis asked.

"You've been getting a little too much sun, that's all. Here's what you do. Outdoors, you keep the arm covered with a long-sleeved shirt. At night, before you go to bed, you can spread a little calamine over it to relieve the itch. Okay?"

Dennis didn't say anything.

"You owe me thirty-seven dollars for the house call."

"Since when do freckles itch?" the kid asked.

"I'm no dermatologist, Denny. You want a skin specialist, it's going to cost you another thirty-seven."

Louise moved in the direction of the kitchen. "I think we should eat. Is anybody hungry?"

"Me," Dennis answered, scratching.

Metger said, "I happened to be in the vicinity. Just thought I'd drop by and see how you folks are settling in." He smiled and raised his coffee cup to his lips. "Besides, I wanted to meet your son. Didn't get the chance last time."

Louise looked at the empty dinner plates on the table. The tatty leftovers of a meal. She wished she'd had time to clean up, but the young cop had just descended on them. She glanced at Max, who was tapping his fingers on the table.

Metger said, "I'm about to have a kid of my own."

"Your wife's pregnant?"

"More than seven months." The cop had a look of pleasure on his face.

"Well, congratulations," Max said.

"Really," Louise said. "You must be very excited."

Metger smiled and looked around the kitchen. It appeared to Louise that there was nothing exactly *idle* in the way he did this—it was almost as if he were looking for something specific, checking on something. He had had the same kind of searching look on his first visit. She remembered that now. It made her feel just a little uneasy, although she couldn't quite say why.

"We just had dinner," she said. "As you can see."

The cop said, "Looks like my place just after dinner," and he smiled, as if to say the mess didn't matter to him.

"Are you familiar with this house, Sheriff?" she asked.

"Familiar?"

"You give the impression that you know this place."

Metger laughed. He had a good-natured, open laugh. "There were some tenants here who had a young daughter. I visited them once. But it's a long time ago. Why do you ask?"

"You seem to be looking for something," Louise said.

"I didn't mean to give that impression," Metger remarked. "I guess I was just trying to remember how much this place has changed, that's all."

"And has it?"

"Different furniture. Different paint." Metger shrugged. "What you might call a face-lift."

He drained his coffee and put the cup on the table and hitched his belt up at his waist. "You folks get into town much?"

"Not often," Max said.

"You ought to take your son to the carnival some night," Metger said. "If he likes that kind of thing. There's a carnival comes here every July for a week. It's not bad. There can't be much for him to do around here."

Louise couldn't help it. She said, "He visits the neighbors a lot."

"Neighbors?"

"The old people."

"The Summers?"

"Dick and Charlotte," she said. "He seems to have formed a close friendship with them."

"You know the Summers well, Sheriff?" Max asked.

"Hardly."

"I guess they've lived here a long time."

"As far back as I remember."

"More coffee, Sheriff?" Louise asked.

Metger shook his head. "It makes me jumpy."

Max, who had lifted the coffeepot in anticipation, smiled and put it down again.

Metger said, "Yeah. The Summers are fixtures in these parts." He moved toward the door now, turning his cap around in his fingers, like somebody nervous. "I'd like to meet your son if he's around. Think I could?"

"I'll call him," Louise said.

"You don't have to go to any trouble." The sheriff was already walking out of the kitchen toward the living room.

"It's no problem." She followed him through the living room and out into the hallway.

There Metger hesitated, gazing ahead at the door of Dennis's room as if he had changed his mind, filled with a sudden reluctance to meet the kid now.

"His room isn't exactly tidy," Louise said. "Could you pretend you don't notice?"

"I'll do that," Metger said. He moved again, as if motion were an afterthought and his attention belonged elsewhere.

Louise knocked on Dennis's door before going in. The boy was sitting on the bed. He looked up at Metger, then he reached out and stuck the stopper in the glass jar that contained the bait. *Thank you for your consideration*, Louise thought. The air in the room was bad, dank. She could hardly breathe. She wondered if Metger noticed. He must have but was too polite to mention it.

"Dennis, meet Sheriff Metger."

Dennis smiled. "Hi," he said.

"Hi, Dennis," the cop said. "How do you like it out here? It's not like what you're used to, huh? It's quite a ways from San Francisco."

Louise detected a note of strain in Metger's voice—he wasn't used to talking with kids, that was all. He spoke with the forced, patronizing cheerfulness of the inexperienced adult. He'd learn soon enough.

"I like it," Dennis said. "I like the trees."

Grinning, like some clumsy uncle on first meeting a niece, Metger moved toward the bed. He was looking around the room, but this time he was trying to take things in more surreptitiously than before. He was no good at subterfuge—it showed all over his face. Louise saw him glance at the bedside table, the lamp, then turn his eyes back to the boy again.

She said, "Sheriff Metger's about to become a father, Denny. Isn't that nice?"

Dennis nodded politely, although she knew this information was of no real interest to him. She'd only mentioned it to fill in a silence she'd suddenly found a touch awkward.

"Well, Dennis, real nice meeting you," he said. There was a strange little break, a crack, in his voice.

"Yeah," the boy answered. He seemed awed by the cop's gun. "Is that loaded? Really?"

"Sure it is," Metger said.

"You ever use it?"

"I've been lucky, Dennis. I've never had to fire this gun. In fact, I only ever took it out of its holster one time."

"When was that? What happened?"

"That was a long time ago."

"If you lived in San Francisco, you'd use it all the time."

Metger smiled. "Carnarvon's a whole other ball game. We don't get big-city action around here. You might be surprised to know that most cops never have to use their weapons."

There was a silence now. Metger appeared to have run out of chitchat. He shook Dennis by the hand, clapped him on the shoulder, then he was ready to leave. Louise walked with him to the front door. Max came out of the living room to the hall.

"You meet Dennis?" he asked.

"Nice kid," the cop said. His face was pale.

"We think so. But we're prejudiced," Louise remarked. She took Max's hand and held it in her own—why did this policeman unnerve her? Beyond the porch, twilight was receding and darkness falling between the trees. A wispy wind tugged at the pines.

Metger leaned against the porch rail. "Well, thanks for the coffee."

"Anytime," Louise said.

"I better be running along. Who knows? There might have been a crime wave in my absence." He laughed at this notion. Carnarvon was safe. Carnarvon was cozy. Nothing ever happened in Carnarvon.

She watched him go toward his car. It backed out and then it was gone, leaving a fading vibration on the air. As she turned to go inside she had the feeling that Metger hadn't entirely wanted to meet Dennis.

That had been an excuse, a pretext for something else.

28 Frog stood on the edge of the clearing.

Earlier, when he had left the Untermeyers, he had gone back up into the forest to nap—to cop, as they used to say, some zzzzs. But when he'd lain down inside the VW his courtship of sleep was a waste of time and so he'd tossed and turned and sipped a little Mondavi he had left in a bottle and then finally, driven by his own need for financial sustenance, he'd strolled through the trees to this place.

He reached up and flicked at the overhanging branch of a pine. It vibrated back and forth.

Then he stepped a little closer to the house, although he was still hidden by a scruffy stand of trees. He could see the trash that was strewn across the yard—somebody had clearly made a small effort to fix the place up. Some of it had been sorted and lay in tidy little mountains. But it was still a bucolic slum, reminding Frog of all the garage sales he'd ever known, all the porch sales and yard sales of North America, those little neighborly enterprises where fat people turned up in rusted wagons to rummage through broken lamps and scuffed sneakers and assorted nuts and bolts, where they dickered over the price of a used shirt or a secondhand set of 1933 encyclopedias, in which there was no entry for penicillin and the far side of the moon was a matter of academic speculation.

He looked at the porch. Nothing, nobody. A whisper here, a rustle there—beneath the mold and humus, creatures stirred.

What you do, he told himself, is you go straight up to the house and introduce yourself and you say, Okay, I'm not a pushy kind of a guy, but I'd like to help you get this slum of yours into some kinda shape, I mean the goddamn neighbors are bitching and the town council is holding a special session and I don't want to see you nice old geezers out on your goddamn asses. . . .

Moreover, Mr. and Mrs. Summer, I come cheap. Five bucks per hour and I might go as low as four-fifty. Be good to me, I am a fugitive from a commune. I know my weeds. I've smoked enough of them.

He puffed his cheeks, made a low whistling sound. He pushed through the trees until he had a side view of the Summer property. Behind the house a small wilderness of weeds proliferated. What that place needed was the services of SuperFrog, Weeder Extraordinaire and all-round Good Neighbor. He wished now he had a business card, something to put the stamp of authenticity on him. Old people like the Summers could be highly suspicious of wandering hippies. Like the last time he'd come here—had they been coldly polite or politely cold? Now he remembered how they must have seen him fucking in the stream and he was a touch embarrassed—perchance they won't remember me. Old memories could be very flaky things.

He headed around the front of the house toward the porch and then he paused because he had the curious sensation of eyes pressed against windows. He was being watched.

But when he glanced at the windows he couldn't see anybody. No watchers. Nothing.

He stuck his hands in the pockets of his jeans to appear nonchalant. Easy Does It. One Day At a Time.

When he reached the bottom of the steps he stopped once again and he looked up at the open doorway. There was a darkness beyond, as if the inside of the house were an open mouth. And he was struck by a sudden weird incongruity: it was an image of young Dennis coming to this place *by choice*, a bizarre juxtaposition of youth and everything antique that this dump stood for. It might have been a framed watercolor: Still Life of Boy with Very Old People.

Cool now, Frog. Turn yourself into a smile.

Sooner or later, like the figures on some Bavarian weather clock, old Dick and Charlotte will appear out of the darkness. At which point you offer the hand of friendship, suggest a freebie to help them with their weed situation, and generally act kind.

He didn't move from the foot of the steps.

But he heard a faint sound from within. A footfall, perhaps. A shuffle. They're coming to greet me.

Forms appeared in the shadows. Ah, yes, Frog thought. In his head he was running through the text of his introductory speech, preparing his attitude, so to speak. A smile, of course. An offer to scythe those weeds out of the earth. Tidy up the entire yard for—shall we say—sixty bucks? Too expensive? Fifty then . . .

They stood in front of him. Dick and Charlotte, hand in hand.

He might have been touched by the sweetness of this affection had it not been for the fact that he found something utterly queer in their appearance.

I get it, he thought. Dressing up, huh? Trying to fit yourselves into very old threads on account of some wild outbreak of nostalgia. Let's break open the old trunks, Charlotte, let's put on the clothes we wore when we were *very young*. . . . Let's see if we can't get into the mood for a little decrepit sex.

The old woman smiled and raised one hand in an ambiguous gesture that might have meant welcome. Frog couldn't be sure. He was still overwhelmed by the antique clothes the pair were wearing. She had on a long satin skirt that covered her feet and a high-collared blouse with a brooch at her throat. And the man, old Dick, wore tight-fitting pinstripe pants, a jacket with very short lapels, and a shirt with a high, detachable collar.

He wasn't sure what to say. He felt a trifle dislocated.

The woman was still smiling at him. It was, Frog thought, a peculiar smile, similar to the kind you saw on the blissed-out faces of Krishna people in airports when they attempted to foist a flower on you or have you purchase a glossy book imprinted with the Wisdom. A spacey thing.

"I'm Bartleby," he said, going with the correct name. It might have been too much for them if he'd introduced himself as Frog.

"We know who you are," the woman said.

"Oh. Well, it's a small neighborhood," and Frog smiled uneasily. There was something here, something he just couldn't fathom.

"We were about to have some tea," the old man said. "Maybe you'd care to join us?"

Frog went up the steps slowly, wiping his clammy palms on the sides of his pants.

Max stood on the sun deck and looked out into the black trees. The tiny breeze that had blown up earlier, feebly stirring branches, had faded now and the darkness was silent. He was conscious of light falling through the sliding glass doors at his back and imposing itself on the slats of the deck. He turned to see Louise emerge from the bedroom. There was a confused scent of toothpaste and cologne and shampoo; she was a moving conglomeration of perfumes. Her hair was piled up inside a towel and her skin glistened.

She stood beside him silently. He put one arm loosely around her shoulder, drawing her toward him. "You smell very good," he said. And he thought, Connie always wears something called Amore, a scent redolent of cut lemons. Why think of her now? You can pretend she doesn't exist, she isn't going to call anymore, nothing ever happened. Ah, indeed—your private Dream Factory. He kissed his wife's shoulder.

Louise said, "I'm glad you got the ball rolling with Denny."

"And I'm glad you're pleased," Max said. The family unit—could he draw it around himself like a fortress? Would it protect him?

"When are you going to take me to Carnarvon to wine and dine me?"

"Any time you like," Max answered. "We only have to make the baby-sitting arrangements."

"Damn, I forgot to mention it to Charlotte when she was out for her nightly stroll. I'll go over there in the morning. Maybe we can do it tomorrow night."

Max looked at the trees. "That's fine," he said.

He had an image of the hotel room overlooking the Bay, a clouded picture of Connie as she stood in front of him, slowly removing her blouse and unbuckling the belt of her pants and stepping out of her clothes as if they were just so much gossamer. He felt a curious tingling in the pit of his stomach.

He turned to Louise. He was suddenly cold, shivery, and he pressed himself against her for warmth. Out in the forest a couple of birds, panicked for God knows what reason, flapped upward through branches, creating a flurry of sound. Max laid his face against Louise's shoulder. The chill passed. He was fine, he was all right, everything was going to be okay—how could it be otherwise? He glanced at the moon, a reassuring silvery presence up there.

Connie Harrison, he thought. It was as if his relationship with her were a sealed bottle he'd thrown into the ocean, something that kept coming back to him on the repetition of tides. I don't want it, don't need it. But there it was again, the hotel room, the girl's wonderful flesh, the sympathetic little light in her eyes, her desire for him. He shut his eyes like a man trying to find a comforting darkness where he might lose himself in amnesia. There it was again—the old tide climbing up on the same old shore. He thought he could feel it knock on his heart. He held Louise tighter.

She slid her hand down between his legs. "Are you so easy to arouse, Max? After all these years?"

Yes, he thought. After all these years.

He kissed his wife there on the sun deck and after a few moments he drew her indoors and lay beside her on the bed, losing himself in the controlled fury of making love.

29

Dennis woke. He reached for the bedside lamp and turned it on and he blinked in the sudden stark light that hit his eyes. Pushing the covers aside, he swung his legs over the edge of the mattress. He'd been dreaming that things were crawling all over his flesh, shapeless dark leeches that no matter how hard he tried to remove still stuck to his skin and sucked at his blood, puncturing his veins with tiny needle-sharp incisors.

Even now, though he was awake, he still felt he was back inside the dream and the bloated shapes were crawling over him and he was plucking at them wildly. He shook his head. Then he rolled up one sleeve of his pajama top and held his bare arm beneath the lamp. The little cluster of freckles itched like crazy. He thought maybe this itching sensation had seeped inside his dream, that the freckles had turned into those gross leeches through some awesome process of the mind. He scratched for a while and it felt better but then the sensation came at him again.

He stared at the spots. It looked as if there were more of them than before.

Goddamn itch, he thought. What he needed was more calamine. It helped for a while anyhow. Calamine, palomine, don't let me down.

He walked across the room and moved out into the hallway, conscious of the silences of the house all around him. He thought of the big dark house as if it were a large silent body, the pulse of which was his parents' room upstairs.

He stepped into the bathroom. His stomach groaned. He took the bottle of pink substance from the cabinet and spread it liberally over his itches, then he stuck out his tongue at his reflection in the mirror. He had small dark circles under his eyes and he leaned closer to the mirror to get a proper look at them. The physician's son examines himself, he thought.

It was a trick of light, nothing more. When he held his face up close to the glass he couldn't see the dark patches any longer. He stuffed his face right against the mirror, breathing over the silver surface. This close, you didn't look remotely like yourself. You became an unfamiliar person. Even to yourself.

He stepped back but the impression of strangeness remained. It was like looking at a single word for a long time—pretty soon it didn't mean anything. He'd done that once with a book when he'd gazed at the word "splash" for more than a minute and then he couldn't recognize it at all, didn't know what it meant—it became gibberish.

He went out of the bathroom and into the kitchen. He opened the refrigerator and found a chicken drumstick, which he ate with the light from the refrigerator door falling across him in a ghostly way. He tossed the bone in the garbage, then found the last piece of Charlotte's fudge. He chewed into it slowly, staring from the kitchen window at the shapeless trees that pressed against the house. He yawned. As he did so he pondered his father's invitation to go camping. It was good of the doctor to suggest it, but Dennis wasn't altogether sure he wanted to go. For one thing, he was at a stage in his life when he didn't feel he had much in common with his father. For another, he didn't really want to leave Dick and Charlotte.

Well, it wasn't really Dick and Charlotte, was it? It was the truck. He wanted to get that damn thing running. Yeah. That was what it came down to.

He tapped his fingers on the door of the freezer compartment. When he yanked it open a gust of icy mist blew out at him. He rummaged amid the Popsicles and ice creams and boxes of frozen veggies. The land of Birds Eye. Jolly Green Giants. A whole frozen wilderness in there. He took out a Popsicle and ripped off the wrapper. Why did he have this gnawing goddamn hunger going on at all hours of the day and night? He launched into the rocket-shaped Popsicle and a variety of stains collected around his mouth— purples and yellows and reds. When he was finished he snapped the stick in two and closed the refrigerator door. He yawned again.

On his way back to the bedroom he decided he'd be good—he'd brush his teeth. He stepped inside the bathroom and took out his brush and a tube of Crest and brushed vigorously. Attack the plaque! Attack the plaque! He imagined the brush was a laser device designed to root out and annihilate the bacterial invaders that threatened the domain known as Oral Hygiene. Scrub brush rotate. He made battle noises as he worked the brush around and around layers of toothpaste foam. Rmmmm, brrmmmm, zooooom, kapowwwww! Then he stopped, placing the brush on the edge of the sink while he rinsed, swirling cold water around his gums and between his teeth.

Tingle. Rinse. Spit!

His saliva was a strange pale pink color.

He spat again. Pink?

He went up close to the mirror and, reaching for his mouth, pulled his upper lip back so that he could check his gums. Just above the left incisor he saw a faint trace of pale blood. It ran over the tooth, discoloring it.

He rinsed again. He recalled that his gums had bled once before, years ago, when he was losing the last of his baby teeth. But he didn't have any baby teeth to lose now. So why the bleeding? He rinsed repeatedly until the last trace of pink was gone. Then he smiled at himself in the mirror.

He went back to bed and turned on his side. He looked at the picture of Dick and Charlotte propped against the base of the lamp. He reached out for it, holding it tipped slightly so it caught the full glare of the electricity. He studied it for a time. Even though both Dick and Charlotte were staring into the camera, they somehow gave the impression—strange—that they were impatient to turn away from the photographer and go on gazing into one another's eyes. Their bodies touched slightly at the hips. Dick's right arm and Charlotte's left were out of the shot, presumably tucked behind their backs. Holding hands, Dennis imagined—they liked to touch one another even now. He set the photograph back in place, a couple of inches away from the jar of bait. It was funny to him how his mother was always bitching about the smell.

He smelled nothing. Maybe he was just used to it. Or somehow immune.

He stared at the brown substance inside the glass. It glistened and, even as he watched it, seemed to move, as though it were breathing very quietly, as though some kind of pulse beat way down deep inside it. Dennis smiled. What was this? The Blob? He sat up on one arm and lifted the glass jar up. It was inert brown matter, lifeless and still. He held it to the light.

And zis, zis in ze glass jar, zis is joost a liddle zomething I am working on, Herr Doctor.

He put the bait back in place, then he switched off the lamp. In the darkness he lay very still; outside, a brief wind rattled the forest. It had a comforting sound to him. He scratched his arm a couple of times and then he was floating down toward sleep, which hurried out of the black places to meet him.

30 Theodore Ronson's office was perched at the top of the municipal building. An aerie, Metger thought, housing the head eagle. It was an expansive room filled with photographs and mementoes of old Carnarvon, historic illustrations of the time when the town had been the center of a thriving silver-mining industry. Wild miners peered bleakly into lenses. Prostitutes who worked the silver circuit eyed the camera coyly, huge-hipped women with painted faces suggestive more of innocence than lewdness. In some pictures horse-drawn wagons trudged the muddy main street.

Metger always found these old pictures interesting, if only because they underlined the absurd transformation of Carnarvon from a wide-open mining town to what it had become today, a genteel tourist trap, complete with imported souvenirs from Taiwan and Hong Kong and Victorian streetlamps and striped canopies hanging above the windows of boutiques. It was the kind of town where the mayor, Theodore Ronson, often came to his office —as he'd done this morning—wearing baggy Bermudas and white shoes and a Hawaiian shirt.

Metger turned from the illustrations and looked at Ronson, who reminded him of a used-car salesman whose tailor had fled Waikiki on account of sartorial crimes.

Ted Ronson said, "Yeah, those old things always fascinate me, Jerry. This town's seen some changes in its time."

Metger sat down facing Ronson's desk. They had met in the parking lot and Ronson had invited Metger up to his office to "shoot the bull." There was nothing unusual in the invitation because Ronson effected a certain folksy manner and was the kind of man who believed in "getting down there" among the people.

Metger trusted none of this. From his point of view Ronson was as fake as the used-car salesman he seemed to model himself on.

"We don't see much of each other, Jerry. We work in the same building. Ships that pass in the night, huh?" Ronson settled in his oversized chair. His shirt flashed. Metger imagined parrots screaming out of the foliage on the material. "How are you these days? How's the job?"

"Job's fine, Ted," Metger said.

"I see your stats. Your reports. They pass across my desk. You run a clean town, Jerry."

Metger shrugged. "It isn't exactly difficult. Traffic violations. Some drunk tourists. A wife beater or two. Petty thefts."

"Yeah, I guess you never run into anything really odd in this little town of ours, do you? You'd imagine that twelve thousand seven hundred people could come up with more imaginative misdemeanors, wouldn't you? More creative ways of breaking the law?"

Metger had an impression that Ronson was fishing. He said, "They don't seem to, Ted. Which makes my job easy."

"Maybe you don't find your work very satisfying, Jerry. Maybe the job doesn't fulfill you."

"I'm perfectly happy," Metger said.

"For now," Ronson said. "What about later on down the line, Jerry? When you've worked your job to where it runs itself and you start to get an itchy feeling? What will you do then? A man's got to think of his future, after all."

"I haven't given it much thought," Metger said. "We'll see what happens then, I guess."

Ronson smiled. He had a smooth, bland face, which reminded Jerry Metger of an underripe tomato. The smile was like a slash in the pink skin.

"When you get bored, Jerry, see me. We'll sit down and together we'll examine your options. Promise me we'll talk."

Metger nodded and said, "Sure," but he thought the whole thing odd. Was Ronson hinting at something here? Some future commitment? Or was he just playing politics?

"I mean, the town's growing, the tourists come, rain or shine they come, a man could have a real nice future here. And you ought to think about joining the Chamber of Commerce. Make some contacts. That's always important in a town like this. Connections. Friends, Jerry. You know what I'm saying?"

Metger wasn't sure. It was as if Ronson's mind were a maze and he'd wandered inside it inadvertently and now he had no true sense of direction.

"They tell me Nora's expecting. Is that right?"

"In a month or two."

"That's terrific. What do you want? Boy? Girl?" Ronson spoke as if he could make certain guarantees as to the sex of the unborn child, as if he could arrange almost anything.

"As long as it's healthy, I don't mind."

"Kids are terrific, Jerry. Expensive though."

"Right."

"They need a lot of care. Clothes. Medical bills. You know that."

Metger shifted in his chair. "Yeah," he said. He was uncomfortable now. He couldn't read between Ronson's lines. But he was sure the man was saying something to him, something that lay just under the surface of his words.

Ronson stood up, his hands deep in his Bermudas. He strolled around behind his desk. "How's your dad, Jerry?"

"Funny you should ask that. I was thinking I'd run over and visit him today."

"He okay?"

"They take good care of him over there, I guess."

"Sure they do, sure they do. Senility's an awful thing. You stop to think about it a moment, it's awful. Can't remember things. Don't know where you are. You get confused easily. Bed-wetting. Bad."

"Some days he's fine, Ted. Other days . . ."

"That's how it goes," Ronson said. "Expensive over there at the nursing home?"

It keeps coming back to money. To my future, Metger thought. "Dad's insurance covers most of it."

"That's a break," Ronson said. "Your dad and me, we go back a long way. He was a hell-raiser when we were younger. He could drink any man under the table." Ronson shook his head. "It's a pity what happened to him. When you see him you say I said hello. Okay? I must get over there and see him sometime."

"I'll do that." Metger, sensing that this whole curious encounter was drawing to a close, got up from his chair.

"It's been nice having this little chat," Ronson said. "I like to keep in touch. We'll do it again soon."

Bermudas flapping against his calves, the mayor walked with Metger to the door of the office. Then he did it, he finally did it—he slung his arm around the cop's shoulders.

"Now remember, Jerry. When you have to make a career choice you see me. Don't forget that. I'd like to just sit down with you and see what we might arrange. Okay?"

"I'll keep it in mind," Metger answered, moving out from under the weight of Ronson's thick arm. He stepped out into the corridor and turned once to see Ronson's smile receding behind the door. *Arrange*, he thought.

Then he was going down the stairs, past the various administrative offices, past desks where typists pounded on IBMs, past the glass-cased historical display that contained late eighteenth-century mining artifacts—picks and dull little samples of silver and more historical daguerreotypes and documents—until he had reached his own white-walled office.

He sat behind his desk and he thought, A waste of time. A waste of goddamn time. He closed his eyes momentarily. What had all that been about anyhow? Why had he been made to feel he was Ronson's blue-eyed boy, his personal protégé, all at once? The sensation disturbed him.

But he had other things on his mind that, when he weighed them against the murky depths of town-hall politics and the motivations of Ted Ronson, were infinitely more important, more urgent. He thought about the Untermeyers and his senses were filled all over again with the dizzying scent that had drifted out of the boy's bedroom.

It's crazy, he told himself.

What kind of smell lingers in a house for twelve years?

3 1   It was a glorious morning of sharp sunlight and warm wind and clouds sailing across the sky like galleons driven to unknown destinations. Louise thought it was more like a morning of early autumn than a day in July—one of those bright yellow days when the two seasons, summer and fall, enter into a brief, doomed partnership.

She paused and turned once to look back the way she had come. All around her the pines shook and the yellow sunlight pressed delicate patterns out of the branches. A day like this could raise your spirits the way a brisk wind flapped laundry on a line.

She came to the dry wash and went down the incline slowly. She thought she remembered the way to the Summers' place. It wasn't very far from the wash. Halfway across, maneuvering around the awkward rocks and boulders that littered the cracked streambed, she saw some bluejays rise out of the foliage and squawk somewhere overhead.

When she reached the clearing the house came into view. She studied it for a time. It looked different from the last time she'd been here. She wondered how. The yard was tidier, that was it. Denny must have helped out; maybe he was doing something more over here than trying to fix an old truck.

At the porch steps she paused. The dead plants she'd noticed before were gone. In the pots that lined the porch there were new growths, shiny fresh leaves. *Someone has been busy here.* A swatch of sunlight slanted into the kitchen, illuminating the edges of things. She climbed the steps, knocked softly on the door, waited. Nobody answered.

She stepped inside the house a little way, calling out, "Charlotte? Charlotte?"

She stood in the awkward manner of the uninvited, reluctant to call any louder for fear of disturbing someone, unwilling to go any farther into the house lest she be rude.

She looked around the kitchen. There had been another transformation. Where there had been cobwebs and dullness before along the shelves, silver sparkled now. The tablecloth was crisp and white and unrumpled and cameo-glass bowls, piled neatly above the shining silver and the row of clean pewter pots, caught traces of sunlight and flashed them back.

Spring cleaning at the heart of summer, Louise thought.

She had a sense of renewed vitality. Looking up, she could see flimsy spiderwebs strung across the ceiling beams, and there were layers of dust on a shelf of old books, and the old stove was still caked with ancient grease and spills—but something had been done in this house, a major effort had been started, an offensive against years of neglect.

She moved toward the table.

There was an old-fashioned stoppered pink glass candy jar in the center of the white cloth. It contained something dark that lay in shadow against the inside of the jar. As she skirted around the table she thought, Don't be nosy. Don't pry, but she went toward the jar anyhow, conscious of light trapped in the density of pink glass.

As she did so she heard a sound from the stairs at her back. She turned away from the candy jar quickly, like someone caught in the act of contemplating petty larceny. A shoplifter's look went across her face and she was embarrassed. Charlotte and Dick appeared halfway down the stairs.

"I . . ." Louise said, then faltered.

She stared at Charlotte. Something was different about the woman. At first Louise couldn't think what. Dick, his hand cupped on his wife's elbow, was smiling in a fashion Louise thought was almost sly, as if he had an enormous secret.

"I knocked," Louise said. "Nobody answered."

The Summers reached the bottom step. Louise smiled at them, and then it struck her that the difference in Charlotte's appearance lay somewhere in the old woman's face, in that general area—but what was it?

"I came to ask if you would mind baby-sitting tonight," Louise said. There was a breathless quality in her voice, a kind of hush, like that of somebody talking in a cathedral. Had they seen her examine the pink glass jar? Had they caught her doing that? But she hadn't really done anything, she'd only looked, she hadn't actually gone and touched the thing or removed the stopper to see what was inside—and now, like a criminal doomed to return to the scene of his crime, she found her attention straying back to the jar. Goddamn, don't even look at the thing.

"Baby-sitting," Charlotte said, and looked at her husband.

Dick was still smiling.

"Only if it's convenient . . ." and Louise heard another sentence trail off into nothing.

"I think we can do that," Charlotte said. "Don't you, Dick?"

"No problem," Dick said. "What time?"

"Seven's fine," Louise said. She looked back at Charlotte. Then she knew. She knew what was different about Charlotte. She had obviously been applying something like Grecian Formula to her hair; there was a darkness rising out of the roots, overshadowing the whiteness of the strands. Louise smiled to herself. *Sly old thing*, she thought. Even at her age there was vanity, an awareness of appearances. Grecian Formula! She was about to say something, perhaps offer a compliment on the change, but she didn't. She had the feeling she wasn't meant to notice. Instead, she remarked on how good the kitchen looked.

"Did a little cleaning," Dick said.

"You sure did," Louise said. "It looks terrific." And despite herself she let her eyes fall once again on the candy jar. "That's a nice little piece. It must be pretty old."

She put her hand out toward it, letting her fingertips touch the ridged contours of the glass surface.

"Quite old," Charlotte said and came to the table, picking the jar up and cradling it in the palms of her hands in a gesture Louise thought was strangely protective.

Louise gazed into the thick pink glass. The dark mass that lay inside seemed to float lightly as Charlotte moved the jar against her body. A dark, weightless mass contained in pink glass.

No, Louise thought. *No . . .*

She held her breath.

Charlotte said, "Seven o'clock's fine. Just perfect."

Dick was coming across the room. "Don't have any plans anyhow."

"Yep," Charlotte said, smiling. "We don't have any other plans at all."

Louise felt crowded by the old couple suddenly, as if they had somehow grown in stature around her, their small stooped bodies changing shape, filling the kitchen and blocking the light. She moved toward the door. The wind blew across the porch and dashed through her hair and then she was going down the steps and the sunlight seemed to have a cutting edge to it all at once, sharp against her face and lips.

She looked back up the steps at the sight of the Summers standing side by side in the doorway.

Charlotte was holding the pink glass jar against her breasts.

"We'll be there by seven," the old woman called out.

"Count on it," Dick added.

Louise blinked in the searing, hostile light. She tried to smile back at the Summers but it was suddenly a terrible effort just to raise her hand and wave.

She turned and went quickly across the yard and when she reached the trees she stopped. She had a tight, clenched feeling around her heart. She opened her mouth and breathed very deeply.

A pink glass jar.

There was a cold sensation in her stomach.

32 Stanley Metger was lost in space, his own strange space in which time and memory had collapsed like a frail house of dominoes. He occupied room number eighteen at the Carnarvon Nursing Home, a new building on the outskirts of town—all sharp edges and angles and glass, a functional place where a functional staff cared for the very old and infirm.

The clean lines of the building, the brisk appearance of it all, made an unpleasant contrast with the ailments of the occupants. You expected this structure to house a computer assembly company, some kind of light, antiseptic industry; you didn't expect it to contain the relics of people who had outlived their social usefulness. As Metger, depressed, crossed the lawn he looked up at the window of his father's room and he remembered the kind of man Stanley Metger used to be.

Strong, with broad shoulders and a red, beery face, the elder Metger had worked his own construction company for years in Carnarvon. He was a man to whom honesty was as important as breathing. He had no tolerance for hypocrites and liars, no place in his life for the pretentious. He reserved in his garrulous heart a special black place for politicians, whom he placed on a level with polyester evangelists, purveyors of junk food, and the people responsible for TV commercials. There was scum on the river of society, he used to say—always wear protective clothing, Jerry, whenever you go out there to swim.

Jerry Metger climbed the stairs to the door of room eighteen. The man he remembered, the man he had loved and admired and been awed by, was not the same man who occupied this room now. Stanley Metger had disappeared, replaced by a stranger, a shadowy substitute, someone the younger Metger didn't always recognize. The muscular arms had wasted. The tattoos, which had seemed mysterious and somehow sinister to a gullible young boy, had lost their flamboyance and now looked like cancers on the man's flesh.

But more than anything else it was the eyes that upset Jerry Metger. They were flat and lifeless and they drifted at times with no apparent object in sight. You never knew what they were seeking or where they were going. They seemed unconnected to the brain, as if wires had burned out. Sometimes Jerry Metger thought he could smell the faint aroma of something that had been scorched a long time ago.

He stepped into the room.

His father sat on the edge of his narrow bed, his face turned toward the TV, which played soundlessly in the corner. It was a sick room, Metger thought, filled with sick smells. Bottles of useless medications littered the bedside table. There were photographs—old family pictures that showed Stanley Metger in his prime. There was one of his dead wife, Jerry's mother. There were several of father and son.

"Dad," Metger said. He moved toward the bed.

The older man turned his face slowly. There was a game show on TV and the colors ran across Stanley Metger's face.

"It's me. It's Jerry." Metger sat down on the bed beside his father.

"Jerry," Stanley Metger said. He seemed to be tasting the name in his mouth, searching for a familiarity of flavor. Obviously it meant nothing to him, because he turned his face back to the TV.

It hurts, Metger thought. It's all such a pain. But you go through the hopeless motions anyhow. "How are you?" he asked. The question floated like cigar smoke in the stale air of the room.

"Jerry." Again the name was pronounced as if it were totally strange. A smile crossed his father's face—it was sly, a sneaky smile. He reached inside the pocket of his gray flannel slacks and produced a cellophane bag that contained M & M's. He rattled these for a moment, popped one in his mouth, then returned his eyes to the noiseless TV.

"Got your little stash, huh?" Jerry Metger asked. There was always a secret cache of candy in the room somewhere.

"They don't know," his father said. "Don't you go telling them."

"I promise I won't."

The older man rubbed his eyes. He got up stiffly and turned the TV off. "You realize there's nothing wrong with me, don't you?"

"Sure, Dad."

"I'm only here for a week tops. No longer."

Jerry Metger nodded. "Yeah, I know."

"They're running some tests. They said. I know what they'd like. To hell with them, I say."

"What would they like, Dad?"

The same sly smile crossed the face. "That's between me and these four walls." Stanley Metger, in a gesture of secrecy, tapped the side of his nose.

Flashes of paranoia. Fear. Secrecy.

Jerry Metger looked at the blank gray face of the TV and tried to fight his depression, but it always went deep when he came to this place. He had to remember that this wasn't just a social call. It was more than simple filial concern that had brought him here. But even as he remembered this, he was swept by a wave of futility. His father was dead—what he saw in front of him was a shell, a lingering shadow, nothing more. You couldn't expect to get anything out of a shell.

Except maybe a pale echo.

Stanley Metger had burned out overnight, without any sign of symptoms, without any warning. During the last lucid conversation Jerry had had with his father, Metger Senior had mentioned something about a book he was writing—an idea so off the wall it took Jerry by surprise. People keep telling me I ought to get some of my stories down on paper before the Grim Reaper silences me, Jerry. I thought to myself, hell, why not give it a try? But Jerry Metger had never seen a page of any manuscript. As far as he knew, his father hadn't committed one word to paper—unless, of course, he'd done so secretively. Then he got sick. Suddenly, irreversibly sick. These things happen sometimes, Lou Pelusi had said at the time. Senility, if you want to call it that, kicks in without warning. The brain just goes. Good old Lou, always a comfort.

Jerry rose from the bed, wandered to the window, and looked down at the lawn. Grass rippled in the wind like a green tide. Then he watched his father roam around the room in the curiously stiff manner of the aged, as if every move were a terrible effort. But he wasn't what you'd call an *old* man. Although he was only in his early sixties, he looked so much older— his skin hanging on his skeleton loosely, his face sunken, a fleck of spit at the corner of his mouth.

Now he said, "They think they got me in this place for life, boy." He laughed, a strange little wheeze that rattled in his throat. For a moment there was a burst of life in his eyes, then the spark died. He moved to the TV, switched it on again. He sat on the edge of the bed and stared at the picture.

Jerry Metger sighed. "Aside from the tests, they treating you okay in here?"

His father nodded. "Food's all right if you like mush. Mush is what you get around here. Not just the food. People's brains. It's all mush. I was telling your mother only yesterday they treat you in here like you're a goddamn baby. Strained peas. For God's sake. I don't need strained peas. Your mother laughed."

Jerry Metger went to his father and sat down beside him. On past visits he'd tried a little truth therapy, as if to shock his father back in the direction of reality. Sometimes there had been a response, more often not. Now he dickered with the notion of saying that his mother had been dead for the past nineteen years, but he decided against it. He clapped his father on the shoulder. "If you don't like the food, I'll bring you something next time I come. Maybe I'll get some Chinese from the Lotus Gardens, or some of Al Trunkey's Down-Home Ribs. You always liked those, didn't you?"

"Best ribs in the world," Stanley Metger said. "Al's secret is in that mesquite he uses. And in the sauce. Special ingredients. He told me one time what he put in that sauce. I forget what the hell he said though."

Memory and forgetfulness. It sometimes seemed that a light bulb went on and off inside his father's brain. Certain dark corners were briefly illuminated, then the light went out again and the older man was left stumbling blindly through his own amnesia. Jerry Metger rubbed his father's shoulder. He could feel the bones through the rice paper of flesh.

"Ted Ronson said to tell you hello."

"Ronson? That carpetbagger? I don't need any message from him. And you can tell him that. I never thought his spit was wet, if you catch my meaning." Stanley Metger was silent a moment. "Wasn't a bad kind of guy until he decided he'd go into politics. Me and him, we used to drink up a goddamn storm. He was here the other night."

"Ronson was *here?*"

Jerry Metger leaned closer to his father. In moments of clarity Stanley Metger was like a man who sees a sudden path opening up in front of him and he follows it until it reaches the confusion of a crossroads and then he's lost once again.

"Are you sure it was Ronson?"

The older man shut his eyes. A nerve worked under his jaw. He didn't answer his son's question and Jerry wondered where his father's reality began and ended. Maybe he was simply confused, maybe it was an illusion. Ted Ronson hadn't mentioned anything about visiting here. Hadn't said he'd been to see Stanley. It was surely something Ronson would have talked about. Instead, he'd given the distinct impression he hadn't seen Stanley in a long time.

"Old Ted Ronson," Stanley said. "I never once voted for him. He tried. Jesus Christ, that man tried. One time I told him I'd give him my vote when hell froze over." He took out his bag of M & M's and put one between his thin lips.

"What did he come here for?" Jerry Metger asked.

"Who?"

"Ronson."

"Did he come here?"

"You said he did."

"It's like a mist sometimes," the older man said. "You can't see through it clearly."

Metger sighed. All the lines in Stanley's mind were blurred. How could he tell if Ted Ronson had actually been here or if Stanley had imagined it?

Metger brought back to his memory how his father had really been once. Not this sickly, skinny person who sat on the bed now, but that other man—the big man with the vast appetite for living, the loud laugh, the infectious zest. He brought back memories of beer parties and empty kegs and smoky rooms filled with laughing people and his mother following his father around as if she were afraid he might drunkenly fall over and would need somebody to catch him. He never did fall.

Prompt him, Metger thought.

Try to prompt him.

"You think about the old days much?" he asked.

Stanley Metger turned to stare at his son. For a moment a blankness crossed his face, as if all possibility of future expression had been bleached out of skin and muscle. Metger thought, *I'm losing him. He's tuning into a different station.* But then the older man smiled.

"It comes and goes," he said.

"You ever remember telling me one time about a boy you knew back in the forties I think it was—"

"What boy? I knew lots of boys—"

"Yeah, well, this kid was a friend of yours, I guess."

"I had lots of friends." An edge of petulance in the voice—that strange impatience sick people sometimes show toward the healthy. "You got a name for this kid?"

Jerry ransacked his memory. He shook his head. He didn't have a name—all he had was a faint recollection, dreamlike in its vagueness—one small legend from a childhood filled with them. His father had always been a great talker, someone who loved to hear the sound of his own voice rambling on. But in the midst of so many old tales, exaggerated stories about the old Welsh miners who'd first come to this place, yarns about colorful characters with names like Evan One-Eye and Tommy the Stiletto and the utterly eccentric Taffy Owens, mines with peculiar names like Deadman's Diggings and the Yellowjack Shaft, and bloody stories of betrayals and double crosses and weird superstitions about ghosts who haunted certain valleys or could be heard to whine in the dark depths of mine shafts—how could Metger truly remember any particular one? Among so many whispers, how could he isolate one?

"I forget the name, Dad."

"So how do you expect *me* to remember anything?"

"This kid died, I remember you telling me he died—"

"Died?"

"He had some strange disease."

Stanley Metger rattled his little bag of candy. The petulance in his voice was more pronounced, like that of an old man who wants to feel that he has better things to do than sit around reminiscing. "What disease? I don't remember shit about any kid with a strange disease."

"You're the one who told me . . ."

Stanley Metger shook his head vigorously. His attention had drifted back to the TV. He got up, turned the set off. He went to the window and stood with his palms upraised against the glass.

"I get tired real easy," he said.

Metger nodded, studying his father there at the window. He'd gone again. It was as if a book had suddenly been shut and all that was left was the dust rising from the pages.

Metger got up from the bed.

His father was still gazing from the window. He said, "You tell your mother she ought to bring me that travel rug I need. It's plaid. We bought it years ago. I need it here because they don't like to give you too many blankets. They want you to be cold, see. They don't want you warm in this place."

"Why's that?"

Stanley Metger looked furtive and when he spoke he whispered. "Cold kills you quicker. That's why. Place like this needs a fast turnover. It's a business. It's all business."

Metger went toward his father. He hugged him for a moment. "I'm pretty sure they don't want to kill anybody quick in here, Dad."

"That's what you think."

Metger let his arms hang at his sides. "Okay. I'll remind her to bring the rug—"

"It's got to be the plaid. Don't forget that. Remind her it's the one we bought in Carmel that time."

A heartbreak, Metger thought. "I'll do that."

He moved toward the door, pulled it open. From his back he could hear the noise of cellophane crinkling and candies rattling again. "I'll come by next week, Dad."

There was no answer.

Stanley Metger had poured all the M & M's into the palm of one hand and was counting them with his fingertip. He stood in the yellowy light at the window like somebody in a fading photograph. He was mumbling to himself. "Yellow . . . red . . . brown . . ."

"You take care of yourself," Metger said.

His father raised his face. His mouth was open and closing silently as he computed the number of his candies.

He smiled.

"Sammy Caskie. Old Sammy, we called him," he said.

"Was that the kid's name?" Metger asked. "Sammy Caskie? Was that it?"

Stanley Metger's hand closed around his candy. He raised the clenched hand to his lips, wiped the saliva from the corner of his mouth. He was already elsewhere, leaving his son behind. "You tell your mother to bring candies when she fetches that rug. I'm getting pretty damn low on them. Okay? Don't you forget now."

"I won't forget," Metger said.

3 3 Louise stared past Max, past the bottle of wine on their table, and looked across the restaurant. It was a pleasant place, decorated in a plum color; the waiters were discreet and hushed and served nouvelle cuisine as if they were administering communion wafers. Louise reached for the wine and poured herself another glass.

"You see some hair inside a glass and you think—" Max said.

"Not any old hair, Max! Denny's hair!"

"Denny's hair then."

"It struck me as very odd. It shocked me."

"Maybe it isn't Denny's hair."

"I know my son's hair when I see it. I know his curls by heart. A mother knows that kind of thing. God, I brushed that hair every day when he was a small boy—"

Max held up one hand. "Okay. It's Denny's hair."

"Yeah, and it shocked me at first. I mean, why save somebody's hair? Why do that? And then Charlotte tried to hide it from me—"

"She was embarrassed." Max shrugged. "Maybe she thought you thought she was some kind of thief."

Louise shrugged and was silent, remembering how she'd felt when she'd seen the hair in the glass jar. It was almost as if she'd been kicked in the stomach, painfully deflated. Now, after a fair meal and several glasses of wine, the whole thing didn't seem very important to her. Puzzling, sure, but not as significant as she'd thought at first.

"Maybe the Summers feel like surrogate grandparents. They wanted to save Denny's hair for sentimental reasons," Max said. "They think they're grandparents for the summer."

"I never heard of grandparents saving reams of discarded hair, Max. That's a new one on me."

"Some people have a thing for keepsakes. Your friend Polly What's-her-name has this baby book. I remember she showed it to me once—it was filled with curls of hair, baby teeth, even a disgusting, dehydrated umbilical cord. The only thing missing was a shriveled placenta. The point is, people keep the strangest things. Sentimentality goes deep."

"Polly Ketchum always went too far with that collection if you ask me."

"She didn't think so," Max said. He topped up his wine, sipped.

"There's something so . . . *personal* about hair, Max."

Louise smiled at their waiter, who was approaching the table to ask about dessert, which both Max and Louise refused. They ordered brandies.

"You're superstitious, Louise."

"I am not superstitious."

"You never walk under ladders. I've noticed that."

"Something might fall on my head. I'm only being practical."

"Certain superstitious people don't like having their photographs taken," Max said. "They think the loss of their image is like having their soul taken away from them. Is that how you feel about hair?"

Louise shook her head and smiled. "You're mocking me again, Doctor."

"Hair," Max said.

"I'm listening. Let's hair what you have to say about it."

"Why is it, when you drink wine, you make terrible puns?"

"Who? Me?"

Max rolled his big brandy glass between the palms of his hands. "Hair's nothing but the outgrowth of the epidermis. It grows out through the sebaceous glands, rising up from the papilla, the bulb, and the follicle, et cetera. When you cut it off it isn't a part of you anymore."

"Big words." Louise sniffed her brandy. She lit a cigarette. Across the restaurant now, on a small upraised platform, a skinny young man was playing piano. "I Get a Kick Out of You." She listened for a moment. When the Summers had appeared that evening to baby-sit—punctually at seven—she hadn't said anything about the hair, nor had Charlotte alluded to it. The Summers were as they always seemed—friendly, anxious to please, kind. And maybe, just maybe, goddamn Max was right—they wanted a souvenir of their summer "grandchild," nothing more than that. Why shouldn't they keep Denny's hair in a glass jar anyhow? After all, there *were* people in the world like Polly Ketchum and perhaps the Summers could be included in that category of keepsake-keepers, collectors, and general sentimentalists.

She shut her eyes and moved her head in time to the music. It flowed over her, soothing, blandly relaxing. She drank some of her brandy, then smiled at Max, reaching across the table for his hand.

"We haven't done this in ages," she said. "We really should do it more often."

Max, dressed in shirt and tie, tasteful sports coat, smiled. "You're right. We should. At least we've got built-in sitters."

Louise set her glass down. From the corner of her eye she was aware of somebody coming across the room to their table. She turned her face slightly and as she did so she was conscious of two things.

One: Max stood up quickly.

Two: He knocked over his brandy glass.

Max opened his mouth, smiled, didn't smile. What went across his face right then was the most curious expression Louise had ever seen, something she couldn't define, a discomfort, maybe a quick suggestion of pain.

The girl wasn't beautiful; she was pretty in a way that suggested the fragility of porcelain and her long hair fell delicately down to her shoulders and she was looking at Max with a smile in which Louise imagined she could read all kinds of concealments, secrets, yearnings. Louise reached out for her brandy even as Max blurted out an introduction:

"This is Connie Harrison," he said and his voice was awfully dry, like one bleached-out old bone being rubbed against another.

The girl smiled.

Louise looked up and blinked and said, "Nice to meet you."

The girl held out one loose hand; her skin was warm as Louise touched it. "Mrs. Untermeyer?" the girl said.

Louise took her hand away. It was funny but she couldn't hear the piano now. The whole restaurant might have been totally silenced. The world went quiet except for an odd ringing in her ears.

"Clumsy of me," Max said, picking up his brandy glass, fussing with the wet tablecloth.

"Very," Connie Harrison said.

Frog's teeth chattered.

He lay shivering inside his sleeping bag in the back of the VW van. Eyelids heavy. Lips cold.

Some time back—he couldn't tell how long—a tape of Bob Dylan had quit playing and he didn't have the strength to get up and change it. The music still echoed in his head, around and around like a thin voice trapped in a marble mausoleum.

> Dr. Frankenstein says
> I need some brain repair . . .

He pulled the sleeping bag up to his beard.

Hot flashes coursed through him. His blood danced and his heartbeat was as sluggish as the stream he could hear in the distance. I am not a well man, Frog thought.

What was it? A virus? Or had his checkered history caught up with him? Had all the casual fornication of the sixties claimed him now? Syphilis, say. He smiled weakly.

He was very conscious of his solitude. You are weak and sick and there's nobody around to attend to you. A sad case, old Frog. *Path-etic.*

He stared up through the skylight of the van at the canopy of the night. Earlier he had downed a couple of aspirins, but they weren't actually doing anything for him. The sickness made his forehead very hot and his limbs weak. An hour back—was it that long ago?—he'd tried to get down to the stream to plunge his face into the brackish water, as if such an immersion might revive him, but he hadn't even made it out of the van.

Was it something you ate, Frog? Something you took inside your body without knowing it was toxic?

He considered rising and stumbling down through the trees to find Max Untermeyer, the physician. Cure me, Max. Make me well. He shuddered inside the sleeping bag. He felt like something trapped inside a pod—an unsprouted bean or something equally distorted.

He found his flashlight and flicked it on, playing the beam around inside the van. As he did so he had a curious sense of his own doom, as if it were looming up on the horizon—black and huge and shuffling down through the pines to get him.

The Boogeyman.

How could he afford to get this sick? He shut his eyes. Maybe the Summers would come by on one of their walks and rescue him. Or maybe Denny would find his way up here. Maybe maybe maybe . . .

Now, through the skylight, he perceived the moon. It hung in the sky like an artificial thing—a counterfeit coin. He struggled up into a sitting position.

What the fuck is wrong with me?

His hands trembling, his whole body shuddering, he had the weird idea of drawing up a will. He found a notepad and a blunt pencil and he started to scribble—then he threw his head back and laughed feebly. I am neither sound of mind nor body, he thought.

He lay back down again. A chill rose from the soles of his feet and advanced upward through his body to the top of his scalp. The pencil and pad slipped out of his fingers.

He thought he knew what it was. One of those twenty-four-hour beauties that rendered your whole system useless. One of those viral babies that just shot you to shit—and then, without so much as a how-do-you-do, it would vanish into the ether and he could get on with his life without this kind of undignified inconvenience.

He was a believer in dignity and the basic rights of man. The right, at least, to pick and choose your own sicknesses.

He stared up at the moon. Tomorrow, he told himself. Tomorrow I will be well.

Every day in every way, I am getting better and better.

Then he lay very silent, listening to the faint meter of his heart and the quiet knocking of his pulses.

34 It was Louise who suggested they stop for a nightcap at the Ace of Spades, a dim place with country-western music pouring out of the jukebox. They stood at the end of the bar watching the woman pour their drinks. Louise sipped her brandy when it came. Max, who had asked—rather curiously Louise thought—for schnapps, swirled his drink around inside the glass.

"I didn't know you liked that stuff," Louise said. What else don't you know about your husband? she wondered. Good old Max. Dear Max. How much do you really know?

Max shrugged. He said nothing. He felt strangely drained, empty inside. In the restaurant he'd gone to the rest room just as soon as Connie Harrison had left and he'd swallowed three Darvon. Three little talismans, pink-orange and attractive to look at. Now, here in the Ace of Spades, they were taking their effect on him. The world might have been glazed over. He saw things as if through glass. Even the music that droned out of the jukebox was thin and distant, a voice crying in another room.

Louise put her glass down. There was something darkly comforting in this tavern, she thought. If she could dig into the secret heart of this place, its unlit pulse, its soul, she understood she would be safe. She shut her eyes a moment.

"She's nice-looking," she said. "If you go for the fragile angular type. Do you go for that type, Max?"

Max didn't speak. He lifted his glass to his mouth and swallowed.

"It's funny," Louise said. "The woman calls you on the telephone one night and then turns up the next. That's funny. Isn't that funny? Why would she come all the way to Carnarvon, Max?"

"I don't know," he said.

"You don't know, huh?" Louise looked across the bar. A drugstore-cowboy type was gazing at her, one eyebrow raised on his thin face. "Max doesn't know. A patient follows him all the way up here and he doesn't know why. Aren't we being obtuse. Aren't we just."

"Louise," Max said. "You read too much into things."

You read too much into things. Poor Louise. Her hyped-up imagination. Poor old thing. Hadn't Max said Connie Harrison was forty and sagging? Why had he lied?

"I don't know what you're talking about—"

"Max Max Max. A pretty girl comes up to you in a restaurant. She *drools* over you. She lays a hand on your arm in a manner a blind man would say was *proprietary*, and she tells you none too nonchalantly the name of the hotel where she's staying, and you don't know what I'm talking about—"

"Jesus, Louise."

"Add to the foregoing that the said Connie Harrison looked at Mrs. Untermeyer only once with something akin to a dagger, and the picture is transparent." Louise pushed her brandy glass away. She felt a claw of tiredness descend on her.

"Sometimes a patient transfers all his or her affections to their physician," Max said. "You know that. You've always known that. It's classic."

"Words, Maxie. Words. I hear emptiness. Sounds signifying nothing. You should have seen your face! Dear God! I would have given a thousand dollars for a Polaroid right then! You looked as if you'd just had a goddamn stroke."

Max shook his head. Why the fuck had Connie Harrison come all the way up here? Why had she presented herself at the fucking table as if she were an old family friend? His head felt as if it were filled with moisture, a swamp sucking him down into its depths. Fuck fuck *fuck*! The horrible thing was not the shock he'd reacted with when she came up to their table. It wasn't even the way color had drained out of his face and his heart had buckled. It was the god-awful yearning for the woman he'd felt when she laid her hand against his arm. Was he to be doomed by that longing? Even now, even as Louise flailed away at him, he wanted to go to Connie Harrison's hotel and get into bed with her. Dismiss it, Max. School's out. Let Connie go.

"Do you see much of her in San Francisco?" Louise asked.

"You're so very wrong about this."

"My head tells me to believe you. My heart's screaming."

"Listen to your head."

Louise called for a second brandy. She saw all over again the face of Connie Harrison looming up in the restaurant. She saw the woman's hand on Max's arm—a casual familiarity, an air of possession, a touch that belonged only to lovers.

"When do you meet her, Max? Is it cozy lunches and midday screwing in motels? Is it like that?"

Max said nothing. He finished his schnapps.

"Did you encourage her, Max? Was it mutual?"

He shook his head from side to side. "There's nothing, Louise. The girl's neurotic. I can't be responsible for the way she feels, can I?"

"I'm struggling here, Max. I'm really struggling to believe you."

He put his hand over hers. Her flesh was warm. "You have to believe me," he said quietly. It was his best voice, his bedside voice. You're going to get well, Mrs. Untermeyer. You have my word on that score. He felt shitty—how the hell had he ever stumbled into all this crap? Lies operate under their own laws—they expand and they fill every vacant space available until you find your whole world is one of fragile fabrication. And he'd told so many that the fact he was compounding them now didn't impress him.

"I want to," Louise said. A couple of tears slipped out from under her closed eyelids. She took a Kleenex from her purse and dabbed it against her face, conscious of the attractive woman behind the bar watching her. Big Scene in Bar! Domestic Strife! Woman Weeps Over Suspected Infidelity! It was just so goddamn cheap, such an epic cliché. Laugh, Louise! Laugh it off! Max is still your husband.

"What does she mean to you?" she asked.

"As much as any patient means."

"And that's it?"

Max nodded. "That's it."

Louise didn't finish her second brandy. "I think I'd like to go home, Max."

He took her by the elbow and steered her out into the parking lot. There he kissed her, but her lips were unyielding and cold against his own. He opened the passenger door for her and she climbed inside and sat staring straight ahead, her eyes wide and her face expressionless and her pale hands lying in her lap like two clay objects. Max turned the key in the ignition.

He said, "I promise you. There's nothing between us, Louise. Nothing."

"I think I heard that part," Louise whispered.

"And I want you to hear it again."

"Don't speak, Max. I think I'd like a little silence right now."

Max drove the Volvo down the dirt road, seeing the colorless branches of trees fly out on either side of the headlights like the wings of shapeless big birds hurrying to unknown destinations.

"The records are a mess, Jerry," Lou Pelusi said. "Miles didn't leave them in the best possible shape when he retired."

Metger watched as the physician opened and closed drawers of filing cabinets and sifted through manila folders. All the folders bore labels, some of them handwritten, others typed.

Pelusi said, "I don't think Miles understood the alphabet as you and I do," and he laughed quietly. He slammed one of the metal drawers shut and turned to look at the sheriff.

Metger folded his arms. He was tired. Through the window of Pelusi's office he could see only darkness—total and inviolate, consuming the night.

"Of course it would help if you could give me a date for that first name," Pelusi said.

"I don't have a date," Metger said. "Only the name. Samuel Caskie. I'd guess it was in the 1940s."

"We could be here all night." Pelusi sighed. He looked at Metger with slight irritation now. "You're talking about a whole decade here, Jerry. Can't you narrow it down for me?"

"I wish I could." Metger rubbed his eyes. It crossed his mind that his father had been deluded, that the old man's memory had been a false one. Who could say for sure that anything Stanley Metger dragged up from the depths of his mind had any veracity? On the other hand, something in the way Miles Henderson had reacted to the sound of the name—a quiet flinch, a flicker of his eyes—had suggested to Metger that Sammy Caskie had indeed lived and died in the town of Carnarvon.

What the hell—all he seemed to hear these days was the noise of straws rattling quietly in the wind. A maze of straws strewn with the names of dead kids. And all of it, every single item of information inside his head, was nebulous.

What possible connections could there be between three deaths over a lengthy period of time?

Pelusi went back to hauling drawers open.

"Caskie, Caskie, Caskie," he muttered to himself. "I don't see anything filed under that name, Jerry."

"Did Miles Henderson take any records with him when he retired?" Metger asked.

"He might have. I don't see why he would, though."

Metger gazed around the office. It was a sterile room whose walls were covered with various charts of a nutritional nature. Two unlit X rays hung like a pair of underexposed photographs. A stethoscope lay curled on Pelusi's desk.

"I'm sorry, Jerry. There doesn't seem to be anything here under the name of Caskie. Sammy or otherwise."

Somehow Metger had known there wouldn't be—maybe there had never been any Sammy Caskie. Or any family known as Caskie for that matter. It wasn't a name he had ever heard around town.

"Try Hann. Robert Hann," Metger said. "Date of death, 1955."

Pelusi shrugged, moving from one cabinet to another.

Metger said, "I thought you people had everything on computer these days."

"Not in Carnarvon," Pelusi answered. He fished through a drawer, flicking files back and forth as he searched. "You did say 1955?"

Metger nodded. He stared at the physician's back. Shadows formed in the folds of the white coat as Pelusi rummaged, small dark ripples crossing the material.

"I always meant to get these things in order," the physician said. "But one gets drawn into other tasks. More important ones. And so the filing system remains inadequate."

Metger walked over to the window.

The surface of his skin felt cold. Somewhere in his mind he heard what sounded to him like the ticking of a clock, muffled, as if it were running down in a room he couldn't quite locate. Three kids, one of whom might not have existed. And nothing else, Jerry. Nothing else.

Lou Pelusi slammed a drawer shut. There was a metallic echo in the office.

"Sorry," the physician said.

"No file on Robert Hann."

"No file."

Metger turned from the window. All at once this office seemed too bright to him, impossibly white, bleached of all color.

"Since I know for sure that Robert Hann existed, and since I also know that he must have received medical treatment here at one time, how do you explain the fact that you don't have any records for the kid? How the hell do you explain that, Lou?"

"It might have been misfiled—"

"Yeah yeah."

"Or you might have the date wrong."

Metger leaned against the desk. He picked up the stethoscope and slapped it up and down against the palm of one hand. Simple mysteries, he thought. Dead kids who never existed. *I dream, therefore I am deluded.*

"Do me one last favor," he said.

Pelusi was smiling, but it was an uncertain expression, a look that seemed ready to slip from his face, as though it were a mask. "I'm pushed for time, Jerry."

"One last thing. Okay? Ackerley. Anthea. Date of death, 1973."

Pelusi, with a show of subdued reluctance, went back to his cabinets. He looked stark against the murky green metal of the boxes. Now, as he opened and closed drawers, he made a great deal of angry noise. At last he turned to face Metger. He didn't say anything.

"Don't tell me," Metger said.

"Where the hell are you getting these names, Jerry?"

"I'm beginning to ask myself that one, Lou."

"There's no record of any one of the three. Are you sure they ever came here for medical treatment?"

"I'm pretty sure they passed this way at least once," Metger said.

"Well." Pelusi was wearing his smile again. "Like I said, Miles Henderson didn't leave a legacy of neatness around here."

Metger hesitated before he moved toward the door. He surveyed the rows of cabinets, remembering a similar collection in Miles Henderson's study. What was hidden in that terrible room? If he were to go back there, what would he find? Ghosts locked away inside metal coffins, he imagined. Ghosts that rattled because he, Metger, was shaking them where they lay.

"If you could give me a hint of what it is you're looking for . . ." Pelusi had an expectant look on his face now.

"I wish I could," Metger said.

He reached the door, opened it, gazed out into the corridor. A nurse passed in front of him, smiling at him casually. Then she was gone, leaving a scent of perfume in the air.

"Thanks anyhow, Lou," and Metger glanced back inside the room. He had a sudden strong urge to get home, see his wife, put his ear against the protuberance of her belly and listen for the unborn kid's movements.

Pelusi was seated behind his desk now, his hands clasped together, his manicured nails as white as the walls that pressed in around him.

"See you, Jerry," the physician said.

Lou Pelusi reached for the telephone, let his hand drift across its smooth plastic surface lightly, didn't pick it up. He was assailed by the feeling that Metger was going to come inside the room again quite unexpectedly and start asking more questions.

So many questions.

He listened to the silences of his office as if beneath the surface of quiet there lay a clamor of unintelligible sounds ready to rush in at him.

Another man in his position might have gone home, packed his bags, and left Carnarvon for good. The problem was—where would he go? He had joined a club whose membership demands were rigid—silence and loyalty were part of the unspoken oath.

Where *could* he go?

Once, he thought, there had been some kind of burning ambition to help the sick. Once, as a premed student, he'd entertained the notion of someday opening a free clinic for charity cases who couldn't afford to pay for treatment. Once—but all that was gone, buried under the weight of years passing. His humanitarianism had yielded to his more secular needs—like money, he thought.

These days he didn't even feel much like a doctor. In unguarded moments he thought of himself as something else—a criminal, a form of assassin. After all, what the hell had he done to Stanley Metger? Wasn't that a kind of assassination?

He leaned back in his chair, breathing deeply. He tried to find solace in something. He took out his lovely Elgin pocket watch and ran his fingertips over it. There had always been a reassuring quality in material possessions.

He picked up the telephone. He dialed Theodore Ronson's home number. The mayor's answering voice was wheezy, like he'd just come from his exercise machine.

"Ted. This is Pelusi."

"What's up, Doc?"

Pelusi frowned. If he'd had a buck for every time he'd heard that question, hell, he wouldn't be sitting here in Carnarvon, scared the way he was.

"Our sheriff was just here—"

"That goddamn busybody," Ronson said. "That boy's heading for a fall. What did he want this time?"

"Certain medical files."

"You didn't have them, of course."

Pelusi said, "Fact is, I don't have them anyway. But Jerry was naming names, Ted. Names. Caskie. Hann. Ackerley." The physician wiped a globule of sweat from his face.

Ronson was silent for a moment. "Leave it with me," he said finally. "I'll mull it over. It's my responsibility now."

3 5   Charlotte said to Louise, "The boy's gone to bed. Guess he was tired."

Louise gazed at the old woman a moment. Dick Summer had one arm around his wife's waist and the old couple leaned together, seeming to fuse, to meld, somewhere in the middle of their bodies. Louise, who had the start of a pounding headache, smiled.

Dick asked, "Nice time? Good food?"

"Good food," Max said. He was standing in the doorway, hands in the pockets of his pants.

Charlotte fussed with her hair a second. She was wearing a pale blue ribbon. "Any time you need us to sit with the boy, don't you hesitate."

"It's very good of you," Louise said. She hoped the Summers weren't going to linger, hoped they wouldn't hang around waiting for a nightcap or something—she wanted to go upstairs and sleep. Just sleep. In the morning light everything was going to be different.

"He's no problem, that boy," Charlotte said. She raised one hand again to adjust her ribbon. As she did so her skin reflected the light from the lamp behind her head. A smooth, soft glistening.

Charlotte's hand.

Louise looked away—there was a hammer beating inside her skull. She was back in the restaurant, surrounded by what she saw as the fact of her betrayal. No. Not Max. Not you, Max. She turned back to the sight of Charlotte's hand. A pulse throbbed in her head, loud and terrifying.

"Going to be taking a trip soon. Better get going," Dick said. He moved Charlotte toward the door, where Max stepped aside to let them pass. Louise went out into the corridor after the old people.

"Thanks again," she said.

Dick and Charlotte went out on the porch, where they turned around in unison and looked at the Untermeyers in the hallway. Two couples, Louise thought. The one old, the other . . . middle-aged. Very middle-aged. Wasn't that the time of one's life when betrayal struck? Wasn't that when it was supposed to happen? Husbands strayed. Found younger women. Wives took up tennis and fucked the club pro. Downhill into forced merriment. Looking impending death and darkness right in the eye.

She went out onto the porch. The Summers started down the steps. There was a bleak moon, yellowy at the edges, hanging above the pines. The night was filled with small currents of electricity, as if out there in the blind darkness all manner of creatures were humming. Louise watched the Summers move toward the trees. Where could they be taking a trip to?

"Do you need a flashlight?" she called after them.

"We know this place like the backs of our hands," Dick answered.

They turned once and waved and then they were gone.

Louise went inside, closing the door. The backs of our hands, she thought—and the image of Charlotte's hand was barely illuminated in her mind, a puzzle of some kind, like something seen through frosted glass. That hand. The skin.

Max was watching her in the hallway.

"Are you okay?" he asked.

"You have a knack for asking inappropriate questions," she said.

"You look pale, Louise."

"Connie's rather pale, too, isn't she?"

"Why don't you leave it alone? Why don't you drop it?"

"Because it's like rancid food, Max. The taste keeps coming back. That's why."

Max sighed. He went to the stairs. "I'm going up," he said. "I'm very tired."

Louise watched him go. Her head was filled with tiny smoking fissures, volcanic in the way they burst open. She heard the bedroom door close at the top of the stairs.

She moved along the hallway. She stepped inside Dennis's room. The lamp was on.

The smell of Dick Summer's bait filled the air—sickly now, sweet as a rotten apple, still strong and objectionable. Louise walked to the bedside table and gazed at the little jar in which Dennis kept the substance.

The boy, who lay on the bed with his head turned away from his mother, had left the lid off as usual.

Louise picked it up, put it on the jar.

The substance had darkened since she'd last seen it. It had changed from a pale brown to something that resembled a dehydrated liver caked with black blood. Along its surface various cracks had developed. She looked closer, inclining her head as she held her breath.

Deep within the cracks she thought she saw something move. Glistening, white as decay, it moved as if it were agitated by the overhead light. Louise picked up the top and jammed it down into the jar, then stepped back in disgust.

The substance in the jar was riddled with maggots. Her stomach turned over. *Maggots.*

"Dennis?" she said quietly.

The boy rolled over on his side and smiled sleepily at her. He looked oddly different in the lamplight, his short hair accentuating the contours of his face. He's growing up, she thought. A warm sense of love coursed through her. This boy. This lovable boy. She sat on the edge of the bed and laid one hand on his forehead. It was warm to her touch.

"I love you," she said. And she knew she was at least uttering the one constant sensation in her life.

"I didn't hear you come in," he said. "I guess I fell asleep."

"You okay?"

"Sure."

"Nice evening?"

"Fine," Dennis said.

Louise hesitated a second. "I hate to bring this up, but don't you think it's time to put that jar outside? It's literally crawling. One day it's going to crawl right out of here anyhow."

Dennis raised his head and squinted at the jar. "I guess," he said. "I could store it under the sun deck."

"Anywhere you like, as long as it's outdoors."

Louise glanced a moment at the photograph of the younger Summers. "What did you do with the Summers?" she asked.

"Watched TV."

"That's all?"

"That's all," the boy said.

Louise placed one hand flat against the side of her head. Pounding now. She needed to go find aspirin. She found her gaze drawn back to the jar, where a single white maggot was undulating just beneath the lid, hanging to the inside of the glass. It curled, slipped, fell back into the brown mass. She shut her eyes. An image of Connie Harrison floated through her mind —Connie stuck inside the jar with all the rest of the maggots. *Connie Harrison! Forty years old and sagging badly! Like hell!*

Dennis was smiling at her. "They're only baby flies," he said. "That's all. They're not really disgusting."

"Ugh," Louise said.

"In South America there are natives who consider larvae a delicacy. They like to eat them live." Dennis sounded cheerful, as if this picture of Indians pigging out on grubs delighted him in some fashion.

"Don't go into details," Louise said. "Just get the jar out of here first thing in the morning."

Dennis sat up, swiveled his body toward the jar. As he reached out to touch it his pajama jacket rode up his spine a little way, laying his back bare.

There were small pink crisscrossing lines on the boy's skin.

"What have you done to your back?" Louise asked. She leaned closer to her son, laying her hand on the boy's spine. The marks suggested the scratches of fingernails.

"What's wrong with my back?"

"These marks. How did you get these marks?"

"What marks?" the boy asked. He attempted to pivot his head around to look.

Louise touched the slender pink lines. "Don't they hurt?"

Dennis shook his head. "I don't feel anything."

"What did you do? Have an argument with a pine tree?"

Dennis laughed. "It must have been when Dick and Charlotte were horsing around—"

"Horsing around?" Louise couldn't imagine the Summers *horsing around*.

"We were rolling on the floor and they were tickling me. I guess it happened then."

"They were *tickling* you?"

"Yeah. It was just their idea of fun."

"They got carried away, Denny. Obviously."

"I guess so."

Louise stood up, smoothing the kid's pajama top back in place. An unexpected shiver went through her—scratch marks on her son's back. She couldn't see the Summers getting so carried away. "Strange games you guys play."

"They thought it was funny," Dennis said.

"Did you?"

The boy shrugged. "Kinda." He had actually been quite frightened by the Summers' persistent, relentless tickling.

The Great Communicator, Louise thought. She bent down and kissed the boy on his forehead. "Maybe I ought to put some ointment on your back."

"I'm fine. Really. It's not like they drew blood or anything. Is it? It's not like I'm going to need a rabies shot."

Louise stepped away from the bed. She moved toward the door. Strange games, she thought. She tried to imagine Dick and Charlotte catching Denny and tickling him like that. She couldn't get the picture in her head.

"Good night," she said.

"Night."

Louise went into the hallway, closing the door of the room. She looked up the stairs, up to the darkness at the top. She climbed, hesitating only when she reached the closed door of the bedroom. Max. Max and that girl. She turned impossibilities around in her mind. She played with fractured notions—Max and that girl in bed together. Max and the girl holding each other intimately. Little secrets.

Not Max, she thought. Not my husband.

She put a small tense smile on her face and opened the bedroom door. Max was sitting up in bed, a book propped open in front of him. He raised his face and looked at her.

How do we play this scene? Louise wondered. What do we do to smooth out the wrinkles, the awkward little creases?

She stepped to the bed, sat on the edge of the mattress, gazed at her husband. What she wished for was infinite understanding, an endless capacity to believe in Max. A whole starry universe of trust. The idea of Max and that girl caused everything to collapse loudly in her mind. Worlds shattered. Mirrors were broken. Everything flew away from a cracked center, like debris flying off into mysterious space.

She licked her dry lips. "Tell me again, Max."

"Tell you what?"

"Tell me I'm sick over nothing."

"You're sick over nothing."

Louise smiled. It was so goddamn hard to believe. She shut her eyes very tightly.

"I can't get over how she touched you."

"She touched *me*. I had no control over that. You might have noticed that I didn't touch *her*."

"True, true." What difference did it make? One small touch suggested all kinds of perfidy. "Did you ever make love to her?"

"Louise."

"Did you?"

Max shook his head emphatically.

"Would you like to?" Louise asked.

"Why are you punishing yourself?"

That isn't an answer, Max.

Louise stood up and wandered restlessly around the room. She threw open the doors that led to the sun deck and went outside, staring up at the misanthropic moon. It hung there with a pitiless look. She had a sense of intimacies from which she was excluded—the betrayed wife.

Max came out on the deck and put his arm around her shoulders.

Her tone one of forced cheerfulness, she said, "This is not the summer I planned. No way."

Max was silent. His arm felt like a lead weight against her.

She looked at the hangdog moon. She felt her whole family unit had become splintered in this place—a son who enjoyed spending his time with strangers, a father who failed to make true connections with the boy, and a husband tracked by a possibly neurotic female patient all the way upstate, a woman who imagined herself in love with him.

These were not the prerequisites for a gorgeous summer. Not remotely. She clenched her hands, frustrated. What was she supposed to believe of Max? Was he capable of treachery? If so, where did that leave her after eighteen years of marriage and trust and mutual support?

She lost herself out there in the depths of the trees, the piebald shadows of the landscape. She had a passing thought of Frog out there someplace— could she go talk to him? Would he understand? Could he help?

She looked into Max's eyes and then she turned and walked into the bedroom. She undressed in front of the bedside lamp. From the sun-deck doorway Max studied her. She tried to ignore the way his eyes scrutinized her body. She lay down, pulling a sheet over her.

Close your eyes. Drift away. Daylight is the great salve.

Max sat beside her and took her hand, clasping it between his own like a flower pressed between pages of a book. She tried to imagine herself and Max when they were as old as Dick and Charlotte. Would they live that long? More important—would they be together still? Kissing dried lips? Holding decrepit hands?

36 Florence Hann's house was located close to the railroad that had once been used to haul silver from the mines around Carnarvon. Now the tracks were rusted and grown over with tangled weeds, and the old signals along the lines were nothing more than stumps of weathered wood. Here and there decayed boxcars sat on the rails, their panels splintered, their numerals defaced by both vandalism and the seasons.

It was a strange neighborhood, a part of Carnarvon the tourists never saw. There were a couple of small bars and corner grocery stores, dimly lit places whose lights barely pecked at the texture of darkness.

Metger parked his car across the street from a tavern called Frank's. It was an old-time neighborhood bar where a TV played constantly in the gloom and men sat at stools with their necks craned in the direction of the moving pictures. He walked past the open doorway, moving along the cracked sidewalk toward Florence Hann's home.

The house was the color of bleached-out green and sat in the dark like a blind toad. The front yard was high with weeds. Metger moved toward the porch, heard the steps creak beneath his feet. Before he had a chance to knock on the door it was opened from inside and Florence Hann stood there with a pale yellow light coming from a place at her back.

"I heard you coming," she said. "I always hear people coming."

From a nearby house a baby cried suddenly and then was silent. Metger said, "I know it's late, but I'd like to talk."

Reluctantly, Florence Hann held the door open and Metger stepped into the living room, where three goldfish scuttled back and forth inside a bowl and an old-fashioned radio played big-band music. The room smelled of soap and fried food.

"I want to talk about Bobby," he said.

The quick expression that crossed the woman's tired, drawn face might have been one of pain. It was extinguished as swiftly as it had arisen. "What about Bobby?"

Metger realized she wasn't looking at him. In fact she was gazing straight past him, her attention welded to something just beyond his head.

"Did Miles Henderson treat Bobby?"

"You can call it treat if you like," she said.

Metger moved slightly. He was uncomfortable in this house. Small, cramped rooms, low ceilings. There was a pressure between the walls of this place, something dense in the very atmosphere. And still Florence Hann wasn't looking at him. She was addressing the same point beyond his face.

"What would you call it, Florence?" he asked.

"Miles Henderson was useless," she said. "It's incurable was all he ever said. Rare and incurable. Never anything else but that." She paused now —she ran the tip of her tongue over her dry lips. She'd pronounced the word "rare" as if there were a film of scum on her tongue. Her eyes glazed over. Metger could see that she had a series of little retreats built into her system, places where she could go without fear of anyone following her.

"You know there's no record of Bobby ever being treated by Henderson?" She said nothing.

"Doesn't that seem strange to you?" he asked.

"Probably he destroyed them," she answered. "Why keep records of your failures? Or maybe he just hid them."

Metger was silent a second. Then: "The other day you said something to me about children being killed. Something like that."

"Did I?"

"Outside the supermarket. You remember?"

"I might," she said. Her face was tight, like a closed fist.

"What did you mean when you said that?"

"I don't remember." She turned over the palms of her hands. "I don't always remember things I say, Sheriff."

"It doesn't seem like the kind of thing you'd forget easily," he said. Why had he come here anyhow? he wondered. It seemed to him suddenly that he was lost, that somewhere along the way he'd misplaced his maps, his sense of direction. If there were arrows he was meant to follow, if there were a spoor he was supposed to catch, they were indetectable. "You must have had something on your mind to make you say what you did, Florence."

Florence Hann adjusted the cuffs of her gray wool cardigan, a shapeless garment that hung around her thin body in deep folds and hollows.

"What difference does it make anyway?" she asked. "My son died. I live with that thought every day of my life. You have any idea what that's like? Living with one thought all the time?"

Metger moved toward the fireplace. He turned, facing the opposite wall—he saw what it was that had taken Florence Hann's attention before.

In frames, bleak beneath dull glass, there were half a dozen or so photographs of Bobby Hann hanging against the floral wallpaper. They showed—like jump cuts in a strip of film—the deterioration of the child. A normal baby. A normal two-year-old. A Christmas picture showing young Bobby sitting beneath a tree of lights surrounded by wrapped packages; his eyes were red from the camera flash. But he was *normal*. There was no sign of any illness. No connection between these pictures and the last two that hung on the wall.

The last pair were dreadful.

Metger couldn't look. He turned his face to the side and shut his eyes briefly and he thought, People are lying to me in this town, people are falsifying or destroying records. In this small town there's some kind of darkness that lies beneath the lights, something scurrying away into unlit corners. . . .

"Try, Florence. Try to remember."

Florence Hann sat down. She held her hands, palms outward, toward the fireplace, as if she thought she might get some heat from the long-dead ashes.

She wished the cop hadn't come here, dredging the past the way he wanted to. Trawling old waters. She stuck a poker into the ashes, twisted it around, saw a pink spark rise up into the hollowed-out dark of the chimney. Try to remember, she thought.

Remember what? Memory had no purpose to it.

Wherever memory went, there were only sinewy trails of pain.

"People come here all the time," she said.

"Come where? To this house?"

"To Carnarvon," she said. "They come and they keep coming. They don't know, do they?"

"What don't they know?"

She covered her face with her hands. "They don't know about the children."

"Suppose you tell me," Metger said. He bent down, staring directly into the woman's face. He felt hot suddenly—a film of warm sweat lay across the surface of his skin. He placed one hand on her cheek and turned her face toward him. But she kept her eyes averted. They were dull and secretive and directed inward.

"Why don't you tell me about the children, Florence?"

"They get sick," she said.

She had the strange sensation all at once of Bobby's small shriveled hand held inside her own—a phantom hand, wrinkled, clutching, desperate.

"Why do they get sick, Florence? Why does it happen?"

She stood up briskly. She moved toward the photographs. She looked at them for a while. Now she couldn't feel Bobby's hand anymore. Instead, there was a terrible emptiness within her, a hollow where her heart should have been.

Metger went toward her. The photographs captured his attention again. Bobby Hann's eyes had a look of inestimable sadness. They stared out at Metger with a pathetic resignation. There was a patch of light on the boy's bare skull and the ears protruded slightly. The skin around the mouth was puckered, drawn into a hundred little lines.

Metger suddenly thought about Anthea Ackerley and the way she'd looked in death and the white hairs matted with freshly spilled blood and the way her hands had been.

He laid his palms on Florence Hann's bony shoulders.

"Does the name Caskie mean anything to you?"

She didn't speak.

"Caskie," he said again. "Sammy Caskie."

She was silent a moment. She strolled to the window and parted the curtain and stared out into the dark street. Then she turned around to face him and asked, "Do you have your car outside, Sheriff?"

"My car?" Puzzled, he nodded. "Sure."

"Take me for a drive."

"Where do you want to go?"

She was already stepping out into the hallway, plucking an overcoat from a rack that sat just inside the front door.

He followed her outside.

When they reached the car he opened the passenger door for her and she climbed in.

"Where do you want to go?" he asked again.

"I'll give you directions," she answered.

He gazed at her face a second. What was it there? Some form of resolve? Purpose? Or just a surge of madness? He got in behind the wheel, drumming his fingers on the rim and waiting for her instructions.

"St. Mary's Road," she said.

He knew then where they were headed.

•   •   •

Dennis Untermeyer woke. His bedside lamp was still lit. He rubbed his eyes, then gazed at his hands under the soft glow of the light.

The nails looked dull and the tiny half-moons were almost gone and the hands themselves appeared bloodless. He brought them back to his side, smuggled them under the blanket. The inside of his mouth was dry. His gums seemed to ache. What had wakened him? He couldn't remember dreaming.

He swung his legs out of the bed, dangling them against the rug. He was oddly breathless, the way he sometimes felt when old Mittelmann, the PE instructor, made his class run six pointless laps of the football field. He needed water; he felt dehydrated.

His attention was drawn a moment to the photograph under the lamp. As he stared at the picture he thought he could actually *feel* the texture of the clothing Dick and Charlotte were wearing, all the small threads and stitches and the depths of the folds. He thought, too, that he could hear the steamship's horn in the background—the low, throaty sound emerging from the vicinity of the funnel. He rubbed his eyes again. When you woke suddenly from sleep you were always kind of spacey and you imagined all manner of things.

He stepped out of bed. He had the feeling the Summers were observing him from the picture. Their eyes appeared to track him. He cracked his knuckles as he moved across the room and out into the hallway, where it was dark save for the small light glowing over the stove in the kitchen. He peered at it, trying to find his bearings. From the upper part of the house he heard the steady drone of Max snoring.

Dennis went inside the bathroom. He filled a glass with water and drank it quickly, spilling the liquid down the front of his pajamas in his haste. The breathlessness he'd felt before was still there, like a claw inside his chest. He took a Vicks inhaler out of the medicine cabinet and inserted it into one nostril and he breathed as deeply as he could, feeling the stuff tickle his nasal passages. It helped for a moment.

Then he removed his pajama jacket—it was damp and unpleasant against his skin—and he twisted around to examine his back in the mirror. It was difficult but he managed to get a look at the marks his mother had mentioned before. They were red now, and they crisscrossed his flesh like the welts that might have been left there after a whipping, but they didn't hurt. They simply itched. Charlotte's fingernails, he thought. He hadn't felt anything at the time.

Dennis stepped out of the bathroom. He paused at the foot of the stairs. He stared in the direction of the stove light—a dark moth beat against the glow in a useless, panicky fashion. Outside, a sudden outburst of wind shook the trees and branches rattled against the side of the house. Dennis moved down the dark hallway and opened the front door. On the porch he breathed the night air into his lungs—he felt like he was choking, like his lungs were suddenly shriveled little things lying prunelike in his chest.

The moon, sucked behind black clouds, threw out a thin light. Dennis gripped the porch rail. The wind came up again, like some big playful dog, and the trees swayed. There was a hint of rain in the air. Tiny drops of moisture struck his face. An owl screamed in the distance. Dennis, who decided that this night—replete with the trappings of a horror movie, owls and whispering trees and black clouds masking a moon—wasn't quite to his liking, went back indoors.

Inside his bedroom he sat for a while on the edge of the mattress. He looked at the bait in the glass jar. Maggots, stirred up by the light from the lamp, crawled all over the inner surface of the jar. As he watched he breathed slowly and deeply, trying to fill his lungs with air, but the restricted feeling persisted. Making a fist of his hand, he struck himself on his rib cage, as if a decent blow might open up clogged passageways. He wondered if maybe he was allergic to something. Between the ages of one and seven he'd been allergic to pollen and cat's fur, he remembered this now, but he'd grown out of them the way his dad had said he would. Had allergies returned to plague him?

He punched himself again, feeling kind of idiotic as he did so. *Boy brutalizes self in effort to breathe!* Sighing, he let his hands dangle against his thighs.

He was sleepy now. He started to lay his head down when he observed strands of his own hair spread across the pillow. Seven or eight sinewy hairs. How could he be going bald at the age of twelve! What was he—some kind of freak!

He smiled, brushing the hairs aside. He realized that what he should have done was wash his hair after Charlotte had cut it—if you didn't do that, you were bound to get loose ends.

He closed his eyes and lay very still. His breathing was shallow and there was a wheeze in his chest. He listened to himself, annoyed with the noise he was making. He yawned and thought, Sleep, beam me up.

Beyond the railroad tracks the narrow road climbed up. It was used mainly by two kinds of vehicles: cars that transported lovers to the furtive leafy places alongside the edges of the road—and hearses. Metger turned on his full beams. Beside him Florence Hann's face was a dark silhouette. The limbs of trees flapped against the windshield.

Ahead, at the crest of the hill, the cemetery came in view. Headstones, catching the lamps of the car, stretched backward into shadows. Then there was gravel and the sound of the tires crunching and Florence Hann was telling him to park. He switched off the engine, pushed his door open, listened to the silences of the night all around him.

"You got a flashlight?" she asked.

He rummaged in the glove compartment. It was a big rubber flashlight with a strong beam.

"What now?" he asked.

"Now we walk, Sheriff."

Metger stood on the gravel, the flashlight glowing in front of him. Florence Hann, as if she knew this place intimately, as if she carried around a mental map to the intricacies of the pathways, was striding ahead of him into the darkness. He hurried to keep up with her, thinking, Why here? Why this place in the dead of goddamn night? Below, between slats of trees, there were lights casting an eerie yellow glow along the central strip of Carnarvon.

"Keep moving like that, Florence, and I'll lose you," he said.

She stopped some way in front of him. In the beam of his light her face was white, her eyes dark smudges. She put one hand up to her eyes. "You trying to blind me?" she said.

He turned the light away.

Through the silences he was suddenly conscious of a sound coming from a distance behind him. It was the noise of weight pressing against chips of gravel, a muted slurring of small stones.

He listened, his head tilted, even as he was aware of Florence Hann calling out to him.

"Come on," she was saying. "Come on. It's this way."

The noise stopped. You're spooked, Metger, he thought. Even at your age, boneyards spook you after dark. He started to move after Florence Hann when he heard a sound again and once more he stopped, turning his flashlight through the dark. The beam, like some big white knife, cut across headstones and through patches of shrubbery, but he couldn't see anything out there even though he had the impression of a presence some yards back.

Shrugging, he followed the woman.

They were going deeper into the cemetery. Florence Hann's overcoat brushed the edges of stones and Metger thought she was like a demented bat, a creature accustomed to that awful combination of darkness and death.

Now a night wind was rising out of the earth, reshaping the shadowy trees around them. And still the woman was hurrying, as if she had the gift of night sight and didn't need Metger's rubber flashlight. Breathing hard, he caught up to her again. He reached out and gripped her elbow and she swung around to face him.

"Where are we going, Florence? Where exactly are we going?"

She shook her arm free, turning away from him. She said nothing. She just kept walking, weaving among the graves, and Metger scurried behind her. Madness, he thought. Madness and all its devious forms.

But now she was slowing. And then she was standing perfectly still, looking from side to side, her hands sunk deep in the pockets of her long overcoat.

"Over here," Florence Hann said. "Give me some light over this way."

Metger did so. A splash of white light fell on a small gray marker, which was surrounded by weeds. The woman went down on her knees, working her fingers through the clumps of weeds, hauling them out of the earth, or pushing them aside when she couldn't tug them from the soil. As he watched her he was aware yet again of another presence nearby. Nervously, he looked behind—but there was nothing, nobody, just the wind scouring the surfaces of the headstones and whispering harshly.

Florence Hann raised her face toward him. She stood upright. Metger could smell the ripe soil on her skin, the perfume of broken stalks of weeds that the ground had released.

He understood that he was meant to look at the stone at his feet. He bent down, turned his light on the granite, read the pale simple inscription cut there in Gothic script.

SAMUEL S. CASKIE
1935–1942

He stood up, looking at Florence Hann, seeing the dark outlines of her face. He was silent—the wind blew against his face and hair, filled his nostrils. He was aware of the woman's hand reaching out to touch his arm. An odd sadness swept through him, a sensation of something broken deep inside. Sammy Caskie, aged six. The kid his dad had called "Old Sammy."

"Tell me about him," he said. "Tell me about Sammy Caskie."

The wind whipped at the woman's hair. "What is there to tell? The thing that killed Bobby killed this child too." She shrugged in the darkness.

"What thing, Florence?"

"Maybe it doesn't have a name, Sheriff. Sure, there's some fancy name doctors give it . . . but that's not its real name."

"What is its real name?" he asked.

She didn't answer his question. She made a sighing sound.

"How did you know about this grave?" he asked.

"I looked for it."

"Why?"

"I saw this boy once. I was twelve years old. I remember thinking how funny he looked. I remember seeing him look out of the window of a passing car and I laughed because . . ." She paused, pushing windblown hair from her eyes. "Because, goddamnit, he looked funny. I was a kid, I didn't know any better. And kids are cruel. They were cruel to Bobby, at least."

Metger wanted more. But it was tricky now because she was drifting in the direction of her own tragedy and when she entered that dark center she might never come out again. He rubbed the back of her arm with the palm of his hand.

"What else do you remember about Sammy Caskie?"

She turned her face toward him and in the oblique angle of the flashlight her eyes were the only things visible in her face. "After he died his family went away. They left Carnarvon. I seem to recall they went back to the Midwest, where they came from, but that's vague and I wouldn't swear to it. . . . Anyhow, they left. Nobody ever saw them again. It was like they wanted to bury the child here in this place and just walk away from the memory of his existence. . . . You can't do that, though, Sheriff. You can't ever just walk away. You can try but you never get very far. Believe me. I know."

Metger shook his head slowly. He stared through the trees. The town, hidden from view, was nothing more than a faint electrical dust in the darkness.

"What else do you remember, Florence?"

"They said the boy was perfectly normal when the family first came to Carnarvon. That's what I heard."

An echo, Metger thought. Wasn't that what Ackerley had implied? That Anthea *changed* after she'd come to Carnarvon? Suddenly the darkness was like a maze to him and he was stumbling through it with all the elegance of a blind man.

She stepped toward the stone. She observed it silently a moment.

"Miles Henderson said it was a rare disease. When Bobby first showed the signs of it he said it was a one-in-a-million thing. One in ten million. I don't remember. He said it was so rare there were barely any studies about it. And nobody had a cure. . . ."

She turned her face toward Metger now, and her mouth hung open, slack with grief. "I remembered this boy. That was different, Miles Henderson said. The two cases were totally different. But they're not. They're exactly the same, Sheriff. Miles Henderson lied about that."

A strange sobbing noise came from her. She swayed a little and Metger had to hold her by the arm.

"If it's so rare, how come it happened twice in the space of fourteen years? How come, Dr. Henderson? Suppose you give me an answer for that one. . . ."

Twice, Metger thought. Add Anthea Ackerley and that makes it three. Three times since 1942.

Florence Hann moved away from him now. She stood staring down at the sad little marker.

Metger was afraid suddenly, afraid of the night, of the impenetrable dark, of the yellowy stardust that floated up from the unseen town below, afraid of the birth of his own child.

He thought of all the dead that lay beneath his feet. He thought of dead children, of something that came up like some god-awful hand and snatched them away.

"Bobby was the sweetest thing," the woman said. "You don't know how sweet that boy was. All you ever saw was what he turned into. You never got to look into that boy's heart, did you?"

"I never did," he answered.

"Probably you found him funny," she said very quietly.

Metger didn't answer. Bobby Hann was a shadow to him now.

Florence Hann stepped backward, out of the range of the flashlight. "Right in front of my eyes, that kid wasted. I watched him waste. Day after day after day." She turned her face up to the sky. "Nobody knows how to cure something like that. All they know around here is how to keep it quiet."

Jerry Metger heard branches part in the dark behind him.

The wind again, he thought.

Just the wind blowing across this damned place. And somewhere a suggestion of rain.

"Let me take you home, Florence."

She stumbled against him. She was no longer so sure of her footing, her surroundings. The darkness was treacherous.

"Seeing them waste," she said. "That's the worst of all."

37 In the hour between darkness and dawn, when the sky is about to crack with the first few splinters of weak light, Louise got out of bed and went downstairs. All night long her sleep had been fitful—dreamless when she found it but shallow at the same time, like floating in four inches of tepid water. She made herself tea in the kitchen and sipped it. She lit a cigarette.

Max had slept like a baby all night long. She'd listened to the steady rhythm of his breathing—unconcerned, carefree sleep. Maybe that was fine, maybe that was okay, because maybe, finally, he had nothing on his conscience and *she* was the one overreacting to a situation that didn't exist. Or had he taken some kind of sleeping pill to carry him over the edge?

She took her tea into the living room. She turned on the lamp and impulsively opened the Carnarvon Telephone Directory, a thin volume with a sprinkling of Yellow Pages at the back. Under the heading of "Motels" she found the name of the place where Connie Harrison said she was staying. The Huckleberry Inn—cute, very cute. Louise stared at the number, then shut the book. Why had she checked that anyhow? To make sure it existed? That last night's encounter in the restaurant had really taken place?

Damn right it had taken place—the recollection was like a wasp's sting. She sat on the sofa, finished both her tea and her cigarette, and hugged herself, rocking her body back and forth because the air in the house was chill. Why didn't Frog have a telephone in his van? She wanted to speak to him—he'd be sympathetic, understanding, he'd listen to her. All at once she was very lonely.

She got up, walked around the room. Shivering in her robe, she looked out the window.

In the sky there was a solitary strip of light now, very pale, slender as a crack in a mirror. The landscape suggested unreality, another world, an unmapped portion of the planet. *I want to be happy*, she thought. Why did that seem so much to ask? She pressed her forehead against the glass, over the surface of which lay streaks of thin rain.

She went down to the kitchen. Dennis was methodically breaking eggs into a mixing bowl.

"You're an early bird," Louise said, surprised.

Dennis appeared not to hear her. He smacked his fourth egg against the rim of the bowl and let it slide out of the shell. Louise went toward him. She laid her hands on his shoulders and the boy, seemingly startled, jumped.

"Got you," Louise said. "The furtive chef."

Dennis said, "You sneaked up on me."

"I'm light on my feet." She made him turn around to face her because she wanted to kiss him. But the kid, as if he were embarrassed, squirmed away from her touch, stepping to one side and dodging her outstretched hands.

"What's up?" she asked. "Don't you want your mother to kiss you? Awww."

He stood beside the stove, egg whisk in one hand. There were small dark circles under his eyes and his skin was pale and tiny pinpoints of sweat glistened on his forehead. She moved closer to him, noticing now how the flesh on the back of his hands was peeling, coming away in small flakes. Too much sun, she thought. Too many hours outdoors working on that damned pickup truck. Freckles and peeling skin. All at once she was glad the Summers were going because then Denny wouldn't have that goddamn truck to keep him outdoors all the time.

"Are you feeling okay? Is something wrong, Denny?"

He shook his head. When he spoke his voice was unusually petulant, even shrill. "I was trying to make my goddamn breakfast in peace!"

"Denny," she said. That tone—where did that come from? "I've never heard you talk to me like that."

He turned his back on her, started whisking the eggs.

"Are you listening to me?" she demanded.

"Yeah yeah yeah," he said, as if he were bored by her presence, her questions, and just wanted to blow her aside.

She caught him by the shoulder and spun him around to face her. There was a terrible urge inside her to raise her hand and slap him, but she caught herself in time. What would she be striking out at anyhow? Her own frustrations? Her own anxieties? Something was bothering the boy—she had to know what. And she saw it in his eyes now, a worry, a muted concern, something he wasn't going to talk about.

"Denny," and she kept her voice quiet. "What's the matter? Tell me. If you're sick, we'll get your father to look at you. Just tell me."

"I'm fine."

"You're sweating and you're pale and you look like you haven't slept in days. Don't tell me you're fine. And your hands—the skin's dry."

The boy stared at her; his look was hard.

She turned away. Leave him alone, she thought. Let him come out of this mood by himself, whatever it is. She walked to the doorway, where she paused and looked back at him. He'd never raised his voice to her before; she'd never seen such a weirdly defiant look on his face either. *Christ, what was going wrong with this family? Her* family? She could hear things crumbling, breaking apart.

"Denny," she said. "Are you sure you're okay?"

"I told you."

She watched him beat the eggs and then she climbed the stairs. Halfway up, she stopped. It's all going wrong, she thought. Everything was falling apart around her and she didn't know how to stop it, how to put things right, how to make good again.

She went on up to the landing, pausing again when she reached the bedroom door. She could hear the steady sound of Max's breathing. She was reluctant to go inside. Reluctant to look at Max. She fidgeted with the cord of her robe.

From downstairs she heard fat sizzling inside a frying pan and after a moment the smell of eggs floated up toward her with nauseating intensity. The cranky boy cooks his greasy breakfast, she thought, and she pushed the door open, stepping inside the bedroom, where Max lay asleep.

An ill-tempered son. A secretive husband. It was a depressing little catalogue.

She moved to the bed, placing herself quietly on the edge of the mattress, thinking—for some reason—of that blue ribbon floating up from Charlotte Summer's skull and the old woman's fingernails scratching the flesh of her son's back. Playful Charlotte. Nice playful Charlotte.

Max opened his puffy eyes.

"Good morning," he said.

Louise smiled wanly.

"No breakfast in bed?" Max asked.

She shook her head.

"No cup of coffee? No San Francisco *Examiner*? What kind of room service is this?"

Louise gathered the edge of the blanket and crumpled it between her fingers. "I want you to do something, Max."

"Sure."

"I want you to take a look at Denny."

"Why? Is he sick?"

Louise hesitated. She gazed in the direction of the sun deck. She said, "I think he may be coming down with something."

"Say aahhh." Max peered inside Dennis's throat, saw nothing out of the ordinary. He placed his long fingers at the sides of his son's neck. There was no swelling. Since Max hadn't thought to bring a stethoscope with him—never imagining any need for the tools of his trade—he couldn't listen to Dennis's chest, but he could hear the boy wheezing a little even without the instrument.

"So what's the scoop?" Dennis asked in an impatient way. "Am I going to live?"

"You've got a long life ahead of you, kid." Max took his son's hands in his own, flipped Dennis's over, looked at the backs of the boy's wrists. The freckles he'd seen there before were more numerous now and the skin was peeling, especially in the spaces between the fingers. "Do these still itch?"

"It's nothing much," the boy answered.

"You're using the calamine?"

"Oh sure."

"I want you to start rubbing moisturizer into your skin as well as the calamine. Your mother's got some in the upstairs bathroom." Max rose from the chair where he'd been sitting. "Use it liberally, work it into your skin as well as you can."

Max gazed into the boy's face. There were dark half-moons hanging under his eyes, which indicated sleeplessness, but the kid had said he was sleeping okay. Maybe what was happening here, Max thought, was a recurrence of allergies. He knew that allergies obeyed no specific laws—they could disappear for years and then, without warning, attack long after you thought they'd been outgrown.

Louise was smoking a cigarette at the kitchen table. She stubbed it out, then stood up. She laid a hand on the boy's shoulder.

Max said, "He's going to be fine."

Louise glanced at Dennis, who seemed anxious to be out of the kitchen. Max's examination had been quick, almost cursory, and she wanted to make a joke about getting a second opinion, but the atmosphere wasn't right for even the mildest kind of humor—she was still tense from the encounter with Dennis. The air in the kitchen reeked from the smell of scrambled eggs and she thought she would choke on it. She pushed the window open, allowing the damp perfume of the pines to infiltrate the house.

"Am I confined to bed or what?" Dennis asked. He looked perfectly sullen, Louise thought.

"You're not confined to bed," Max replied. "But you ought to stay out of the sun."

"I won't have much trouble doing that," and Dennis indicated the swollen gray sky that was lit now by a muted, indistinct sun behind clouds.

Max poured himself a cup of coffee. Cup rattled against saucer, a small cacophony. Everything is nervy today, Louise thought. Everything has an edge against which you might cut yourself. She longed to step out of the house and go up through the trees, aimless and free and unconcerned. She was thinking about Frog again. Could she ever find the place where he lived? Or would she lose herself in the green-gray forest? She envisaged a skeleton of herself found, fifty years later, by some passing hiker—an assembly of bones with no identifying peculiarities.

Dennis went out of the kitchen. After a moment she heard the sound of the front door closing and the boy's footsteps creaking on the porch and then he was gone. She looked at Max. He isn't here in this room with me, Louise thought. He's miles away, elsewhere, receding like a flimsy thing on a strong tide. He was thinking about Connie Harrison—what else could make him so utterly distracted?

"I think I'll take a walk," she said.

"Any place in particular?"

She shrugged. She wanted to come back with something sharp, like *Yeah, Carnegie Hall* or *Sure, Fisherman's Wharf,* but at the same time she didn't see much point in being abrasive. Basically, what she really wanted was to get out of this house, out of Max's company. She wanted the deep forest around her and the sounds of birds filling the air and some sense of liberation, even if it were illusory. She looked at Max's face. He was gazing down inside his cup, like some old biddy trying to tell the future from the pattern of coffee grounds or tea leaves.

"Are you sure Denny's okay?"

Max sighed. "I'm sure."

"It just seemed . . ." She hesitated.

"Seemed what?"

"You examined him quickly, that's all. You didn't take your time over it. It wasn't like you, that's what I'm trying to say."

Max frowned. Restlessly now, he moved up and down the kitchen. He rubbed his hands together. "He's all right, Louise. Believe me."

"He doesn't even *sound* like himself."

With a motion of his hand, Max dismissed her—her concerns, her worries, he dismissed everything with one slight karate chop in the air. She heard his hand *swish* through space. She stepped out into the hallway and stood at the foot of the stairs.

All around her the house made dripping sounds—the recent rain slithered out of eaves, rolled down the cedar roof, dropped from the sun deck and trickled off the roof of the porch—and Louise thought of a large dark dog, a very damp dog, shaking itself free of moisture.

She went outside.

38 Theodore Ronson said, "My point is, I don't think it looks very good for the sheriff of our town to be visiting strange places in the company of—shall we say—a woman whose mental condition is known to be more than just a tad odd, Jerry."

Ronson, with the scrubbed pink look of a man who has come straight from a sauna, wore white shorts and a white Izod shirt. He had a pair of Vans on his feet—black and white checks.

Behind him stood his chief administrative assistant, Bryce Dunning, with his prominent Adam's apple and vacant sky-blue eyes. Dunning's hair was wet and slicked back and there were little patches of dampness on his beige shirt.

They must have come from the Carnarvon Health Club, Metger thought. There, in the privacy of the steam room, they must have discussed the nocturnal comings and goings of their appointed sheriff. Metger closed the door of the living room; he was conscious of Nora out in the kitchen, moving back and forth between the sink and the stove. A smell of bacon drifted through the air. .

"Why don't you both sit down?" Metger asked.

Neither man moved. Ronson said, "Are you hearing me, Jerry? Are you listening to me?"

"I'm listening," Metger said. He glanced at the TV a second. A Saturday morning movie was playing. Randolph Scott was talking to Ronald Reagan and they were both dressed like West Point cadets. "Maybe *you* ought to listen to *me*, Ted. I don't like the idea of being followed. It doesn't agree with me. If I choose to go anywhere, that's my business."

Ronson smiled. "Jerry, Jerry, this is a small town. People talk."

"They don't talk enough," Metger said. "Some things they don't talk about at all."

"Is that so?" Ronson asked.

"That's so." Metger killed the TV. He looked at Bryce Dunning. Those pale blue eyes, set in some other face, would have broken ladies' hearts. But on Bryce Dunning they just seemed pallid and bleached.

Ted Ronson moved. His new Vans made cracking sounds. "What are you working on, Jerry? What case are you working on that takes you out to the cemetery at night? I mean, can we expect a request for an exhumation order or something pretty soon?" Ronson and Dunning laughed, those quietly conspiratorial laughs common to bureaucrats who share a lot of memos together.

Ronson knows, Metger thought. Ronson and Dunning. They both know. They know it as well as Miles Henderson. Presumably Lou Pelusi too. And who else? Where in the name of God does it stop?

They know about the dead children and they want it kept locked inside a box that nobody's ever going to be allowed to open.

Three children had died over thirty years. From the same ailment. But what did it mean? What did it *really* mean?

"You want to know what I'm working on, Ted?" he said. "You've got your spies. Ask them."

"Spies," Bryce Dunning said. "We don't have spies, Jerry. This is just a small friendly town, for heaven's sake. You've seen our slogan as you drive in—CARNARVON, TOWN WITH A WELCOME IN ITS HEART? What's all this about spies?"

"We just happen to be curious, Jerry," Ted Ronson said.

Bryce Dunning nodded. "Curious about our sheriff running around graveyards in the dead of night."

They're quite a double act, Metger thought. He wondered if they rehearsed until they got it down pat and neat. And then he wondered about the conspiracy of silence and how far down it might go. Did they all get together in silent rooms and discuss the comings and goings of their sheriff in solemn tones? Or was it more lighthearted than that? Did they meet and laugh about how good old Jerry was running around like a jackrabbit with a firecracker up its ass?

"You said the other day you liked your job," Ronson remarked. "Am I to assume you might be looking for a change now? Like a gravedigger's job?"

"Droll," Metger said.

Ronson shrugged and glanced at Bryce Dunning. Dunning, shifting the weight of his body from one foot to the other, cleared his throat. "You go up to the Ace of Spades much, Jerry?"

Metger gazed at the mayor's assistant. What was coming down now? he wondered.

"Now and again," he answered. "Why?"

"Pretty woman up there," Dunning said. "Can't put my finger on her name, though." He looked at Ronson for help.

"Martine," Ronson said. "Fine-looking thing."

"Right, Martine," Dunning said. "You and her used to be an item, didn't you, Jerry? Or is that just scuttlebutt?"

"I know the woman," Metger said. He could see it—a whole new angle was opening out in front of him.

Ronson spread his hands and said, "Nobody would blame you, Jerry. I mean, pregnant wife and all. You don't have what you'd call an outlet, do you? And she's one hell of a looker, that Martine. Hell, Jerry, *I* understand all that. You think Nora would?"

"Fuck you," Metger said.

Bryce Dunning smiled. "Touchy, touchy. You know what they say. There's no smoke without fire. Especially in this town."

Metger said nothing. They could come at him from any direction they liked. They could smear him any way they wanted. He flexed his hands—there was an anger rising inside him. But it was a blind thing going nowhere.

"I mean, Jerry, we like having you as sheriff," Ronson said.

Bryce Dunning smiled in agreement. "Nora doesn't need to know a thing about Martine. She sure won't hear it from us, I'll tell you that."

Sure, hell, we're all men of the world in here, Metger thought. He moved around the room. He could hear Nora in the kitchen, the clatter of knives, dishes. He had a strange feeling of powerlessness right then—his home, wife, and child menaced in a way he wasn't sure how to fight against.

Bryce Dunning said, "Florence Hann took sick last night."

"Oh, yeah, we forgot to mention that," Ronson said.

"Took sick? How?"

"Had one of them nervous attacks," Ronson said.

"She was okay when I dropped her off," Metger said. "She wasn't sick then."

"Sudden, sudden," Dunning said quietly.

"What have you done with her? Made her disappear? Buried her?"

Ronson laughed. "Jerry, you got this funny notion in your head about some people around here. I mean, this ain't the goddamn Mafia, Jerry. People don't disappear. She needed some treatment and now she's getting it. Plain and simple. She's nicely settled in the nursing home. Not too far from your father, matter of fact."

Not too far from your father. A small sensation of panic rose inside Metger, then subsided. Not too far from your father! Was he supposed to glean something from this simple sentence, something underlying the words themselves? Another kind of meaning? That was the trouble with people like Ronson and Dunning—they made the English language as slippery as bathtub soap. Their meanings kept slipping, kept sliding. Not too far from your father, matter of fact. Was Ronson telling him something?

Metger's sudden anger was a wild thing. He felt a tightness in his throat and his fists clenched and the room seemed to turn blood red in front of his eyes. He fought the sensation away—it wasn't going to do any good to yield to brute anger with these guys. They were warning him, that much was clear. But the implication of this warning was shocking to him. Were they saying that they were responsible for Stanley Metger's condition? For Florence Hann's? Was Lou Pelusi the hatchet man?

Now the door opened and Nora came inside the room, asking a question about how many bacon sandwiches were required. Both Ronson and Dunning laughed and said they'd come from the steam room and they weren't about to put on more calories and they were all laughing. So ordinary, Metger thought. So very ordinary.

When they were gone Metger went inside the kitchen.

Nora folded her arms across the lump the baby made in her body.

Metger watched her a second and then he went toward her and held her closely against him. His mind was filled with the dark of graveyards, with old tombstones, with a sad woman scratching at weeds, with his father counting M & M's in a sterile room inside a nursing home.

And with a life as yet unborn.

Uncertain of her direction, Louise remembered Frog having said something about how—if you followed the wash—you would reach a stream that flowed in an east-west direction. Traveling due west for a quarter of a mile, you would find his VW van. It had seemed at the time very simple, but now, faced with the density of the trees and the fact that she understood left and right better than she grasped east and west, she hesitated.

Maybe Frog had left the vicinity anyhow.

People like him, people without ties, didn't stay too very long in one place, did they?

She followed a bend around the trees. She had the weird feeling that she was alone in all the world.

She followed the bank of the wash, carefully clambering around boulders and rubble. Silences and shadows stalked her. The funnel in the land curved again and when she stopped she realized she was very close to where the Summers lived.

Which was where Denny was bound to be right now. Why did that suddenly worry her? Because Denny is not himself, she thought. He is not the same boy I first came up here with—and this perception, which surprised her, caused her to shiver. It didn't matter what Dr. Max said, it didn't matter that the boy had been given a clean bill of health, because when you got right down to it a mother's instinct was worth a damn sight more than the eye of a distracted physician, and that's what Max was—distracted, distant, functioning on what she thought of as automatic pilot.

On an impulse, she took a detour.

When she came to the clearing she saw the small log house before her. In the branches of a tree a bird shrieked.

That house, Louise thought. It looked so damned gloomy to her now, so washed out, bleak under a sunless sky.

She moved through the clearing, noticing differences around her. The Summers—presumably with Dennis's help as unpaid labor—had made their yard as tidy as it could possibly be, given all the junk lying around. Wood had been sorted into a neat pile. The sprawling collection of tires had been transformed into a pyramid. Rolls of chicken wire were neatly stacked. Everything was in its place, almost as if there were some design intended here, a pattern that perhaps only the Summers might understand.

She paused, gazing at the house.

Drab, she thought. It hadn't looked so drab before. It didn't matter that flowers were blooming around the porch, that the windows were clean, that the porch itself—which used to slope—had been shored up with fresh planks of pine, the place was still drab.

She moved in the direction of the porch.

There was the incongruous sound of music, scratchy music filtering out of the house. It was a polka. Louise couldn't remember its name, but it was faintly recognizable. She hated polkas, hated the forced jollity of them. She hated them now especially. And then there was another noise—laughter. It floated down toward her. Simple clear laughter. It sounded so . . . incongruous. Laughter in the gloom. A polka emerging from the shadows.

She climbed the steps to the porch.

From the doorway she peered inside the gloomy kitchen. She felt vibrations underfoot and then, as her eyes grew accustomed to the dim light, she saw—Dick and Charlotte dancing.

Charlotte had an arm around Dick's waist and her head was thrown back and she was laughing even as she moved her feet nimbly, quickly, to the crazy rhythm of the music. Dick clapped his hands and Charlotte danced around him. Louise, amazed by the outburst of energy, didn't move for a while. There was a vitality here, a sense of life being lived with gaiety. The music forced itself inside her head.

Where was Denny? She couldn't see her son. She stepped inside the kitchen, knocking on the door. But the music smothered any sound she made.

And Dick and Charlotte danced on, around and around, the old woman kicking up her heels and Dick smacking the palms of his hands together. The floor of the kitchen shook. Plates trembled on shelves.

They don't see me, Louise thought. I don't exist. Only the dance is real.

The ribbon in Charlotte's hair flew backward as she whirled and her mouth was open in laughter and her dark hair flopped untidily, wildly, while she spun around her husband's body. *Dark* hair? Louise wondered.

The music stopped. The silence was sudden, eerie. Dick and Charlotte collapsed against one another and Louise had a sudden insight into the love they felt—it came at her out of nowhere, with all the ferocity of an arrow. A perpetual love, she thought. Undeniable and strong, something that the passage of time didn't erode. A love that rejuvenated these old people.

She blinked in the dim kitchen. All around her everything was clean, sparkling, tidy. Even the old Acme stove, which had been crusted with spillage, shone in the corner of the room.

Where was Denny? she wondered.

"Louise!" Charlotte said. "We didn't hear you."

Dick smiled at Louise. Charlotte ran a hand across her hair, which, Louise saw now, wasn't quite as dark as it had seemed. It was gray, streaked with darker strands. It comes out of a bottle, Louise thought. It's a dye, a cosmetic. She wants to make herself look younger for her husband. That's what it is. That's what it comes down to. Love's little vanity—nobody in love should ever age.

"I hope I didn't interrupt," Louise said.

"Of course you didn't," Dick said. He was panting a little. His chest rose and fell. Louise moved farther inside the kitchen.

She saw now how the Summers were dressed. Dick wore a rather formal dark suit and Charlotte was dressed in a long white dress into which had been crocheted the most amazing floral detail. Louise couldn't help herself —she simply had to reach out and touch it. She fingered the flowers, feeling the upraised petals, the sinewy stalks.

"I made it," Charlotte said.

"It's beautiful," Louise said. And it was. The details were astonishing. She stepped back, admiring it.

It was the gown Charlotte Summer had been wearing in the photograph.

Louise looked around the kitchen, but there was no sign of her son. How could it be the same gown? It had to be a replica, a duplicate, because the original would be yellowed by this time, wouldn't it? Why would Charlotte Summer go to the trouble of duplicating a garment she'd worn—how long ago? How many years ago?

"She worked hard on it," Dick was saying.

"I can tell," Louise said. *Where's Denny?*

"It took a while," Charlotte remarked.

"She enjoys working with her hands," Dick added, his voice proud.

Her hands, Louise thought.

Right then Charlotte had her hands behind her back, hidden out of sight.

"Is . . ." Louise was about to ask where Dennis was when she stopped. There was a sound from the stairs and she looked up into the gloom, seeing Dennis descend slowly. What was he doing up there? He appeared halfway down, his hand on the rail.

"Mom," he said, bored.

"I was just passing. Thought I'd say hello . . ."

Dennis smiled weakly. His hand gripped the rail. He looked at the Summers and asked, "Do you want me to change the record?" His voice was hoarse.

That's it, Louise thought. The phonograph is up there and Dennis is the deejay. That's it. She squinted at her son. He looked—she struggled for the right word—depressed? Unhappy? Maybe the Summers had told him they were planning a trip and the information had made him miserable. Maybe he was already anticipating his loneliness. There was a strange little reversal of roles going on here, she thought. It was Dennis who was down and the Summers who were up. Before, when he'd first started to visit them, she'd had the impression that *he* was the one bringing a certain cheer into *their* lives—but it was different now, it had shifted.

Dennis reached the foot of the stairs.

Charlotte said, "I don't think we have the strength to dance anymore."

"Sure we do," Dick said. "Put on something lively, Dennis."

Dennis nodded and climbed the stairs again and Louise watched him ascend slowly, carefully, into the shadows. After a moment music floated down. Another polka. Charlotte and Dick danced again.

As if she had ceased to exist for them, as if the dance had consumed them to the exclusion of all else, Louise turned away and went out onto the porch and moved across the clearing. The polka tracked her, sharp little notes pecking around her head like a flock of demented birds.

39 Inside the tiled corridor of the nursing home, Metger asked the nurse at the desk which room Florence Hann occupied. The nurse was a middle-aged woman with dyed platinum hair and a huge chest, presumably held up by a cantilevered bra. She ruffled papers and looked at the sheriff.

"Twenty-three," the woman said. "Just along the corridor from your father, Sheriff."

"I'm going up to see her."

The nurse smiled. She had immaculately capped teeth—she might have had a forty-watt bulb in her mouth. "She's probably sleeping, Sheriff. Came in very early this morning, I believe. Had some kind of breakdown, I gather."

"I bet she did," Metger mumbled.

The nurse watched him stride toward the stairs.

Metger climbed up, taking the steps two at a time. Outside the door of room eighteen, he hesitated. He heard a TV play inside his father's room. *Their cases are remarkably similar.* . . . Florence Hann and his own father, neighbors in the Loony Palace. Two people who had both been well at one moment, then sick at the next—how had such a thing happened?

Don't think, Jerry. You don't want to know.

But his mind came back again and again, as a moth will circle the candle of its own doom, to the notion that both Florence Hann and his father had been—*had been* deliberately made sick by Ronson or Ronson's cronies, made sick and brought to this wretched place with their brains fused, where they might spend the rest of their days as harmlessly confused vegetables.

Victims, Metger thought, of the people who run Carnarvon, the keepers of the secrets.

Metger continued down the hallway. He knocked on the door of twenty-three. Receiving no answer, he went inside anyhow.

Florence Hann lay on the bed, arms clasped in front of her body, her eyes shut. She was breathing in a very shallow way and her face was bleached of color. What she reminded him of was a corpse he'd once seen fished out of Canyon Lake after having been in the water for four long days. He approached the woman, pulled a chair up to the bed, sat down.

"Florence"—in a whisper.

Zero.

He reached out and touched the back of her hand. He'd never felt flesh so cold. *Some kind of breakdown.* He took his fingers away from her.

"Florence," he whispered again.

Nothing.

How had it been done? An injection of some kind? Heavy drugs? But they wouldn't last forever, would they? They'd wear off sooner or later and Florence would be coherent again—so what then?

An operation. Open the skull, a small incision, a tiny knife. Was Lou Pelusi the technician? Was that the way it worked? Did Ronson and his cronies see danger in a dotty woman like Mrs. Hann and a garrulous old guy like his own father? Were they enemies of the status quo? Yeah, Metger thought, a pair of revolutionaries, terrorists bent on bringing down the delicate system known as Carnarvon. And so they were silenced. And so they were shut in these awful rooms for the rest of their lives—senility, nervous breakdowns, convenient labels easily attached.

Jerry Metger stood up. Florence Hann was motionless. He turned away, went out into the corridor. He stepped into his father's room.

Stanley Metger didn't look up.

"Dad," he said.

Metger felt useless. "Dad," he said again. "Before you got sick . . . did Ted Ronson come to see you? Did Lou Pelusi visit you? Did he give you anything? A drug? Anything like that?"

Hopeless questions—why bother asking them?

He wasn't going to get anything answered here.

Metger tried to imagine himself as a small boy sitting up in his bed while Stanley—half drunk, a cigarette staining his fingers orange-brown—told him a story in that rambling way he always used. Did I tell you about the time Taffy Owens decided to steal the Carnarvon Baptist Church? Not the collection plate, Jerry. Not the Bibles. Not the stained-glass window. No, nothing so small, Taffy wanted to steal the *whole goddamn church*! He went down there in the middle of the night with a big wagon and a team of horses and a couple of guys to help him out and they tried to get that church up on the wagon and haul the sucker right outta town—all because Taffy decided the preacher was an asshole! Tried to steal the whole *church*, Jerry! Taffy Owens never thought small. Didn't know the meaning of the word!

Stories, Metger thought. All those old narratives that adhered to his father the way glue sticks to wood. And he'd wanted to write them down in book form.

Jerry Metger gazed at the TV. There was a cartoon showing a cat flattened by a bulldozer. The sound effects were shrill. Stanley was looking at it without really seeing it.

"Dad," Metger said. "I need to know . . ."

Stanley Metger poked a finger inside his mouth, brought out a scrap of food, and wiped it against his pants.

Did you ever write your stories down, Dad? Did you put them on paper? Did you write down something that certain people in this town didn't want to read, something that revealed the secrets? Was that it? All these questions—and Jerry Metger wasn't going to get an answer to any one of them.

He leaned forward and kissed his father on the side of the face and the older man—as if some faint memory moved inside him—caught the sheriff by the wrist.

"You be careful," Stanley Metger said.

"Why?"

"Because."

"Because what?"

Stanley shut his eyes.

"Because they'll come and take your fucking candies away from you, boy."

Metger sighed and moved toward the door.

He glanced once across the room, seeing his father silhouetted against the gray window, and then he left.

A bird hopped overhead, chattered, rose up into the cold sky. Louise watched it go.

She continued to walk. The forest nudged against her with a pressure she could feel. The wash curved once more.

She pushed her hands into the pockets of her pale blue jeans. Cold air cut through the folds of her plaid flannel shirt.

She continued along the wash and wondered if she'd gone off in the wrong direction. But she'd tracked the hollow in the land religiously—so how come she didn't hear the sound of the stream Frog had mentioned?

She slithered over pebbles. The wash was becoming narrower the farther she walked. There were more tiny stones inside her sneakers and they rolled under the soles of her feet, but she didn't stop now to remove them.

She wished the sun would fill this landscape with the comfort of warmth, but it remained a cold flat cloudy disk of white on the horizon.

She kept moving. The wash, although deeper, was now so narrow that it was little more than a gash in the earth. Then she thought she heard the distant noise of sluggish water. A rattling, a slow sloughing over stones.

Quite abruptly the trees thinned out and she found herself on the low bank of a stream. Green, opaque water, its surface scummy against the bank, flowed slowly past. Water beetles skidded back and forth and some kind of swift birds—more bats than birds, she thought—darted against the dark surface before they disappeared.

East. West.

She followed the bank for a while. The VW was parked on an incline, thirty or forty feet away from the stream, an incongruous contraption out here in the pines.

She went toward it and called out Frog's name. The side doors of the van were open and some of Frog's belongings lay around the vehicle. A Coleman stove and some cooking utensils and a plastic container of Dove dishwashing liquid.

"Frog?"

She went around to the front of the van.

"Frog?"

She looked in, seeing tattered upholstery. Some kind of charm hung from the rearview mirror—a small fuzzy thing on a string. It was a frog—what else?—with large protruding eyes. A child's toy.

"Frog?"

She stuck her head inside the van.

There was a pile of blankets, a pillow, a couple of flies buzzing in the white sunlight that streaked inside the van. She saw a bottle of Old Spice, hair conditioner, Head & Shoulders Shampoo, toothpaste.

And for a moment she had the bizarre, unsettling feeling that she was taking an inventory of a dead man's estate. That Frog was somewhere nearby, lying dead and neglected, maybe facedown in the stream.

She stepped away from the van.

Some aspect of the sun slanted at broken angles through the trees. She called Frog's name again. She heard a sound close to her and she swung around.

Frog was coming up the bank from the stream, moving toward her.

"Hi," she said.

At the top of the bank he paused, looking in her direction. Then he moved again, silent in such a way that the quiet he carried hung around his body like an extra shadow.

"Hi there," she said again.

Now he was only a few feet away.

"Louise," he said.

His face was thin and his eyes vacant and his smile odd—it might have been someone else's expression fixed there.

"Are you okay, Frog?" she asked. His appearance surprised her.

He gazed at her curiously. "What do you mean?"

"I don't know," and she shrugged, because she didn't really know—there was just something out of synch. His face lacked color and his hair—usually held back neatly in a ponytail—fell without luster over his shoulders. Strands were matted, unwashed. Streaks of dirt smeared his T-shirt and his bare feet were grubby. He looked as if he'd fallen into the stream.

Now he poked around inside his van, stuck a tape into his cassette deck. The music was loud and Neanderthal—it was an old recording of The Who.

Substitute, me for him
Substitute, my coke for gin . . .

He increased the volume and the whole van vibrated. He sat down on the ground beside the passenger door and beat his fingertips in the soil in time to the music.

He lay back now, his hands clasped behind his head, his eyes fixed to the sky. His voice a flat monotone, he said, "I got sick, Louise. I got pretty sick. But I'm okay now."

He turned his face toward her and smiled and she thought she'd seen that look before—way back, back when she'd been a student and everybody around her was dropping this or that kind of drug and people went around in a haze for day after goddamn day. Was that it? Had Frog taken a bad drug? The music blasting out of the van drowned her thoughts. She wanted to go inside and turn the damn thing off so that she could talk to him.

"How did you get sick?" she asked.

"Huh?"

"You said you got sick, Frog! How?" Louise was shouting to be heard.

He cupped a hand to his ear. "I guess it was something I ate."

> *The simple things you see are all complicated*
> *I look pretty young but I'm just backdated . . .*

"Maybe we could get Max to take a look at you, Frog."

He shook his head. "I'm okay now. I'm in prime condition."

"You might have food poisoning," she said. "You ought to let Max examine you."

"Uh-huh," and he dismissed the suggestion. He lay flat on his back and looked up at the sky. Louise thought, I came up here to see him, I came this way for sympathy, for friendship—and somehow he's lost to me. She had wanted, even in an indirect fashion, to talk to Frog about Max and Connie Harrison, her suspicions, her fears, that whole bit. But now . . . her sense of loneliness was suddenly an acute thing. She stared bleakly toward the trees. The music from the van throbbed through her.

Frog coughed. He sat up and covered his mouth with his hand. When the spasm was over he lay back down again. I don't exist for him, Louise thought. I might as well not be here. She glanced at him, dismayed by his appearance. Even the lids of his eyes seemed transparent to her now—she saw frail blue veins beneath the surface of the skin.

"I don't care what you say, Frog. Somebody ought to examine you."

The music stopped. The forest was silent.

Suddenly Frog said, "I went to see the Summers. And you know something? They're really okay people."

Louise looked at the man. She had the impression of somebody locked into a fever, somebody whose train of thought was forever being derailed. She saw Frog lick his lips, which were dry and pale. How gaunt he looked—he seemed more bone than flesh. She had the urge to cradle him against her body and nurse him back to health.

"We drank tea," he said.

"Tea?"

"Dandelion tea." Frog smiled in a thin way. "They told me they would have all kinds of work for me to do around their place. At the end of summer, they said. When they return."

Louise was silent. She plucked a blade of grass from the ground and held it against her lips. Tea with Dick and Charlotte. Dandelion tea yet.

Frog tugged on his little beard, cleared his throat. "They're really okay. I could learn a lot from them, Louise. They know this forest. They know an incredible amount about all this. . . ." He gestured with his hand, indicating the vast reaches of the trees.

She looked into his eyes. His pupils were dark and enormous. The irises were mere pale rims. Learn what? she wondered. And where was the Frog who'd used the term "Wrinkle City"? The Frog who'd entertained her with his banter? Where was that man now?

Dandelion tea. She stared toward the trees.

Frog said, "Good people. Let me tell you. They make fine tea."

Fine tea and excellent cookies and amazing apple pies and fudge and it doesn't stop there with their culinary wonders—no, they baby-sit at the drop of a hat and they cut Denny's hair and they give little presents like photographs and Wonder Bait and they dance, God they dance, Frog, how they dance, you should see them.

"They're going on a honeymoon," Frog said.

"A honeymoon?"

"They're in love."

"I don't doubt that. But a *honeymoon?*"

"Love has no age, Louise," and Frog grinned in a beatific way. It was a look she'd seen on one of her old girlfriends, Sally Haskowitz, who'd given up her studies at UCLA and followed the Maharishnu and had panhandled, for the greater good of the guru and his fleet of Rolls-Royces, in airport terminals and on street corners. Poor Sally. Poor Frog. What in the name of God had he eaten?

"Love has no age," he said again. "The Summers are living proof of that."

The old Frog would have been skeptical, mocking himself for uttering such a thing. The old Frog—what did that mean? Who was this person she was sitting with now? She reached out and rubbed his arm. A honeymoon? The idea was preposterous, and yet she wasn't quite sure why—Charlotte, the dancing Charlotte, had looked like a girl, for God's sake. And Dick, in his darkly formal suit—what else did he resemble but the beau who came calling? The Summers. Dick and Charlotte. Why did she find herself suddenly disliking them? It had something to do with Denny, how Denny had looked back at their house, anxious to please them, scurrying up and down the stairs to change their music for them, his voice hoarse and his breathing labored. Something to do with that. He looked like some pale facsimile of himself. Just the way Frog does right now. She turned the thought aside. The Summers would be gone soon. Away. On their absurd honeymoon.

"Why don't you walk back with me to my house?" she asked. "We can sit down and have some of that good coffee you like." She paused. Why was she talking to him the way she'd talk to a very small kid?

"I don't feel like moving."

"Please, Frog."

He shook his head.

She was silent for a long time. Frog goes to see the Summers. They drink dandelion tea. And then Frog gets sick. Was that the sequence of events? Why would she think that? She gazed across the stream and into the trees.

Something was churning at the back of her mind, something inarticulable, a movement of specters. She saw once again the sight of Dick and Charlotte caught up in their frenzied polka. Then she remembered the slow-motion old couple they'd been when she'd first met them.

How did you effect such a transformation? *Love has no age, Louise.* Blah blah blah—what had turned Frog into such a Pollyanna? Now she thought of her son going up the stairs in the Summers' home, shuffling as he moved, his hand squeaking on the rail while he climbed. What had happened to all his energy?

She took a cigarette out of her jeans and lit it, gazing down to the stream, watching the steady flow of slow water.

Frog stared up at the sky, saying nothing. And Louise thought how lonely she really was with Frog acting like this. How alone. How empty.

And very unhappy.

Frog watched her lazily.

"I'm going home," she said. "When you feel up to it, Frog, come over."

"How's Denny?"

"Okay . . ." she lied.

"Dick and Charlotte really like him, you know. They have this picture of him in their living room. What they call their parlor."

"Picture? You mean a photograph?" Louise asked.

"Like one of those school shots. You know the kind? It sits on the mantelpiece. It's framed."

A school photo? Louise wondered.

Where would Dick and Charlotte get a picture of Denny? How could they possess something like that? Puzzled, she gazed into Frog's face. "You sure it's Denny?"

"Hey, I know what I saw, Louise."

"You said it looked a school picture, didn't you?"

"Yeah. The kind that makes the kid look like he's made out of plastic," and Frog smiled.

She shook her head. "They must have taken it themselves," she said.

"I doubt it. Looks like a studio job to me," Frog replied. "Looks professional. Check it out for yourself if you don't believe me. Anyhow, what's the big deal?"

Louise moved away. *A photograph of Denny, what's the big deal?* echoed in her throbbing brain.

She walked close to the stream, which trapped murky images of the sky. A framed photograph of her son. Why did that bother her?

She turned to look back at Frog. Sitting cross-legged beside his van, he wasn't even gazing in her direction.

40

Charlotte sat in front of the big dressing-table mirror inside her bedroom. Before her lay a variety of tubes and pots and little brushes: creams, lipsticks, eye makeup. She leaned close to her reflection and then, with lavish care, began to paint her face. She puckered her lips, applied the tube of lipstick, drawing a thick red line. And then, using a small brush, she dusted her cheeks with pink blush.

Dennis watched all this. Sometimes he caught his own reflection in the mirror. He shuffled his feet in the rug.

Fetch this. Do that. Change the record. Make tea.

All morning long the Summers had talked to him the way they might have ordered a servant around. And now he was simply standing there waiting for further instructions. Why weren't they being kind to him the way they usually were? Why were they treating him like this? If it hadn't been for the lousy way he felt in general—his aching chest, the odd numbness in his hands, the way his eyes hurt—he might have had the strength to be even more offended than he was. Maybe they just didn't want him hanging around today, although he couldn't think why that would be the case. Maybe they were tired of him—after all, he'd been coming here every day. People needed a break from company at times, didn't they? They wanted to be alone. It was as if he didn't exist except as a somebody to perform little tasks for them.

But they'd always been good to him and he felt he owed them something and so he stood around waiting for them to impose a function on him.

Charlotte looked at him in the mirror.

Dennis turned his eyes down to the floor. He could hear Dick coming up the stairs. Dennis pulled on his fingers, cracking the bones in his knuckles. A few flakes of his dried skin floated to the floor.

Dick appeared in the doorway, humming a quiet tune through his closed lips. He stared at Dennis. "There's some final things need doing to the truck, boy."

Dennis moved his body slightly. There was a short stabbing pain in his hips.

"Let's get out there and take a look."

"Sure," Dennis answered.

He followed Dick down the stairs. Charlotte, her face covered with makeup, her lips bright red and her eyes dark with shadow and her cheeks glowing, descended after them.

All three went out onto the porch, where the potted flowers bloomed richly and the leaves of plants were waxen and healthy. Dennis looked out at the Dodge.

"Let's get this show on the road," Dick said.

Dennis rubbed his fingers together and slowly followed Dick across the yard to where the pickup stood—gleaming and white and wonderful and as waxy as any of the plants on the porch.

Charlotte stood watching her husband and the boy as they dickered around under the upraised hood of the truck. After a moment there was the satisfying sound of the motor turning over. She smiled, clasping her hands in front of her white gown.

She felt it happen suddenly. She had been expecting it, but even so it took her by surprise.

It was moist and warm between her legs. She felt it trickle against her inner thighs. The warm discharges of her womb.

She shut her eyes. Bliss.

She went back indoors, locking herself inside the bathroom.

41 It was not the best of ideas, Max told himself. It was not the most worthy of notions—stepping out of the empty house and getting inside the Volvo and driving to Carnarvon and searching for the place known as the Huckleberry Inn, but he was doing it

anyhow. Floating along on a cocktail of Valium and Darvon, washed down by a double scotch, he felt he could keep the situation at bay with these fortifications. His driving was a little erratic. He almost ran the station wagon into a ditch near the Ace of Spades and when he hit Carnarvon he failed to see a stoplight and he ran through the intersection quickly, drawing harsh stares from pedestrians who were milling around all the nifty little boutiques of the town. And then he became confused, losing himself in cobbled streets, bedazzled by colored parasols outside shops selling iced yogurt and fashionable ice creams and little terraced pubs where tourists sipped their drinks and breathed the good air inside their city lungs. It was not, he told himself again, a wise notion to be here. What was he going to do anyhow? What was he going to say to Connie?

Dazed by his chemical imbalance, he found the Huckleberry Inn beyond the shopping precinct, a squat building constructed mainly of glass and erected on stilts, so that it seemed to perch precariously in midair, looking rather like a surreal oceangoing liner. He parked the Volvo, squeezing it with some difficulty between a Jaguar and a Porsche, and he got out—unsteady on his feet, he noticed, his motor reflexes functioning at a low level.

Inside the lobby of the inn, a grand foyer with a fountain trickling in the middle of the floor and a uniformed doorman scrutinizing everything that moved, Max went to the reception desk and asked for Connie's room number. He was instructed to call her on the house phone because it was the policy of the Huckleberry—so the red-faced clerk told him—not to give out room numbers to any Tom, Dick, or Harry who asked.

He found a white telephone and asked for Mrs. Harrison and after a moment he heard Connie's voice on the line.

"I'm downstairs," Max said.

"Come on up. Room one zero seven. Second floor. And hurry."

Hurry, Max thought. Indecent haste. He climbed the stairs to the second floor and when he found room one zero seven he paused. What the fuck was he doing, running to this woman who had threatened to tear his goddamn marriage apart? What am I but a simple GP, happily married, with some kind of career ahead of me? What am I doing, rushing like a schoolboy to his first encounter in a hotel? Writing prescriptions for myself? What the hell am I doing with my life?

Connie opened the door before Max had time to knock. She was wearing her hair up on top of her head, piled there in a series of little curls; he'd never seen it that way before. She was dressed in a black mini-skirt and knee-length black boots and a string of red glassy gems hung around her neck. She had very little makeup on her face. It was subtle—a touch of eyeliner, a dim suggestion of shadow, and that was it. Max was filled with an old hunger, despite himself and any good intentions he might have had. He reached out and drew her toward him and when they kissed he lost himself in her touch.

She drew away from him. She sat down on the bed, taking off her boots.

Her perfume, the fragrance of lemon, assailed him.

"You almost gave me a heart attack," he said.

Connie smiled. "In the restaurant, you mean?"

"You know what I mean."

"Ah," she said. She kicked the boots across the room and laughed. "I don't give up easily. I stick to things. I have a stubborn streak this wide," and she spread her hands like an angler indicating the size of the one that got away.

"It wasn't a judicious thing to do, Connie. What the hell are you doing here?" *Judicious*—what kind of word was that? He gazed at her bare legs, at how shadows formed in her thighs. "First you call me. Next thing, you show up in Carnarvon. How in God's name am I supposed to explain all that to my wife?"

"She probably imagines we're having an affair," Connie Harrison said, her voice filled with mock innocence. She lay back. She was wearing nothing under her mini-skirt. Max had to look elsewhere for a moment, even as he was conscious of how she was spreading her legs and allowing her fingers to rest against her thighs. What are you here for, Max? he asked himself. To end this nefarious business? Or to make love to this woman?

"I'm amazed by your cunning," he said. "What do you really want? You'd like me to leave my family? Throw everything up for you?"

Connie didn't speak.

"You really screwed things up," Max said.

"You poor thing. Did I put you in a bad place?"

"Yeah. Very bad. I've been struggling to reassure Louise." Max turned back to face the woman. "It isn't exactly easy."

"So why bother?"

"Because she happens to be my wife and because we happen to have a kid—"

"You're so old-fashioned." And Connie frowned, gazing past Max at some point on the wall.

"Look, before you came along . . ." He let his sentence fade out. He felt wretched, uneasy, being here in this place with Connie, seeing her lie there with her knees upraised and her legs apart and her short skirt lifted up to

her thighs. He also felt, in some other way, excited—such were the con-
tradictions of The Big Dilemma. What was he supposed to do? He could
bury himself between Connie's legs and in that place all problems would,
at least on a temporary basis, resolve themselves in a brief amnesia. He paced
around the room, conscious of how her eyes followed him. He saw her stretch
to the bedside table and find a cigarette, and her skirt rose up. He went
back and took her in his arms.

She moved out of his embrace. "I don't want to ruin your marriage," she
said.

"You could have fooled me."

"Seriously, Max." Her voice was unusually solemn now, dry and serious
in a way that surprised him.

"If you don't want to do a demolition number on my life, then why the
hell are you here in Carnarvon?" he asked. Tell her to go, Max. Tell her
it's over. Finito. The End. His hand fell against her thigh.

"What do you think of me, Max? I mean, what do you *really* think?"

He smiled. "It keeps changing. It's always in flux. I can't answer that
question properly. I think about you a lot of the time. Sometimes what I
feel is downright dread. At other times there's this intense longing for you."
He shrugged. It wasn't a satisfactory answer to a somewhat unexpected
question, but it was honest, the best he thought he could do.

The girl got up from the bed and walked to the window, where she looked
out for a time, smoking her cigarette. Max watched her. Without turning
to him, she said, "I like you. I genuinely like you, Max. I'm not so sure I
care so much for myself. . . ."

Why was she so solemn?

"I shouldn't have come here," she said.

Max walked across the floor toward her.

"It was wrong to come up here," and she shook her head from side to
side. "Look at the way I'm dressed, Max. The black mini-skirt. Those boots.
Look at me. I feel like some kind of cheap hooker."

He placed his hands on her shoulders—why was she talking this way?
Guilt? Second thoughts about their entire relationship? He didn't understand
the sudden change in her mood. When he'd first come through the door,
everything had been different—the way she'd welcomed him, her provocation
in lying back across the bed and kicking her boots off and touching herself,
arousing him. But now. What was going on now?

"I feel sorry for your wife," she said.

"Connie—"

"This is a sham, Max. A fucking sham."

"What is?" Perplexed, he realized Connie was moving away from him yet again, slipping out from beneath his hands and going back across the room where she paused by the bed and swung her face around to look at him.

"A sham," he echoed. "I don't understand."

"You're not supposed to."

"Connie, you're losing me."

"That's the whole idea."

Max sighed, spread his hands out. "I was never good with conundrums, sweetheart."

Connie Harrison sat down, lit another cigarette. "I'm not a home wrecker, Max. It doesn't come easy to me. Do you understand that? And what you called cunning a moment ago—that doesn't come easy to me either, Max."

He nodded. There was a strange little lump in his throat and his mouth was very dry. He realized he wanted a drink. He went to the tiny refrigerator in the corner of the room, opened it, found a couple of miniatures of liquor. He snapped one of them open, without bothering to read the label, and he drank straight out of the small bottle. Rum. It smarted at the back of his throat. What the hell was Connie trying to tell him?

"Maybe if you could spell this out for me," he suggested. He tossed the empty miniature inside the wastebasket.

Connie Harrison sighed. "It isn't easy."

"Try."

"It's been a lie from the beginning."

"What has?" Bewildered, Max sat down. He hated narrative of events that lost him, made him founder.

"You. Me." She had a Kleenex in one hand and she was crumpling it uneasily. "I genuinely thought I could go through with it. I thought it would be the simplest thing in the world." She paused. Max stared at her.

"I'm still in the dark," he said. "I don't know what you're trying to tell me."

"What do you know about me, Max?"

"You're a graduate assistant at City College. English Department. You're divorced—"

"You know only what I told you."

"I didn't go hire a private detective to check you out, Connie." Max smiled weakly. Where was this leading anyhow?

"Max," she said. "I don't even know where City College is! I couldn't find it without a goddamn map, Max. And I've never been married. Lies, Max. Lies. One after the other. I made all that up."

"Why?"

Connie Harrison moved to where he sat. She went down on her knees and took one of his hands, clasping it between her own, then laid her face against the side of his leg. He reached out to touch her hair. She'd lied— so what? He wasn't altogether an innocent in that department himself. "You must have had a good reason—"

"Yeah. The best," she replied. "Only I can't follow the whole thing through."

"Follow what?" Max asked. "What whole thing are you talking about?"

Connie Harrison clutched the fabric of her black skirt. "I guess it happened when I saw your wife's face in the restaurant. See, up until then, she'd been an abstraction. A name. I didn't know what she looked like. And then I saw her and I guess that's when it happened. . . ."

Max raised his hands in exasperation. Around and around, going nowhere—what was she driving at? He felt a sense of slippage. Was she, in her own roundabout manner, telling him the whole thing was over just because she'd seen Louise? Was that it? He wasn't sure what to feel, whether relief or pain.

Connie opened the small refrigerator and removed a can of ginger ale. She popped it open. She sipped a little, dabbed her lips with the Kleenex. "It paid well, that's the best I can say about the whole thing."

Paid well? Max gripped her wrist. "What the hell are you talking about? Paid well? What is that supposed to mean?"

"Money, Max. Cash."

"Money."

"The first payment was five hundred dollars. I needed cash. What does an out-of-work actress do, Max? I was waiting tables. I wanted out of that."

"Wait. Hold on." Max let her arm go. An actress?

"The second payment was another five hundred," she said.

Max shook his head from side to side. "Somebody gave you money—"

"You got it. Somebody gave me money."

"For what?"

Connie Harrison was very quiet. She looked at Max and he couldn't tell if her expression were pity or regret or some other emotion he just couldn't identify.

"For what?" he asked again.

"To sleep with you."

"You're joking."

"I don't have the kind of humor you'd call weird," she said. "I'm not joking."

"I don't see it. I don't get it."

"Don't ask me to explain it all, Max, because I'm not sure I understand it myself. The guy said he wanted me to interfere with your marriage. Okay? He said he wanted the whole marriage shaken up. He said he needed to drive a wedge between you and your wife. He wanted the marriage . . . Look, I don't remember the exact words he used."

"What guy?" Max asked.

Connie didn't answer the question. "A crisis. Something like that. He wanted a crisis in your marriage. Something that would cause chaos. Something to distract you and Louise. Listen, I didn't stop to ask about his motives. I took the money and I performed my duties and I think I did that side of it pretty well."

"Who are you talking about, for God's sake?"

She crushed the aluminum can in her hand. "I can't follow through, that's the trouble. I'm supposed to go see Louise and tell her about our . . . affair. Specific details, dates and places—those are my instructions. Like I say, I can't goddamn do it!"

Max asked the question again. *"What guy?"*

"Your tenant," she answered this time. "The man who lives in your house."

Max was silent for a long time. A darkness crossed his mind, eclipsed his thoughts. He didn't even hear Connie Harrison telling him how sorry she was, didn't listen to the flow of her words, didn't feel her hand as she laid it against the side of his face. Because nothing made sense. Nothing added up. Nothing computed. What faced him was an abacus whose beads kept slipping from the wires, making any calculation impossible.

The girl had to be lying. That's what it came down to. She *had to be lying.*

He said so.

Connie looked hurt. "Why would I make anything like that up, Max? I've told you the truth. I've told you everything. I could've gone on with the whole scheme. I could have gone to see your wife, the way he wanted me to. But I didn't, did I? I didn't have the heart for the rest of it."

"It doesn't make any fucking sense," Max said.

Connie Harrison shrugged. "My feelings exactly."

"Why would Zmia want to . . . what were those words you used?"

"Chaos. Distraction."

"Why would he want to introduce chaos into my life?" Max walked the room—his puzzlement had given way to a shapeless anger, something that lay unfocused inside him. He was angry with the girl for misleading him.

Angry with himself. Angry with Zmia. And with the game, the strange game of deception that was going on. "Why would he want my marriage to be in a state of crisis?"

Connie Harrison sat on the bed. "I'm sorry, Max."

"I bet you are."

"I don't blame you for being angry."

Max went to the window, clenched his hands, raised them up to the pane. Why why why—he couldn't bring himself to look at the woman now. All the things he'd ever said to her, all the intimacies they'd ever shared, these things made him feel utterly foolish, totally used. What was this strange alliance of Professor Zmia and Connie Harrison, waitress and unemployed actress?

"How did Zmia find you?"

"He came to the place where I was working," she answered. "We got talking. He can be quite charming, you know. He came back a few times. One thing led to another. He knew I needed money. . . ." She put a hand to her mouth. "I thought I could be more cold-blooded than I am, Max."

"You've been cold-blooded enough," he snapped at her.

She smoothed her skirt over her thighs. "I don't blame you for saying that. The trouble is, I started to like you. I was only instructed to seduce you. Liking you wasn't part of the strategy."

"Strategy," Max said, his voice filled with scorn. "I don't see any goddamn reason for all this."

"Zmia didn't mention any either. I can't help you there."

"Goddamn it. Goddamn you and him." Bluster, Max thought. Bluster and confusion and outrage. He felt as a laboratory animal might—led inside a labyrinth and manipulated by flashing lights, bells, and ultimate rewards. In this case, Connie Harrison's willing body. But what kind of experiment was it intended to be? He slammed his hands together.

What did Zmia want?

The question went around and around in his mind, trapped there like a god-awful echo.

"There's one other thing," Connie said. "I don't know what it means exactly."

Max looked at her. What else could there be?

"He asked me to make a delivery for him."

"A delivery?"

"Yeah," she said.

He was silent. The tension inside him was intolerable.

"It seemed perfectly harmless," she said.

"I'm listening."

Connie lit a cigarette.

Then she told him.

42 Louise stepped inside the house. She was thinking about Frog still, the way she'd been thinking about him all the way back through the forest. She went inside the kitchen, heated up some old coffee, sat at the table. Distracted, she wondered about the photograph Frog had mentioned.

There was, so she thought, an easy explanation. If the Summers hadn't taken it themselves, then obviously Dennis had given it to them. Didn't that make good sense?

Yes, of course.

Provided the kid had brought his own picture here from San Francisco.

She closed her eyes. She couldn't remember.

Why would Dennis carry a photograph of himself all the way up here? Why would he stash such a thing in his luggage? She couldn't remember ever seeing a photograph. Besides, like any number of kids his age, he was never exactly enamored of having his picture taken and usually did so only under duress. He never expressed much of an interest in the finished result, either, so why *would* he carry a picture in his luggage? Dammit.

Frog wasn't well. Maybe he only thought he'd seen such a thing. She worried about him. On her second cup of coffee, she decided she'd talk to Max about him. Maybe he'd go up through the forest and examine the man. *If he could be bothered.*

Louise moved out into the hallway. From the foot of the stairs she called Max's name. There wasn't an answer. She called a second time.

And then she remembered. In her preoccupation, her absentmindedness, she hadn't really absorbed the fact that the Volvo wasn't in the driveway, which meant Max had gone out, which meant—as far as she was concerned—Carnarvon.

Which meant—that girl. The Huckleberry Inn. Yes, she thought. That's where. She tried to be calm. Carnarvon. Connie Harrison.

She drained her coffee. She smoked a couple of cigarettes in quick succession. Don't think about it. Don't let your imagination run riot. Be good and calm and take it easy! Do something to keep yourself occupied!

What does any housewife do at a time like this, Louise?

They clean, don't they? They look for busywork, which is said to be good for the soul, don't they?

She stepped into Dennis's room. The boy had forgotten to remove the jar of Dick Summer's bait, as she'd known he would. At least it was stoppered, so the smell in the room wasn't altogether unbearable, but the sight of the maggots clinging to the inside of the jar upset her. She moved toward it. She couldn't quite bring herself to handle the thing.

Sighing, she sat down on the edge of the boy's unmade bed. She didn't have the energy to do anything. She shut her eyes and hugged herself and wondered what she could do to fight off the loneliness that assailed her.

This place. This empty house. And then there was Frog, sick but refusing to admit it. Christ, why had they ever come to this place? She wept. It was sudden, a quick collapse, a few tears which she wiped against the cuff of her shirt. She dried her eyes, smiled, tried to shake the mood out of herself. Who needs this?

Not you, Louise.

Everything is going to be . . . *fine.*

She gazed around the kid's room. Crumpled shirts, discarded jeans, socks—everything lay in casual disarray. Would he ever learn to pick up after himself? She moved from the bed, gathered up some clothing, whistled to herself. Inducing cheer, she thought. Welcome to this empty house.

She paused. She listened to the silences. She whistled again. *How did it all go so wrong?*

Not that way, Louise. Think bluebirds and sunshine and nice summery days.

She stopped by the bedside table. She picked up the photograph of Dick and Charlotte and stared at the gown Charlotte was wearing. It was identical to the one she'd been dancing in. What did it all mean? This repetition of clothing. This honeymoon they apparently planned. What did all that mean?

The photograph. Louise turned it over in her hand and wondered how long ago it had been taken. She studied the photographer's name imprinted on the back of the picture, then she stared once more at the faces of Dick and Charlotte Summer. There was, she thought, a dark kind of beauty about Charlotte, and yet it was somehow touched with a sadness, an indefinable sorrow. And Dick's smile, even though it suggested cheerfulness, seemed more than just a little forced, as if he'd had to hold that expression a long time.

She was about to set the picture back on the bedside table when she found herself drawn back down into it, drawn down beyond the faces of Dick and Charlotte, beyond the quay where they stood. There, in the background, was some kind of blurry shadow imposed between the Summers and the steamship, something that must have been moving at the precise moment when the photographer took this picture.

Louise screwed her eyes, held the picture toward the light falling at the window, stared hard. At first she thought it was smoke blown from the funnels of the ship, because it looked more like a shapeless drift of dark cloud than anything else. But when she examined it even more closely she realized that the amorphous shadow had some kind of recognizable form. She watched it emerge from the murky background, watched it take shape in front of her narrowed eyes.

She thought she knew what it was. A horse. A horse hauling some kind of cart, a flurry of motion that had defied the photographer.

Maybe it was pulling luggage for the steamship. Maybe it carried coals for the ship's engine room.

A goddamn horse. When did they stop using horses and start using motorized vehicles? Trucks?

She returned the photograph to its place beneath the bedside lamp, picked up Dennis's discarded clothing, then left the room. A horse, she thought. How old did that make the picture?

She dumped the dirty clothing in the washing machine in the kitchen, then she stood for a long time looking out the window at the pines. The Summers and Dennis must have exchanged photographs, if indeed Dick and Charlotte did have a picture of the boy. Well, wasn't that nice and cozy, tit for tat, trading keepsakes?

She moved listlessly through the house, room to room, upstairs, down, paused once to examine her reflection in the downstairs bathroom, absently noticed tufts of hair adhering to Dennis's hairbrush. She roamed without purpose through the emptiness of this forest house, seeing herself—as if from a place above—as little more than a mere domestic speck, the disenchanted wife, the betrayed woman.

She ran a hand across her face. A project. She needed a project. Maybe she'd brew up some soup and take it up to Frog in a flask. A whole Care Package. She'd be the lady from the Welcome Wagon, Forest Branch. She'd be a regular rustic Florence Nightingale, trudging up through the forest to repair a sick, superannuated hippy. Poor Frog. And his dandelion tea.

She sat down in the living room. An image of Max and Connie Harrison floated through her mind, a little wispy thing she didn't want to pay attention to—a tableau in wax. Max Wax. Was he at this moment humping the woman? Were they both barebacked and clinging sweatily to one another in Connie's room at the Fuckleberry Inn?

Louise rose. The house was silent.

Horse-drawn carts. What was it about horse-drawn carts that came back to her? She went to the liquor cabinet and poured herself a shot of scotch. She felt it spread throughout her body as she drank it. If you could consume enough of this, you'd never need to think about your wandering husband or your absent son or your sick friend out there in the forest. No, you'd have oblivion, for which she could make out a pretty decent case right now.

She strolled to the window. Stood there. Blanked out her mind. Observed the pines. Finished her drink. Poured another.

Then she went inside Dennis's room, took the photograph, and carried it back to the living room, where she propped it up on the mantelpiece.

A horse-drawn cart. An old steamship. A young couple. Guess the date. Pin the tail on the fashion.

Mrs. Louise Untermeyer, of San Francisco, California, this is your chance to win $64,000. . . . Are you ready?

1920?

1910?

Louise shook her head from side to side.

This was absurd. Even so, she continued to stare at the picture. She finished her scotch and uncorked the bottle, pouring herself a third glass somewhat more generous than the previous two. She stood at the mantelpiece. Charlotte and Dick looked out at her.

She saw them as she'd last seen them, caught up in the crazed whirl of the polka. The old couple dancing. As if they might dance forever. And Dennis, Denny lingering in the shadows of the stairs.

She turned away from the picture. Her brain felt fogged. She set her glass down on the coffee table, noticing how she spilled tiny slicks of scotch on the polished wood.

She drew a deep breath, held it. And then she reached out to pick up the telephone.

Lou Pelusi said, "I really don't appreciate you barging into my office, Jerry. I've got patients to see. People are waiting for me."

The sheriff sat down facing Pelusi's desk. He had a look of dark determination on his face—a man, the physician thought, in something of a hurry. Pelusi fingered his Elgin timepiece, stared at the hands, then flipped the lid shut.

"I won't take up too much of your precious time, Lou."

Pelusi stood up. "Is it your wife? Is something wrong with Nora?"

Metger shook his head. "Nora's fine."

"Good." Pelusi moved meaninglessly around his office, his white coat brushing against things. He saw himself pick things up and set them down again, as if the mere act of touching and readjusting gave his movements some kind of significance. He was conscious of Jerry Metger staring at him. He wanted to get out from under that *look* because it was making him uncomfortable. More than uncomfortable—downright *miserable*.

"I don't have a lot of time, Jerry."

The sheriff said nothing for a while.

Pelusi opened and closed the drawer of a filing cabinet. Unnerved, he walked back to his desk and his white coat billowed behind him.

"Florence Hann," Metger said.

Pelusi looked down at his desk calendar. He tore off a sheet, crumpled it. "What about her?"

"It seems she was stricken by a mysterious malady, Lou. I'm interested in hearing your diagnosis."

Pelusi managed a small smile. Florence Hann, he thought. A sense of dread touched him—the small hairs on the back of his neck quivered. A darkness moved in front of his eyes. "She collapsed early this morning," he said. "I haven't made a thorough diagnosis, Jerry. I'll see her later today. I gave her some Thorazine to help her relax, get some sleep. . . ."

"Thorazine," Metger said.

"It's standard," Pelusi remarked. "My educated guess is she's suffering from some kind of strain, some kind of nervous pressure. Like I say, I'll look in on her later, then I'll know more."

Metger touched the butt of his gun lightly. "It's funny," he said. "It's funny how something similar happened to my father. One day he was fine. The next—knock-knock, nobody's at home. Doesn't that strike you as funny, Lou?"

"Coincidence," Pelusi said.

"Yeah. Sure." Metger stared at the papers strewn across Pelusi's desk. Pamphlets from pharmaceutical houses, brochures, notepads, prescription blanks. "How do you explain this coincidence, Lou?"

"What's to explain?"

Metger stood up. "Two healthy adults become zombies overnight—"

Pelusi studied his timepiece again. "You can annoy certain people behaving this way."

"That's what I keep hearing."

Metger was silent for a time.

"I'll go on barking, Lou. And it's going to get louder before I'm through."

Pelusi frowned. He fiddled impatiently with a small metal nail clipper.
He watched Metger go toward the door, where the sheriff stopped and,
smiling, turned his head.

"You know what I wonder, Lou?"

Pelusi said nothing.

"I wonder what they pay you. . . . Mainly, I wonder if it's worth it all
in the end."

And then Metger was gone.

Pelusi gazed at the closed door and what he remembered now was how
—in the early morning dark before the damp dawn had come up—he'd
gone to Florence Hann's house and how he'd thrust his needle inside the
woman's arm and the way Bryce Dunning had smothered her scream with
a pillow. He remembered this now and a sense of despair went through
him.

He hadn't meant to get in this deep. Even when he'd first agreed to come
to this place and Ted Ronson had shaken his hand and winked and mentioned
something about an old sickness that kept recurring, something that had
everybody puzzled, something nobody really wanted to talk about because
that kind of talk didn't do much but scare people anyway, even then Pelusi
hadn't *dreamed* he'd do the things he'd done.

But now. . . .

He could hear it falling apart. He could hear the whole thing crumble
around him. A desperate tidal sound, coming again and again and again.

43

"I just couldn't go through with it, that's all."

Professor Pyotr Zmia watched the woman sling her clothes
untidily into her suitcase. She did so quickly, with a hasty
disorder he found distasteful. He wanted to tell her how she had failed him,
but he thought better of it—people had their weaknesses, which sometimes
they liked to think of as scruples.

"I assume you're leaving," he said. There was a weariness in his voice.
This same tiredness echoed throughout his body. He had known it before,
of course, had known when his strength was leaving him and he was assailed
by a sense of his own time running out. The internal clock, he thought.
Periodically it had to be rewound, it had to find a fresh source of energy.

"I want to put some distance between myself and this dump," she answered. "As quickly as I can."

He observed her. She smoked a cigarette furiously.

"I still don't get it," she said. "You pay me to try and ruin a guy's marriage. It's sick. Sick. And I went along with it."

Sick, the professor thought. It was not an apt description.

He smiled at Connie Harrison. The cycle was almost ended. The woman had, up to a point, played her part admirably. What did it matter that she'd failed at the end? The thing was in motion and there was no way of stopping it now. As for himself, he would disappear as he always did and after a while he'd be little more than a mystery, quickly forgotten. And who could say he'd ever played any kind of role at all? Other than Connie Harrison, who could really point a finger at him?

"I don't think I want to know," she said. "Even if you wanted to tell me. Which I doubt."

The professor stepped out onto the balcony of the hotel room. Carnarvon had grown during the last twelve years. In their haste to push forward the frontiers of progress—ah, terrible misconception!—Americans covered woodlands and fields with their hideous dwelling places and their playgrounds.

He considered Everett Banyon a moment. He thought about the thousands and thousands of acres around here that had been in Banyon's family for generations. Banyon had created a whole slew of corporations, an entire maze of companies, whose single purpose was that of wheeling and dealing in land. Everett Banyon's worst nightmare would be to lose his holdings, to see his dreams of condominiums and hotels and health spas crumble under him.

Which would not happen, of course. Not as long as Banyon and his successors kept to their part of a bargain that had been forged a very long time ago. The professor remembered now how one of the early Banyons, Clarence II, had come to him with a certain proposition concerning the Summers.

Immortality was how Clarence Banyon II had put it. If a way could be found to bestow immortality on the Summers, whom Clarence considered a very odd pair making an even odder request, then several thousand acres of fine real estate would remain in the Banyon family in perpetuity.

Pyotr Zmia had found a way. It wasn't altogether pleasant and it involved grief for a number of innocent families, but until he could discover some other means of prolonging lives—his own as well as the Summers—then it would have to do. He leaned against the balcony rail, feeling very feeble indeed. He knew these signs in himself only too well and he was filled with a sense of urgency. Time, as it always did, was running out. A day would come, he thought, when he'd find a more permanent solution to the whole problem, but so far that hadn't happened.

The professor closed the balcony door. He gazed in the woman's direction. She could not possibly understand the role she had played. She could never be made to see it. When one created cracks in the facade of a marriage, when one introduced fault lines, when one brought a small *chaos* into play, a stress that was filled with doubts and anxieties—then what parents, so preoccupied with the state of their union, could *possibly* pay attention to the needs and concerns of a small boy? What parents could help but neglect their offspring, when they were so utterly absorbed in questions of infidelity, in matters of the heart? When they were so totally afraid for their own relationship—and when their future looked uncertain? It had been a little psychic manipulation, bruising the flesh of the marriage, the professor thought.

Poor Dennis. Lonely and overlooked and neglected, he had naturally been obliged to find companionship elsewhere. Poor Dennis, whose very substance had been eaten out. Yes, poor Dennis, who would provide for himself as well as the Summers.

It had been rather a good scheme as far as it went, the professor thought. But now it was coming to an end.

The woman looked at him. "If I ever see you on the street, I'll cross to the other side. If I ever run into you, I'll look the other way. I don't know you. I've never known you."

"Admirable," said the professor. But not quite good enough.

"I don't think I've ever felt so bad. . . ." The woman shut her suitcase. "Nothing makes sense. And those old people . . ."

"Forget. Forget it all." The professor smiled.

"I've already forgotten. I'm splitting."

Pyotr Zmia nodded his head. For a second he felt a strange little sympathy toward Connie Harrison. She had participated in events that would forever lie just beyond her understanding.

Zmia stroked the side of his smooth face. She would never know about the ritual and conspiracy that had been at the foundation of this town for more years than even Zmia wanted to remember. She'd never know about the succession of mayors and city officials who'd been so well rewarded for their ability to contain and control a conspiracy. She'd never learn about the physicians who had been duped into participation, those fine medical doctors who had been bought and paid for and who thought they were keeping secret some strange *ailment* that occurred periodically in Carnarvon. She would understand the basic greed underlying the silences since she was greedy herself, but she'd never see down into the other levels of darkness that were the reality of this town. The delicate architecture of everything here: the Summers, the town officials who protected them, the misguided physicians who thought they were dealing with a problem that one day medical science could solve—all the intricate moving parts.

He watched the woman move toward the door, lugging her case. Smoke from her cigarette made her screw up her pretty eyes. "We won't be meeting again," she said, "I hope."

He stepped in front of her and asked, "As a matter of my own curiosity, dear lady, how much *did* you actually convey to our mutual friend Max?"

"Enough," Connie Harrison answered.

"Indeed, indeed."

The professor flexed his fingers. "By that, I take it you mentioned my name?"

"Yeah. Wasn't that naughty of me?"

Professor Zmia smiled his most dazzling smile. He clamped his hands together, sighed, moved a little closer to the woman.

"If you don't mind," she said, stepping to one side to pass him.

"I don't mind in the least," he answered.

He was quick, astonishingly quick, his movement a blur. He fastened his delicate hands quickly around her neck.

Her eyes widened—it was always the way. The eyes widened, then popped. After that the mouth fell open—creating a perfect oval, the professor noticed—and her suitcase dropped from her limp hands and she twisted her head backward in a curious manner and when finally he released her, stepping back from the woman, she slid to the floor as if her clothing were filled not with flesh and bone but potatoes, a sack of vegetables.

Professor Zmia stared down at her. Then he went inside the bathroom and came back carrying a glass. Bending, he took a small knife from his pocket and made an incision in the woman's wrist. He filled the glass with her blood, which he drank slowly. It was at best a temporary solution since the woman wasn't exactly young and her body had been badly used and she'd never taken great care of herself—but it would have to do for the time being, despite the fact he considered it more than a little barbaric.

He set the glass down. He looked at the woman as he wiped his lips with the back of his hand.

If she had ever known his name, she was most certainly in no position now to repeat it to anyone.

44

Louise put the telephone down. She was very cold. She went upstairs to the bedroom, where she found a sweater, which she draped over her shoulders. Then she went out on the sun deck. There was a faint moist wind blowing up out of the trees and bloated clouds scudded overhead. She leaned against the handrail. The trees shook.

Of course none of it made sense.

How could it?

She smiled to herself. People make mistakes all the time. And that's what this was. A simple error of fact.

She moved around the deck, which vibrated very slightly underfoot. When the wind whipped up again she huddled deep in her sweater. She knew she should go indoors, light a fire, get warm. But she was reluctant to go back inside the house, go down the stairs to the living room.

A simple little mistake.

She shivered. She tried to light a cigarette and the wind snuffed out her match. What she ought to do, she told herself, is go back inside and pick up the telephone and say *I really think you've got this all wrong, would you be so kind as to check it again, please?*

The voice in San Francisco had been extremely polite. And insistent. Louise shut it out of her mind.

It's going to rain, she thought.

She stared in the direction of the Summers' property.

It's going to rain.

Check it again, please. . . .

She placed the palms of her hands flat together. The voice from San Francisco rolled inside her mind.

You must be talking about my grandfather. . . .

Louise roamed the deck. Denny was out there in the forest someplace. She wished he was home, standing right beside her at this very moment.

Some of his pictures are collector's items. . . .

But but but

Are you absolutely sure it says J. Durstewitz on the reverse of the photograph?

absolutely

J. for Jeffrey?

yes yes i'm sure, jay for jackass

Well, he died in 1914. . . .

nineteen fourteen

He had a stroke, which really put an end to his career. . . .

a stroke

He took his last pictures . . .
his last pictures
Louise held her breath and the landscape turned over. Down there, between
the pines, somebody was moving. She leaned forward over the rail, narrowing
her eyes, staring hard.
He took his last pictures around . . .
yes? Yes?
In the summer of 1899 . . .
that was the last year of the last century
Louise saw a figure emerge from the trees.
Eighteen ninety-nine, she thought.
A mistake. That's all. She'd been fed the wrong information by the voice
in San Francisco.
Because if what she'd heard was *true*, then . . .
Then . . .
She swayed slightly, her hands gripping the rail.
The figure below, its face turned up to the sun deck, was Denny.
And yet it wasn't.

45   Jerry Metger thought it might rain because the flat washed-
      out sky was filling with clouds to the west, great dark masses
      that moved inexorably toward Carnarvon. He drove down the
central strip where the big tour buses were emptying the usual herds of
visitors into the street, people who'd wander from one small store to the
next with all the unhurried innocence of the casual sightseer.

He stopped at the only red light on the street, staring through his windshield at two Asian women crossing in front of him. They were jabbering
together, making expansive hand gestures and laughing. When the light
changed to green he slid the car forward slowly, edging past the buses and
the campers and the Winnebagos that crowded the curbs.

Tourism, he thought. Carnarvon's sustenance. The thing that kept it
alive, made it grow. If these people stopped coming, if the buses stopped
running, if everything quit, then Carnarvon would break down and disin-
tegrate into a ghost town the way it almost had in the past when the silver
mines no longer produced and the earth had been stripped and the shafts
emptied.

A ghost town. A dying place. Nothing but maybe a solitary decrepit gas station, such as one saw alongside the forsaken highways of America, and a general store where old men whittled on sticks or drank beer and traded stories of the Good Old Days.

No overpriced boutiques, no classy restaurants. No expensive real estate. He turned along Delaney Street. It swarmed with tourists, cars with out-of-state plates. Wisconsin. Nebraska. Arkansas.

All of this—the streets, the stores, the tourists, which had been familiar to Metger for so many years—now seemed completely strange to him. It was as if what he saw around him was nothing more than a surface, that there existed on some other plane a second Carnarvon, a town where prominent men zealously guarded old secrets, where they lied and cheated and obfuscated, where they distorted history and concealed truths and buried all their corpses silently and without regret.

And for what? So that Joe Smith from Hot Springs, Arkansas, could buy his kids Carnarvon T-shirts? So that Adeleine Bloggs out of Des Moines, Iowa, could spend her tourist dollars on funny little souvenirs of the old silver mines or pay top dollar for a shrimp cocktail at La Chaumière? So that the smart money could pour in from L.A. and San Francisco and Vegas and inflate the price of real estate?

Metger gunned his car hard, making the tires squeal as he turned out of Delaney Street. He glanced up at St. Mary's Cemetery as he drove and he thought, Poor Florence Hann. Poor fucking Florence. His anger had changed now to something that resembled loathing. This whole town and those men that ran it contaminated him.

He went out several miles past the nursing home, stopped, pulled over to the side of the road. He got out of his car and smoked a cigarette and he looked up at the sky—it was about to become another rainy day and he was pricked by the tiny needles of memory. *The way his sodden cigarette had fallen apart in his fingers on that terrible day. The way the redwood house had seemed as lifeless as any morgue.*

And that dead child who had taken a shotgun to her own face because . . .

Because she couldn't stand the thing she was turning into.

He tossed his cigarette away. A solitary drop of rain, cold and unwelcome, struck the back of his hand.

He looked back the way he had come. The loneliness of this stretch of road disturbed him now, the gray sky filling with cloud, the first smears of rain on his jacket, his dark shoes, the roof of his car. And now there was a slight wind hurrying the clouds over Carnarvon, darkening the landscape.

He got back in his car and swung it around toward town again. He drove fast, hard, carelessly.

When he reached Miles Henderson's house he stopped the car, left the engine running, stared out through his windshield at the way rain made a drizzling shroud around the facade of the house.

He squeezed his eyes shut. Think think think. Imponderable things.

Those cabinets in Henderson's study. They had to contain records. And he was filled with a hard urge to know how long this thing had been going on and what was causing it to happen and why it happened the way it always did. And perhaps Miles Henderson would have all the answers stuffed away in those cold gunmetal cabinets.

He stepped out of his car and moved toward the house.

Halfway up the path he stopped and he thought, *What good would it do to know? It couldn't bring those dead children back. And how could knowing anything prevent it from ever happening again?*

And then there was Florence Hann and his own father—what good could he do for them now?

He knocked on the door.

Miles Henderson answered, standing there in shapeless gray slacks and a short-sleeved plaid shirt. So goddamn ordinary, Metger thought. It was this perception that appalled him—all these men were so goddamn commonplace with their Bermuda shorts and their alligator shirts and their gray flannel pants—how could anything evil spring out of such utter banality?

"Why, it's Sheriff Metger," Henderson said, with mock surprise. "Come to shelter from the rain?"

Metger stepped inside the hallway. His shirt was already damp, sticking to his skin.

"Or have you come for a medical consultation?" Henderson bowed slightly, the way an ingratiating butler might. "I ought to tell you, though, I don't know a whole lot about psychiatry, Sheriff, and if you want the name of somebody who might help you with your graveyard obsessions, hell, I might come up with something for you."

"Your information network's outstanding, Miles," Metger said.

At the end of the hallway Henrietta Henderson appeared, carrying a basket of dirty clothes on her way to the laundry room. She nodded in Metger's direction, then was gone.

"It's a small town," Miles Henderson said. "Word gets around."

A small town, Metger thought. It was a phrase that covered a multitude of sins. He followed Henderson into a room that was located off the hallway. It was a big unused room—you got the impression that the furniture was normally covered with dust sheets, that you'd never find a fingerprint anywhere here.

"Last time, I asked you not to come back, Jerry," Henderson said.

"I don't remember any agreement on my part, Miles."

Miles Henderson shrugged. He sat down in a wing-back chair and crossed his legs and looked at Metger with an expression of amused tolerance.

Metger watched rain slide down the window a moment.

"I want to see your files," he said.

"What files?"

"The ones you keep upstairs, Miles."

Henderson smiled and said, "You get a sudden interest in medicine, Jerry? Being a cop not good enough for you these days? Huh?"

Metger stuck his thumbs in his belt. He was tired of it all now, all the lies, the games. He was tired of feeling that he was the butt of an enormous joke.

He had the feeling now, as he stared at Miles Henderson, that he was trying to look through an opaque window inside a secret chamber where a bizarre freemasonry assembled, a cloaked sect who spoke in a jargon he'd never understand.

"I'm only interested in seeing what you've got on the kids, Miles," he said.

"Kids, kids, kids. You're still ranting about those damn kids. Look, if there are any records, go see Lou Pelusi, he's the local medicine man these days. I retired, Sheriff. I quit."

"Pelusi doesn't have them."

"Then he's a goddamn liar."

"He says you left the whole record system in such a mess he can't find anything these days—"

"Asshole," Henderson said. He got up out of his chair and for the first time Metger realized the man wasn't exactly sober. He gave a passable impersonation of sobriety but now Metger noticed the indecisive movements and the slack motions of the lips. "I knew he was an asshole first time I ever saw him."

Metger listened to the rain. A quiet drumming on glass.

"Well, Miles. You going to let me see these records of yours or do I need to get a court order?"

Henderson threw his head back and laughed. "A court order? Here? In Carnarvon? You're in Disneyland, Jerry. You're way up there with the cuckoos, sonny."

Maybe, Metger thought. Maybe the conspiracy went everywhere, like a sequence of subterranean tunnels, all of them linked, all of them dark.

"You know, I just realized I don't need a court order. I could walk up the stairs right now, Miles. And I could tear your private little room apart. What could you do to stop me? Call the cops?"

Henderson flapped his arms in the air. "You'd find nothing. Not a god-damn thing."

Metger moved toward the door. He wasn't sure how serious he was about tearing anything apart, he wasn't certain if he was bluffing. But he let the threat hang on the air inside this pristine room and waited to see how Henderson would respond.

The physician looked up at the ceiling a moment, hands in his pockets, body swaying. "Let me ask you a question, Jerry. Let me ask you what you expect to find in my cabinets up there. Okay? Answer me that."

Metger said nothing. He was thinking of lost children, thinking of the burned-out man who'd been his father, thinking of Florence Hann, who was wandering down the same avenues his father had been forced to walk.

"I have some choice tidbits tucked away, Sheriff. Some real ripe material. I have medical records that might be embarrassing to some of our more illustrious local residents, past and present." Henderson wandered around the room now, chair to window, window to bookcase. "There's a wealth of material up there on certain social diseases. You'd be surprised—"

"None of that would interest me," Metger said.

"I have intriguing information on scandals. Abortions. Bastard offspring. Who brought what kind of disease back from a trip to Vegas. Who knocked up whose fourteen-year-old daughter. That kind of thing. Just some of the stuff I happened to save to spare some people a lot of embarrassment. . . ."

"Like I said, I wouldn't be interested." Metger opened the door now and looked along the hallway. There was the ordinary domestic sound of a washing machine running, clothes tumbling in water. He moved in the direction of the stairs, conscious of Miles Henderson following him breathlessly.

Henderson grabbed him by the arm as Metger put his foot on the bottom step. "Don't do this, Jerry," he said. His voice was unexpectedly grim, hushed. "Play their game. Go along with them. Just don't look any harder. You stop now, turn around, run along home, everything's going to be okay. Nobody will know you've ever been here. You go any farther up those stairs, Jerry, then you take the consequences yourself. You understand me?"

Metger brushed the physician's hand away. He climbed to the third step.

Miles Henderson said, "Your wife's expecting a child, Jerry. She could have a real nice easy delivery. Or there could be complications."

Metger stopped. He looked back down at Miles Henderson.

"I'm getting tired of threats, Miles."

"All you have to do is mind your own goddamn business. Go home. Just go home. Put all this shit out of your mind."

Metger hesitated a moment longer, then he continued to climb and Henderson came scrabbling up after him. When Metger reached the landing he paused. Henderson, out of breath now, his chest heaving hard, caught at his sleeve.

"They'll put you away, Jerry. They'll lock the door and forget the key. They're good at that. They're goddamn experts at misplacing people."

Metger moved toward the door of Henderson's study.

Nora. The baby.

They're goddamn experts at misplacing people. . . .

Scared, he pushed the door and stepped into the room. He wasn't going to be afraid, though—he wasn't going to let his fears distort his purpose.

"Which cabinet, Miles?"

Henderson said nothing. He followed Metger into the room, where he collapsed in the chair behind the desk. He was gasping and his face was red.

"Which fucking cabinet? Didn't you hear me, Doc?"

Henderson said, "I can't, I can't . . ."

Metger surveyed the cabinets a second, then he turned to look at the physician.

There was a long, awkward silence, and Metger wondered if he'd really use force if it came right down to it.

Henderson opened the middle drawer of his desk and took out a bunch of keys, which he tossed down on the blotter. As Metger picked them up he watched Henderson rummage deeper in his desk for a bottle and a glass.

"The last cabinet," Henderson said. "The one that's unmarked. Go on. Pick up the key. That's what you want, isn't it?"

And Henderson picked up the keys and tossed them through the air at Metger, who snatched them nimbly in the palm of his hand.

Henderson poured his glass full of gin.

He raised it in the air before he swallowed.

"Go ahead, Sheriff. Go look for yourself. They ever ask me I'll tell them you had a gun, I'll tell them you threatened me with it, that's what I'll say. They'll believe that." There was doubt in his voice.

"Tell them anything you like," Metger said, and he stared a second at the physician, who sat with his glass in hand, eyes shut, face drained of color—a sorry specimen.

Metger fitted one of the keys into the lock and slid the cabinet drawer open. A stale dusty smell rose up from inside.

•   •   •

Max stood in the Ace of Spades, where he drank his third martini. The alcohol wasn't having any effect on him—it seemed not to obfuscate, but instead to clarify, as if his brain were afloat in pure, clear liquid. He had been on his way back to the redwood house, but then he'd stopped, drawn inside the bar, and with each drink he consumed the house appeared to drift farther away from him, like a very thin memory. He studied the attractive woman who served him, albeit in an absent way, because what kept coming back to him was the confrontation with Connie.

Somewhere, he knew, there had to be sense to it all. Somewhere, if he could find it. If he had a map.

The woman saw his empty glass and asked if he needed a refill, and he nodded. He turned, staring across the big bar to the door that hung open. Outside, slanting through the grim trees, there was rain. It fell over the forest in the fashion of a misted shroud. Everything shook, vibrated, pine-cones trembled and branches stirred as the rain came down.

"Nasty day," said the woman.

Max didn't entirely hear her. He drummed his fingers on the side of his glass.

"We're getting into the rainy season," the woman said. She was silent a moment. "Aren't you the tenant of the old Joe Lyons house?"

Max nodded. Why did this woman want conversation now? He wasn't up for it.

"Nice place. Too lonely for my liking, though. Isolated." She was leaning against the bar, smiling at him.

Dick and Charlotte Summer and Professor Zmia, Max thought. Why would there be a connection between these three people? He played with the notion that Connie Harrison had been lying to him, that she wanted the relationship to end so she'd simply made a whole story up—but this didn't convince him. If she'd been lying, how would she know about the Summers down there in the forest?

And why had she run a seemingly pointless errand for Zmia? Why had she done that?

Max turned to the woman behind the bar.

"You like it down there?" she was asking.

Like it? he wondered. What could he possibly say to that? A sense of urgency assailed him. He should leave this place, get inside his car, hurry down the dirt road.

But . . . I'm afraid, he thought. It scares me.

"It was okay at first," he heard himself say.

"But now it's not?"

He shook his head uncertainly. "It's too . . ." And he let his sentence go. Too what?

The woman was watching him with sympathy. "I think I know what you mean. You going to stay for the whole summer?"

Max gazed back out at the rain. "Do you know the old people?" he asked.

The woman shrugged. "I know they're down there somewhere." She laughed a moment. "But I've never actually seen them. I don't think the Ace is the kind of place where they'd hang out."

Max stared at the olive in his drink, then he fished it out, examined it. Again, he was beset by urgency. He'd finish this drink, then he'd go. But what then? Was he going to get to the bottom of the mystery?

He drained the glass, set it down on the bar, refused a refill. But still he didn't move. The rainy landscape outside wasn't exactly welcoming. He tried to imagine Connie Harrison going deep into the forest, carrying her little package from Professor Zmia to Dick and Charlotte Summer. An errand girl.

On a most curious errand.

The puzzles shifted around inside his head like broken glass.

Why in the name of God would Zmia send such a thing to Dick and Charlotte?

Why would Dick and Charlotte Summer want a photograph of Denny?

It eluded him, it shimmered before him then it shifted away, and he was lost in the stratosphere, where unanswerable questions were the most natural things in all the world.

He stepped away from the bar and stood in the doorway, watching the rain fall over the parking lot and the impenetrable forest beyond.

The boy stood in the hallway, the open door behind him. Watching him, Louise didn't move. She could hear rain ticking all around the house as she stared at her son.

Denny, she said, and her voice was filled with hollows.

The boy stood very still. He had his hands stretched out in front of his body and he was looking at them, extending them as if they didn't belong to him.

Denny, she said again.

The boy raised his face to look at her. She had a sense of nightmare, a viscous feeling, like that of treading through warm molasses.

Those outstretched hands. That small upturned face.

Louise put a hand to her throat, conscious of the way her mouth hung open, aware of how a paralysis had rendered her immobile. She wanted to step along the hallway and catch the boy in her arms and hold him but she couldn't move, couldn't take a single step, she could do nothing but simply stare at him with an expression she knew was one of complete bewilderment. And pain, somewhere there was pain. His eyes. Those hands.

This isn't Denny. This is some kind of substitute. This isn't the kid who left this morning to go visit Dick and Charlotte and they sent a poor replica back in his place, so where was the real boy, where was her real son?

She began to tremble. She felt it begin in her legs and move upward through her body, this shaking. Her mouth was dry and there was a pressure behind her eyes.

Denny.

She shut her eyes. Because she'd wake in a moment. She'd wake up and they'd be in their house in San Francisco and they'd never have heard of this forest, this house, their neighbors. There would be no old people. No photograph taken before the turn of the century. Nothing like that. There would just be the ordinary, Max's practice, Denny roller-skating, herself perched over her easel, newspaper headlines about the Strangler—it would all be wonderfully banal.

When she opened her eyes nothing had changed. The boy still stood there, framed by the open door. Rain fell through the trees behind him. Dripped on the porch. Tick tick tick.

"Mom," he said.

She stepped slowly toward him. Her heart raged. All her pulses were haywire.

Tick tick tick.

He held his hands out to her, palms turned downward.

"Look," was what he said. Look, Mom.

You step forward. Encounter unreality. Distortions of the world you thought you knew.

Dear God!

She reached out and touched his hands. She drew him toward her, pressing his body against her own. A thin scent rose up from him, filling her nostrils. It was musty, the perfume of decay.

Nothing's real. None of this. It's a universe turned upside down, inverted so that everything slips away from you and goes falling out into the depths of space.

You hold the boy, who isn't the boy. Who isn't your son.

"Mom," he said.

She moved with him into the living room, her arm placed gently around his shoulders, and she made him lie down on the sofa, conscious of the photograph on the mantelpiece and how the Summers stared down at her.

She looked away from the picture. Because it seemed to her now that the expressions on those young faces—which before she'd thought somehow sorrowful—were nothing of the kind.

They were the sly, furtive smiles of people who win small victories, tiny triumphs. People who are in touch with secrets known to nobody else.

Denny looked at his mother from where he lay on the sofa.

She stared at him. This stranger. She clenched her hands together. It wasn't anger she felt. It wasn't sadness or puzzlement or hatred. It was an emotion she couldn't name, as if inside her the capacity for feeling had become completely splintered and there were fragments of different sensations spinning madly through her mind.

She looked at the boy's hands. Then away.

The knuckles. Those knuckles. And his face. That face.

Fumbling, she flicked the pages of the telephone directory, looking under the heading for "Physicians," thinking of Max as she did so, the absent Max, the doctor who wasn't here to make the most important house call of his entire life.

She dialed the number, got it wrong, dialed again. She heard herself say something about an emergency, something about a sick boy, and the woman who answered was slow, so goddamn slow, wanting to know about the boy's temperature and if he'd been throwing up, wanting to know all kinds of useless things even as Louise tried to hurry her.

When she hung up she turned to look again at her son. And she realized something that made her whole body cold. What could a physician do for this kid? What could medical science accomplish here? This was something else. Something with no name.

She picked up his limp, swollen hand between her own. She gazed into his face and swept a strand of hair from his forehead. A gray-brown strand.

"Mom," the boy said. "Am I dying?"

The voice, she thought. It was thick, hoarse. It wasn't a boy's voice. It belonged to somebody else.

And suddenly she was filled with fleeting impressions, disjointed little memories that came rushing at her so quickly she couldn't pin them down and make sense out of them. Her son's hair in a glass jar. The worm-ridden bait in the bedroom. The scratch marks on the boy's back. All the food Charlotte and Dick had fed him. And the picture Frog said they had.

All these things flooded through her, as if they were narrow tributaries rushing toward one central river—but it was a river whose course she couldn't chart, a river going nowhere.

"Am I dying?" the boy asked again in the strange voice.

She knew whose voice it was.

"What you've got there," Miles Henderson was saying, "is a photocopy of a journal written by a Welsh immigrant called Thomas Owens, who came this way in 1899. Quite an adventurer, Tommy Owens—or 'Taffy' as he sometimes called himself. A swashbuckler. You'll see that the appropriate passage is marked, Metger. For your convenience." There was a definite sarcasm in his voice, although there was also a certain resigned weariness— as if, having yielded the keys to his file to Metger, he was no longer interested in anything except the bottle of gin that sat in front of him.

Metger strained to interpret the crabbed handwriting. Thomas "Taffy" Owens, Metger thought. The central figure in many of his father's yarns. Taffy the Amazing. Taffy the Eccentric. The wild one. . . . He read:

Later on the same afternoon, at around three o'clock, we came across a family of settlers whose personal tragedy affected us most deeply. Their name was Dower, out of Cardiff, and they were seeking their fortune in silver. Of their three infants, one was most peculiar in form and appearance. Although he was said to be only seven years of age, his features were wizened, his head devoid of hair, and he was deformed in the manner befitting a person of very advanced years. We were told that no treatment had allayed his symptoms, which were growing more pronounced daily.

"That was written in 1899," Henderson said. "It's the first record we have of a disease that had no name until very recently."

Metger set the journal down a moment, then picked it up again. He continued to read:

A physician is sometimes in attendance, a small man whose labors appear to be in vain. It is said that he has traveled from the East to attend this sick child. The family, however, is very poor since Dai Dower, the father, is unable to find work. He has in some way offended Clarence Banyon, who owns the silver mines and much of the immediate territory. It is said that the mines and the land were deeded by the former owners, a family known as Summer. The reason for the transfer is not fully understood, although there is speculation amongst the Welsh that Banyon is heavily indebted to the Summers and has made promises to them of an evil nature.

"A family known as Summer?" Metger asked.

"Ancestors of those old folks down in the forest, I guess," Henderson answered.

"And they gave the land away?"

"That's how it sounds."

Metger put the journal down. "I wonder why. I also wonder what kind of promises Owens is talking about here. Of an evil nature?"

"Hyperbole. Superstition. The early Welsh settlers were a superstitious crew."

"And who's this small man?"

"A traveling quack, I'd say," Henderson answered. "The West was full of them back then. Probably still is."

Metger glanced down at certain phrases again.

Features wizened, head devoid of hair, deformed in the manner befitting a person of very advanced years. It might have been an accurate description of Bobby Hann. Of Anthea Ackerley—at least what little had been left of her. And presumably Sammy Caskie also.

Miles Henderson stood up, clutching the edge of his desk. "You'll find, in that little drawer, our first illustration of the disease. It's dated 1910."

Metger took out an old sepia picture.

The face that stared back at him was ancient. The lips had collapsed in the face, so that they were nothing more than very thin lines surrounded by wrinkles. The ears protruded from the bald head. The neck was sunken and scrawny. The eyes were Bobby Hann's eyes.

"That's Lincoln MacIvor, aged nine. Taken three months before his death," Henderson said. "A pretty picture, huh? He had the misfortune to have the kind of caring parents who sold him to a traveling freak show."

Metger raised his eyes from the photograph and squinted at Henderson. On the physician's face was an expression of subdued sadness, as if he had tested the integrity of the human race and found it sadly lacking in decency, himself included. A freak show, Metger thought.

"You'll find the entry for 1928 in the file so marked," Henderson said. He filled his glass, sighed. He sat down and plumped his feet up on the desk and laughed, a strange little sound that was oddly nervous. "It's not so bad, sonny. It's not so bad, after all. I didn't want to show you these things, but it doesn't feel half as bad as I thought it would. It's probably what a Catholic feels inside the confessional, huh?"

1928.

There was a photograph of an old woman, taken against a wooded background. A very small old woman. On the back of the photograph somebody had written in faded blue ink the words *Georgina Monmouth, aged six, July, 1928.*

Henderson said, "Georgina died when she was seven. The physician at the time wrote up the case for publication. However, as bad luck would have it, his house burned down and his notes were lost and he himself seemingly suffered a stroke. It happened just about the time the last silver was gone and folks were thinking up ways of finding occupants for the Silver Queen Hotel and the Carnarvon Inn and the other hostelries that prevailed in those days. . . . There's an awful lot of bad luck in this town, Jerry."

Metger didn't speak.

"The next case is Caskie. The one you asked about the other day. This one's a little more comprehensively documented. The physician at the time was my predecessor, Daniel Jenkins. A private old man who retired in 1943, one year after Sammy Caskie died. Surprising, don't you think, that Jenkins never wanted to publicize the case of Sammy Caskie? Could it have had something to do with the fact that Carnarvon was beginning to emerge from a ruined old mining town into a thriving tourist center, Jerry? Could it be connected to the fact that people were stopping here in this picturesque little town to take in the sights? Bringing their wives and families with them and breathing the air that was as sweet as any man ever breathed? And contributing to a general new prosperity? I've often wondered about that. . . ."

There was more than sarcasm in the physician's voice. There was bitterness. A tone in which was barely concealed Miles Henderson's own complicity, his own regrets.

Metger found himself looking at several photographs of the Caskie child taken over a period of a few months. In each picture the child looked markedly different. In the last one the boy appeared to be eighty years old, sad and wasted and dying. Like Bobby Hann.

"I was in Carnarvon when the Caskie child was dying," Henderson said. "I was working as old Dan Jenkins's apprentice, so to speak. I was still a med student in those days. When I mentioned to Jenkins that he publish this case, it was suggested to me, in no uncertain terms, that some things were not to be bruited about. . . . Bruited about, Jerry. Are you catching my drift?"

Henderson moved toward the filing cabinets now. Liquid spilled from his glass. It slithered down the front of his shirt and over his crotch. He appeared not to notice it. He waved the glass in the air precariously.

"You'll find Robert Hann in there. And Anthea Ackerley, your own private little obsession, although in poor Anthea's case the documentation is incomplete since the child found her own tragic release from the death that faced her. It's all in there, Jerry. Be my guest. Poke around as much as you like."

Metger stared inside the open drawer. The photographs, the documents lay around in disarray, like the pieces of a puzzle out of which no sense, no total pattern, might ever be created. He turned his face toward the window, watching rain slither down the glass.

Between 1899 and now, six kids.

Miles Henderson had gone back to his desk, where he contrived to knock his glass over and spilled gin made small puddles across papers. "Ooops," he said. "*Ooops.*" He straightened up the glass, wiped up a puddle from under the telephone with an old handkerchief, laughed quietly to himself.

Metger listened to the rain. In less than a hundred years, six kids.

Henderson raised his face from the desk. "They've got a fancy name for it, Sheriff. Nowadays they call it *progeria.* A fancy name for an ugly sickness. It's like pretty frosting on a cake that's rancid. Progeria . . . the rapid advancement of senility in young people. The hell of it is, they don't know what causes it and they don't know how to cure it." He paused. He drew the back of a hand over his lips. "But you only have to look at those pictures to see that if there's a disease straight out of hell, progeria is the one. A six-year-old kid can turn into an eighty-year-old man and . . ." Henderson didn't have to finish his sentence.

"Progeria," Henderson said again, as if the word awed him. "This profession of mine is real good at coming up with names. Hell, we can put names to almost anything, Sheriff. That's the easy part. The tough part is finding out what lies behind some of those five-dollar labels. *Progoddamngeria.* Senile kids . . ." He seemed to drift away now into his own shroud of silences.

The only sound in the room was the click of rain on glass. Metger dropped the pictures of Samuel Caskie back inside the cabinet drawer.

"Maybe one in ten million kids catches this thing. Maybe it's closer to one in twenty million. I don't know the numbers, Jerry. All I know is that the statistics in this town are wrong as all hell. It shouldn't be happening here with anything like this kind of regularity. Six kids in less than a century! One, maybe. Two would be farfetched. Three's unthinkable!"

Metger shut the drawer. He saw Sammy Caskie's ancient face—like that of some sorrowful man who has witnessed too many terrors—slide away from him, back into the tomb of the filing cabinet. What struck him suddenly was the sheer random awfulness of the disease—a healthy child succumbs, ages, grows old and weary, small bones brittle, face etched with all the deep lines of a life that hasn't even been *lived,* for Christ's sake.

"Why does it happen here like this, Miles? Why does it keep happening *here?*"

Henderson shrugged. "Over the years wiser men than you and me have tried to answer that question, sonny. Highly paid specialists have come to town and secretly tested the drinking water and analyzed the air and dissected the beef we eat and the milk we drink. They've prodded around in our sewage and run tests on our garbage and dug holes in our landfill and shoved our excrement under microscopes and put our piss inside bottles. They've been down in the old mine shafts and run dirt samples through their computers. They've done so many tests in this goddamn town there aren't any more left to do."

Henderson wandered around his study now, shuffling back and forth. "Healthy kids, Jerry," he muttered. "It takes a healthy kid, it sneaks up on it in the dead of night, it takes control. Processes in the kid's body that ought to take a lifetime happen in a matter of weeks, maybe months, maybe at best a few short years. . . . Only one outcome is certain. The kid dies. That's the only sure thing. The kid dies. Then the years go past. And the whole sonofabitching thing starts up again."

Henderson turned to Metger with a look of pain on his face. "And what do we do, Jerry? What do the authorities in this town do? Why, we keep our mouths shut, don't we? A slip of the pen here. A slip there. A record that isn't quite right. A document that doesn't make sense. A hasty burial. We've been keeping our mouths shut a long time now, Jerry. That's what we're good at in Carnarvon. Tourism and secrecy. Twin pillars of this neat little society we call home. . . ."

Metger stood by the window now. He felt curiously numb, his brain empty. It was as if his mind had closed down, shutters drawn over his awareness. "Did any of these victims have anything in common, Miles? Did they live in the same house, the same spot, anything like that?"

"That's a cop's question," Henderson said. "This isn't a cop's problem. You're looking for connections, you won't find any. Don't think I haven't tried myself. Don't think I haven't stayed awake nights wondering whether there was some factor in common—because I have, I sure as hell have. I've been over it all, Jerry. It's old ground to me. I've run the gamut from some kind of undetectable pollution to explanations that involve occult happenings."

Metger leaned against the desk. "Occult?" he asked.

"Sure. Why not? When science doesn't have an answer you start looking anywhere you can. I've asked myself some pretty odd questions. Were there old curses around Carnarvon? Some kind of ancient horror?"

"What did you find?"

Miles Henderson looked into his glass, as if he hadn't heard Metger's question. "I'm a man of science, Jerry. Anything that smacks of the occult leaves me pretty damn cold. Science wants to call this disease progeria and leave it at that. Who am I to contradict it?"

"You still haven't answered me, Miles," Metger said.

Henderson shrugged. "I first realized I was going soft in the brain when I found myself sitting up here, drunk as a lord, going over these records for hour after hour looking for some occult explanation. Jesus Christ, Jerry! Spooks. Witches. Curses." Henderson shook his head from side to side. "These concepts don't mean anything to a physician. You can't X-ray them. You can't take tissue samples and analyze them. And if you can't do these things then you go back to the scientific explanation and you forget all the other nonsense and maybe you make a resolution to cut down on your drinking for a while. I quit chasing ghosts."

Henderson paused, smiling. "Progeria. That's the official line, Jerry. The question you have to ask yourself is what you're going to do with this knowledge. Publicize it? Empty the whole town? Chase everybody away in some general exodus, something like that? Choke the highways with frightened people? Forget it. Do you think you'll even get the *chance* to tell your little narrative of doom? The prospect ahead of you, sonny, is silent and nasty." Henderson smiled wearily. "You're not the first person who wants to open this particular can of worms, Jerry. Your own father . . ."

Metger was very still.

"Stan wanted to be an author, for God's sake! He wanted to write his stories down! Which included . . . these children. Just imagine the consequences for this town if he published his little histories! He wasn't an easy person to shut up, I'm sure you know that."

"How did you manage it?" Metger asked.

"Don't look at me, Jerry. I didn't do a damn thing to your father. Remember, I retired. I quit the club. I'm old and weary and sad. I'm the town drunk. I don't belong in clubs. Lou Pelusi replaced me. Lou's the conspiratorial type. Up to a point anyhow. One day he's going to weaken, but for the time being he goes along with Ronson."

"How did he manage to silence my father?" Metger asked again.

"Lou just keeps pumping drugs into Stanley. Later, I guess he thinks he'll go inside the brain itself with a laser, so that he won't need to continue with his injections. Lou's hungry. He likes the nicer things in life. So he goes along, like I said. And he keeps up with all those nifty advances in medical technology. Like lasers. It's double Dutch to me, Jerry, but Lou knows all that good stuff."

A laser, Metger thought. A beam of concentrated light to burn the cells of Stanley Metger's brain. Was that the plan with Florence Hann as well? And were there others locked away in rooms in the nursing home? Others who'd stumbled onto the truth that the children of this picturesque town were all potential victims of an incurable disease?

Children, Metger thought. Always the children. It kept coming back to Anthea Ackerley and the redwood house. To the scents and pictures that had dogged him for years. He saw Dennis Untermeyer's face float into his mind and he was filled with a sudden fear. That kid. That house. The rainswept pines.

"Will it happen again?" he asked. There was a hoarseness in his voice.

Henderson nodded. "As sure as the sun rises. It could be happening right now, Jerry."

Metger felt the tension rise inside him. "I've got to put a stop to it," he said.

"How, Jerry? How do you propose to do that?"

Metger went toward the door. He didn't look back. He stepped out onto the landing. He heard Miles Henderson's voice follow him all the way down the stairs.

46 "I don't know how. I can't explain how. I only know the Summers caused this. Some way. Some way they *caused* this thing to happen, Max," and Louise watched her husband, who had just come inside the house, as he examined the kid. He looked in the boy's mouth, peered down into the darkness of the throat, then studied Denny's hands, turning them over, feeling the upraised knuckles, the swelling.

Max touched his son's hair. He did this tentatively, as if he doubted the evidence of his senses.

Puzzled, scared, he looked down at the boy on the sofa. There was a certain receding of the lower gums and small specks of blood at the base of each tooth. The hands were swollen, the knuckles distended and reddened, and brown spots—spots he'd thought were freckles before—spread across the backs of the hands and extended along the arm. The face . . .

It was the face and the hair that shocked him most. Small lines spread out from the corners of the eyes—wrinkles, tiny wrinkles. And the hair was discolored, as if bleached in some weird way, the brown intermingled with streaks of gray. The eyes themselves, usually so lively, were flat and glazed and dead.

"They did this," Louise said again. *"They did this to him!"*

Max looked at his wife. He wanted to say no, wanted to say that the old people couldn't possibly have anything to do with this, and yet at the same time, how could he claim anything with certainty? He bent down, lowering himself over his son. He had heard of a disease that produced accelerated aging in young children, but he'd never encountered it—it was textbook stuff, things he'd read in journals and magazines, a few isolated case studies here and there. It was rare, so rare that it was never encountered by an ordinary GP in the general run of business. Jesus, he couldn't even remember the name of the damned thing!

He laid his hands on the boy's arms.

Louise, pacing around the room, said, "I called a doctor. You weren't here, I had to do something. Christ knows what good a doctor can do!"

Max felt numb, useless. A broken bone, a strep throat, a bad case of influenza, acne, even a heart seizure—he could have dealt with any of these things without even thinking, but the thing that faced him now was more than he could cope with.

"The Summers," Louise said again. "*They* did this!"

"How? How could they?"

She shook her head. "I don't know how!"

Max turned to look at the kid. "Denny," he said.

The boy rolled his eyes toward his father.

"How do you feel?" Max asked. A physician's question—padding out silences. Even when the answer to the question was obvious.

"Awful," the kid mumbled.

"Pain?"

"Everywhere. All over."

Louise stood on the other side of the sofa. "Can't you hear, Max? He doesn't even sound like himself! That's not his voice!"

Hoarseness, Max thought, but didn't say so. He looked at the boy hopelessly. Those hands—Jesus, those hands were not the hands of a twelve-year-old kid, and how could you explain the gum disease and the hair and the small lines running out from the corners of the eyes and the spots on the arm, those dark brown marks you normally saw only on . . .

The old.

Louise went to the fireplace. She picked up the picture of Dick and Charlotte.

"They did this," she said again. "Nobody else."

"How?" Max asked. A weariness went through him. A fatigue, an edge of fear. "Tell me how, Louise."

Louise didn't answer the question. "You know when this picture was taken, Max?"

What was she babbling about now? he wondered. What difference did it make?

"Before the turn of the century, Max!"

"Don't," he said. Hysteria.

"Around 1899, Max."

"Louise—"

"If the Summers were in their twenties when it was taken, you figure out how old they are right now!"

Max didn't say anything. He clasped Denny's hand in his own, running his thumb over the swollen knuckles, and he thought, Arthritis. This boy has arthritis. But how? How the fuck could that be? Max's eyes watered and he felt a tightness at the back of his throat. What he recalled, from the few things he'd ever read about cases like this, was the fact that it was invariably fatal. . . . No—it was something else, it was something other than the disease whose name he couldn't recollect. It had to be. It *had to be*. . . .

"A hundred and ten," Louise was saying. "A hundred and twenty, Max."

"Do you know what you're saying? You're not making any goddamn sense!" The boy is sick, sick in the weirdest way imaginable, sick beyond all Max's experience—and all Louise can talk about is some fucking photograph! He laid his hand on his son's forehead—the skin was hot, feverish.

"And whatever it is that's happened to Denny doesn't make any goddamn sense either, Max."

Max focused his attention on the boy, who moaned and shifted his body a little. Louise knelt on the rug beside the sofa, tugging at her husband's arm.

"Okay, you're a doctor," she said. "You don't want to think about things that just don't fit into your narrow little medical framework. I understand that. But look at the boy, Max! Look at his face and his hands!"

Max thought of Connie Harrison now, going down into the pine trees with Dennis's photograph. What were the connections there? What did Zmia have to do with the Summers? Everything shifted—what Louise had called his "narrow little medical framework" wasn't equipped to carry the weight of this mystery. It sagged, buckled—he was at a loss.

Louise covered her face with her hands. "Maybe . . ."

"Maybe what?"

"I don't know, Max. . . ."

Max lifted his hands in despair. They were debating the Summers, when all their attention should have been given to Dennis. To this wretched boy. This *creature* . . .

Louise said, "Look, they fed him all the time, didn't they? Charlotte was always baking things for him. How do we know she didn't put something into that food? How do we know that? You said yourself her cooking was bitter, didn't you?"

"Bitter, yeah," he said. "I don't remember mentioning anything about potions, which is what I think you're getting at."

Louise nodded. "And she cut his hair, Max."

"Well?"

"She cut his hair and she kept it—"

"I'm not with you, Louise."

Louise sighed in dismay. She could go on, she supposed. She could run through her little list. She could talk about the scratch marks on the kid's back, those crisscrossing marks left by Charlotte's fingers, the boy's skin that must have adhered to the woman's fingernails, perhaps even minuscule samples of his blood. She could speak about the sickening bait, which must have polluted the very air the boy breathed. She could mention the photograph the Summers were supposed to have, Dennis's image locked inside their dreary little log house. And she could tell Max about how Charlotte's hands had changed and how she'd seen the Summers dance and the way the old woman's hair had seemed to grow darker, she could tell her husband all of these things—but he couldn't help himself, he couldn't overcome his training, the way he thought, he couldn't get around science and into some other realm of experience, where logic didn't have all the explanations, where common sense didn't cover it all, where events happened that couldn't be duplicated in the sterile controlled conditions of a laboratory.

Max said, "You're talking witchcraft, Louise. Isn't that where you're leading? Potions. Spells. Isn't that your direction?"

Louise stood up. She looked at her son. His hair. His flesh and blood. The food he ate. The air he breathed in his bedroom. The Summers had touched almost every aspect of her son.

She turned her face to one side. All I know, she thought, is what I see. Denny grows older. The Summers get younger. That's all I know.

She peered through the window into the dismal rain that seeped throughout the forest. They'd said they were going away. On a honeymoon. She looked around at Dennis and she understood what it was that Dick and Charlotte—eternal lovers—were taking with them on their trip.

Was it too late? she wondered. Too late to stop it?

Drifting, dreaming, sliding in and out of a leaden sleep, Dennis realized that his father was sitting beside him on the sofa and that his mother had gone out into the rain. Distantly, he'd heard the door close and the sound of her feet slapping across the porch; then he was conscious of rain hammering against the house, a wild sound, wind-driven and bleak.

His limbs were heavy, his mouth dry. Sometimes he tasted his own blood on his tongue. When he looked up into his father's face the man's features were somehow misty, seen through a fog.

He'd been about to leave the Summers, he remembered, because the work on the truck was finished and he felt a little out of place, a little *superfluous*, since neither Dick nor Charlotte seemed to notice him very much. And then, just as he'd stepped out onto the porch, they'd called him back.

Which was when they told him they were going away for a while. The information, which somehow hadn't surprised him altogether, was vaguely depressing just the same. All the time they talked to him they were holding his hands, Dick on one side of him, Charlotte on the other.

And he felt . . . he wasn't sure . . . wasn't sure what he felt . . . something he couldn't define.

They held his hands. They formed a tight little circle. And he had felt . . .

He blinked his eyes; the eyelids were heavy.

You'll always be with us, Charlotte had said.

Part of you will, Dick had added.

It was so hard to remember this now—tiny, broken pictures floated in and out of his mind.

As Dick and Charlotte had held his hands, he'd felt . . . something flow out him. Something ebb away.

It was as if a lively bird, which had occupied a space in his brain, had suddenly risen upward and flapped away, and he'd felt it go and the sensation was one of the most horrible emptiness imaginable.

Then he'd seen himself through Dick and Charlotte's eyes. A small boy with puffy hands and a wrinkled face. A boy whose arms and legs were stiff and painful. A boy who had risen and dragged himself back through the trees without once looking back at the house where the Summers lived, that place of music and laughter where a man and a woman loved and danced, danced and loved, and planned still another honeymoon.

The wind that ripped through the trees pushed rain against her face, soaked her hair, entered her eyes. This whole forest, which had seemed to her at one time the most peaceful, the most relaxing place imaginable, had become hostile and sly. Sounds made by trees—the creak of trunks and the thrust of rain through branches—were voices crying aloud in anguish.

When she reached the wash, where water was already beginning to create a quick-foaming stream, her clothes were sodden, her flannel shirt stuck to her skin, her jeans were cold and uncomfortable, water seeped inside her sneakers.

A day for drowning. For dying.

She forded the wash carelessly, slipping now and then, shoving her hand into the fast water for balance.

Now the trees crowded her as she reached the far bank. Her long hair, whipped at by wind and water, blew into her eyes and stung her.

She paused, breathless, and clung for a moment to a tree. All this, this landscape, this forest, the sky overhead, the deluge—she understood now that what lay out here in the deep black heart of the forest was malignant and cruel and powerful.

And it had taken her son from her. It had taken her boy away, dragged him into an area she couldn't understand, couldn't follow. She knew only that she felt deranged here in this forest.

She clenched her hands, making two small hard fists.

She had brought innocence into this place and it had been corrupted. Purity had been altered, youth stolen away.

The weave of rain through the dense trees made a travesty of her sense of direction.

The ground beneath her feet had the texture of swamp. It sucked at her sneakers and she kicked them off and moved barefoot, her soles hurting from blades of wood and pinecones and fallen needles.

Was she insane? Was she simply imagining the ugly sorcery of the Summers? The theft of a life? Was that something which—in her grief—she'd fabricated?

Her son. Her son's face.

She lowered her face to keep the rain out of her eyes but the wind, raging without true direction, blew it against her cheeks and forehead anyway. When she raised her face to check her surroundings, like somebody in an unfamiliar environment hoping for a landmark, the rain came at her with a tidal force. She kept moving, hurrying as much as she could, her mind empty save for some cold hard notion of saving her son.

But how? How did she fight?

And then she stopped. Energy had gone out of her.

It must have gone out of Dennis in just this same way, she thought. *The Summers must have sucked the kid dry of life and vitality exactly like this, leaving him empty and useless and old. While they, like vampires of the spirit, replenished themselves on his young life. . . .*

It was madness time again. She was dreaming things. All this—a dream. A big bad one.

The wind knocked her sideways into soaking shrubbery. Thorns and barbs penetrated the limp flannel of her shirt, piercing her flesh. She pressed her face into the damp bark of a tree and smelled moist wood rise into her nostrils. *You can't afford fatigue. Not now. Not now . . .*

She pushed on.

A honeymoon.

This notion, which had only seemed bizarre before, was now utterly horrible to her. She shut it out of her mind. All she knew was that if the Summers had taken Dennis from her, then only the Summers could give him back.

But how? How how how?

And what if they were gone already and that wretched wooden house was empty? And what if she couldn't find the Summers again?

She stopped, caught her breath. She had reached the edge of the clearing.

In the scattered rain, the small house appeared abandoned. Abandoned, scary, as if it were more than merely wood and glass, light, and shadow— the entrance to a dimension where she'd never traveled before.

She moved across the yard.

Rain fell on the roof with the sound of a hammer knocking the heads of nails.

Dripping, she climbed the steps of the porch. The damp wood underfoot creaked quietly, its resonance stifled by moisture. She pushed the front door open and the kitchen, shadowy and indistinct, appeared before her.

She moved inside.

It wasn't the same place as it had been once. Everything shone. Everything glittered. Everything was clean and free of dust and dirt and cobwebs. Everything was changed.

She went toward the table.

The pink glass jar, which had so distressed her before, was now an object of total horror. Against it a photograph of Dennis had been propped. There was a meaning, a design, in the way the picture stood against the jar—only she wasn't sure what.

She went closer. She knew that photograph. It had been taken on the last day of the recent school year. She recognized it—the pose, the forced smile, even the goddamn frame! How did the Summers get it? How did they manage to get ahold of that particular picture? But these were questions whose answers were unimportant—she was thinking only of Dennis.

The picture, the hair inside the jar—she felt she was gazing at relics of a dead child. It was an arrangement that somehow reminded her of a shrine.

She stood very still. The house was silent except for the rain, always the rain banging against the roof.

They've gone, she thought. It's already too late.

She went inside the living room. An old upright piano, its wood gleaming, stood against the wall. The keys were as white as a baby's first teeth. There was an oval coffee table with a lace cover placed across it. Logs had been stacked neatly alongside the empty fireplace and the hearth was filled with kindling. A brass fireside set stood alongside the wood—a poker, a brush, an ashpan. A short-handled ax was propped against the cut logs.

They've gone, she thought again.

Everything had been left neat and tidy in a way she thought was unwholesome, like a tableau in a museum. She didn't move.

She could feel this house all around her. She could feel it touch her, reach out to her.

Slowly she turned her face back in the direction of the kitchen. A noise, a faint noise reached her, some soft sound that lay quietly under the relentless pounding of rain. Something that originated indoors—a paper rustling, something stirring in the chimney, brushing across wood. She wasn't certain.

She looked down at her hands, splaying her bloodless fingers.

She gripped the handle of the ax.

She went back inside the kitchen and gazed at the dark stairs that rose to the upper part of the house.

Noise again. A soft sound filtered down those shadowy stairs, light as a whisper.

The ax was heavy in her hand.

They are up there, she thought. Up there in the dim reaches of this awful house.

She moved toward the stairs and placed her foot on the first step and listened again and what she heard float down toward her this time was the unmistakable sound of laughter.

Melodic and terrible.

She began to climb.

With blind purpose.

The husband stood in the hallway, in an attitude of puzzled defeat, as if he had lost to forces he couldn't understand. Metger stared at him and thought,

It's twelve years ago, nothing has changed, the same rain falls in the same forest and a kid dies. . . .

"I don't know," Untermeyer said. "I don't know what's happened to the boy. My wife . . . my wife telephoned for a doctor. I don't have any experience of this kind of thing."

Max Untermeyer moved his face in an unreadable gesture and Metger remembered Ackerley and how Ackerley had looked all those years ago on a day the same as this one. The sense of repetition appalled him, filled him with the dread whose source he'd been seeking for a long time now.

Metger moved down the hallway. He glanced inside the living room. He didn't want to go look at the kid. He couldn't bring himself to enter the room. The gunshot. Anthea Ackerley. The faces of her parents. The past crowded him.

A doctor is coming, he thought. Probably Pelusi. Lou Pelusi. And the conspiracy rolls on.

"Where is your wife?"

"I don't know. I could hazard a guess. She's probably gone to the Summers."

"The Summers?"

"The boy spends a lot of time there. My wife has some funny ideas . . ." Untermeyer didn't finish his sentence.

Metger thought, Anthea Ackerley, too, had spent a lot of time with the Summers.

Echoes. Too many echoes. This house. The rain. The sick boy. The Summers.

"What funny ideas?" Metger asked.

Max Untermeyer shook his head. He didn't want to talk—that much was obvious. An expression of great fatigue went through him and he leaned back against the wall, his eyes shut and his mouth open and his hands dangling loosely at his sides.

Jerry Metger watched him for a time. And then he went outside, out into the rain, even as he felt all the years fall away. He stepped into the forest, and he thought, You knew you'd come this way again, Jerry. You've always known that.

There was a half-open door at the top of the stairs. Louise stood on the landing. She didn't move.

The ax was heavy against her side.

Through the space she saw a pale oval mirror in which was trapped gray light. She saw the edge of a dressing table, an old phonograph.

I dream this, she thought. None of this is real.

She pushed the door and it swung quietly and she stood on the threshhold of the room, the blade of the ax hanging against her thigh.

I dream all this. I dream I am walking into a bedroom, a mad woman carrying an ax.

The room opened out before her. Its details came at her in one burst of rainy light falling from the window. A chest of drawers, polished cherry wood. The fullness of the oval mirror, hanging against the wall, catching faint images in its glass.

Louise swayed in the doorway. The blade of the ax knocked against her thigh.

This room. This dreadful room. There was a large double bed with a brass headboard and the room was filled with a sense of weird serenity, the kind of silence that is intimate in its intensity, as if what had recently taken place here was an act of love.

Louise leaned against the doorjamb. The weight of the ax was impossible. She blinked against the rainy light.

The two shapes that lay on the large bed were naked, limbs coiled together, hands touching. The two shapes that lay there saw nothing but each other because everything else in the world had been frozen out of their awareness. They touched—fingertips, lips, feet—like things trapped in some lovely web of their own making. Lovely and beautiful and obscene.

Louise moved into the room. She was outside her own body, dreaming. A dream without end.

She saw Dick and Charlotte turn their faces toward her and the dream intensified, shifted, moved down into deeper layers of unreality. She felt the room tilt and go floating away from her, as if everything it contained were being sucked toward that gray rainy light at the window. Furniture. People. Air, especially air. Because she couldn't breathe.

Dick and Charlotte.

Moaning, Louise swung the ax down at the bed and the people moved away from her and the sharp cutting blade went through the material of the mattress and the air was suddenly filled with feathers, as if hunters had come this way and made the air dance with the feathers of dead birds.

Dick and Charlotte.

And the dream deepened.

It didn't matter to her that they were not the old people anymore, it didn't matter that they looked exactly like the two people in the photograph taken on the quay in San Francisco with a steamship and the blurred shape of a horse, none of this mattered because she was going deeper and deeper

inside a dream of lunacy, a place where she had the strength to raise and
swing the ax again, missing a second time, feeling the clash of blade upon
the brass of the bed, seeing a small spark rise up out of metal.

Feathers floated before her. The air parted with her third swing of the ax
and she heard Charlotte laugh, saw the woman—her body glistening and
her mouth open—roll away from the falling blade. And Dick was rising, a
pale white bedsheet half wrapped around him, Dick was rising and moving
toward her with his arms outstretched.

Which was when she groaned and brought the ax up through the air,
catching the side of the man's thigh. Blood soaked through the bedsheet
and suddenly even the settling feathers were red. The man moaned, clutched
the side of his leg, slid to the floor beside the bed.

Charlotte had something that flashed in her hand.

Vaguely, Louise was aware of scissors coming at her and, before she could
move her head aside, felt their awful blades puncture the place where neck
joined shoulder and the pain, which should have been unbearable, was hardly
anything at all, because this was all still a dream. Dick staggered up to his
feet and somehow managed to get his hands around her neck and she felt
the air being squeezed out of her body, a darkness dancing in front of her
eyes, before she brought the ax up with an enormous effort and the blade
sank somewhere between his legs and he screamed, falling away from her
now.

Charlotte struck again.

A flash of blades.

Louise was aware of blood flowing out of her own wrist and suddenly she
thought, I can't hold the ax now, it's slipping out of my fingers, I don't
have strength, even in my own mad dream I can't find strength. Even here.
In my own insanity.

Charlotte came at her again. Louise stepped to one side. She brought the
ax up sideways, the only way she could, with the only strength she could
find, and the blade rose up into Charlotte's breasts and the woman slithered
back, back across the room, striking the wall and holding her hands up to
the place where her flesh had been laid open.

Louise slumped against the door.

Dick Summer, who barely moved, gazed across the room at the place
where his wife lay. His eyes were moist. His mouth opened and closed in
silence and yet it seemed to Louise he was saying something like *Do it.
Finish it. What are you waiting for?*

Louise pushed herself across the room and brought the blade down once,
twice, a third time, driving it into Charlotte's skull and hearing the thud

of sharp metal upon bone, again and again and again until Charlotte Summer no longer moved and her face was covered entirely with blood and even the saliva that dripped from her open mouth was scarlet.

Louise thought, I wake up now. Numb, unfeeling, I wake up.

Dick Summer slowly lifted a hand. He pointed a finger at Louise, as if the gesture were a threat he was in no position to carry out, and then his head tilted to an angle and he sat motionless on the floor, his eyes wide, his stare fixed directly at Louise.

And the dream moved into another horror. Here in this dark red room it shifted.

As wax will melt in flame, as paper will curl in fire, as flesh will turn to dust with the passage of time, so it seemed to Louise that Dick and Charlotte Summer, lying some ten feet from each other—although how could you measure distances in a nightmare?—were undergoing changes even as she watched them. Flesh shriveled. A darkness touched their bodies. Their faces altered. Beneath flesh there was the motion of skeletons, subtle differences in how they appeared in death, as if the whole process they had worked to stop, the passage of time they had tried to still, had caught up with them now.

Louise shut her eyes. She backed out of the room. Numbly, she started to go down the stairs.

She trailed the ax in her hand, hearing it bump against each step as she descended.

The man who was rising to meet her looked vaguely recognizable. It didn't matter. Vaguely recognizable, a stranger, whatever—it didn't matter.

He blocked her way. He gripped her by the arm.

"What have you done?" he asked.

Louise said nothing. She was aware of her own wounds, but only from some distant place, as if she were removed from her sense experiences and stood—small and hollow—at the end of a dark tunnel.

"What in the name of God have you done?" the man asked again.

Louise moved her lips. She said nothing.

"You killed them," and it wasn't a question.

Louise shut her eyes, swayed, imagined for a moment that she might fall and go on falling down this flight of stairs.

"Dear God," the man said. His expression was one of hopelessness.

What was he doing here? she wondered. What was Professor Zmia doing in this place? If there were answers, they hardly seemed to matter.

"They had lived for two hundred years," the man said. "Have you any idea what it is you've done? What it is you've destroyed?"

Louise shook her head.

"When they needed a child, I brought them one. When they needed fresh blood, when they needed young flesh, I brought it to them. When they needed a soul, if you like, I arranged it for them. . . ." The small brown man drew one hand across his face in fatigue, despair. "Immortality becomes an addiction. There is no death, no fear of death. You can have absolutely no idea of what that is like. . . ."

The man was silent. His hand fell away from his face.

"The need to feed. The need to devour to stay alive. Their need. And mine, my dear lady. Mine."

Louise let the ax fall from her hand at last. It slipped down the stairs and lay somewhere at the bottom, making a sound she barely heard.

"I gave them Dennis," the man said.

Dennis, she thought. It didn't matter what this man had to say, it didn't matter if what he had to tell her was every secret in the universe, she had only one thought—her son.

Denny.

"Your boy's blood. His spirit." The man stared up past Louise at the gray rectangle of the bedroom door where the terrible light lay still and framed. "There is a hunger. A wanting. A lust to live. For two hundred years I have been bringing them young children. For two hundred years all three of us have cheated death. For two hundred years we have been renewing ourselves whenever we needed to. . . ."

The man paused. When he smiled the expression was a weary one. "Dear lady. Dear lady. Your son was enough for all three of us. One small boy, filled with life and vitality, that was sufficient for all of us. . . . We shared the gift of immortality. We knew its secrets. *What have you done?*"

Louise looked past the man. Whatever he was telling her, whatever he was saying, it didn't matter remotely. She stared down into the kitchen at the foot of the stairs.

Denny.

The thought of the boy was creating a pressure inside her head.

"Are you sure that what you've done will have saved your son?" the man asked. "Are you sure it's over?"

Louise moved past him, pushing him aside. She heard him come down after her.

"Are you sure it's finished?" he shouted.

She didn't look back. She rushed out through the kitchen, went out onto the porch, stepped toward the yard—and still Pyotr Zmia's voice pursued her.

You don't know what you've done!
Louise walked into the trees. She felt the rain fall against her face. Felt it mix with her own blood. She didn't look back.

She entered the forest, which dripped all around her.

Halfway back to the redwood house, she saw Jerry Metger coming through the trees.

He gave the woman his jacket because her plaid shirt was limp, soaked right through with rain and smeared with blood. Her face had streaks of blood on it, which looked to Metger like something almost tribal, as if she'd dipped her fingers in the liquid and daubed herself with it. And her hand, badly punctured, would need bandaging, but that was something her husband could do.

As they moved across the clearing in the direction of the trees, he placed one arm tenderly around her shoulders. He was aware of her fragility—she seemed to him like something sculpted out of fine glass, a creature that would crack and break under the pressure of wind and rain. And yet . . .

She appeared quite unaware of her surroundings. She let the rainy wind blast her. She made no effort to lower her face or resist the weather in any way. She talked.

All she did was talk. About her son.

Yes, Metger thought. Let her talk. Don't interrupt her now. She needs to talk.

They reached the trees. Already the sound of the foaming wash could be heard. In his mind's eye Metger could see water clutch at branches, pinecones, anything nature had left loose and untidy, and sweep it along in its crazed rush to nowhere.

He paused. He wasn't in any hurry to get to the redwood house. He wasn't in any hurry to see the boy. No matter what Louise Untermeyer said, no matter what she'd made herself believe, he wasn't in any hurry to go back to that house by the side of the dirt road.

There was a weird buoyancy in her voice. Her eyes were bright, lit by some inner flame.

He's going to be fine, she said. The boy is going to be fine.

He smiled and nodded. The woman was traveling in zones to which he was denied access. But that was all right—let her believe what she needs to. She's going to need every resource she can find.

Now she was talking about Dick and Charlotte Summer and it was babble that he couldn't understand, it was wild talk of spells and potions and immortality, it was insane chatter about how the old people had drained life out of her son, but he was going to be okay now, he was going to be just fine, because she'd killed the Summers, she'd taken an ax and she'd chopped them apart, and that was why they couldn't harm Denny anymore.

It was, Jerry Metger thought, pitiful. It was the raving of a madwoman. But he could understand that. He could understand how she'd broken down this way. The blood, though—how was all that blood to be explained?

Unless—he didn't want to think it. Unless she'd really snapped and she really *had* killed the old people.

He escorted her to the redwood house. The front door was open.

Max Untermeyer stood in the hallway, pale, watchful.

Louise hurried up the steps. "How is he?" she asked. "How's Denny?"

Metger saw the door shut behind her, didn't hear how Max Untermeyer answered his wife's question.

He stood at the foot of the porch for a while, feeling the rain on his face and the wind buffet him. And then he turned and went back into the forest, back in the direction of the Summers' property, like a creature tracking the spoor of blood.

He found Dick and Charlotte Summer in their bedroom. He stood motionless, his awareness filled with violence, with echoes of violence. An ax lay at the foot of the stairs, its blade smeared with stains of blood. And this room, this terrible room—death and feathers, an old couple lying on the floor. Metger shut his eyes. The aftermath of violence had its own noise, a low kind of buzzing, a sound that filled his mind.

He crossed the room. A pair of scissors lay near Charlotte Summer's body.

And Dick.

Metger moved to the window, pushed it open, listened to the way rain drummed out there in the forest.

And Dick.

Leaving behind him a trail of blood, Dick Summer had somehow crawled across the stained wood floor to die alongside his wife. His body touched hers; his hand was pressed to her hand. Metger studied the trail. It led from the bed to the other side of the room. What kind of effort had it cost the old guy to crawl to the side of his dead wife?

Charlotte's eyes were wide open. Dick looked as if he were peacefully asleep.

Metger sucked the damp air deep inside his lungs. Louise Untermeyer had come here and killed these two harmless old people, an insane woman unhinged by the condition of her son. Mitigating circumstances—how could violence like this ever be excused?

He turned, looked down at the bodies. Something in the way they lay, locked in that bloody contact of flesh, touched him. He felt a cold emptiness around his heart, as if all blood had drained out of the organ and it had filled up with ice.

He'd have to arrest the woman. He'd have to go back to the redwood house where the sick boy lay and arrest Louise Untermeyer. The prospect numbed him. How in the name of God could he take her away from the boy's side at such a time?

From the window he gazed down over the yard. He had a sense that somebody was moving out there beyond the trees, but it was probably only the rain and the damp gesture of a bird. These woods, these woods had a way of driving anybody crazy. He thought of Anthea Ackerley, the roar of a shotgun, the rocking chair going back and forth in a room of death.

Sighing, he went back across the room. There were suddenly so many things to do—he was crowded by the future. This time he'd make sure there was no cover-up, no conspiracy perpetuated by Ted Ronson and Lou Pelusi and Bryce Dunning—this time he'd force it out into the open. Whatever it was, whatever it was in Carnarvon that made children sick, he'd open all the doors and let fresh air blow the secrets away.

Then there was his father. And Florence Hann. Could they be restored?

He looked once around the bedroom, noticed how the wind coming through the window stirred Charlotte Summer's white hair. Then he went down the stairs and out of the house and back into the forest, back to a situation he didn't have the heart for.

He understood why they were watching. They were waiting. Waiting for his condition to change.

He clasped his hands together under the quilt his mother had laid over his body. He ached. His pulses felt very weak. His hands were raw. The swelling hadn't gone down. Strange little thoughts drifted in and out of his mind, pictures of Dick and Charlotte, Charlotte baking things inside her big iron stove, Dick pottering around his yard, sifting through junk, the upraised hood of the Dodge truck—so many inconsequential little pictures.

Then he felt very cold, as if ice were crushed suddenly against his heart, and he knew that Dick and Charlotte were dead. Somehow he knew that his mother had gone over there and killed them. The pressure of ice inside him increased and the cold rose up into his head like some great chilly fist.

They were dead but then he thought he could still feel them somewhere very close to him and when he realized this the ice inside him dissolved and he was warm again and a strange sense of peace came over him. The Summers *were* close to him. It was almost as if they stood in the shadows at the back of his head. They were telling him something, calling to him.

He heard Max whisper, *What in the name of God have you done, Louise?* Then Louise said, *Wait, just wait. You'll see.*

Max sighed. *Christ, oh Christ*, he said.

The boy listened to the rain. Under the sound there was something else, some other movement. Footsteps on the porch. And then inside the hallway.

He heard the cop's voice. Louise, it said. Louise, I went to the Summers' place . . . and—

A great silence filled up the house.

Dennis opened his eyes just a little way, squinting out at the cop, who was staring at him. The policeman's face was very pale. Drained of blood, Dennis thought. Through narrowed eyes, Dennis observed the policeman. And something came back to him. Something he'd just remembered. This policeman was about to become a father.

Yes . . .

His wife was pregnant. Pregnant, bloated, throbbing with unborn life. A whole new life in her womb.

Dennis thought about this baby, tucked inside its mother's body. And then he shut his eyes because Dick and Charlotte were still calling to him and he knew he could see them only if he looked inside his own mind. There, locked in the darkness, they were holding their hands out toward him. He listened very carefully to what they were telling him and the warmth he'd felt before spread through his entire body, filling every corner of his system.

He understood. He knew what he had to do. He knew what the Summers were telling him. The Summers loved him.

"Look," Louise said. "He's smiling."

Dennis wasn't aware of any change in his expression, wasn't conscious of his facial muscles moving.

Maybe he *was* smiling.

Because he was thinking—

He was thinking about the fetus, plump and succulent, filled with fresh vitality, lying there inside its mother's womb.

He opened his eyes.